Presented to

Texarkana Public Library

By

The Fraternal
Order of the Eagles

March 1992

HIGHGATE
RISE

Also by Anne Perry
in Thorndike Large Print

The Face of a Stranger

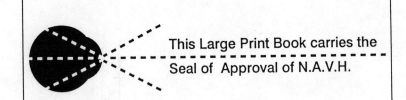

This Large Print Book carries the
Seal of Approval of N.A.V.H.

HIGHGATE RISE

Anne Perry

Thorndike Press • Thorndike, Maine

Library of Congress Cataloging in Publication Data:

Perry, Anne.
  Highgate rise / Anne Perry.
    p. cm.
  ISBN 1-56054-268-3 (alk. paper : lg. print)
  I. Large type books. I. Title.
[PR6066.E693H54   1991b]   91-30347
823'.914—dc20   CIP

Thorndike Press Large Print edition published in 1991
by arrangement with MBA Literary Agents, Ltd.

Cover design by James R. Harris.
Cover painting by Mitzura Salgian.

The tree indicium is a trademark of Thorndike Press.

This book is printed on acid-free, high opacity paper. ∞

To Meg MacDonald, for her friendship
and her unfailing faith in me,
and
to Meg Davis, for her friendship
and her guidance and work.

CHAPTER ONE

Inspector Thomas Pitt stared at the smoking ruins of the house, oblivious of the steady rain drenching him, plastering his hair over his forehead and running between his turned-up coat collar and his knitted muffler in a cold dribble down his back. He could still feel the heat coming from the mounds of blackened bricks. The water dripped from broken arches and sizzled where it hit the embers, rising in thin curls of steam.

Even from what was left of it he could see that it had been a gracious building, somebody's home, well constructed and elegant. Now there was little left but the servants' quarters.

Beside him Constable James Murdo shifted from one foot to the other. He was from the local Highgate station and he resented his superiors having called in a man from the city, even one with as high a reputation as Pitt's. They had hardly had a chance to deal with it themselves; there was no call to go sending for help this early — whatever the case proved to be. But his opinion had been ignored, and here was Pitt, scruffy, ill-clad apart from his boots, which were beautiful. His pockets bulged with nameless rubbish, his gloves were odd, and his face was smudged with soot and creased with sadness.

"Reckon it started almost midnight, sir," Murdo said, to show that his own force was efficient and had already done all that could be expected. "A Miss Dalton, elderly lady down on St. Alban's Road, saw it when she woke at about quarter past one. It was already burning fiercely and she raised the alarm, sent her maid to Colonel Anstruther's next door. He has one of those telephone instruments. And they were insured, so the fire brigade arrived about twenty minutes later, but there wasn't much they could do. By then all the main house was alight. They got water from the Highgate Ponds" — he waved his arm — "just across the fields there."

Pitt nodded, picturing the scene in his mind, the fear, the blistering heat driving the men backwards, the frightened horses, the canvas buckets passed from hand to hand, and the uselessness of it all. Everything would be shrouded in smoke and red with the glare as sheets of flame shot skywards and beams exploded with a roar, sending sparks high into the darkness. The stench of burning was still in the air, making the eyes smart and the back of the throat ache.

Unconsciously he wiped at a piece of smut on his cheek, and made it worse.

"And the body?" he asked.

Suddenly rivalry vanished as Murdo remembered the men stumbling out with the stretcher, white-faced. On it had been grotesque remains, burned so badly it was no longer even whole — and yet hideously, recognizably human. Murdo found his voice shaking as he replied.

"We believe it was Mrs. Shaw, sir; the wife of the local doctor, who owns the house. He's also the police surgeon, so we got a general practitioner from Hampstead, but he couldn't tell us much. But I don't think anyone could. Dr. Shaw's at a neighbor's now, a Mr. Amos Lindsay." He nodded up the Highgate Rise towards West Hill. "That house."

"Was he hurt?" Pitt asked, still looking at the ruins.

"No sir. He was out on a medical call. Woman giving birth — Dr. Shaw was there best part of the night. Only heard about this when he was on the way home."

"Servants?" Pitt turned away at last and looked at Murdo. "Seems as if that part of the house was the least affected."

"Yes sir; all the servants escaped, but the

butler was very nastily burned and he's in hospital now; the St. Pancras Infirmary, just south of the cemetery. Cook's in a state of shock and being looked after by a relative over on the Seven Sisters Road. Housemaid's weeping all the time and says she should never 'ave left Dorset, and wants to go back. Maid of all work comes in by the day."

"But they are all accounted for, and none hurt except the butler?" Pitt persisted.

"That's right, sir. Fire was in the main house. The servants' wing was the last to catch, and the firemen got them all out." He shivered in spite of the smoldering wood and rubble in front of them and the mild September rain, easing now, and a watery afternoon sun catching the trees across the fields in Bishop's Wood. The wind was light and southerly, blowing up from the great city of London, where Kensington gardens were brilliant with flowers, nursemaids in starched aprons paraded their charges up and down the walks, bandsmen played stirring tunes. Carriages bowled along the Mall and fashionable ladies waved to each other and displayed the latest hats, and dashing ladies of less than perfect reputation cantered up Rotten Row in immaculate habits and made eyes at the gentlemen.

The Queen, dressed in black, still mourning

the death of Prince Albert twenty-seven years ago, had secluded herself at Windsor.

And in the alleys of Whitechapel a madman disemboweled women, mutilated their faces and left their bodies grotesque and blood-drenched on the pavements — the popular press would soon call him Jack the Ripper.

Murdo hunched his shoulders and pulled his helmet a little straighter. "Just Mrs. Shaw that was killed, Inspector. And the fire seems, from what we can tell, to have started in at least four different places at once, and got a hold immediately, like the curtains had lamp oil on them." The muscles tightened in his young face. "You might spill oil on one curtain by accident, but not in four different rooms, and all of them catch alight at the same time and no one know about it. It has to be deliberate."

Pitt said nothing. It was because it was murder that he was standing here in the mangled garden beside this eager and resentful young constable with his fair skin soot-smudged and his eyes wide with shock and the pity of what he had seen.

"The question is," Murdo said quietly, "was it poor Mrs. Shaw they meant to kill — or was it the doctor?"

"There are a great many things we shall have to find out," Pitt answered grimly. "We'll begin with the fire chief."

"We've got his statement in the police station, sir. That's about half a mile back up the road." Murdo spoke a little stiffly, reminded of his own colleagues again.

Pitt followed him and in silence they walked. A few pale leaves fluttered along the pavement and a hansom cab rattled by. The houses were substantial. Respectable people with money lived here in considerable comfort on the west side of the road leading to the center of Highgate, with its public houses, solicitors' offices, shops, the water works, Pond Square, and the huge, elegant cemetery spreading to the southeast. Beyond the houses were fields on both sides, green and silent.

In the police station they welcomed Pitt civilly enough, but he knew from their tired faces and the way the juniors avoided his eyes that, like Murdo, they resented the necessity of having to call him in. All the forces in the London area were short staffed and all police leaves had been canceled to draft as many men as possible into the Whitechapel district to deal with the fearful murders which were shocking all London and making headlines across Europe.

The fire chief's report was all laid out waiting for him on the superintendent's desk, cleared for Pitt. He was gray-haired, quietly

12

spoken and so civil that it accentuated rather than hid his resentment. He had a clean uniform on, but his face was pinched with weariness and there were burn blisters on his hands he had not had time to treat.

Pitt thanked him, making little of it so as not to draw attention to their sudden reversal of roles, and picked up the fire report. It was written in a neat, copperplate hand. The facts were simple, and only an elaboration of what Murdo had already told him. The fire had started simultaneously in four places, the curtains of the study, the library, the dining room and the withdrawing room, and had caught hold very swiftly, as if the fabric had been soaked in fuel oil. Like most others, the house was lit by gas, and as soon as the supply pipes had been reached they had exploded. The occupants would have had little chance of escape unless they had woken in the earliest stages and left through the servants' wing.

As it happened, Mrs. Clemency Shaw had probably been suffocated by smoke before she burned; and Dr. Stephen Shaw had been out on a medical emergency over a mile away. The servants had known nothing until the fire brigade bells had disturbed them and the firemen had set ladders at their windows to help them out.

It was nearly three o'clock and the rain had

stopped when Pitt and Murdo knocked at the door of the neighbor immediately to the right of the burned house. It was opened less than a minute afterwards by the owner himself, a small man with a fine head of silver hair brushed back from his forehead in leonine waves. His expression was very earnest. There was a furrow of anxiety between his brows, and not a vestige of humor in the lines round his gentle, precise mouth.

"Good afternoon. Good afternoon," he said hastily. "You are the police. Yes, of course you are." Murdo's uniform made the observation unnecessary, although the man looked askance at Pitt. One did not recall the faces of police, as one did not of bus conductors, or drain cleaners, but lack of uniform was unexplained. He stood back and aside to make way for them readily.

"Come in. You want to know if I saw anything. Naturally. I cannot think how it happened. A most careful woman. Quite dreadful. Gas, I suppose. I have often thought perhaps we should not have abandoned candles. So much more agreeable." He turned around and led the way through the rather gloomy hall and into a large withdrawing room which over a space of years had been used more and more often as a study.

Pitt glanced around it with interest. It was

highly individual and spoke much of the man. There were four large, very untidy bookshelves, obviously stocked for convenience and not ornament. There was no visual order, only that of frequent use. Paper folios were poked in next to leather-bound volumes, large books next to small. A gilt-framed and very romantic picture of Sir Galahad kneeling in holy vigil hung above the fireplace, and another opposite it of the Lady of Shallott drifting down the river with flowers in her hair. There was a fine model of a crusader on horseback on a round wooden table by the leather armchair, and open letters scattered on the desk. Three newspapers were piled precariously on the arm of the couch and clippings lay on the seats.

"Quinton Pascoe," their host said, introducing himself hastily. "But of course you know that. Here." He dived for the newspaper clippings and removed them to an open desk drawer, where they lay chaotically skewed. "Sit down, gentlemen. This is quite dreadful — quite dreadful. Mrs. Shaw was a very fine woman. A terrible loss. A tragedy."

Pitt sat down gingerly on the couch and ignored a crackle of newspaper behind the cushion. Murdo remained on his feet.

"Inspector Pitt — and Constable Murdo," he said, introducing them. "What time did

15

you retire last night, Mr. Pascoe?"

Pascoe's eyebrows shot up, then he realized the point of the question.

"Oh — I see. A little before midnight. I am afraid I neither saw nor heard anything until the fire brigade bells disturbed me. Then, of course, there was the noise of the burning. Dreadful!" He shook his head, regarding Pitt apologetically. "I am afraid I sleep rather heavily. I feel a fearful guilt. Oh dear." He sniffed and blinked, turning his head towards the window and the wild, lush garden beyond, the tawny color of early autumn blooms still visible. "If I had retired a little later, even fifteen minutes, I might have seen the first flicker of flames, and raised the alarm." He screwed up his face as the vision became sharp in his mind. "I am so very sorry. Not much use being sorry, is there? Not now."

"Did you happen to look out at the street within the last half hour or so before you retired?" Pitt pressed him.

"I did not see the fire, Inspector," Pascoe said a trifle more sharply. "And for the life of me I cannot see the purpose in your repeatedly asking me. I mourn poor Mrs. Shaw. She was a very fine woman. But there is nothing any of us can do now, except — " He sniffed again and puckered his lips. "Except do what we can for poor Dr. Shaw — I suppose."

16

Murdo fidgeted almost imperceptibly and his eyes flickered to Pitt, and back again.

It would be common knowledge soon and Pitt could think of no advantage secrecy would give.

He leaned forward and the newspaper behind the cushion crackled again.

"The fire was not an accident, Mr. Pascoe. Of course the gas exploding will have made it worse, but it cannot have begun it. It started independently in several places at once. Apparently windows."

"Windows? What on earth do you mean? Windows don't burn, man! Just who are you?"

"Inspector Thomas Pitt, from the Bow Street station, sir."

"Bow Street?" Pascoe's white eyebrows rose in amazement. "But Bow Street is in London — miles from here. What is wrong with our local station?"

"Nothing," Pitt said, keeping his temper with difficulty. It was going to be hard enough to preserve amicable relations without comments like this in Murdo's hearing. "But the superintendent regards the matter as very grave, and wants to have it cleared up as rapidly as possible. The fire chief tells us that the fire started at the windows, as if the curtains were the first to catch alight, and heavy curtains burn very well, especially if soaked in candle oil or paraffin first."

"Oh my God!" Pascoe's face lost every shred of its color. "Are you saying someone set it intentionally — to kill — No!" He shook his head fiercely. "Rubbish! Absolute tommyrot! No one would murder Clemency Shaw. It must have been Dr. Shaw they were after. Where was he anyway? Why wasn't he at home? I could understand it if — " He stopped speaking and sat staring at the floor miserably.

"Did you see anyone, Mr. Pascoe?" Pitt repeated, watching his hunched figure. "A person walking, a coach or carriage, a light, anything at all."

"I — " He sighed. "I went for a walk in my garden before going upstairs. I had been working on a paper which had given me some trouble." He cleared his throat sharply, hesitated a moment, then his emotion got the better of him and the words poured out. "In rebuttal of a quite preposterous claim of Dalgetty's about Richard Coeur de Leon." His voice caressed the romance of the name. "You don't know John Dalgetty — why should you? He is an utterly irresponsible person, quite without self-control or a proper sense of the decencies." His expression crumpled with revulsion at such a thing. "Book reviewers have a duty, you know." His eyes fixed Pitt's. "We mold opinion. It matters what we sell to the public, and what we praise or condemn. But Dalgetty would rather allow all the values of chivalry and honor to be mocked or ignored, in the name of liberty, but in truth he means license." He jerked up and waved his hands expansively, wrists limp, to emphasize the very slackness he described. "He supported that fearful monograph of Amos Lindsay's on this new political philosophy. Fabians, they call themselves, but what he is writing amounts to anarchy — sheer chaos. Taking property away from the people who rightfully own it is theft, plain and simple, and people won't stand for it. There'll be blood in the streets if it gains any number of followers." His jaw tightened with the effort of controlling his anguish. "We'll see Englishmen fighting Englishmen on our own soil. But Lindsay wrote as if he thought there were some kind of natural justice in it: taking away people's private property and sharing it out with everyone, regardless of their diligence or honesty — or even of their ability to value it or preserve it." He stared at Pitt intensely. "Just think of the destruction. Think of the waste. And the monstrous injustice. Everything we've worked for and cherished — " His voice was high from the constriction of his throat by his emotions. "Everything we've inherited down the generations, all the beauty, the treasures of the past, and of course that fool Shaw was all for it too."

His hands had been clenched, his body tight, now suddenly he remembered that Pitt was a policeman who probably possessed nothing — and then he also remembered why Pitt was here. His shoulders slumped again. "I am sorry. I should not so criticize a man bereaved. It is shameful."

"You went for a walk . . ." Pitt prompted.

"Oh yes. My eyes were tired, and I wished to refresh myself, restore my inner well-being, my sense of proportion in things. I walked in my garden." He smiled benignly at the memory. "It was a most agreeable evening, a good moon, only shreds of cloud across it and a light wind from the south. Do you know I heard a nightingale sing? Quite splendid. Could reduce one to tears. Lovely. Lovely. I went to bed with a great peace within me." He blinked. "How dreadful. Not twenty yards away such wickedness, and a woman struggling for her life against impossible odds, and I quite oblivious."

Pitt looked at the imagination and the guilt in the man's face.

"It is possible, Mr. Pascoe, that even had you been awake all night, you would not have seen or heard anything until it was too late. Fire catches very quickly when it is set with intent; and Mrs. Shaw may have been killed in her sleep by the smoke without ever waking."

"Might she?" Pascoe's eyes opened wide. "Indeed? I do hope so. Poor creature. She was a fine woman, you know. Far too good for Shaw. An insensitive man, without ideals of a higher sort. Not that he isn't a good medical practitioner, and a gentleman," he added hastily. "But without the finer perceptions. He thinks it witty and progressive to make mock of people's values. Oh dear — one should not speak so ill of the bereaved, but truth will out. I profoundly regret that I cannot help you."

"May we question your resident servants, Mr. Pascoe?" Pitt asked only as a formality. He had every intention of questioning them whatever Pascoe said.

"Of course. Of course. But please try not to alarm them. Reasonable cooks are so extremely hard to get, especially in a bachelor household like mine. If they are any good they want to give dinner parties and such things — and I have little occasion, just a few literary colleagues now and then."

Pitt rose and Murdo stood to attention. "Thank you."

But neither the cook nor the manservant had seen anything at all, and the scullery maid and housemaid were twelve and fourteen, respectively, and too horrified to do anything but twist their aprons in their hands and deny even being awake. And considering that their duties required them to be up at five in the morning, Pitt had no difficulty in believing them.

Next they visited the house to the south. On this stretch of Highgate Rise the fields opposite fell away towards a path, which Murdo said was called Bromwich Walk, and led from the parsonage of St. Anne's Church to the south, parallel with the Rise, and ended in Highgate itself.

"Very accessible, sir," Murdo finished gloomily. "At that time o' the night a hundred people with pocketsful o' matches could have crept down here and no one would have seen them." He was beginning to think this whole exercise was a waste of time, and it showed in his frank face.

Pitt smiled dryly. "Don't you think they'd have bumped into each other, Constable?"

Murdo failed to see the point. He had been sarcastic. Could this inspector from Bow Street really be so unintelligent? He looked more carefully at the rather homely face with its long nose, slightly chipped front tooth and untidy hair; then saw the light in the eyes, and the humor and strength in the mouth. He changed his mind.

"In the dark," Pitt elaborated. "There might have been enough moon for Mr. Pascoe to gaze at, but a cloudy night, and no house lights — curtains drawn and lamps out by midnight."

"Oh." Murdo saw the purpose at last. "Whoever it was would have had to carry a lantern, and at that time of night even a match struck would show if anyone happened to be looking."

"Exactly." Pitt shrugged. "Not that a light helps us much, unless anyone also saw which way it came from. Let us try Mr. Alfred Lutterworth and his household."

It was a magnificent establishment, no expense spared, the last one on this stretch of the road, and twice the size of the others. Pitt followed his custom of knocking at the front door. He refused to go to the tradesmen's entrance as police and such other inferiors and undesirables were expected to. It was opened after a few moments by a very smart parlormaid in a gray stuff dress and crisp, lace-edged cap and apron. Her expression betrayed immediately that she knew Pitt should have been at the scullery door, even if he did not.

"Trade at the back," she said with a slight lift of her chin.

"I have called to see Mr. Lutterworth, not the butler," Pitt said tartly. "I imagine he receives his callers at the front?"

"He don't receive police at all." She was just as quick.

"He will today." Pitt stepped in and she was obliged to move back or stand nose-to-chest with him. Murdo was both horrified and struck with admiration. "I am sure he will wish to help discover who murdered Mrs. Shaw last night." Pitt removed his hat.

The parlormaid went almost as white as her apron and Pitt was lucky she did not faint. Her waist was so tiny her stays must have been tight enough to choke a less determined spirit.

"Oh Lor'!" She recovered herself with an effort. "I thought it were an accident."

"I am afraid not." Pitt followed up his rather clumsy beginning as best he could. He should be past allowing his pride to be stung by a maid by now. "Did you happen to look out of your window around midnight and perhaps see a moving light, or hear anything unusual?"

"No I didn't — " She hesitated. "But Alice, the tweeny, was up, and she told me this morning she saw a ghost outside. But she's a bit daft, like. I don't know if she dreamt it."

"I'll speak to Alice," Pitt replied with a smile. "It may be important. Thank you."

24

Very slowly she smiled back. "If you'll wait in the morning room, I'll tell Mr. Lutterworth as you're 'ere . . . sir."

The room they were shown to was unusually gracious, not merely that the owner had money, but he also had far better taste than perhaps he knew. Pitt had time only to glance at the watercolors on the walls. They were certainly valuable, the sale of any one of them would have fed a family for a decade, but they were also genuinely beautiful, and entirely right in their setting, wooing the eye, not assaulting it.

Alfred Lutterworth was in his late fifties with a fresh complexion, at the moment considerably flushed, and a rim of smooth white hair around a shining head. He was of good height and solidly built, with the assured stance of a self-made man. His face was strong featured. In a gentleman it might have been considered handsome, but there was something both belligerent and uncertain in it that betrayed his sense of not belonging, for all his wealth.

"My maid tells me you're 'ere about Mrs. Shaw bein' murdered in that fire," Lutterworth said with a strong Lancashire accent. "That right? Them girls reads penny dreadfuls in the cupboard under the stairs an' 'as imaginations like the worst kind o' novelists."

25

"Yes sir, I'm afraid it is true," Pitt replied. He introduced himself and Murdo, and explained the reason for their questions.

"Bad business," Lutterworth said grimly. "She was a good woman. Too good for most o' the likes o' them 'round 'ere. 'Ceptin' Maude Dalgetty. She's another — no side to 'er, none at all. Civil to everyone." He shook his head. "But I didn't see a thing. Waited up till I 'eard Flora come 'ome, that were twenty afore midnight. Then I turned the light down and went to sleep sound, until the fire bells woke me. Could 'a marched an army past in the street before that an' I'd not 'ave 'eard 'em."

"Flora is Miss Lutterworth?" Pitt asked, although he already knew from the Highgate police's information.

"That's right, me daughter. She was out with some friends at a lecture and slide show down at St. Alban's Road. That's just south of 'ere, beyond the church."

Murdo stiffened to attention.

"Did she walk home, sir?" Pitt asked.

"It's only a few steps." Lutterworth's deep-set, rather good eyes regarded Pitt sharply, expecting criticism. "She's a healthy lass."

"I would like to ask her if she saw anything." Pitt kept his voice level. "Women can be very observant."

"You mean nosey," Lutterworth agreed

26

ruefully. "Aye. My late wife, God rest 'er, noticed an 'undred things about folk I never did. An' she was right, nine times out o' ten." For a moment his memory was so clear it obliterated the police in his house or the smell of water on burnt brick and wood still acrid in the air, in spite of the closed windows. From the momentary softness in his eyes and the half smile on his lips they bore nothing but sweetness. Then he recalled the present. "Aye — if you want to." He reached over to the mantel and pulled the knob of the bell set on the wall. It was porcelain, and painted with miniature flowers. An instant later the parlormaid appeared at the door.

"Tell Miss Flora as I want 'er, Polly," he ordered. "To speak to the police."

"Yes sir." And she departed hastily, whisking her skirts around the door as she closed it again.

"Uppity, that lass," Lutterworth said under his breath. "Got opinions; but she's 'andsome enough, and that's what parlormaids 'as to be. And I suppose one can't blame 'er."

Flora Lutterworth must have been impelled as much by curiosity as her servants, because she came obediently even though her high chin and refusal to meet her father's eyes, coupled with a fire in her cheeks equal to his, suggested they had very recently had a heated difference

27

of opinion about something, which was still unresolved.

She was a fine-looking girl, tall and slender with wide eyes and a cloud of dark hair. She avoided traditional beauty by the angularity of her cheekbones and surprisingly crooked front teeth. It was a face of strong character, and Pitt was not in the least surprised she had quarreled with her father. He could imagine a hundred subjects on which she would have fierce opinions at odds with his — everything from which pages of the newspaper she should be permitted to read to the price of a hat, or the time she came home, and with whom.

"Good afternoon, Miss Lutterworth," he said courteously. "No doubt you are fully aware of the tragedy last night. May I ask you, did you see anyone on your way home from the lecture, either a stranger or someone you know?"

"Someone I know?" The thought obviously startled her.

"If you did, we should like to speak to them in case they saw or heard anything." It was at least partly the truth. There was no point in making her feel as if she would automatically be accusing someone.

"Ah." Her face cleared. "I saw Dr. Shaw's trap go past just as we were leaving the Howards'."

"How do you know it was his?"

"No one else around here has one like that." She had no trace of Lancashire in her voice. Apparently her father had paid for elocution lessons so she should sound the lady he wished her, and even in his temper, now that her attention was engaged elsewhere, his eyes rested on her with warmth. "Anyway," she continued, "I could see his face quite clearly in the carriage lamps."

"Anyone else?" Pitt asked.

"You mean coming this way? Well, Mr. Lindsay came a few moments after us — I was walking with Mr. Arroway and the Misses Barking. They went on up to the Grove in Highgate itself. Mr. and Mrs. Dalgetty were just ahead of us. I don't recall anyone else. I'm sorry."

He pressed her for further descriptions of the evening and the names of everyone attending, but learned nothing that he felt would be of use. The occasion had ended a little too early for the fire setter, and in all probability he, or she, would have waited until such a function was well over before venturing out. They must have supposed themselves to have several hours at least.

He thanked her, asked permission to speak to the tweeny and the rest of the staff, and accordingly he and Murdo were shown to the housekeeper's sitting room, where he heard the twelve-year-old between maid's story of seeing a ghost with burning yellow eyes flitting between the bushes in next-door's garden. She did not know what time it was. The middle of the night. She had heard the clock in the hall strike ever so many times, and there was no one else about at all, all the gas lamps on the landing below were dimmed right down and she daren't call anyone, terrified as she was. She had crept back to bed and put the covers over her head, and that was all she knew, she swore it.

Pitt thanked her gently — she was only a few years older than his own daughter, Jemima — and told her she had been a great help. She blushed and bobbed a curtsey, losing her balance a little, then retreated in some confusion. It was the first time in her life that an adult had listened to her seriously.

"Do you reckon that was our murderer, Inspector?" Murdo asked as they came out onto the footpath again. "That girl's ghost?"

"A moving light in Shaw's garden? Probably. We'll have to follow up all the people Flora Lutterworth saw as she left the lecture. One of them may have seen somebody."

"Very observant young lady, very sensible, I thought," Murdo said, then colored pink. "I mean she recounted it all very clearly. No, er, no melodrama."

"None at all," Pitt agreed with the shadow of a smile. "A young woman of spirit, I think. She may well have had more to say if her father were not present. I imagine they do not see eye to eye on everything."

Murdo opened his mouth to reply, then found himself in confusion as to what he wanted to say, and swallowed hard without saying anything.

Pitt's smile widened and he increased his rather gangling pace up the pavement towards the house of Amos Lindsay, where the widower Dr. Shaw was taking refuge, being not only bereaved but now also homeless.

The house was far smaller than the Lutterworths', and as soon as they were inside they could not help being aware it was also of highly eccentric character. The owner was apparently at one time an explorer and anthropologist. Carvings of varied nature and origin decked the walls, crowded together on shelves and tables, and even stood in huddles on the floor. From Pitt's very restricted knowledge he took them to be either African or central Asian. He saw nothing Egyptian, Oriental or from the Americas, nothing that had the subtle but familiar smoothness of the classicism that was the heritage of western European culture. There was something alien in it, a barbaric

31

rawness at odds with the very conventional Victorian middle-class interior architecture.

They were conducted in by a manservant with an accent Pitt could not place and a skin no darker than many Englishmen's, but of an unusual smoothness, and hair that might have been drawn on his head with India ink. His manners were impeccable.

Amos Lindsay himself was eminently English in appearance, short, stocky and white-haired, and yet totally unlike Pascoe. Where Pascoe was essentially an idealist harking back to an age of medieval chivalry in Europe, Lindsay was a man of insatiable and indiscriminate curiosity — and irreverence for establishment, as his furnishings showed. But his mind was voyaging outward to the mysteries of savagery and the unknown. His skin was deep furrowed both by the dominant nature of his features and by the severity of tropical sun. His eyes were small and shrewd, those of a realist, not a dreamer. His whole aspect acknowledged humor and the absurdities of life.

Now he was very grave and met Pitt and Murdo in his study, having no use for a morning room.

"Good evening," he said civilly. "Dr. Shaw is in the withdrawing room. I hope you will not ask him a lot of idiotic questions that anyone else could answer."

"No sir," Pitt assured him. "Perhaps towards that end you might answer a few for us before we meet Dr. Shaw?"

"Of course. Although I cannot imagine what you think there is to learn from us. But since you are here, you must suppose, in spite of the unlikelihood of it, that it was in some way criminal." He looked acutely at Pitt. "I went to bed at nine; I rise early. I neither saw nor heard anything, nor did my domestic staff. I have already asked them because quite naturally they were alarmed and distressed by the noise of the fire. I have no idea what manner of person might do such a thing with intent, nor any sane reason why. But then the mind of man is capable of almost any contortion or delusion whatever."

"Do you know Dr. and Mrs. Shaw well?"

Lindsay was unsurprised. "I know him well. He is one of the few local men I find it easy to converse with. Open-minded, not pickled in tradition like most around here. A man of considerable intelligence and wit. Not common qualities — and not always appreciated."

"And Mrs. Shaw?" Pitt continued.

"Not so well. One doesn't, of course. Can't discuss with a woman in the same way as with a man. But she was a fine woman; sensible, compassionate, modest without unctuousness, no humbug about her. All the best female qualities."

"What did she look like?"

"What?" Lindsay was obviously surprised. Then his face creased into a comic mixture of humor and indecision. "Matter of opinion, I suppose. Dark, good features, bit heavy in the — " He colored and his hands waved vaguely in the air. Pitt judged they would have described the curve of hips, had not his sense of propriety stopped him. "Good eyes, intelligent and mild. Sounds like a horse — I apologize. Handsome woman, that's my judgment. And she walked well. No doubt you'll talk to the Worlingham sisters, her aunts; Clemency resembles Celeste a trifle, not Angeline."

"Thank you. Perhaps we should meet Dr. Shaw now?"

"Of course." And without further speech he led them back into the hall, and then with a brief warning knock he opened the withdrawing room door.

Pitt ignored the remarkable curios on the walls, and his eyes went immediately to the man standing by the hearth, whose face was drained of emotion, but whose body was still tense, waiting for some action or demand upon it. He turned as he heard the door latch, but there was no interest in his eyes, only acknowledgment of duty. His skin had the pallor of shock, pinched at the sides of the lips and bruised around the eye sockets. His features were strong, and even bereavement in such fearful circumstances could not remove the wit and intelligence from him, nor the caustic individualism Pitt had heard others speak of.

"Good evening, Dr. Shaw," Pitt said formally. "I am Inspector Pitt, from Bow Street, and this is Constable Murdo from the local station. I regret it is necessary that we ask you some distressing questions — "

"Of course." Shaw cut off his explanations. As Murdo had said, he was a police surgeon and he understood. "Ask what you must. But first, tell me what you know. Are you sure it was arson?"

"Yes sir. There is no possibility that the fire started simultaneously in four different places, all accessible from the outside, and with no normal household reason, such as a spark from the hearth or a candle spilled in a bedroom or on the stairs."

"Where did they start?" Shaw was curious now and unable to remain standing on the spot. He began to move about, first to one table, then another, automatically straightening things, compulsively making them tidier.

Pitt stood where he was, near the sofa.

"The fire chief says it was in the curtains," he replied. "In every case."

Shaw's face showed skepticism, quick and even now with a vestige of humor and critical perception which must normally be characteristic in him. "How does he know that? There wasn't much" — he swallowed — "left of my home."

"Pattern of the burning," Pitt answered gravely. "What was completely consumed, what was damaged but still partially standing; and where rubble and glass falls shows to some extent where the heat was greatest first."

Shaw shook himself impatiently. "Yes, of course. Stupid question. I'm sorry." He passed a strong, well-shaped hand over his brow, pushing straight fair hair out of his way. "What do you want from me?"

"What time were you called out, sir, and by whom?" He was half aware of Murdo by the door, pencil and notebook in hand.

"I didn't look at the clock," Shaw answered. "About quarter past eleven. Mrs. Wolcott was in childbirth — her husband went to a neighbor's with a telephone."

"Where do they live?"

"Over in Kentish Town." He had an excellent voice with clear diction and a timbre that was unique and remarkably pleasing. "I took the trap and drove. I was there all night until the child was delivered. I was on the way home about five o'clock when the police met me — and told me what had happened — and that Clemency was dead."

Pitt had seen many people in the first hours of loss; it had often been his duty to bear the news. It never failed to distress him.

"It's ironic," Shaw continued, not looking at anyone. "She had intended to go out with Maude Dalgetty and spend the night with friends in Kensington. It was canceled at the last moment. And Mrs. Wolcott was not due for another week. I should have been at home, and Clemency away." He did not add the obvious conclusion. It hung in the silent room. Lindsay stood somber and motionless. Murdo glanced at Pitt and his thoughts were naked for a moment in his face. Pitt knew them already.

"Who was aware that Mrs. Shaw had changed her mind, sir?" he asked.

Shaw met his eyes. "No one but Maude Dalgetty and myself," he replied. "And I assume John Dalgetty. I don't know who else they told. But they didn't know about Mrs. Wolcott. No one did."

Lindsay was standing beside him. He put his hand on Shaw's shoulder in a steadying gesture of friendship. "You have a distinctive trap, Stephen. Whoever it was may have seen you leave and supposed the house empty."

"Then why burn it?" Shaw said grimly.

Lindsay tightened his grip. "God knows! Why do pyromaniacs do anything? Hatred of those who have more than they? A sense of power — to watch the flames? I don't know."

Pitt would not bother to ask whether the home was insured, or for how much; it would be easier and more accurate to inquire through the insurance companies — and less offensive.

There was a knock on the door and the manservant reappeared.

"Yes?" Lindsay said irritably.

"The vicar and his wife have called to convey their condolences to Dr. Shaw, sir, and to offer comfort. Shall I ask them to wait?"

Lindsay turned to Pitt, not for his permission, of course, but to see if he had finished any painful questioning and might now retreat.

Pitt hesitated for a moment, uncertain whether there was anything further he could learn from Shaw now, or if in common humanity he should allow whatever religious comfort there might be and defer his own questions. Perhaps he would actually learn more of Shaw by watching him with those who knew him and had known his wife.

"Inspector?" Lindsay pressed him.

"Of course," Pitt conceded, although from the expression of defiance and something close to alarm in Shaw's face, he doubted the vicar's religious comfort was what he presently desired.

Lindsay nodded and the manservant withdrew, a moment later ushering in a mild, very earnest man in clerical garb. He looked as if he had been athletic in his youth, but now in his forties had become a little lax. There was too much diffidence in him for good looks, but there was nothing of malice or arrogance in his regular features and rather indecisive mouth. His surface attempt at calm masked a deep nervousness, and the occasion was obviously far from being his element.

He was accompanied by a woman with a plain, intelligent face, a little too heavy of eyebrow and strong of nose to be appealing to most people, but a good-natured mouth. In contrast to her husband she projected an intense energy, and it was all directed towards Shaw. She barely saw Lindsay or Pitt, and made no accommodation to them in her manner. Murdo was invisible.

"Ah . . . hem — " The vicar was plainly confused to see the police still there. He had prepared what he was going to say, and now it did not fit the circumstances and he had nothing else in reserve. "Ah . . . Reverend Hector Clitheridge." He introduced himself awkwardly. "My wife, Eulalia." He indicated the woman beside him, waving his hand, thick

39

wristed and with white cuffs a size too large.

Then he turned to Shaw and his expression altered. He was apparently laboring under some difficulty. He wavered between natural distaste and alarm, and hard-won resolution.

"My dear Shaw, how can I say how sorry I am for this tragedy." He took half a step forward. "Quite appalling. In the midst of life we are in death. How fragile is human existence in this vale of tears. Suddenly we are struck down. How may we comfort you?"

"Not with platitudes, dammit!" Shaw said tartly.

"Yes, well — I'm sure . . ." Clitheridge floundered, his face pink.

"People only say some things so often because they are true, Dr. Shaw," Mrs. Clitheridge said with an eager smile, her eyes on Shaw's face. "How else can we express our feelings for you, and our desire to offer consolation."

"Yes quite — quite," Clitheridge added unnecessarily. "I will take care of any — any, er . . . arrangements you care to — er . . . Of course it is soon — er . . ." He tailed off, looking at the floor.

"Thank you," Shaw cut across. "I'll let you know."

"Of course. Of course." Clitheridge was patently relieved.

40

"In the meantime, dear doctor . . ." Mrs. Clitheridge took a step forward, her eyes bright, her back very straight under her dark bombazine, as if she were approaching something exciting and a little dangerous. "In the meantime, we offer you our condolences, and please feel you may call upon us for anything at all, any task that you would prefer not to perform yourself. My time is yours."

Shaw looked across at her and the ghost of a smile touched his face. "Thank you, Eulalia. I am sure you mean it kindly."

The blush deepened in her face, but she said no more. The use of her Christian name was a familiarity, particularly in front of such social inferiors as the police. Pitt thought from the lift of Shaw's brows that even now he had done it deliberately, an automatic instinct to sweep away pretense.

For a moment Pitt saw them all in a different light, six people in a room, all concerned with the violent death of a woman very close to them, trying to find comfort for themselves and each other, and they observed all the social niceties, masked all the simplicity of real emotion with talk of letters and rituals. And the old habits and reactions were there too: Clitheridge's reliance on quoting predictable Scriptures, Eulalia's stepping in for him. Something in her was wakened to a sharper

41

life by Shaw's personality, and it both pleased and disturbed her. Duty won. Perhaps duty always won.

From Shaw's tight body and restless movements none of it reached more than a surface, intellectual humor in him. The ache underneath he would bear utterly alone — unless Lindsay had some frank expression that could bridge the gulf.

Pitt stepped back out of the center of the floor and stood next to the patterned curtains, watching. He glanced at Murdo to make sure he did the same.

"Are you going to remain here with Mr. Lindsay?" Eulalia inquired solicitously of Shaw. "I assure you, you would be most welcome at the parsonage, if you wish. And you could remain as long as suited you — until . . . er, of course you will purchase another house — "

"Not yet, my dear, not yet," Clitheridge said in a loud whisper. "First we must, er, organize — deal with the — er, spiritual — "

"Nonsense!" she hissed back at him. "The poor man has to sleep somewhere. One cannot deal with emotions until one has accommodated the creature."

"It is the other way 'round, Lally!" He was getting cross. "Please allow me — "

"Thank you." Shaw interrupted, swinging

around from the small table where he had been fingering an ornament. "I shall remain with Amos. But I am sensible of your kindness — and you are perfectly correct, Eulalia, as always. One can grieve far more adequately in some physical comfort. There is no advantage whatsoever in having to worry about where to sleep or what to eat."

Clitheridge bridled, but offered no demur; the opposition was far too much for him.

He was saved from further argument by the manservant's reappearance to announce yet more callers.

"Mr. and Mrs. Hatch, sir." There was no question as to whether they should be received. Pitt was curious.

"Of course." Lindsay nodded.

The couple who were admitted a moment later were soberly, even starkly dressed, she in total black, he in a winged collar, black tie and high-buttoned suit of indeterminate dark shade. His face was composed in extreme gravity, tight-lipped, pale, and his eyes brilliant with contained emotion. It was a countenance that caught Pitt's attention with its intensity as passionate as Shaw's, and yet by every innate inclination different — guarded and inward of thought where Shaw was rash and quickly expressive; abstemious and melancholy where Shaw was full of vitality and

43

a wild humor; and yet the possibilities of depth were the same, the power of emotion.

But it was Mrs. Hatch who came forward first, ignoring everyone else and going straight to Shaw, which seemed to be what he expected. He put both arms around her and held her.

"My dear Prudence."

"Oh, Stephen, this is quite dreadful." She accepted his embrace without hesitation. "How can it have happened? I was sure Clemency was in London with the Bosinneys. At least thank God you were not there!"

Shaw said nothing. For once he had no answer.

There was an uncomfortable silence as if others who felt the emotions less deeply were embarrassed by their exclusion and would rather not have witnessed them.

"Mrs. Shaw's sister," Murdo whispered, leaning closer to Pitt. "Both ladies are daughters of the late Theophilus Worlingham."

Pitt had never heard of Theophilus Worlingham, but apparently he was a person of some repute from the awe in Murdo's voice.

Josiah Hatch cleared his throat to draw the episode to a conclusion. Proprieties must be observed, and he had become aware of the shadowy figures of Pitt and Murdo in the unlit corner of the room, not part of the event, and yet intrusively present.

"We must comfort ourselves with faith," he continued. He looked sideways at Clitheridge. "I am sure the vicar has already spoken words of strength to you." It sounded almost like a charge, as if he were not sure at all. "This is a time when we call upon our inner resources and remember that God is with us, even in the valley of the shadow, and His will shall be done."

It was a statement at once banal and unarguable, and yet he was painfully sincere.

As if catching some honesty in the man, Shaw pushed Prudence away gently and answered him.

"Thank you, Josiah. It is a relief to me to know you will be there to sustain Prudence."

"Of course," Hatch agreed. "It is a man's godly duty to support women through their times of grief and affliction. They are naturally weaker, and more sensitive to such things. It is their gentleness and the purity of their minds which make them so perfectly suited to motherhood and the nurturing of tender youth, so we must thank God for it. I remember dear Bishop Worlingham saying so much to that effect when I was a young man."

He did not look at any of them, but to some distance of his own memory. "I shall never cease to be grateful for the time in my youth

I spent with him." A spasm of pain crossed his face. "My own father's refusal to allow me to enter the church was almost offset by that great man's tutelage of me in the ways of the spirit and the path of true Christianity."

He looked at his wife. "Your grandfather, my dear, was as close to a saint as we are like to see in this poor world. He is very sadly missed — sadly indeed. He would have known precisely how to deal with a loss like this, what to say to each of us to explain divine wisdom so we should all be at peace with it."

"Indeed — indeed," Clitheridge said inadequately.

Hatch looked at Lindsay. "Before your time, sir, which is your misfortune. Bishop Augustus Worlingham was quite remarkable, a great Christian gentleman and benefactor to uncounted men and women, both materially and spiritually. His influence was incalculable." He leaned forward a fraction, his face creased with earnestness. "No one can say how many are now following a righteous path because of his life here on this earth. I know of dozens myself." He stared at Lindsay. "The Misses Wycombe, all three of them, went to nurse the sick entirely on his inspiration, and Mr. Bartford took the cloth and set up a mission in Africa. No one can measure the domestic happiness resulting from his counsel on the proper place and duties of women in the home. A far wider area than merely Highgate has been blessed by his life . . ."

Lindsay looked nonplussed, but did not interrupt. Perhaps he could think of nothing adequate to say.

Shaw clenched his teeth and looked at the ceiling.

Mrs. Hatch bit her lip and glanced nervously at Shaw.

Hatch plunged on, a new eagerness in his voice, his eyes bright. "No doubt you have heard of the window we are dedicating to him in St. Anne's Church? It is planned already and we need only a little more money. It is a representation of the bishop himself, as the prophet Jeremiah, teaching the people from the Old Testament; with angels at his shoulders."

Shaw's jaw clenched, and he refrained from saying anything with apparent difficulty.

"Yes — yes, I heard," Lindsay said hastily. He was patently embarrassed. He glanced at Shaw, now moving as if he could barely contain the pent-up energy inside him. "I am sure it will be a beautiful window, and much admired."

"That is hardly the point," Hatch said sharply, his mouth puckering with anger. "Beauty is not at issue, my dear sir. It is the upliftment of souls. It is the saving of lives from sin and ignorance, it is to remind the faithful what journey it is we make, and to what end." He shook his head a little as if to rid himself of the immediacy of the very solid materiality around him. "Bishop Worlingham was a righteous man, with a great understanding of the order of things, our place in God's purpose. We permit his influence to be lost at our peril. This window will be a monument to him, towards which people will raise their eyes every Sunday, and through which God's holy light will pour in upon them."

"For heaven's sake, man, the light would come through whatever window you put in the wall," Shaw snapped at last. "In fact you'd get most of it if you stood outside in the graveyard in the fresh air."

"I was speaking figuratively," Hatch replied with suppressed fury in his eyes. "Must you see everything in such earthbound terms? At least in this terrible time of bereavement, lift your soul to eternal things." He blinked fiercely, his lips white and his voice trembling. "God knows, this is dreadful enough."

The momentary quarrel vanished and grief replaced anger. Shaw stood motionless, the first time he had been totally still since Pitt had arrived.

"Yes — I — " He could not bring himself to apologize. "Yes, of course. The police are here. It was arson."

"What?" Hatch was aghast. The blood fled from his face and he swayed a little on his feet. Lindsay moved towards him in case he should fall. Prudence swung back and held out her arms, then the meaning of what Shaw had said struck her and she also stood appalled.

"Arson! You mean someone set fire to the house intentionally?"

"That is right."

"So it was" — she swallowed, composing herself with difficulty — "murder."

"Yes." Shaw put his hand on her shoulder. "I'm sorry, my dear. But that is what the police are here for."

For the first time both she and Hatch turned their attention to Pitt with a mixture of alarm and distaste. Hatch squared his shoulders and addressed Pitt with difficulty, ignoring Murdo.

"Sir, there is nothing whatsoever that we can tell you. If indeed it was deliberate, then look to some vagabond. In the meantime, leave us to bear our grief in private, in the name of humanity."

It was late and Pitt was tired, hungry and weary of pain, the stench of stale smoke, and the itch of ash inside his clothes. He had no more questions to ask. He had seen the forensic evidence and learned what little there was to be concluded from it. It was no vagabond responsible; it was carefully laid with intent to destroy, probably to kill — but by whom? Either way the answer would lie in the hearts of the people who knew Stephen and Clemency Shaw, perhaps someone he had already seen, or heard mentioned.

"Yes sir," he agreed with a sense of relief. "Thank you for your attention." He said this last to Shaw and Lindsay. "When I learn anything I shall inform you."

"What?" Shaw screwed up his face. "Oh — yes, of course. Goodnight — er — Inspector."

Pitt and Murdo withdrew and a few minutes later were walking up the quiet street by the light of Murdo's lantern, back towards Highgate Police Station, and for Pitt a long hansom ride home.

"Do you reckon it was Mrs. Shaw or the doctor they were after?" Murdo asked after they had gone a couple of hundred yards and the night wind was blowing with a touch of frost in their faces.

"Either," Pitt replied. "But if it was Mrs. Shaw, then it seems so far only Mr. and Mrs. Dalgetty, and the good doctor himself, knew she was at home."

"Lot of people might want to kill a doctor, I suppose," Murdo said thoughtfully. "I imagine doctors get to know a lot of folks' secrets, one way or another."

"Indeed," Pitt agreed, shivering and quickening his pace a little. "And if that is so, the doctor may know who it is — and they may try again."

CHAPTER
TWO

Charlotte had done half the linen and her arm was tired with the weight of the flatiron. She had stitched three pillowcases and mended Jemima's best dress. Now she had stuffed it in her needlework basket and pushed it all away where it could not be seen, at least not at a casual glance, which was the most Pitt would give the corner of the room when he came in.

It was already nearly nine o'clock and she had long been straining at every creak and bump waiting for him. Now she tried to take her mind from it, and sat on the floor in a most undignified position, reading *Jane Eyre*. When Pitt did come at last she was quite unaware of it until he had taken off his overcoat and hung it up and was standing in the doorway.

"Oh, Thomas!" She put the book aside and scrambled to her feet, disentangling her skirt with considerable difficulty. "Thomas, where on earth have you been? You smell terrible."

"A fire," he replied, kissing her, touching

only her face with his lips, not holding her where the smut and grime would soil her dress.

She heard the weariness in his voice, and something more, an experience of tragedy.

"A fire?" she asked, holding his gaze. "Did someone die in it?"

"A woman."

She looked up at his face. "Murder?"

"Yes."

She hesitated, seeing the crumpled, grimy clothes, still wet in places from the afternoon's rain, and then the expression in his eyes.

"Do you want to eat, wash, or tell me about it?"

He smiled. There was something faintly ludicrous in her candor, especially after the careful manners of the Clitheridges and the Hatches.

"A cup of tea, my boots off, and then later hot water," he replied honestly.

She accepted that as declining to talk, and hurried through to the kitchen, her stockinged feet making no sound on the linoleum of the passage, or the scrubbed boards of the kitchen floor. The range was hot, as always, and she put the kettle back on the hob and cut a slice of bread, buttered it and spread it with jam. She knew he would want it when he saw it.

He followed her through and unintentionally stood in her way.

"Where was it?" she asked.

"Highgate," he said as she walked around him to get the mugs.

"Highgate? That's not your area."

"No, but they are sure this was arson, and the local station sent for us straightaway."

Charlotte had deduced that much from the smell of smoke and the smudges on his clothes, but she forbore from mentioning it.

"It was the home of a doctor," he went on. "He was out on a call, a woman in childbirth unexpectedly early, but his wife was at home. She had canceled a trip to the city at the last moment. It was she who was burned."

The kettle was boiling and Charlotte heated the pot, then made the tea and set it to brew. He sat down gratefully and she sat opposite him.

"Was she young?" she said quietly.

"About forty."

"What was her name?"

"Clemency Shaw."

"Could it not have been an accident? There are lots of accidental fires, a candle dropped, a spark from an unguarded hearth, someone smoking a cigar and not putting it out properly." She poured the tea and pushed one of the mugs towards him.

"On the curtains of four separate rooms,

54

downstairs, at midnight?" He took his tea and sipped it and burned his tongue. He bit into the bread and jam quickly.

"Oh." She thought of waking in the night to the roar and the heat, and knowing what it was, and that you were trapped. How much more dreadful to think someone else had lit it deliberately, knowing you were there, meaning to burn you to death. The thought was so fearful that for a moment she felt a little sick.

Pitt was too tired to notice.

"We don't know yet if they meant to kill Mrs. Shaw — or her husband." He tried the tea again.

She realized he must have felt all that she was now imagining. His mind would have conjured the same pictures, only more vividly; he had seen the charred rubble, the heat still radiating from it, the smoke still filling the air and stinging the eyes and throat.

"You can't do any more tonight, Thomas. She isn't in any pain now, and you cannot touch the grief," she said gently. "There is always somebody hurting somewhere, and we cannot take their pain." She rose to her feet again. "It doesn't help." She brushed his hand with hers as she passed. "I'll get a bowl of hot water and you can wash. Then come to bed. It will be morning soon enough."

Pitt left as soon as he had eaten breakfast, and Charlotte began the routine of domestic chores. The children, Jemima and Daniel, were seen off to their respective lessons at the same school along the road, and Gracie the maid began the dusting and sweeping. The heavy work, scrubbing floors, beating the carpets and carrying the coal and coke for the cooker, was done by Mrs. Hoare, who came in three days a week.

Charlotte resumed the ironing, and when she had finished that, began on pastry baking, the daily making of bread, and was about to begin washing and preparing jars for jam when there was a clatter at the door. Gracie dropped her broom and ran to answer it, and returned a moment later breathless, her thin little face alight with excitement.

"Oh, ma'am, it's Lady Ashworth back — I mean, Mrs. Radley — back from 'er 'oneymoon — an' lookin' so grand — an' 'appy."

Indeed, Emily was only a few steps behind, laden with beautiful parcels wrapped in paper and ribbons, and swirling huge skirts of noisy taffeta in a glorious shade of pale water green. Her fair hair showed in the fine curls Charlotte had envied since childhood, and her skin was rosy fair from sun and pleasure.

She dropped everything on the kitchen table, ignoring the jars, and threw her arms around Charlotte, hugging her so fiercely she almost lost her balance.

"Oh, I have missed you," she said exuberantly. "It's wonderful to be home again. I've got so much to tell you, I couldn't have borne it if you had been out. I haven't had any letters from you for ages — of course I haven't had any letters at all since we left Rome. It is so boring at sea — unless there is a scandal or something among the passengers. And there wasn't. Charlotte, how can anyone spend all their lives playing bezique and baccarat and swapping silly stories with each other, and seeing who has the newest bustle or the most elegant hair? I was nearly driven mad by it." She disengaged herself and sat down on one of the kitchen chairs.

Gracie was standing rooted to the spot, her eyes huge, her imagination whirling as she pictured ships full of card-playing aristocrats with marvelous clothes. Her broom was still propped against the wall in the passageway and her duster stuffed in the waist of her apron.

"Here!" Emily picked up the smallest of the packages and offered it to her. "Gracie, I brought you a shawl from Naples."

Gracie was overcome. She stared at Emily

as if she had materialized by magic in front of her. She was too overwhelmed even to speak. Her small hands locked onto the package so tightly it was fortunate it was fabric, or it might have broken.

"Open it!" Emily commanded.

At last Gracie found words. "Fer me, my lady? It's fer me?"

"Of course it's for you," Emily told her. "When you go to church, or out walking, you must put it 'round your shoulders, and when someone admires you, tell them it came from the Bay of Naples and was a gift from a friend."

"Oh — " Gracie undid the paper with fumbling fingers, then as the ripple of blue, gold and magenta silk fell out, let her breath go in a sigh of ecstasy. Suddenly she recalled her duty and shot off back to the hallway and her broom, clutching her treasure.

Charlotte smiled with a lift of happiness that would probably not be exceeded by any other gift Emily might bring, even for Jemima or Daniel.

"That was very thoughtful," she said quietly.

"Nonsense." Emily dismissed it, a trifle embarrassed herself. She had inherited a respectable fortune from her first husband, the shawl had cost a trifle — it was so small a thing to give so much pleasure. She spread out the other parcels and found the one with Charlotte's name on it. "Here — please open it. The rest are for Thomas and the children. Then tell me everything. What have you done since your last letter? Have you had any adventures? Have you met anyone interesting, or scandalous? Are you working on a case?"

Charlotte smiled sweetly and benignly, and ignoring the questions, opened the parcel, laying aside the wrapping paper neatly, both to tantalize Emily and because it was far too pretty to tear. She would keep it and use it at Christmas. Inside were three trailing bouquets of handmade silk flowers that were so lush and magnificent she gasped with amazement when she saw them. They would make the most ordinary hat look fit for a duchess, or in the folds of a skirt make a simple taffeta dress into a ball gown. One was in pastel pinks, one blazing reds, and the third all the shades between flamingo and flame.

"Oh, Emily. You're a genius." Her mind raced through all the things she could do with them, apart from the sheer pleasure of turning them over and over in her hand and dreaming, which was a joy in itself if she never got any further. "Oh, thank you! They are exquisite."

Emily was glowing with satisfaction. "I shall bring the paintings of Florence next time. But now I brought Thomas a dozen silk handkerchiefs — with his initials on."

"He'll adore them," Charlotte said with absolute certainty. "Now tell me about your trip — everything you can that isn't terribly private." She did not mean to ask Emily if she were happy, nor would she have. Marrying Jack Radley had been a wild and very personal decision. He had no money and no prospects; after George Ashworth, who had had both, and a title as well, it was a radical social change. And she had certainly loved George and felt his death profoundly. Yet Jack, whose reputation was dubious, had proved that his charm was not nearly as shallow as it appeared at first. He was a loyal friend, with courage as well as humor and imagination, and was prepared to take risks in a cause he believed right.

"Put on the kettle," Emily ordered. "And have you got pastry baking?" She sniffed. "It smells delicious."

Charlotte obeyed, and then settled to listen.

Emily had written regularly, except for the last few weeks, which had been spent at sea on the long, late-summer voyage home from Naples to London. They had sailed slowly by intent, calling at many ports, but she had not mailed letters, believing they would not reach Charlotte before she did herself. Now the words poured out in descriptions of Sardinia, the Balearic Isles, North Africa, Gibraltar, Portugal, northern Spain and the Atlantic coast of France.

To Charlotte they were magical places, immeasurably distant from Bloomsbury and the busy streets of London, housework and domestic duties, children, and Pitt's recounting of his day. She would never see them, and half of her regretted it and would love to have watched the brilliant light on colored walls, smelled the spice and fruit and dust in the air, felt the heat and heard the different rhythm of foreign tongues. They would have filled her imagination and enriched her memory for years. But she could have the best of them through Emily's recounting, and do it without the seasickness, the weariness of long cramped coach rides, highly irregular sanitation and a wide variety of insects which Emily described in repulsive detail.

Through it all there emerged a sharper, kinder and less romantic picture of Jack, and Charlotte found many of her anxieties slipping away.

"Now that you're home, are you going to stay in the city?" she asked, looking at Emily's face, flushed with color from sun and wind but tired around the eyes. "Or are you going to the country?" She had inherited a large house in its own parklands, in trust for her son from her marriage to Lord Ashworth.

"Oh, no," Emily said quickly. "At least — " She made a small, rueful face. "I don't know. It's very different now we're not on a planned journey with something new to see or to do each day, and somewhere we have to be by nightfall. This is the beginning of real life." She looked down at her hands, small and strong and unlined on the table. "I'm a little frightened in case suddenly we're not sure what to say to each other — or even what to do to fill the day. It's going to be so different. There isn't any crisis anymore." She sniffed rather elegantly and smiled directly at Charlotte. "Before we were married there was always some terrible event pressing us to act — first George's death, and then the murders in Hanover Close." She raised her fair eyebrows hopefully and her blue eyes were wide, but they knew each other far too well for even Emily to feign innocence. "I don't suppose Thomas has a case we could help with?"

Charlotte burst into laughter, even though she knew Emily was serious and that all the past cases in which they had played a part were fraught with tragedy, and some danger as well as any sense of adventure there may have been.

"No. There was a very terrible case while

you were away."

"You didn't tell me!" Emily's expression was full of accusation and incredulity. "What? What sort of case? Why didn't you write to me about it?"

"Because you would have been too worried to enjoy your honeymoon, and I wanted you to have a perfect time seeing all the glories of Paris and Italy, not thinking about people having their throats cut in a London fog," Charlotte answered honestly. "But I will certainly tell you now, if you wish."

"Of course I wish! But first get me some more tea."

"We could have luncheon," Charlotte suggested. "I have cold meat and fresh pickle — will that do?"

"Very well — but talk while you're getting it," Emily instructed. She did not offer to help; they had both been raised to expect marriage to gentlemen of their own social status who would provide them with homes and suitable domestic servants for all house and kitchen labor. Charlotte had married dreadfully beneath herself — to a policeman — and learned to do her own work. Emily had married equally far above herself, to an aristocrat with a fortune, and she had not even been *in* a kitchen in years, except Charlotte's; and although she knew how to approve or disapprove a menu for anyone from a country squire to the Queen herself, she had no idea, and no wish for one, as to how it should be made.

"Have you been to see Great-Aunt Vespasia yet?" Charlotte asked as she carved the meat.

Great-Aunt Vespasia was actually George's aunt, and no immediate relative to either of them, but they had both learned to love and admire her more deeply than any of their own family. She had been one of the great beauties of her generation. Now she was close to eighty, and with wealth and social position assured she had both the power and the indifference to opinion to conduct herself as she pleased, to espouse every cause her conscience dictated or her sympathies called for. She dressed in the height of fashion, and could charm the prime minister, or the dustman — or freeze them both at twenty paces with a look of ice.

"No," Emily replied. "I thought of going this afternoon. Does Aunt Vespasia know about this case?"

Charlotte smiled smugly. "Oh yes. She was involved. In fact she lent me her carriage and footman for the final confrontation — " She let it hang in the air deliberately.

Emily glared at her.

Blithely Charlotte refilled the kettle and turned to the cupboard to find the pickle. She even thought of humming a little tune, but decided against it on the ground that she could not sing very well — and Emily could.

Emily began to drum her fingers on the scrubbed-clean wooden tabletop.

"A member of Parliament was found lashed to a lamppost on Westminster Bridge. . . ." Charlotte began to recount the whole story, at first with relish, then with awe, and finally with horror and pity. When she had finished the meal was done and it was early afternoon.

Emily said very little, reaching her hands across the table to clasp Charlotte's arm with her fingers. "You could have been killed!" she said angrily, but there were tears in her eyes. "You must never do such a mad thing again! I suppose whatever I think of to say to you, Thomas will already have said it? I trust he scolded you to within an inch of your life?"

"It was not necessary," Charlotte said honestly. "I was quite aware of it all myself. Are you ready to go and see Aunt Vespasia?"

"Certainly. But you are not. You must change out of that very plain stuff dress and put on something more appealing."

"To do the ironing?"

"Nonsense. You are coming with me. It will do you good. It is a lovely day and the drive will be excellent."

Charlotte gave duty a brief thought, then

submitted to temptation.

"Yes — if you wish. It will only take me a few moments to change. Gracie!" And she hurried out to find the maid and request her to prepare the children's tea for their return and peel the vegetables for the main evening meal.

Lady Vespasia Cumming-Gould lived in a spacious, fashionable house, and her door was opened by a maid in a crisp uniform with lace-trimmed cap and apron. She recognized Charlotte and Emily immediately and showed them in without the usual formalities of prevarication. There was no question as to whether they would be received. Her ladyship was not only very fond of them both, she was also acutely bored with the chatter of society and the endless minutiae of etiquette.

Vespasia was sitting in her private withdrawing room, very sparsely furnished by current standards of taste — no heavy oak tables, no overstuffed sofas and no fringes on the curtains. Instead it was reminiscent of a far earlier age, when Vespasia herself was born, the high empire of Napoleon Bonaparte, before the Battle of Waterloo, the clean lines of the Georgian era and the austerity of a long, desperate war for survival. One of her uncles had died in Nelson's navy at Trafalgar. Now even the Iron Duke was dead and Wellington a name in history books, and those who fought in the Crimea forty years later were old men now.

Vespasia was sitting upright on a hard-backed Chippendale chair, her dove-gray gown high at the neck, touched with French lace, and four ropes of pearls hanging almost to her waist. She did not bother with the pretense of indifference. Her smile was full of delight.

"Emily, my dear. How very well you look. I'm so pleased you have come. You shall tell me everything you enjoyed. The tedious parts you may omit, no doubt they were just the same as when I was there and it is quite unnecessary that any of us should endure them again. Charlotte, you will live through it all a second time and ask all the pertinent questions. Come, sit down."

They both went to her, kissed her in turn, then took the places she indicated.

"Agatha," she commanded the maid. "You will bring tea. Cucumber sandwiches, if you please — and then have Cook make some fresh scones with — I think — raspberry jam, and of course cream."

"Yes, my lady." Agatha nodded obediently.

"In an hour and a half," Vespasia added. "We have much to hear."

Whether they would stay so long was not open to argument, nor if any other chance caller should be admitted. Lady Vespasia was not at home to anyone else.

"You may begin," Vespasia said, her eyes bright with a mixture of anticipation and laughter.

Nearly two hours later the tea table was empty and Emily finally could think of nothing else whatever to add.

"And now what are you going to do?" Vespasia inquired with interest.

Emily looked down at the carpet. "I don't know. I suppose I could become involved in good works of some sort. I could be patron of the local committee for the care of fallen women!"

"I doubt it," Charlotte said dryly. "You are not Lady Ashworth anymore. You'd have to be an ordinary member."

Emily made a face at her. "I have no intention of becoming either. I don't mind the fallen women — it's the committee members I cannot abide. I want a proper cause, something to do better than pontificate on the state of others. You never did answer me properly when I asked you what Thomas was doing at the moment?"

"Indeed." Vespasia looked at Charlotte hopefully also. "What is he doing? I trust he is not in Whitechapel? The newspapers are being very critical of the police at the moment.

Last year they were loud in their praises, and all blame went to the mobs in Trafalgar Square in the riots. Now the boot is on the other foot, and they are calling for Sir Charles Warren's resignation."

Emily shivered. "I imagine they are frightened — I think I should be if I lived in that sort of area. They criticize everyone — even the Queen. People are saying she does not appear enough, and the Prince of Wales is far too light-minded and spends too much money. And of course the Duke of Clarence behaves like an ass — but if his father lives as long as the Queen, poor Clarence will be in a bath chair before he sees the throne."

"That is not a satisfactory excuse." Vespasia's lips moved in the tiniest smile, then she turned to Charlotte again. "You have not told us if Thomas is working on this Whitechapel affair."

"No. He is in Highgate, but I know very little about the case," Charlotte confessed. "In fact it has only just begun — "

"The very best place for us to become acquainted with it," Emily said, her enthusiasm returning. "What is it?"

Charlotte looked at their expectant faces and wished she had more to tell.

"It was a fire," she said bleakly. "A house was burned and a woman died in it. Her husband was out on a medical call — he is a doctor — and the servants' wing was the last to be damaged and they were all rescued."

"Is that all?" Emily was obviously disappointed.

"I told you it was only the very beginning," Charlotte apologized. "Thomas came home reeking of smoke and with fine ash in his clothes. He looked drained of all energy and terribly sad. She was supposed to have gone out, but it was canceled at the last moment."

"So it should have been the husband who was at home," Vespasia concluded. "I assume it was arson, or Thomas would not have been called. Was the intended victim the husband — or was it he who set the fire?"

"It would seem that he was the intended victim," Charlotte agreed. "With the best will in the world, I cannot see any way in which we could" — she smiled with a touch of self-mockery — "meddle."

"Who was she?" Emily asked quietly. "Do you know anything about her?"

"No, nothing at all, except that people spoke well of her. But then they usually do of the dead. It is expected, even required."

"That sounds totally vacuous," Vespasia said wearily. "And tells neither Thomas nor us anything about her at all — only that her friends are conventional. What was her name?"

"Clemency Shaw."

"Clemency Shaw?" Vespasia's voice quickened with recognition. "That name is familiar, I believe. If it is the same person, then she is — was — indeed a good woman. Her death is a tragedy, and unless someone else takes over her work, a great many people will suffer."

"Thomas said nothing of any work." Charlotte was acutely interested herself now. "Perhaps he doesn't know. What work was it?"

Emily sat forward in her chair, waiting eagerly.

"It may not be the same person," Vespasia warned.

"But if it is?"

"Then she has begun a fight to get certain laws changed regarding the ownership of slum housing," Vespasia answered gravely, her face expressing what she knew from her own experience of the near impossibility of overcoming such vested interests. Many of the worst, where there is appalling overcrowding and no sanitation at all, are owned by people of wealth and social standing. If it were more readily known, some minimal standards might be enforced."

"And who is in its way?" Emily was practical as always.

"I cannot give you a detailed answer," Vespasia replied. "But if you are determined to pursue it, then we should go and visit Somerset Carlisle, who will be able to tell us." Even as she spoke she was already rising to her feet and preparing to leave.

Charlotte caught Emily's eye with a flash of amusement, and they also rose.

"What an excellent idea," Charlotte agreed.

Emily hesitated only a moment. "Is it not an unsuitable time to call upon anyone, Aunt Vespasia?"

"Most unsuitable," Vespasia agreed. "That is why it will do very well. We shall be highly unlikely to find anyone else there." And without continuing the discussion she rang the bell for her maid to call Emily's carriage so they might travel together.

Charlotte had a moment's hesitation; she was not dressed well enough to call upon a member of Parliament. Usually for anything approaching such formality in the past she had borrowed a gown from Emily, or Aunt Vespasia herself, suitably made over to fit her, even if by strategic pins here and there. But she had known Somerset Carlisle for several years, and always in connection with some passionate cause when there was little thought of social niceties, only the matter in hand. Anyway, neither Emily nor Vespasia were taking the slightest notice of protests and if she did not catch them up she would be left behind, and she would have gone in her kitchen pinafore rather than that.

Somerset Carlisle was at home in his study working on papers of some political importance, and for anyone less than Vespasia his footman would politely have refused them entrance. However, he had an appreciation for the dramatic and a knowledge of his master's past crusades in one cause or another, and he was quite aware that Lady Vespasia Cumming-Gould had frequently been involved in them one way or another; indeed she was an effective ally for whom he had great regard.

Accordingly he conducted all three ladies to the study door and knocked before opening it and announcing their presence.

Somerset Carlisle was not young, nor yet middle-aged; quite possibly he never would be, but would pass directly from where he was now into a wiry and unmellowed old age. He was full of nervous energy, his winged eyebrows and thin, mercurial face never seemed completely in repose.

His study reflected his nature. It was full of books on all manner of subjects, both for his work and for his wide personal interests. The few spaces on the walls were crammed with paintings and curios, beautiful, and probably of financial value. The deep Georgian windows shed excellent light, and for winter or evening work there were several gas brackets both on the walls and pendant from the ceiling. A long-legged marmalade cat was stretched out in ecstatic sleep in the best chair in front of the fire. The desk itself was piled with papers in no imaginable sort of order.

Somerset Carlisle put his pen into the stand and rose to greet them with obvious delight, coming around the desk, knocking off a pile of letters and ignoring them completely as they cascaded to the floor. The cat did not stir.

He took the immaculately gloved hand that Vespasia offered him.

"Lady Cumming-Gould. How very nice to see you." He met her eyes with a spark of humor. "No doubt you have some urgent injustice to fight, or you would not have come without warning. Lady Ashworth — and Mrs. Pitt — now I know something is afoot! Please sit down. I — " He looked around for some place of comfort to offer them, and failed. Gently he removed the cat and placed it on the seat of his own chair behind the desk. It stretched luxuriously and resettled itself.

Vespasia took the chair and Charlotte and Emily sat on the upright chairs opposite. Carlisle remained standing. No one bothered to correct him that Emily was now plain Mrs. Jack Radley. There was time enough for that later.

Vespasia came to the point quickly.

"A woman has died in a fire which was not accidental. We know little other than that, except that her name was Clemency Shaw — " She stopped, seeing the look of distress that had touched his face the moment she said the name. "You knew her?"

"Yes — mostly by repute," he answered, his voice low, his eyes searching their faces, seeing the surprise and the heightened tension as he spoke. "I only met her twice. She was a quiet woman, still uncertain of how best to achieve her aims and unused to battling the intricacies of civil law, but there was an intense dedication in her and an honesty I admired very much. I believe she cared for the reforms she desired more than her own dignity or the opinions of her friends or acquaintances. I am truly grieved that she is dead. Have you no idea how it happened?" The last question he addressed to Charlotte. He had known Pitt for many years, in fact since he himself had been involved in a bizarre murder.

"It was arson," she replied. "She was at home because a trip into town had been unexpectedly canceled, and her husband was out on a medical emergency. Otherwise he would have died, and not she."

"So her death was accidental." He made it

almost a question, but not quite.

"Someone might have been watching and known." Charlotte would not leave it so quickly. "What was she fighting for — what reforms? Who would want her to fail?"

Carlisle smiled bitterly. "Almost anyone who has invested in slum property and raked in exorbitant rents for letting it to whole families a room at a time, sometimes even two or three families." He winced. "Or for sweatshops, gin mills, brothels, even opium dens. Very profitable indeed. You'd be surprised by some of the people who make money that way."

"How did Mrs. Shaw threaten them?" Vespasia asked. "Precisely what did she wish to do about it? Or should I say, what did she have the slightest realistic prospect of doing?"

"She wanted to change the law so that owners could be easily traced, instead of hiding behind companies and lawyers so they are virtually anonymous."

"Wouldn't it be better to make some law as to occupancy and sanitation?" Emily asked reasonably.

Carlisle laughed. "If you limit occupancy all you would do is put even more people out into the street. And how would you police it?"

"Oh — "

"And you'd never get a law passed on sanitation." His voice hardened. "People in power tend to believe that the poor have the sanitation they deserve, and if you gave them better, within a month they would have it back to its present state. It is easier for them to take their own luxury with a quiet conscience. Even so, to do anything about it would cost millions of pounds — "

"But each individual owner — " Emily argued. "They would have millions. At least over time — "

"Such a law would never be passed through Parliament." He smiled as he said it, but there was anger in his eyes and his hands by his sides were tight. "You forget who votes for them."

Again Emily said nothing. There were only two political parties with any chance of forming a government, and neither of them would espouse such a law easily, and no women had the franchise, the poor were ill organized and largely illiterate. The implication was too obvious.

Carlisle gave a little grunt that was almost a laugh. "That is why Mrs. Shaw was attempting to make it possible to discover without difficulty who owned such places. If it were public, social pressure would do a great deal that the law cannot."

"But don't social pressures come from the same people who vote?" Charlotte asked; then knew the moment she had said it that it was not so. Women did not vote, and subtle though it was, a very great deal of society was governed one way or another by women. Men might do all manner of things if they were sufficiently discreet, indulge tastes they would not acknowledge even to their fellows. But publicly and in the domestic tranquillity of their homes they would deplore such affronts to the fabric of a civilized people.

Carlisle saw the realization in her face and did not bother to explain.

"How perceptive of Mrs. Shaw," Vespasia said quietly. "I imagine she made certain enemies?"

"There was some . . . apprehension," he agreed. "But I don't believe she had as yet succeeded well enough to cause actual anxiety."

"Might she have, had she lived?" Charlotte asked with intense seriousness. She found herself regretting Clemency Shaw's death not only with the impartial pity for any loss but because she could never meet her, and the more she heard, the more strongly she felt she would have liked her very much.

Carlisle considered for a moment before replying. It was not a time for empty compliments. He had known enough of political life and the power of financial interests, and had been close enough to several murders, not to dismiss the possibility that Clemency Shaw had been burned to death to keep her from continuing in a crusade, however unlikely it seemed that she would affect the course of law, or of public opinion.

Charlotte, Emily and Vespasia all waited in silence.

"Yes," he said eventually. "She was a remarkable woman. She believed passionately in what she was doing, and that kind of honesty sometimes moves people where logic fails. There was no hypocrisy in her, no — " He frowned very slightly as he searched for precisely the words to convey the impression upon him of a woman he had met only twice, and yet who had marked him indelibly. "No sense that she was a woman seeking a cause to fight, or some worthy works to fill her time. There was nothing she wanted for herself; her whole heart was on easing the distress of those in filthy and overcrowded housing."

He saw Vespasia wince and knew it was pity rather than distaste.

"She hated slum landlords with a contempt that could make you feel guilty for having a roof over your own head." He smiled awkwardly, a crooked gesture very charming in his oddly crooked face. "I am very grieved that she is dead." He looked at Charlotte. "I presume Thomas is on the case, which is why you know about it?"

"Yes."

"And you intend to meddle?" The last observation was addressed to all three of them.

Vespasia sniffed a little at his choice of word, but she did not disagree in essence. "You could have expressed yourself more fortunately," she said with a very slight lift of her shoulders.

"Yes we do." Emily was forthright. Unlike Clemency Shaw, she was quite definitely looking for something to do, but that was no reason why she should not do it well. "I don't yet know how."

"Good." He had no doubts. "If I can be of assistance, please call on me. I had a great admiration for Clemency Shaw. I should like to see whoever murdered her rot in Coldbath Fields, or some similar place."

"They'll hang him," Vespasia said harshly. She knew Carlisle did not approve of the rope; it was too final, and there were too many mistakes. She did not herself, but she was a realist.

He looked at her levelly, but made no remark. The issue had been discussed before and they knew each other's feelings. A wealth of experience lay in common, other tragedies, errors and knowledge of pain. Crime was seldom a single act, or the fault of a single person.

"That is not a reason to leave it undone." Charlotte rose to her feet. "When I learn more I shall tell you."

"Be careful," Carlisle warned, going to the door ahead of her and holding it open while they went through, first Vespasia, her head high, her back very stiff, then Emily close behind, lastly Charlotte. He put his hand on her arm as she passed him. "You will be disturbing very powerful people who have a great deal at stake. If they have already murdered Clemency, they will not spare you."

"I shall be," she said with conviction, although she had no idea what she was going to do that would be the slightest use. "I shall merely gather information."

He looked at her skeptically, having been involved in several of her past meddlings, but he relaxed his grip and escorted them to the door and out into the sunlit street where Emily's carriage was waiting.

As soon as the horses began to move Emily spoke.

"I shall discover whatever I can about Mrs. Shaw and her struggles to have new laws passed to disclose who owns derelict property. I am sure if I think hard I must have some acquaintances who would know."

"You are a new bride," Vespasia cautioned

her gently. "Your husband may have rather different expectations of his first weeks at home from honeymoon."

"Ah — " Emily let out her breath, but it was only a hesitation in her flight of thought. "Yes — well that will have to be got around. I shall deal with it. Charlotte, you had better be discreet about it, but discover everything you can from Thomas. We must be aware of all the facts."

They did not wait at Vespasia's house but wished Vespasia good-bye and watched her alight and climb the steps to the front door, which was opened before her by the waiting maid. She went in with an absentminded word of thanks, still deep in thought. There were many social evils she had fought against in the long years since her widowhood. She enjoyed battle and she was prepared to take risks and she no longer cared greatly what others thought of her, if she believed herself to be in a just cause. Which was not that the loss of friends, or their disapproval, did not hurt her.

But now it was Emily who occupied her mind. She was far more vulnerable, not only to the emotions of her new husband, who might well wish her to be more decorous in her behavior, but also to the whims of society, which loved innovations in fashion, something to marvel at and whisper about, but hated anything that threatened to disturb the underlying stability of its members' familiar and extremely comfortable lives.

Charlotte parted from Emily at her own door after a brief hug, and heard the carriage clatter away as she went up the scrubbed steps into the hall. It smelled warm and clean; the sounds of the street were muffled almost to silence. She stood still for a moment. She could just hear Gracie chopping something on a board in the kitchen, and singing to herself. She felt an overwhelming sense of safety, and then gratitude. It was hers, all of it. She did not have to share it with anyone except her own family. No one would put up the rent or threaten her with eviction. There was running water in the kitchen, the range burned hot, and in the parlor and bedrooms there were fires. Sewage ran away unseen, and the garden was sweet with grass and flowers.

It was very easy to live here every day and forget the uncounted people who had no place warm enough, free of filth and smells, where they could be safe and have privacy enough for dignity.

Clemency Shaw must have been a most unusual woman to have cared so much for those in tenements and slums. In fact she was remarkable even to have known of their existence. Most well-bred women knew only what they were told, or read in such parts of the newspapers or periodicals as were considered suitable. Charlotte herself had not had any idea until Pitt had shown her the very edges of an utterly different world, and to begin with she had hated him for it.

Then she'd felt angry. There was a horrible irony that Clemency Shaw should be murdered by the destruction of her home, and whoever had caused it, Charlotte intended to find and expose, and their sordid and greedy motives with them. If Clemency Shaw's life could not bring attention to the evil of slum profiteers, then Charlotte would do all in her power to see that her death did.

Emily was bent on a similar purpose, but for slightly different reasons, and in an utterly different fashion. She entered the hallway of her spacious and extremely elegant house in a swirl of skirts and petticoats and flung off her hat, rearranging her hair to look even more casually flattering, fair tendrils curling on her neck and cheeks, and composed her face into an expression of tenderness touched with grief.

Her new husband was already at home, which she knew from the identity of the footman who had opened the door for her. Had Jack been out, Arthur would have been with him.

She pushed open the withdrawing room doors and made a dramatic entrance.

He was sitting by the fire with a tea tray on the low table and his feet up on the stool. The crumpets were already gone; there was only a ring of butter on the plate.

He smiled with warmth when he heard her and stood up courteously. Then he saw the expression on her face and suddenly his pleasure turned to concern.

"Emily — what is it? Is something wrong with Charlotte? Is she ill — is it Thomas?"

"No — no." She flew to his arms and put her head on his shoulder, partly so he would not meet her eyes. She was not entirely sure how far she could deceive Jack successfully. He was too much like her; he also had survived on his charm and very considerable good looks and he was aware of all the tricks and how to perform them. And it was also because she found herself still very much in love with him, and it was a most comfortable feeling. But she had better explain herself before he became alarmed. "No, Charlotte is perfectly well. But Thomas is engaged on a case which distresses her deeply — and I find I feel the same. A woman was burned to death — a brave and very good woman who was fighting to expose a vicious social evil. Great-Aunt Vespasia is most upset as well." Now she could abandon subterfuge and face him squarely.

"Jack, I feel we should do what we can to help — "

He smoothed her hair gently, kissed her, then with wide eyes and barely the beginning of a smile, met her gaze.

"Oh yes? And how shall we do that?"

She made a rapid change of tactics. Drama was not going to win. She smiled back. "I'm not sure — " She bit her lip. "What do you think?"

"What social evil?" he said guardedly. He knew Emily better than she realized.

"Slum owners who charge exorbitant rents for filthy and crowded tenements — Clemency Shaw wanted to make them answerable to public opinion by not being able to be anonymous behind rent collectors and companies and things."

He was silent for so long she began to wonder if he had heard her.

"Jack?"

"Yes," he said at last. "Yes we will — but together. You cannot do anything alone, Emily. We shall be threatening some very powerful people — there are millions of pounds — you'd be surprised how many fortunes are seated in St. Giles and the Devil's Acre — and the misery there."

She smiled very slightly; the thought was ugly and there flashed through her mind the faces of people she had known in her days with George. She had accepted them easily then; it never occurred to her to wonder where their incomes were generated. Certain people simply had money; it was a state of affairs that had always existed. Now she was less innocent, and it was not a comfortable feeling.

Jack was still holding her. He brushed one finger gently over her forehead, pushing back a wisp of hair.

"Still want to go on?" he asked.

She was startled how clearly he had understood her thoughts, and the twinges of both guilt and apprehension they had aroused.

"Of course." She did not move; it was extremely pleasant remaining in his arms. "There is no possible way to retreat now. What should I say to Great-Aunt Vespasia, or Charlotte — and more important, what should I say to myself?"

His smile widened and he kissed her gently, and then gradually with passion.

When she thought about money again, it was a faraway thing to be dealt with another day, real and important then, but for now there were other, better things.

CHAPTER THREE

Because Pitt had been sent for from the Bow Street station, and did not belong to Highgate, he reported the incident to his own superior officer, a man whom he both respected for his professional ability and liked for his candor and lack of pretension. Perhaps because Drummond was a gentleman by birth and had sufficient financial means not to have to concern himself with it, he did not feel the compulsion to prove his position.

He greeted Pitt with pleasure, interest quickening his lean face.

"Well?" he asked, standing up from his desk, not as a courtesy, which would have been absurd to a junior, even though he had offered Pitt considerable promotion. Pitt had declined it, because although he could dearly have used the money, he would have hated being behind a desk directing other men in the investigations. He wanted to see the people, watch faces, hear the inflections of a voice, the gestures and movements of the body. It was people who gave him both his pleasure and his pain, and the reality of his work. To give instructions to others and shuffle reports would rob him of the chance to exercise the real skills he possessed. To decline it had been Charlotte's decision as well as his, made because she knew him well enough to understand his happiness, and prefer it to the extra salary. It was one of those rarely-spoken-of generosities which deepened his sense of sharing with her and the knowledge that her commitment was still one of love.

Micah Drummond was regarding him with curiosity.

"Arson," Pitt replied. "I have looked through the physical evidence, such as it is, and there seems no doubt. There is too little left of the body to learn anything useful, but from the remains of the building the firemen say at least four separate fires were started, so whoever it was was determined to succeed."

Drummond winced and his eyes reflected his distress.

"And you say it was a woman who was found?"

"There seems little doubt it was a Mrs. Clemency Shaw." And he explained what they had learned from the brief investigations in the community of the immediate area, and from the Highgate police, including their natural inquiry into all the members of the small crowd which had turned out in the alarm and commotion to stand huddled in the background and stare. Perhaps among the sympathizers and offerers of help there had been one there to thrill at the glory of the flames and feel a vicarious power in their consuming destruction? Arsonists did not stay, but those touched with a certain madness did.

Drummond resumed his own seat behind his desk and waved Pitt to the most comfortable leather-upholstered chair opposite. It was an agreeable room, full of light and air from the large window. The walls were lined with bookshelves, except for the area around the fireplace, and the desk was polished oak, as beautiful as it was functional.

"Was it intended to have been the husband?" Drummond came straight to the point. "What do you know about him?"

Pitt tilted back in the chair and crossed his legs. "A doctor. An intelligent, articulate man, apparently open-minded and outspoken, but I haven't found time to look into his medical reputation yet."

"Your own feelings?" Drummond looked at him a little sideways.

Pitt smiled. "I liked the man, but then I've liked a few people who have committed murder, when desperate, frightened or injured enough. It would be so much easier if we could either like or dislike people and be decided about it; but I keep having to change my mind, and complicate my feelings by doing both at the same time in wildly differing proportions, as each new act and explanations for it emerge. It's such hard work." His smile broadened.

Drummond sighed and rolled his eyes upward in mock exasperation.

"A simple opinion, Pitt!"

"I should think he's an excellent candidate for murder," Pitt replied. "I can think of dozens of reasons why someone might want to silence a doctor, especially this one."

"A medical secret?" Drummond raised his eyebrows high. "Surely doctors keep such confidences anyway? Are you thinking of something discovered inadvertently and not bound by such an ethical code? For example . . . ?"

"There are many possibilities." Pitt shrugged, choosing at random. "A contagious disease which he would be obliged to report — plague, yellow fever — "

"Rubbish," Drummond interrupted. "Yellow fever in Highgate? And if that were so he would have reported it by now. Possibly a congenital disease such as syphilis, although that is unlikely. How about insanity? A man might well kill to keep that out of public knowledge, or even the knowledge of his immediate family, or prospective family, if he planned an advantageous marriage. Look into that, Pitt."

"I will."

Drummond warmed to the subject, leaning back a little in his chair and putting his elbows on the arms and his fingertips together in a steeple. "Maybe he knew of an illegitimate birth, or an abortion. For that matter maybe he performed one!"

"Why wait until now?" Pitt said reasonably. "If he's just done it, it will be among the patients he's visited in the last day or two; and anyway, why? If it was illegal he would be even less likely to speak of it, or make any record, than the woman. He has more to lose."

"What about the husband or father?"

Pitt shook his head. "Unlikely. If he didn't know about it beforehand, then he would probably be the one she was most anxious to keep it from. If he then discovered it, or learned it from her, the last way to keep it discreet would be to murder the doctor and cause all his affairs to be investigated by the police."

"Come on, Pitt," Drummond said dryly. "You know as well as I do that people in the grip of powerful emotions don't think like that — or half our crimes of impulse would never be committed, probably three quarters. They don't think; they feel — overwhelming rage, or fear, or simply confusion and a desire to lash out at someone and blame them for the pain they are suffering."

"All right," Pitt conceded, knowing he was right. "But I still think there are lots of other motives more probable. Shaw is a man of passionate convictions. I believe he would act on them, and devil take the consequences — "

"You do like him," Drummond said again with a wry smile, and knowledge of some unspoken hurt in his own past.

No reply was called for.

"He may have knowledge of a crime," Pitt said instead, following his own thoughts. "A death, perhaps of someone in terminal illness and great pain — "

"A merciful killing?" Drummond's expression quickened. "Possible. And occurring to me as someone who likes him less and perhaps has a clearer view, he may have assisted in a killing for less unselfish reasons, and the principle mover has grown nervous lest his accomplice becomes careless, or more likely from your description of Shaw as a man with nerve and passion, blackmail him. That would be an excellent cause for murder."

Pitt would like to have denied such a thought, but it was eminently logical, and to dismiss it would be ridiculous.

Drummond was watching him, his eyes curious.

"Perhaps," Pitt agreed aloud, and saw a small smile curl Drummond's lips. "But knowledge gained simply because of his professional skill is in my opinion more likely."

"What about a purely personal motive?" Drummond asked. "Jealousy, greed, revenge? Could there be another woman, or another man in love with his wife? Didn't you say he was expecting to be at home, and she not?"

"Yes." Pitt's mind was filled with all sorts of ugly possibilities, dark among them the Worlingham money, and the pretty face of Flora Lutterworth, whose father resented her frequent, private visits to Dr. Shaw.

"You need to have a great deal more." Drummond stood up and walked over towards the window, his hands in his pockets. He turned to face Pitt. "The possibilities are numerous — either for the murder of the wife, which happened, or for the murder of Shaw, which may have been attempted. It could be a very long, sad job. Heaven knows what other sins and tragedies you'll find — or what they will do to hide them. That's what I hate about investigation — all the other lives we overturn on the way." He poked his hands deeper into his pockets. "Where are you going to begin?"

"At the Highgate police station," Pitt replied, standing up also. "He was the local police surgeon — "

"You omitted to mention that."

Pitt smiled broadly. "Makes the knowledge without complicity look a trifle more likely, doesn't it?"

"Granted," Drummond said graciously. "Don't get carried away with it. What then?"

"Go to the local hospital and see what they think of him there, and his colleagues."

"You won't get much." Drummond shrugged. "They usually speak well of each other regardless. Imply that any one of them could have made an error, and they all close ranks like soldiers facing the enemy."

"There'll be something to read between the lines." Pitt knew what Drummond meant, but there was always the turn of a phrase, the overcompensation, the excessive fairness that betrayed layers of meaning and emotion beneath, conflicts of judgment or old desires. "Then I'll see his servants. They may have direct evidence, although that would be a lot to hope for. But they may also have seen or heard something that will lead to a lie, an inconsistency, an act concealed, someone where they should not have been." As he said it he thought of all the past frailties he had unearthed, foolishness and petty spites that had little or nothing to do with the crime, yet had broken old relationships, forged new ones, hurt and confused and changed. There were occasions when he hated the sheer intrusion of investigation. But the alternative was worse.

"Keep me advised, Pitt." Drummond was watching him, perhaps guessing his thoughts. "I want to know."

"Yes sir, I will."

Drummond smiled at the unusual formality, then nodded a dismissal, and Pitt left, going downstairs and out of the front doors to the pavement of Bow Street, where he caught a hansom north to Highgate. It was an extravagance, but the force would pay. He sat back inside the cab and stretched out his legs as far as possible. It was an agreeable feeling bowling along, not thinking of the cost.

The cab took him through the tangle of streets up from the river, across High Holborn to the Grey's Inn Road, north through Bloomsbury and Kentish Town into Highgate.

At the police station he found Murdo waiting for him impatiently, having already sifted through all the police reports of the last two years and separating all those in which Shaw had played a significant part. Now he stood in the middle of the room, uncarpeted, furnished with a wooden table and three hard-backed chairs. His fair hair was ruffled and his tunic undone at the neck. He was keen to acquit himself well, and in truth the case touched him deeply, but at the back of his mind was the knowledge that when it was all over Pitt would return to Bow Street. He would be left here in Highgate to resume working with his local colleagues, who were at present still acutely conscious of an outsider, and stung by resentment that it had been considered necessary.

"There they are, sir," he said as soon as Pitt was in the door. "All the cases he had the slightest to do with that could amount to anything, even those of disturbing the Queen's peace." He pointed his finger to one of the piles. "That's those. A few bloody noses, a broken rib and one broken foot where a carriage wheel went over it, and there was a fight afterwards between the man with the foot and the coachman. Can't see anybody but a madman murdering him over that."

"Neither can I," Pitt agreed. "And I don't think we're dealing with a madman. Fire was too well set, four lots of curtains, and all away from the servants' quarters, none of the windows overlooked by a footman or a maid up late, all rooms that would normally be closed after the master and mistress had gone to bed, no hallways or landings which might be seen by a servant checking doors were locked or a maid fetching a late cup of tea for someone. No, Murdo, I think our man with the oil and the matches is sane enough."

Murdo shivered and his face lost a little of its color. "It's a very ugly thing, Mr. Pitt. Someone must have felt a great passion to do it."

"And I doubt we'll find him in this lot." Pitt picked up the larger pile which Murdo had sorted for him. "Unless it's a death Shaw knew something very odd about. By the way, did you look into the demise of the late Theophilus Worlingham yet?"

"Oh, yes sir." Murdo was eager now. Obviously it was a task he had performed well and was waiting to recount it.

Pitt raised his eyebrows expectantly.

Murdo launched into his account, and Pitt sat down behind the desk, crossing his legs.

"Very sudden," Murdo began, still standing and hunching his shoulders a trifle in dramatic concentration. "He had always been a man of great physical energy and excellent health, what you might call a 'muscular Christian' I believe — " He colored slightly at his own audacity in using such a term about his superiors, and because it was an expression he had only heard twice before. "His vigor was a matter of some pride to him," he added as explanation, as the thought suddenly occurred to him that Pitt might be unfamiliar with the term.

Pitt nodded and hid his smile.

Murdo relaxed. "He fell ill with what they

98

took to be a slight chill. No one worried unduly, although apparently Mr. Worlingham himself was irritated that he should be no stronger than most. Dr. Shaw called upon him and prescribed aromatic oils to inhale to reduce the congestion, and a light diet, which did not please him at all, and that he should remain in bed — and give up smoking cigars, which also annoyed him very much. He made no comment as to a mustard plaster — "

Murdo screwed up his face in surprise and shook his head. "That's what my mam always used on us. Anyway, he got no better, but Shaw didn't call again. And three days later his daughter Clemency, the one who was murdered, visited and found him dead in his study, which is on the ground floor of his house, and the French doors open. He was lying stretched out on the carpet and according to the bobby as was called out, with a terrible look on his face."

"Why were the police sent for?" Pitt asked. After all, it was ostensibly a family tragedy. Death was hardly a rarity.

Murdo did not need to glance at his notes. "Oh — because o' the terrible look on his face, the French doors being open, and there was a great amount of money in the house, even twenty pounds in Treasury notes clutched in his hand, and they couldn't unlock

99

his fingers of it!" Murdo's face was pink with triumph. He waited for Pitt's reaction.

"How very curious." Pitt gave it generously. "And it was Clemency Shaw who found him?"

"Yes sir!"

"Did anyone know whether any money was missing?"

"No sir, that's what's so peculiar. He had drawn out seven thousand, four hundred and eighty-three pounds from the bank." Murdo's face was pale again and a little pinched at the thought of such a fortune. It would have bought him a house and kept him in comfort till middle age if he never earned another penny. "It was all there! In Treasury notes, tied up in bundles in the desk drawer, which wasn't even locked. It takes a lot of explaining, sir."

"It does indeed," Pitt said with feeling. "One can only presume he intended to make a very large purchase, in cash, or to pay a debt of extraordinary size, which he did not wish to do in a more usual manner with a draft. But why — I have no idea."

"Do you suppose his daughter knew, sir — I mean, Mrs. Shaw?"

"Possibly," Pitt conceded. "But didn't Theophilus die at least two years ago?"

Murdo's triumph faded. "Yes sir, two years

and three months."

"And what was the cause on the death certificate?"

"An apoplectic seizure, sir."

"Who signed it?"

"Not Shaw." Murdo shook his head fractionally. "He was the first on the scene, naturally, since Theophilus was his father-in-law, and it was his wife who found him. But just because of that, he called in someone else to confirm his opinion and sign the certificate."

"Very circumspect," Pitt agreed wryly. "There was a great deal of money in the estate, I believe. The amount withdrawn was only a small part of his total possessions. That's another thing you might look into, the precise degree and disposition of the Worlingham fortune."

"Yes sir, I will immediately."

Pitt held up his hand. "What about these other cases Shaw was involved with? Do you know about any of them?"

"Only three firsthand, sir; and none of them is anything out of the way. One was old Mr. Freemantle, who got a bit tiddley at the mayor's Christmas dinner party and got into a quarrel with Mr. Tiplady and pushed him down the steps of the Red Lion." He tried to keep his expression respectful, and failed.

"Ah — " Pitt let out his breath in a sigh

of satisfaction. "And Shaw was called to attend to the resulting injuries?"

"Yes sir. Mr. Freemantle fell over by hisself and had to be helped home. I reckon if he'd been a less important gentleman he'd 'ave cooled off the night in a cell! Mr. Tiplady had a few bruises and a nasty cut on his head, bled all over the place and gave them all a fright. Looked as white as a ghost, he did. Sobered him up better than a bucket of cold water!" His lips curled up in a smile of immeasurable satisfaction and his eyes danced. Then full memory returned and the light died. "Filthy temper the next day. Came in here shouting and carrying on, blamed Dr. Shaw for the headache he had, said he hadn't been properly treated, but I reckon he was just furious 'cause we'd all seen him make a right fool of hisself on the town hall steps. Dr. Shaw told him to take more water with it next time, and go home till he'd slept it off."

Pitt did not bother to pursue it. A man does not murder a doctor because the doctor speaks rather plainly about his debauchery and the consequent embarrassments.

"And the others?"

"Mr. Parkinson, Obadiah Parkinson, that is, got robbed up Swan's Lane one evening. That's up by the cemetery," he added in case Pitt did not know. "He was hit rather hard and the bobby that found him called Dr. Shaw, but there's nothing in that. He just took a good look at him, then said it was concussion and took him home in his own trap. Mr. Parkinson was very obliged."

Pitt put the two files aside and picked up the third.

"Death of the Armitage boy," Murdo said. "Very sad indeed, that. Dray horse took fright at something and bolted. Young Albert was killed instantly. Very sad. He was a good lad, and not more than fourteen."

Pitt thanked him and dispatched him to go and pursue the Worlingham money, then he began to read the rest of the files on the desk in front of him. They were all similar cases, some tragic, some carrying an element of farce, pomposity exposed by the frailties of the flesh. Perhaps domestic tragedy lay behind some of the reports of bruising and broken bones, it was even possible that some of the autopsies which read as pneumonia or heart failure concealed a darker cause, an act of violence; but there was nothing in the notes here in front of him to indicate it. If Shaw had seen something he had not reported it in any official channel. There were seven deaths in all, and even on a second and third reading, Pitt could find nothing suspicious in any of them.

Finally he abandoned it, and after informing the desk sergeant of his intention, he stepped out into the rapidly chilling afternoon air and walked briskly to the St. Pancras Infirmary, glancing briefly across the road at the Smallpox Hospital, then climbed the steps to the wide front entrance. He was already inside when he remembered to straighten his jacket, polish his boots on the backs of his trouser legs, transfer half the collected string, wax, coins, folded pieces of paper and Emily's silk handkerchief from one pocket to the other to balance the bulges a trifle, his fingers hesitating on the handkerchief's exquisite texture just a second longer than necessary. Then he put his tie a little nearer center and ran his fingers through his hair, leaving it conspicuously worse. Then he marched to the superintendent's office and rapped sharply on the door.

It was opened by a young man with fair hair and a narrow, anxious face.

"Yes?" he said, peering at Pitt.

Pitt produced his card, an extravagance which always gave him a tingle of pleasure.

"Inspector Thomas Pitt, Bow Street Police," the young man read aloud with alarm. "Good gracious. What can you possibly want here? There is nothing amiss, I assure you, nothing at all. Everything is in most excellent order." He had no intention of allowing Pitt in. They remained standing in the doorway.

"I do not doubt it," Pitt soothed him. "I have come to make some confidential inquiries about a doctor who I believe has worked here — "

"All our doctors are fine men." The protest was instant. "If there has been any impropriety — "

"None that I know of," Pitt interrupted. Drummond was right, it was going to be exceedingly difficult to elicit anything but panicky mutual defense. "There has been a most serious threat against his life." That was true, in essence if not precisely the way he implied it. "You may be able to help us discover who is responsible."

"Against his life? Oh, dear me, how monstrous. No one here would dream of such a thing. We save lives." The young man picked nervously at his tie, which was apparently in danger of throttling him.

"You must occasionally have failures," Pitt pointed out.

"Well — well, of course. We cannot work miracles. That would be quite unreasonable. But I assure you — "

"Yes — yes!" Pitt cut across him. "May I speak with the governor?"

The man bridled. "If you must! But I assure

you we have no knowledge of such a threat, or we should have informed the police. The superintendent is a very busy man, very busy indeed."

"I am impressed," Pitt lied. "However if this person succeeds in carrying out his threat, and murders the doctor in question, as well as his current victim, then your superintendent will be even busier, because there will be fewer physicians to do the work . . ." He allowed the train of thought to tail off as the man in front of him was alternately pink with annoyance and then white with horror.

However, the harassed superintendent, a lugubrious man with long mustaches and receding hair, could tell Pitt nothing about Shaw that advanced his knowledge. He was far more agreeable than Pitt expected, having no sense of his own importance, only of the magnitude of the task before him in battling disease for which he knew no cure; ignorance that swamped the small inroads of literacy; and a perception of cleanliness where there was too little pure water, too many people, no sanitation and frequently no outlet to a sewer, drains overflowed and rats were everywhere. If the Queen's consort could die of typhoid carried by poor drains, living in his own palace, what struggle was there to be waged in the houses of the ordinary, and the poor, let alone the slums of the destitute?

He escorted Pitt into his small, untidy office, which smelled faintly of soap and paper. The window was very small, and both gas lamps were lit and made a slight hissing sound. He invited Pitt to sit down.

"Nothing," he said regretfully. "Shaw is a damn good doctor, sometimes gifted. Seen him sit up all day and all night and all the next day with a sick man, and weep when he loses a mother and child." A smile spread across his lantern face. "And seen him bawl out a pompous old fool for wasting his time." He sighed. "And worse than that to a man who could have fed his children on milk and fruit, and didn't. Poor little beggars were twisted up with rickets. Never seen a man so furious as Shaw that day. He was shaking with passion and white to the lips." He took a deep breath and tilted back in his chair and looked at Pitt with surprisingly sharp eyes. "I like the man. I'm damned sorry about his wife. Is that why you're here — because you think the fire was meant for him?"

"It seems possible," Pitt replied. "Did he have any deep differences of opinion with his colleagues, that you know of?"

"Ha!" The superintendent barked out his laughter. "Ha! If you can ask that you don't know Shaw. Of course he did — with every-

one: colleagues, nurses, administrative staff —
me." His eyes were alive with a dark amusement. "And I knew of them all — I should
imagine everyone within earshot did. He
doesn't know the meaning of discretion — at
least where his temper is concerned." He slid
down off the tilt of his chair and sat up straight,
looking at Pitt more intently. "I don't mean
on medical matters, of course. He's closer than
an oyster with a confidence. Never betrayed
a secret even in consultation for another opinion. I doubt he's ever spoken a word of gossip
in his life. But got a temper like an Indian curry
when he sees injustice or humbug." He
shrugged his bony shoulders. "He's not always
right — but when he's proved wrong he'll usually come 'round, albeit not immediately."

"Is he well liked?"

The superintendent smiled at Pitt. "I'll not
insult you with a generous fiction. Those who
like him, like him very much. I am one of
them. But there are a good few he's offended
with what they consider uncalled-for brusque-
ness or frankness when it amounts to rudeness,
interference or undermining their position."
His gaunt, good-humored face showed the tolerance of years of battles and defeats. "There
are many men who don't care to be proved
wrong and shown a better way, especially in
front of others. And the harder and longer

they stick to their first position, the bigger fools they look when they finally have to back away from it and turn around." His smile grew broader. "And Shaw is frequently less than tactful in the way he goes about it. His wit is often quicker than his perception of people's feelings. More than once I've seen him set the room laughing at someone's expense, and known from the look on a man's face that he'd pay for it dearly one day. Few men care to be the butt of a joke; they'd rather be struck in the face than laughed at."

Pitt tried to make his voice casual, and knew immediately that it was a wasted effort. "Anyone in particular?"

"Not enough to set fire to the man's house," the superintendent replied, looking at Pitt wide-eyed and candid.

There was no point in fencing with the man and Pitt did not insult him by trying. "The names of those most offended?" he asked. "It will be something at least to eliminate them now. The house is gutted and Mrs. Shaw is dead. Someone set the fires."

The superintendent's face lost its humor as if it had been wiped away with a sponge, and somberness replaced it. He made no struggle.

"Fennady couldn't abide him," he replied, leaning back and beginning what was obviously a catalogue, but there was still more comprehension than judgment in his voice. "They quarreled over everything from the state of the monarchy to the state of the drains, and all issues between. And Nimmons. Nimmons is an old man with old ideas which he had no inclination to change. Shaw taught him some better ways, but unfortunately he did it in front of the patient, who promptly transferred his custom, bringing his very large family with him."

"Tactless," Pitt agreed.

"His middle name." The superintendent sighed. "But he saved the man's life. And there's Henshaw — he's young and full of new ideas, and Shaw can't be bothered with them either, says they are untried and too risky. The man's as contrary as an army mule at times. Henshaw lost his temper, but I don't think he really bears any resentment. That's all I can give you."

"No tact, no discretion with his colleagues, but how about impropriety with his patients?" Pitt was not yet ready to give up.

"Shaw?" The superintendent's eyebrows rose. "Damn your realism, but I suppose you have to. Not that I know of, but he's a charming and vigorous man. Not impossible some woman imagined more than there was."

He was interrupted by a sharp tap on the door.

"Come in," he said with a glance of apology at Pitt.

The same fair young man who had so disapproved of Pitt poked his head around the door with a look of equal distaste on his face.

"Mr. Marchant is here, sir." He ignored Pitt very pointedly. "From the town hall," he added for good measure.

"Tell him I'll be there in a few minutes," the superintendent replied without any haste.

"From the town hall," the young man repeated. "It is important — sir."

"So is this," the superintendent said very distinctly, without shifting his position at all. "Man's life might hang on it." Then he smiled lugubriously at the double meaning. "And the longer you stand there, Spooner, the longer it will be before I am finished here and can come and see Marchant! Get out man, and deliver the message!"

Spooner withdrew with umbrage, closing the door as sharply as he dared.

The superintendent turned to Pitt again with a slight shake of his head.

"Shaw . . ." Pitt prompted.

"Not impossible some woman fell in love with him," the superintendent resumed, shaking his head. "It happens. Odd relationship, doctor and patient, so personal, and yet so practical and in some ways remote. Wouldn't be the first time it has got out of hand, or been misunderstood by a husband, or a father." He pushed out his lip. "It's no secret Alfred Lutterworth thinks his daughter sees a damned sight too much of Shaw, and insists on doing it alone, and won't discuss what passes between them or what her ailment might be. Handsome girl, and great expectations. Old Lutterworth made a fortune in cotton. Don't know if anyone else has his eyes on her. Don't live in Highgate myself."

"Thank you, sir," Pitt said sincerely. "You've given me a great deal of your time, and been some help at least in eliminating certain possibilities."

"I don't envy you your job," the superintendent replied. "I thought mine was hard, but I fear yours will be harder. Good day to you."

When Pitt left the hospital the autumn evening was dark and the gas lamps were already lit. It was now October, and a few early leaves crunched under his feet as he strode towards the intersection where he could get a cab. The air had a clarity and sharpness that promised frost in a week or two. The stars shone in pinpricks of light infinitely far away, flickering and sparking in the cold. Out here in Highgate there was no fog from the river, no smoke in the air from factories or densely packed

112

houses huddled back-to-back. He could smell the wind blowing off the fields and hear a dog barking in the distance. One day he must take Charlotte and the children for a week in the country. She had not been away from Bloomsbury for a long time. She would love it. He began to think of small economies he could make, ways he could save enough for it to be possible, and the expression on her face when he could tell her. He would keep it to himself until he was sure.

He strode out along the footpath and was so lost in thought that the first cab passed him by and was over the rise in the hill and disappearing before he realized it.

In the morning he returned to Highgate to see if Murdo had discovered anything of interest, but he was already out hot on the scent, and had left only the briefest notes to that effect. Pitt thanked the desk sergeant, who still grudged him his interference in a local matter which he believed they could well have handled themselves. Pitt left and went back to the hospital to speak to the Shaws' butler.

The man was propped up in bed looking haggard, his eyes deep socketed with shock and pain, his face unshaved and his left arm bound in bandages. There were raw grazes on his face and one scab beginning to form.

It was unnecessary for the doctor to tell Pitt that the man had been badly burned.

Pitt stood by the bedside and in spite of the fact that it was blood, carbolic, sweat and the faint odor of chloroform that he could smell in the air, the sharp stench of smoke and wet cinders came back to him as if he had stood by the ruined house only a few minutes since, and then seen the charred wreck of Clemency Shaw's body lying on a stretcher in the morgue, barely recognizable as human. The anger inside him knotted his stomach and his chest till he found it hard to form the words in his mouth or force the breath to make speech.

"Mr. Burdin?"

The butler opened his eyes and looked at Pitt with no interest.

"Mr. Burdin, I am Inspector Pitt of the Metropolitan Police. I have come to Highgate to find out who set the fire that burned Dr. Shaw's house — " He did not mention Clemency. Perhaps the man had not been told. This would be a cruel and unnecessary shock. He should be informed with gentleness, by someone prepared to stay with him, perhaps even to treat his grief if it worsened his condition.

"I don't know," Burdin said hoarsely, his lungs still seared by the smoke. "I saw nothing, heard nothing till Jenny started screaming out. Jenny's the housemaid. Her bedroom's nearest the main house."

"We did not imagine you had seen the fires started." Pitt tried to sound reassuring. "Or that you knew anything obvious. But there may have been something which, on reflection, could be of importance — perhaps when put together with other things. May I ask you some questions?" It was a polite fiction to seek permission, but the man was badly shocked, and in pain.

"Of course." Burdin's voice dropped to a croak. "But I've already been thinking, turning it over and over in my mind." His face furrowed now with renewed effort. "But I don't remember anything different at all — not a thing. Everything was just as — " The breath caught in his throat and he began to cough as the raw lining hurt anew.

Pitt was confused for a moment, panic growing inside him as the man's face suffused with blood as he struggled for air, tears streaming down his cheeks. He stared around for help, and there was none. Then he saw water on the table in the corner and reached for it, tipping it into a cup clumsily in his haste. He clasped Burdin around the shoulders and eased him up and put the cup to his lips. At first he choked on it, spluttering it over himself, then at last enough trickled down his burning throat and cooled it. The pain was eased and he lay back, exhausted. It would be cruel and pointless to require him to speak again. But the questions must be asked.

"Don't speak," Pitt said firmly. "Turn your hand palm up if the answer is yes, and down if it is no."

Burdin smiled weakly and turned his palm up.

"Good. Did anyone call on the doctor at his house that day, other than his surgery appointments?"

Palm up.

"Tradesmen or business?"

Palm down.

"Personal acquaintance?"

Palm on its side.

"Family?"

Palm up.

"The Worlingham sisters?"

Palm down, very definitely.

"Mr. or Mrs. Hatch?"

Palm up.

"Mrs. Hatch?"

Palm down.

"Mr. Hatch? Was there a quarrel, raised voices, unpleasantness?" Although Pitt could think of nothing that could aggravate a temperamental difference into murder.

Burdin shrugged fractionally and turned his

hand on its side.

"Not more than usual?" Pitt guessed.

Burdin smiled and there was a flicker of something like humor in his eyes, but again he shrugged. He did not know.

"Anyone else call?"

Palm up.

"Local person?"

Palm up and raised a little.

"Very local? Mr. Lindsay?"

Burdin's face relaxed in a smile, the palm remained up.

"Anyone else that you know of?"

Palm down.

He thought of asking if there was any mail that might be unusual or of interest, but what would such a thing be? How could anyone recognize it?

"Did Dr. Shaw seem anxious or disturbed about anything that day?"

The palm was down, but indecisive, hovering above the bed cover.

Pitt took a guess, drawn from what he had observed of Shaw's temperament. "Angry? Was he angry about something?"

The palm came up quickly.

"Thank you, Mr. Burdin. If you think of anything else, comments, a letter, unusual arrangements, please tell the hospital and write it down for me. I shall come immediately. I hope you recover quickly."

Burdin smiled and closed his eyes. Even that small effort had tired him.

Pitt left, angry himself at so much physical pain, and helpless because he could do nothing for it, and he had learned little he felt of use. He imagined Shaw and Hatch probably quarreled fairly regularly, simply because their natures were utterly different. They would almost certainly perceive any issue with opposite views.

The Shaws' cook was in a far less serious state of health, and he left the hospital and took a hansom for the short ride down Highgate Hill and through Holloway to the Seven Sisters Road and the house of her relatives, which Murdo had given him. It was small, neat and shabby, exactly what he expected, and he was permitted in only with reluctance and after considerable argument.

He found the cook sitting up in bed in the best bedroom, wrapped around more against the indecency of being visited by a strange man than to prevent any chill. She had been burned on one arm and had lost some of her hair, giving her a lopsided, plucked look which had it been less tragic would have been funny. As it was Pitt had difficulty in maintaining a perfectly sober expression.

The niece, bustling with offense, remained

obtrusively present every moment of the time.

"Mrs. Babbage?" Pitt began. All cooks were given the courtesy title of "Mrs." whether they were married or not.

She looked at him with alarm and her hand flew to her mouth to stifle a shriek.

"I mean you no harm, Mrs. Babbage — "

"Who are you? What do you want? I don't know you." She craned upwards as if his mere presence threatened her with some physical danger.

He sat down quickly on a small bedroom chair just behind him and tried to be disarming. She was obviously still in an extreme state of shock, emotional if not from her injuries which appeared to be relatively slight.

"I am Inspector Pitt," he said, introducing himself, avoiding the word *police*. He knew how respectable servants hated even an association with crime as tenuous as the presence of the police. "It is my duty to do what I can to discover how the fire started."

"Not in my kitchen!" she said so loudly it startled her niece, who drew her breath in in a loud gasp. "Don't you go accusing me, or Doris! I know how to tend a stove. Never had so much as a coal fall out, I 'aven't; never mind burnin' down an 'ole 'ouse."

"We know that, Mrs. Babbage," he said soothingly. "It did not begin in the kitchen."

She looked a trifle mollified, but still her eyes were wide and wary and she twisted a rag of a handkerchief around and around in her fingers till the flesh of them was red with the friction. She was afraid to believe him, suspecting a trap.

"It was begun deliberately, in the curtains of four different ground-floor rooms," he elaborated.

"Nobody would do such a thing," she whispered, winding the handkerchief even more tightly. "What do you come to me for?"

"Because you might have seen something odd that day, noticed someone unusual hanging around — " Even as he said it he knew it was hopeless. She was too shocked to recall anything, and he himself did not believe it had been a tramp or a casual vagrant. It was too careful; it spoke of a deep hatred, or insatiable greed, or fear of some intolerable loss. It came back to his mind again with renewed force: what did Stephen Shaw know — and about whom?

"I didn't see nothin'." She began to weep, dabbing at her eyes, her voice rising again. "I mind me own business. I don't ask no questions an' I don't listen be'ind no doors. An' I don't give meself airs to think things about the master nor the mistress — "

"Oh?" Pitt said instantly. "That's very

commendable. I suppose some cooks do?"

" 'Course they do."

"Really? Like what, for example?" He endeavored to look puzzled. "If you were that sort, what may you have wondered?"

She drew herself up in virtue and glared at him over the top of her large hand, wrapped around with the sodden handkerchief.

"Well, if I were that sort — which I in't — I might 'ave wondered why we let one of the maids go, when there weren't nothin' wrong wiv 'er, and why we 'aven't 'ad salmon like we used to, nor a good leg o' pork neither — an' I might 'ave asked Burdin why we 'aven't 'ad a decent case o' claret come inter the 'ouse in six months."

"But of course you didn't," Pitt said judiciously, hiding the shadow of a smile. "Dr. Shaw is very fortunate to have such a discreet cook in his household."

"Oh, I don't know as I can cook for 'im anymore!" She started sniffing again violently. "Jenny's given 'er notice an' as soon as she's fit she'll go back 'ome ter Somerset where she comes from. An' Doris in't no more'n a chit of a thing — thirteen mebbe. An' poor Mr. Burdin's so bad who can say if 'e'll ever be the same again? No, I got ter be in a respectable 'ouse, for me nerves."

There was no purpose in arguing with her,

121

and for the time being Shaw had no need of servants — there was no house for them to live in or to wait upon. And apart from that, Pitt's mind was racing with the very interesting fact that the Shaws had apparently reduced their standard of living recently, to the degree that the cook had noticed it and it had set her mind wondering.

He stood up, wished her well, thanked the niece, and took his departure. Next he went in search of Jenny and Doris, neither of whom were burned more than superficially and more suffering from shock and fright and some considerable pain, but not in danger of relapse, as might be the case with Burdin.

He found them in the parsonage, in the care of Lally Clitheridge, who needed no explanation of his call.

But even after careful questioning they could tell him nothing of use. They had seen no one unusual in the neighborhood; the house had been exactly as it was at any other time. It had been a very ordinary day until they were roused, Jenny by the smell of smoke as she lay awake, thinking of some matter she blushed to recall and would not name, and Doris by Jenny's screams.

He thanked them and went out as dusk was falling and walked briskly southwards to Woodsome Road and the home of the woman who came in daily to do the heavy work, a Mrs. Colter. It was a small house but the windows were clean and the step scrubbed so immaculately he avoided putting his boots on it out of respect.

The door was opened by a big, comfortable woman with a broad-cheeked face, an ample bosom, and an apron tied tightly around her waist, the pocket stuffed full of odds and ends and her hair trailing out of a hasty knot on the back of her neck.

"Who are you?" she said in surprise, but there was no ill nature in it. "I dunno you, do I?"

"Mrs. Colter?" Pitt removed his rather worn hat, now a little crooked in the crown.

"That's me. It don't tell me who you are!"

"Thomas Pitt, from the Metropolitan Police — "

"Oh — " Her eyes widened. "You'll be about poor Dr. Shaw's fire, then. What a terrible thing. She was a good woman, was Mrs. Shaw. I'm real grieved about that. Come in. I daresay you're cold — an' 'ungry, mebbe?"

Pitt stepped in, wiping his feet carefully on the mat before going onto the polished linoleum floor. He almost bent and took his boots off, as he would have done at home. A smell of rich stew assailed him, delicate with onions and the sweetness of fresh carrots and turnips.

"Yes," he said with feeling. "Yes I am."

"Well I don't know as I can 'elp you." She led the way back and he followed after. To sit in a room with that aroma, and not eat, would be very hard. Her generous figure strode ahead of him and into the small, scrubbed kitchen, a huge pot simmering on the back of the stove filling the air with steam and warmth. "But I'll try," she added.

"Thank you." Pitt sat down on one of the chairs and wished she meant the stew, not information.

"They say it were deliberate," she said, taking the lid off the pot and giving its contents a brisk stir with a wooden ladle. "Although 'ow anybody could bring theirselves to do such a thing I'm sure I don't know."

"You said 'how,' Mrs. Colter, not 'why,' " Pitt observed, inhaling deeply and letting it out in a sigh. "You can think of reasons why?"

"In't much meat in it," she said dubiously. "Just a bit o' skirt o' mutton."

"You have no ideas why, Mrs. Colter?"

" 'Cos I in't got the money for more, o' course," she said, looking at him as if he were simple, but still not unkindly.

Pitt blushed. He was well used enough to poverty not to have made such an idiotic remark, or one so condescending.

"I mean why anyone should set fire to Dr.

124

and Mrs. Shaw's house!"

"You want some?" She held up the ladle.

"Yes please, I would."

"Lots o' reasons." She began to dish up a generous portion in a large basin. "Revenge, for one. There's them as says 'e should'a looked after Mr. Theophilus Worlingham better'n 'e did. Although I always thought Mr. Theophilus would wind 'isself up into a fit and die one day. An' 'e did. But then that don't mean everyone sees it that way." She put the bowl down in front of him and handed him a spoon to eat with. It was mostly potatoes, onions, carrots and a little sweet turnip with a few stray ends of meat, but it was hot and full of flavor.

"Thank you very much," he said, accepting the bowl.

"Don't think it'd 'ave much to do wiv it." She dismissed the notion. "Mr. Lutterworth was fair furious with Dr. Shaw, on account of 'is daughter, Miss Flora, nippin' ter see 'im all hours, discreet like, not through the reg'lar surgery. But Mrs. Shaw weren't worried, so I don't suppose there were nothin' in it as there shouldn't 'a bin. Leastways, not much. I think Dr. Shaw and Mrs. Shaw kept their own ways a lot. Good friends, like, but maybe not a lot more."

"That's very observant of you, Mrs. Colter," Pitt said doubtfully.

"Need more salt?" she asked.

"No thank you; it's perfect."

"Not really." She shook her head.

"Yes it is. It doesn't need a thing added," he assured her.

"Don't take much ter see when people is used ter each other, and respects, but don't mind if the other gets fond o' someone else."

"And Dr. and Mrs. Shaw were fond of someone else?" Pitt's spoon stopped in midair, even the stew forgotten.

"Not as I know of. But Mrs. Shaw went off up to the city day after day, and 'e wished 'er well and never cared nor worried as who she went wiv; or that the vicar's wife came all over unnecessary every time Dr. Shaw smiled at 'er."

This time Pitt could not dismiss his amusement, and bent his head over the dish at least to conceal the worst of it.

"Indeed?" he said after another mouthful. "Do you think Dr. Shaw was aware of this?"

"Bless you, no. Blind as a bat, 'e is, to other people's feelin's o' that nature. But Mrs. Shaw, she saw it, an' I think she were kind o' sorry for 'er. 'E's a bit of a poor fish, the Reverend. Means well. But 'e's no man, compared wi' the doctor. Still," she sighed, "that's 'ow it is, in't it?" She regarded his empty bowl. "You want some more?"

He considered the family she had to feed and pushed the plate away from him.

"No thank you, Mrs. Colter. That answered the need perfectly. Very fine flavor."

She colored a little pink. She was unused to compliments, and pleased and awkward at the same time.

"It's nuthin' but ordinary." She turned away to give it a fierce stir.

"Ordinary to you, maybe." He rose from the table and pushed the chair back in, something he would not have bothered to do at home. "But I'm much obliged to you. Is there anything else you can think of that might have bearing on the fire?"

She shrugged. "There's always the Worlingham money, I suppose. Though I don't see 'ow. Don't think the doctor cared that much about it, and they ain't got no children, poor souls."

"Thank you, Mrs. Colter. You've been most helpful."

"Don't see that I 'ave. Any fool could'a told you as much, but if it pleases you, then I'm glad. I 'ope you catch whoever done it." She sniffed hard and turned her back to stir the pot again. "She were a fine woman, an' I grieve sorely that she's gorn — an' in such an 'orrible way."

"I will, Mrs. Colter," he said rather recklessly, and then when he was out on the footpath in the sharp evening air, wished he had been more reserved. He had not the faintest idea who had crept around cutting the glass, pouring oil on curtains and lighting those fires.

In the morning he returned to Highgate immediately, turning the case over and over in his mind on the long journey. He had told Charlotte of the progress he had made, largely negative, because she had asked him. She had taken an interest in the case beyond his expectations, because as yet there was little human drama of the sort which usually engaged her emotions. She gave him no explanation, except that she was sorry for the dead woman. It was a fearful way to die.

He had assured her that in all probability Clemency Shaw had been overcome by smoke long before any flames reached her. It was even possible she had not woken.

Charlotte had been much comforted by it, and since he had already told her his progress was minimal, she had asked him no more. Instead she turned to her own business of the day, giving volleys of instructions to Gracie, who stood wide-eyed and fascinated in the kitchen doorway.

Pitt stopped the hansom at Amos Lindsay's

house, paid him off and walked up to the front door. It was opened by the black-haired manservant again and Pitt asked if he might speak with Dr. Shaw.

"Dr. Shaw is out on call" — the briefest of hesitations — "sir."

"Is Mr. Lindsay at home?"

"If you care to come in I shall inquire if he will receive you." The manservant stood aside. "Who shall I say is calling?"

Did he really not remember, or was he being deliberately condescending?

"Inspector Thomas Pitt, of the Metropolitan Police," he replied a little tartly.

"Indeed." The manservant bowed so slightly only the light moving across his glistening head determined it at all. "Will you be so good as to wait here? I shall return forthwith." And without bothering to see if Pitt would do as he was bidden, he walked rapidly and almost silently towards the back of the house.

Pitt had time to stare again around the hall with its fierce and exotic mixture of art and mementos. There were no paintings, nothing of the nature of European culture. The statuary was wooden or ivory, the lines alien, looking uneasy in the traditional dimensions of the room with its paneling and squared windows letting in the dull light of an October morning. The spears should have been held in dark hands, the headdresses moving, instead of pinned immobile against the very English oak. Pitt found himself wondering what an unimaginably different life Amos Lindsay had lived in countries so unlike anything Highgate or its residents could envision. What had he seen, and done; whom had he known? Was it something learned there which had prompted his political views which Pascoe so abhorred?

His speculation was cut short by the manservant reappearing, regarding him with mild disapproval.

"Mr. Lindsay will see you in his study, if you will come this way." This time he omitted the "sir" altogether.

In the study Amos Lindsay stood with his back to a brisk fire, his face pink under his marvelous white hair. He did not look in the least displeased to see Pitt.

"Come in," he said, ignoring the manservant, who withdrew soundlessly. "What can I do for you? Shaw's out. No idea how long, can't measure the sick. What can I add to your knowledge? I wish I knew something. It's all very miserable."

Pitt glanced back towards the hallway and its relics. "You must have seen a good deal of violence at one time and another." It was more an observation than a question. He thought of Great-Aunt Vespasia's friend, Zenobia Gunne, who also had trekked into Africa, and sailed uncharted rivers and lived in strange villages, with people no European had seen before.

Lindsay was watching him curiously. "I have," he conceded. "But it never became ordinary to me, nor did I cease to find violent death shocking. When you live in another land, Mr. Pitt, no matter how strange it may seem at first, it is a very short time until its people become your own, and their grief and their laughter touches you as deeply. All the differences on earth are a shadow, compared with the sameness. And to tell you the truth, I have felt more akin to a black man dancing naked but for his paint, under the moon, or a yellow woman holding her frightened child, than I ever have to Josiah Hatch and his kind pontificating about the place of women and how it is God's will that they should suffer in childbirth." He pulled a face and his remarkably mobile features made it the more grotesque. "And a Christian doctor doesn't interfere with it! Punishment of Eve, and all that. All right, I know he is in the majority here." He looked straight at Pitt with eyes blue as the sky, and almost hidden by the folds of his lids, as if he were still screwing them up against some tropical sun.

Pitt smiled. He thought quite possibly he would feel the same, had he ever been out of England.

"Did you ever meet a lady named Zenobia Gunne on your travels — " He got no further because Lindsay's face was full of light and incredulity.

"Nobby Gunne! Of course I know her! Met her in a village in Ashanti once — way back in '69. Wonderful woman! How on earth do you know her?" The happiness fled from his face and was replaced by alarm. "Dear God! She's not been — "

"No! No," Pitt said hastily. "I met her through a relative of my sister-in-law. At least a few months ago she was in excellent health, and spirits."

"Thank heaven!" Lindsay waved at Pitt to sit down. "Now what can we do about Stephen Shaw, poor devil? This is a very ugly situation." He poked at the fire vigorously, then replaced the fire iron set and sat down in the other chair. "He was extremely fond of Clemency, you know. Not a great passion — if it ever was, it had long passed — but he liked her, liked her deeply. And it is not given to many men to like their wives. She was a woman of rare intelligence, you know?" He raised his eyebrows and his small vivid eyes searched Pitt's countenance.

Pitt thought of Charlotte. Immediately her face filled his mind, and he was overwhelmed with how much he also liked his wife. The friendship was in its own way as precious as the love, and perhaps a greater gift, something born of time and sharing, of small jokes well understood, of helping each other through anxiety or sorrow, seeing the weaknesses and the strengths and caring for both.

But if for Stephen Shaw the passion had gone, and he was a passionate man, then could it have been kindled elsewhere? Would friendship, however deep, survive that whirlwind of hunger? He wanted to believe so; instinctively he had liked Shaw.

But the woman, whoever she was — she would not feel such constraints. Indeed she might seethe with jealousy, and the fact that Shaw still liked and admired his wife might make that frail outer control snap — and result in murder.

Lindsay was staring at him, waiting for a response more tangible than the thoughtful expression on his face.

"Indeed," Pitt said aloud, looking up again. "It would be natural if he found it hard at present to think of who might hold him in such enmity, or feel they had enough to gain from either his death or his wife's. But since you know him well, you may be able to give more suggestions, unpleasant as it would be. At least we might exclude some people . . ." He left the sentence hanging in the air, hoping it would be unnecessary to press any further.

Lindsay was too intelligent to need or wish for any more prompting. His eyes wandered over the relics here in the room. Perhaps he was thinking of other lands, other peoples with the same passions, less colored and confused by the masks of civilization.

"Stephen has certainly made enemies," he said quietly. "People of strong convictions usually do, especially if they are as articulate about them as he is. I am afraid he has little patience with fools, and even less with hypocrites — of which this society provides a great many, in one form or another." He shook his head. A coal settled in the fire with a shower of sparks. "The more we think we are sophisticated sometimes the sillier we get — and certainly the more idle people there are with nothing to fill their minds except making moral rules for everyone else, the more hypocrisy there is as to who keeps them and who doesn't."

Pitt envisioned a savage society in the sun on vast plains with the flat-topped trees he had seen in paintings, and grass huts, drum music and imprisoning heat — a culture that had not changed since memory's record began.

What had Lindsay done there, how had he lived? Had he taken an African wife, and loved her? What had brought him back to Highgate on the outskirts of London and the heart of the Empire with its white gloves, carriages, engraved calling cards, gas lamps, maids in starched aprons, little old ladies, portraits of bishops, stained-glass windows — and murder?

"Whom in particular may he have offended?" He looked at Lindsay curiously.

Lindsay's face was suddenly wreathed in smiles. "Good heavens, man — everyone. Celeste and Angeline think he failed to treat Theophilus with proper attention, and that if he had not, the old fool would still be alive — "

"And would he?"

Lindsay's eyebrows shot up. "God knows. I doubt it. What can you do for an apoplectic seizure? He couldn't sit 'round the clock with him."

"Who else?"

"Alfred Lutterworth thinks Flora is enamored of him — which she may well be. She's in and out of the house often enough, and sees Stephen on her own, out of normal surgery hours. She may imagine other people don't know — but they most certainly do. Lutterworth thinks Stephen is seducing her with an eye to the money, of which there is

135

a very great deal." The bland look of slight amusement on his face made Pitt think that the idea of Shaw murdering his wife because she stood in the way of such a marriage had not crossed his mind. His weathered face, so lined it reflected every expression, was touched with pity and a shadow of something like contempt, without its cruelty — but there was no fear in it.

"And of course Lally Clitheridge is appalled by his opinions," Lindsay went on, his smile broadening. "And fascinated by his vitality. He is ten times the man poor old Hector is, or ever will be. Prudence Hatch is fond of him — and frightened of him — for some reason I haven't discovered. Josiah can't abide him for a dozen reasons that are inherent in his nature — and Stephen's. Quinton Pascoe, who sells beautiful and romantic books, reviews them, and quite genuinely loves them, thinks Stephen is an irresponsible iconoclast — because he supports John Dalgetty and his avant-garde views of literature, or at least he supports his freedom to express them, regardless of whom they offend."

"Do they offend people?" Pitt asked, curious for himself as well as for any importance it might have. Surely no literary disapproval could be powerful enough to motivate murder? Ill temper, dislike, contempt, but surely only a madman kills over a matter of taste?

"Grossly." Lindsay noted Pitt's skepticism and there was a light of irony in his own eyes. "You have to understand Pascoe and Dalgetty. Ideals, the expression of thought and the arts of creation and communication are their lives." He shrugged. "But you asked me who hated Stephen from time to time — not who I thought would actually set fire to his house with the intent of burning him to death. If I knew anyone I thought would do that I should have told you long before you came to the door asking."

Pitt acknowledged it with a grimace, and was about to pursue the matter when the man-servant reappeared to announce that Mr. Dalgetty had called to ask if Lindsay would receive him. Lindsay glanced at Pitt with a flash of amusement, then indicated his agreement.

A moment later John Dalgetty came in, obviously having assumed Lindsay was alone. He launched into speech immediately, his voice ringing with enthusiasm. He was a dark man of medium stature and high, almost vertical forehead, fine eyes, and a shock of hair which was now receding a little. He was very casually dressed with a loose black cravat tied in what had probably been a bow when he set out that morning. Now it was merely a bundle. His jacket was overlong and loose, and the whole effect was extremely untidy, but had a certain panache.

"Quite brilliant!" He waved his hands. "Just what Highgate needs — indeed the whole of London! Shake up some of these tired old ideas, make people think. That's what matters, you know — freedom from the rigid, the orthodox that ossifies the faculties of invention and discovery." He frowned, leaning a little forward in his urgency. "Man is a creature full of the power of the mind, if only we free it from the shackles of fear. Terrified of the new, quaking at the prospect of making a mistake. What do a few mistakes matter?" He hunched his shoulders high. "If in the end we discover and name some new truth? Cowards — that's what we're fast becoming. A nation of intellectual cowards — too timorous to undertake an adventure into unknown regions of thought or knowledge." He swung one arm wide towards an Ashanti spear on the wall. "How would our Empire be if all our voyagers of the seas or explorers of the lands had been too afraid of anything new to circumnavigate the earth, or venture into the dark continents of Africa and India?" He poked his fingers at the floor. "Right here in England, that's where! And the world" — he flung out his hand dramatically — "would belong to the French, or the Spanish, or God knows whom. And here we are leaving all the voyages of the mind to the Germans, or whomever, because we are afraid of treading on a few toes. Have you seen Pascoe? He's practically foaming at the mouth because of your monograph on the wrongs of the ownership of the means of production! Of course it's brilliant. Full of new ideas, new concepts of community and the proper division of wealth. I shall review it as widely as — oh — " Suddenly he noticed Pitt and his face fell with amazement, then as quickly filled with curiosity. "I beg your pardon, sir, I was unaware Mr. Lindsay had company. John Dalgetty." He bowed very slightly. "Seller of rare books and reviewer of literature, and I hope, disseminator of ideas."

"Thomas Pitt," Pitt replied. "Inspector of police, and I hope discoverer of truth, or at least a measurable portion of it — we will never know it all, but sometimes enough to assist what serves as justice."

"Good gracious me." Dalgetty laughed aloud, but there was considerable nervousness in it as well as humor. "A policeman with an extraordinary turn of phrase. Are you making fun of me, sir?"

"Not at all," Pitt replied sincerely. "The truth of a crime, its causes and its effects, are far beyond us to reach. But we may, if we are diligent and lucky, discover who committed it, and at least some portion of why."

"Oh — ah — yes, indeed. Very terrible." Dalgetty drew his black brows down and shook his head a little. "A fine woman. Didn't know her closely myself, always seemed to be busy with matters of her own, good works and so forth. But excellent reputation." He looked at Pitt with something almost like a challenge. "Never heard a word against her from anyone. Great friend of my wife's, always conversing with one another. Tragic loss. I wish I could help, but I know nothing at all, absolutely nothing."

Pitt was inclined to believe him, but he asked a few questions in case there was some small fact in among the enthusiasm and opinions. He learned nothing, and some fifteen minutes after Dalgetty departed, still muttering praises of the monograph, Stephen Shaw himself returned, full of energy, coming in like a gale, flinging doors open and leaving them swinging. But Pitt saw the shadows under his eyes and the strain in the lines around his mouth.

"Good afternoon, Dr. Shaw," he said quietly. "I am sorry to intrude again, but there are many questions I need to ask."

"Of course." Shaw absentmindedly

140

straightened the Ashanti spear, and then moved to the bookcase and leveled a couple of volumes. "But I've already told you everything I can think of."

"Someone lit those fires deliberately, Dr. Shaw," Pitt reminded him.

Shaw winced and looked at Pitt. "I know that. If I had the faintest idea, don't you think I'd tell you?"

"What about your patients? Have you treated anyone for any disease that they might wish to conceal — "

"For God's sake, what?" Shaw stared at him, eyes wide. "If it were contagious I should report it, regardless of what they wished! If it were insanity I should have them committed!"

"What about syphilis?"

Shaw stopped in mid movement, his arms in the air. "Touché," he said very quietly. "Both contagious and causing insanity in the end. And I should very probably keep silence. I certainly should not make it public." A flicker of irony crossed his face. "It is not passed by shaking hands or sharing a glass of wine, nor is the insanity secret or homicidal."

"And have you treated any such cases?" Pitt smiled blandly, and had no intention of allowing Shaw to sidestep an answer.

"If I had, I should not break a patient's confidence now." Shaw looked back at him with candor and complete defiance. "Nor will I discuss with you any other medical confidence I may have received — on any subject."

"Then we may be some considerable time discovering who murdered your wife, Dr. Shaw." Pitt looked at him coolly. "But I will not stop trying, whatever I have to overturn to find the truth. Apart from the fact that it is my job — the more I hear of her, the more I believe she deserves it."

Shaw's face paled and the muscles tightened in his neck and his mouth pulled thin as if he had been caught by some necessary inner pain, but he did not speak.

Pitt knew he was wounding, and hated it, but to withhold now might make it worse in the close future.

"And if, as seems probable, it was not your wife the murderer was after," he went on, "but yourself, then he — or she — will very possibly try again. I assume you have considered that?"

Shaw's face was white.

"I have, Mr. Pitt," he said very quietly. "But I cannot break my code of medical ethics on that chance — even were it a certainty. To betray my patients would not necessarily save me — and it is not a bargain I am prepared to make. Whatever you learn, you will have to do it in some other way."

Pitt was not surprised. It was what he had expected of the man, and in spite of the frustration, he would have been at least in part disappointed had he received more.

He glanced at Lindsay's face, pink in the reflected firelight, and saw a deep affection in it and a certain wry satisfaction. He too would have suffered a loss had Shaw been willing to speak.

"Then I had better continue with it in my own way," Pitt accepted, standing a little straighter. "Good day, Mr. Lindsay, and thank you for your frankness. Good day, Dr. Shaw."

"Good day, sir," Lindsay replied with unusual courtesy, and Shaw stood silent by the bookshelves.

The manservant returned and showed him out into the autumn sunlight, thin and gold, and the wind scurrying dry leaves along the footpath. It took him half an hour's brisk walk before he found a hansom to take him back into the city.

CHAPTER FOUR

Charlotte did not enjoy the public omnibus, but to hire a hansom cab all the way from Bloomsbury to her mother's home on Cater Street was an unwarranted extravagance; and should there be any little surplus for her to spend, there were better things that might be done with it. Particularly she had in mind a new gown on which to wear Emily's silk flowers. Not, of course, that a cab fare would purchase even one sleeve of such a thing, but it was a beginning. And with Emily home again, there might arise an occasion to wear such a gown.

In the meantime she climbed aboard the omnibus, gave the conductor her fare, and squeezed between a remarkably stout woman with a wheeze like a bellows and a short man whose gloomy stare into the middle distance of his thoughts threatened to take him beyond his stop, unless he were traveling to the end of the line.

"Excuse me." Charlotte sat down firmly, and they were both obliged to make way for her, the large woman with a creak of whalebone and rattle of taffeta, the man in silence.

She alighted presently and walked in mild, blustery wind the two hundred yards along the street to the house where she had been born and grown up, and where seven years ago she had met Pitt, and scandalized the neighbors by marrying him. Her mother, who had been trying unsuccessfully to find a husband for her ever since she had been seventeen, had accepted the match with more grace than Charlotte had imagined possible. Perhaps it was not unmixed with a certain relief? And although Caroline Ellison was every bit as traditional, as ambitious for her daughters, and as sensitive to the opinions of her peers as anyone else, she did love her children and ultimately realized that their happiness might lie in places she herself would never have considered even tolerable.

Now even she admitted to a considerable fondness for Thomas Pitt, even if she still preferred not to tell all her acquaintances what he did as an occupation. Her mother-in-law, on the other hand, had never ceased to find it a social disaster, nor lost an opportunity to say so.

Charlotte mounted the steps and rang the bell. She had barely time to step back before it opened and Maddock the butler ushered her in.

"Good afternoon, Miss Charlotte. How very pleasant to see you. Mrs. Ellison will be delighted. She is in the withdrawing room, and at the moment has no other callers. Shall I take your coat?"

"Good afternoon, Maddock. Yes, if you please. Is everyone well?"

"Quite well, thank you," he replied automatically. It was not expected that one would reply that the cook had rheumatism in her knees, or that the housemaid had sniffles and the kitchen maid had twisted her ankle staggering in with the coke scuttle. Ladies were not concerned in such downstairs matters. He had never really grasped that Charlotte was no longer a "lady" in the sense in which she had been when she grew up in this house.

In the long-familiar withdrawing room Caroline was sitting idly poking at a piece of embroidery, her mind quite absent from it; and Grandmama was staring at her irritably, trying to think of a sufficiently stinging remark to make. When she was a girl embroidery was done with meticulous care, and if one were unfortunate enough to be a widow with no husband to please, that was an affliction to be borne with dignity and some grace, but one still did things with proper attention.

"If you continue in that manner you will stitch your fingers, and get blood on the linen," she said just as the door opened and Charlotte was announced. "And then it will be good for nothing."

"It is good for very little anyway," Caroline replied. Then she became aware of the extra presence.

"Charlotte!" She dropped the whole lot, needle, linen, frame and threads, on the floor and rose to her feet with delight — and relief. "My dear, how nice to see you. You look very well. How are the children?"

"In excellent health, Mama." Charlotte hugged her mother. "And you?" She turned to her grandmother. "Grandmama? How are you?" She knew the catalogue of complaint that would follow, but it would be less offensive if it were asked for than if it were not.

"I suffer," the old lady replied, looking Charlotte up and down with sharp, black eyes. She snorted. She was a small, stout woman with a beaked nose, which in her youth had been considered aristocratic, at least by those most kindly disposed towards her. "I am lame — and deaf — which if you came to visit us more often you would know without having to ask."

"I do know, Grandmama," Charlotte replied, determined to be agreeable. "I asked only to show you that I care."

"Indeed," the old woman grunted. "Well sit down and tell us something of interest. I am also bored. Although I have been bored ever since your grandfather died — and for some time before, come to that. It is the lot of women of good breeding to be bored. Your mother is bored also, although she has not learned to resign herself to it as I have. She has developed no skill at it. She does bad embroidery. I cannot see well enough to embroider anymore, but when I could, it was perfect."

"You will have tea." Caroline smiled across her mother-in-law's head. These conversations had been part of her life for twenty years, and she accepted them with good grace. Actually, she was seldom bored; when the first grief of her widowhood had passed she had discovered new and most interesting pursuits. She had found herself free to read the newspapers for the first time in her life, any pages she wished. She had learned a little of politics and current affairs, social issues of debate, and she had joined societies which discussed all manner of things. She was finding time heavy this afternoon simply because she had decided to spend the time at home with the old lady, and they had until now received no callers.

"Please." Charlotte accepted, seating herself in her favorite chair.

Caroline rang for the maid and ordered tea, sandwiches, cakes and fresh scones and jam, then settled to hear whatever news Charlotte might have, and to tell her of a philosophical group she had recently joined.

The tea came, was poured and passed, and the maid retired.

"You will have seen Emily, no doubt." Grandmama made it a statement, and her face was screwed up with disapproval. "In my day widows did not marry again the moment their poor husbands were cold in the ground. Unseemly haste. Most unseemly. And it's not even as if she were bettering herself. Stupid girl. That I could understand, at least. But Jack Radley! Who on earth are the Radleys? I ask you!"

Charlotte ignored the whole matter. She was confident Jack Radley would flatter the old lady and she would melt like butter on a hot crumpet. It was simply not worth trying to argue the point now. And of course whatever Emily had brought her from Europe she would criticize, but she would be pleased all the same, and show it off relentlessly.

As if aware of Charlotte's well-controlled temper the old lady swiveled around and glared at her over the top of her eyeglasses.

"And what are you doing with yourself these

days, miss? Still meddling in your husband's affairs? If there is anything in the world that is totally and inexcusably vulgar, it is curiosity about other people's domestic tragedies. I told you at the time no good would come of it." Again she snorted spitefully and settled back a little in her seat. "Detective, indeed!"

"I am not involved in Thomas's present case, Grandmama." Charlotte took a fifth cucumber sandwich and ate it with relish. They really were delicious, thin as wafers, and sweet and crisp.

"Good," the old woman said with satisfaction. "You eat too much. It is unladylike. You have lost all the refinement of manner you used to have. I blame you, Caroline! You should never have allowed this to happen. If she had been my daughter she would not have been permitted to marry beneath her!"

Caroline had long ago ceased to defend herself from such remarks, and she did not wish to quarrel, even though she was provoked. In fact it gave her a certain satisfaction to catch her mother-in-law's beady eyes and smile sweetly back at her, and see the irritation in them.

"Unfortunately I had not your skill," she said gently. "I managed very well with Emily — but Charlotte defeated me."

The old lady was temporarily beaten.

"Hah!" she said, at a loss for words.

Charlotte hid her smile, and took another sip of tea.

"Given up meddling, have you?" The old lady renewed the attack. "Emily will be disappointed!"

Charlotte sipped her tea again.

"All cutpurses and thieves, I suppose," Grandmama continued. "Been demoted, has he?"

Finally Charlotte was drawn, in spite of her resolution.

"No. It is arson and murder. A very respectable woman has been burned to death in Highgate. In fact her grandfather was a bishop," she added with something unpleasantly like triumph.

The old lady looked at her guardedly. "What bishop would that be? Sounds unlikely to me."

"Bishop Worlingham," Charlotte replied immediately.

"Bishop Worlingham! Augustus Worlingham?" The old lady's eyes snapped sharp with interest; she leaned forward in her chair and thumped her black walking stick on the ground. "Answer me, girl! Augustus Worlingham?"

"I imagine so." Charlotte could not remember Pitt having mentioned the bishop's Christian name. "There surely cannot be two."

"Don't be impertinent!" But the old lady was too excited to be more than cursorily critical. "I used to know his daughters, Celeste and Angeline. So they still live in Highgate. Well why not? Very fortunate area. I should go and call upon them, convey my condolences upon their loss."

"You can't!" Caroline was appalled. "You've never mentioned them before — you cannot have called upon them in years!"

"And is that any cause not to comfort them now in their distress?" the old lady demanded, eyebrows high, searching for reason in an unreasonable house. "I shall go this very afternoon. It is quite early. You may accompany me if you wish." She hauled herself to her feet. "As long as you do not in any circumstances display a vulgar curiosity." And she stumped past the tea trolley and out of the withdrawing room without so much as glancing behind her to see what reaction her remarks had provoked.

Charlotte looked at her mother, undecided whether to declare herself or not. The idea of meeting people so close to Clemency Shaw was strongly appealing, even though she believed the person who had connived her death, whoever had lit the taper, was someone threatened by her work to expose slum profiteers to the public knowledge.

Caroline drew in her breath, then her expression of incredulity turned rapidly through contemplation to shamefaced interest.

"Ah — " She breathed in and out again slowly. "I really don't think we should permit her to go alone, do you? I have no idea what she might say." She bit her lip to suppress a smile. "And curiosity is so vulgar."

"Perfectly terrible," Charlotte agreed, rising to her feet and clasping her reticule, ready for departure.

They made the considerable ride to Highgate in close to silence. Once Charlotte asked the old lady if she could inform them of her acquaintance with the Worlingham sisters, and anything about their present situation, but the reply was scant, and in a tone that discouraged further inquiry.

"They were neither prettier nor plainer than most," the old lady said, as if the question had been fatuous. "I never heard any scandal about them — which may mean they were virtuous, or merely that no opportunity for misbehavior offered itself. They were the daughters of a bishop, after all."

"I was not seeking scandal." Charlotte was irritated by the implication. "I simply wondered what nature of people they were."

"Bereaved," came the reply. "That is why

I am calling upon them. I suspect you of mere curiosity, which is a character failing of a most distasteful sort. I hope you will not embarrass me when we are there?"

Charlotte gasped at the sheer effrontery of it. She knew perfectly well the old lady had not called on the Worlinghams in thirty years, and assuredly would not now had Clemency died in a more ordinary fashion. For once a suitably stinging reply eluded her, and she rode the remainder of the journey in silence.

The Worlingham house in Fitzroy Park, Highgate, was imposing from the outside, solid with ornate door and windows, and large enough to accommodate a very considerable family and full staff of indoor servants.

Inside, when they were admitted by a statuesque parlormaid, it was even more opulent, if now a little shabby in various places. Charlotte, well behind her mother and grandmother, had opportunity to glance around with a more lingering eye. The hall was unusually large, paneled in oak, and hung with portraits of varying age, but no plates underneath to tell their names. An instant suspicion crossed Charlotte's mind that they were not ancestral Worlinghams at all, merely dressing to awe a visitor. In the place of honor where the main light shone on it was by far the largest portrait, that of an elderly gentleman in very current dress. His broad face was pink fleshed, his silver hair grew far back on his sloping forehead and curled up over his ears, forming an almost luminous aureole around his head. His eyes were blue under heavy lids, and his chin was wide; but his most remarkable feature was the benign, complacent and supremely confident smile on his lips. Under this the plate was legible even as Charlotte walked past it to the morning room door. BISHOP AUGUSTUS T. WORLINGHAM.

The maid departed to inquire whether they would be received, and Grandmama bent herself stiffly to sit in one of the chairs, staring around at the room critically. The pictures here were gloomy landscapes, framed samplers with such mottoes as "Vanity, vanity, all is vanity," in cross-stitch; "The price of a good woman is above rubies," framed in wood; and "God sees all," with an eye in satin and stem stitches.

Caroline pulled a face.

Charlotte imagined the two sisters as girls sitting on a sabbath afternoon in silence, carefully sewing such things, all fingers and thumbs, hating every moment of it, wondering how long until tea when Papa would read the Scriptures to them; they would answer dutifully, and then after prayers be released to go to bed.

Grandmama cleared her throat and looked with disfavor at an enormous glass case filled with stuffed and mounted birds.

The antimacassars were stitched in brown upon linen, and all a trifle crooked.

The parlormaid returned to say that the Misses Worlingham would be charmed to receive them, and accordingly they followed her back across the hall and into the cavernous withdrawing room hung with five chandeliers. Only two of these were lit, and the parquet wooden floors were strewn with an assortment of Oriental rugs of several different shades and designs, all a fraction paler where the pile had been worn with constant tread, from the door to the sofa and chairs, and to a distinct patch in front of the fire, as if someone had habitually stood there. Charlotte remembered with an odd mixture of anger and loss how her father had stood in front of the fire in winter, warming himself, oblivious of the fact that he was keeping it from everyone else. The late Bishop Worlingham, no doubt, had done the same. And his daughters would not have raised their voices to object, nor would his wife when she was alive. It brought a sharp flavor of youth, being at home with her parents and sisters, the callowness and the safety of those times, taken for granted then. She glanced at Caroline, but Caroline was watching Grandmama as she sailed up to the elder of the Misses Worlingham.

"My dear Miss Worlingham, I was so sorry to hear of your bereavement. I had to come and offer my condolences in person, rather than simply write a letter. You must feel quite dreadful."

Celeste Worlingham, a woman in her late fifties with strong features, dark brown eyes and a face which in her youth must have been handsome rather than pretty, now looked both confused and curious. The marks of shock were visible in the strained lines around her mouth and the stiff carriage of her neck, but she had admirable composure, and would not give in to unseemly grief, at least not in public, and she considered this public. Obviously she did not recall even the barest acquaintance with any of her visitors, but a lifetime of good manners overrode all.

"Most kind of you, Mrs. Ellison. Of course Angeline and I are very grieved, but as Christians we learn to bear such loss with fortitude — and faith."

"Naturally," Grandmama agreed, a trifle perfunctorily. "May I introduce to you my daughter-in-law, Mrs. Caroline Ellison, and my granddaughter, Mrs. Pitt."

Everyone exchanged courtesies and Grandmama fixed her eyes on Celeste, then changed her mind and looked at Angeline, a younger, fairer woman with mild features and a comfortable, domestic look. Grandmama swayed back and forth on her feet and planted her stick heavily on the carpet and leaned on it.

"Please sit down, Mrs. Ellison," Angeline said immediately. "May we offer you some refreshment? A tizanne, perhaps."

"How kind," Grandmama accepted with near alacrity, pulling Caroline sharply by the skirt so she also was obliged to sit on the fat red sofa a step behind her. "You are as thoughtful as ever," Grandmama added for good measure.

Angeline reached for the hand bell and rang it with a sharp, tinkling sound, and almost as soon as she had replaced it on the table the maid appeared. She requested a tizanne, then changed her mind and asked for tea for all of them.

Grandmama sank back in her seat, set her stick between her own voluminous skirts and Caroline's, and rather belatedly masked a look of satisfaction with concern again.

"I imagine your dear brother will be a great strength to you, and of course you to him," she said unctuously. "He must be most distressed. It is at such a time that families must support each other."

"Exactly what our father the bishop used

to say," Angeline agreed, leaning forward a little, her black dress creasing across her ample bosom. "He was such a remarkable man. The family is the strength of the nation, he used to say. And a virtuous and obedient woman is the heart of the family. And dear Clemency was certainly that."

"Poor Theophilus passed on," Celeste said with a touch of asperity. "I am surprised you did not know. It was in *The Times*."

For an instant Grandmama was confounded. It was no use saying she did not read obituaries; no one would have believed her. Births, deaths, marriages and the Court calendar were all that gentlewomen did read. Too much of the rest was sensational, contentious or otherwise unsuitable.

"I am so sorry," Caroline murmured reluctantly. "When was it?"

"Two years ago," Celeste answered with a slight shiver. "It was very sudden, such a shock to us."

Caroline looked at Grandmama. "That will have been when you were ill yourself, and we did not wish to distress you. I imagine by the time you were recovered we had forgotten we had not told you."

Grandmama refused to be obliged for the rescue. Charlotte was moved to admiration for her mother. She would have allowed the old lady to flounder.

"That is the obvious explanation," Grandmama agreed, staring at Celeste and defying her to disbelieve.

A flicker of respect, and of a certain dry humor, crossed Celeste's intelligent face.

"Doubtless."

"It was very sudden indeed." Angeline had not noticed the exchange at all. "I am afraid we were inclined to blame poor Stephen — that is, Dr. Shaw. He is our nephew-in-law, you know? Indeed I almost said as much, that he had given Theophilus insufficient care. Now I feel ashamed of myself, when the poor man is bereaved himself and in such terrible circumstances."

"Fire." Grandmama shook her head. "How can such a thing have happened? A careless servant? I've always said servants are nothing like they used to be — they're slovenly, impertinent and careless of detail. It is quite terrible. I don't know what the world is coming to. I don't suppose she had this new electrical lighting, did she? I don't trust that at all. Dangerous stuff. Meddling with the forces of nature."

"Oh, certainly not," Angeline said quickly. "It was gas, like ours." She barely glanced at the chandelier. Then she looked wistful and a little abashed. "Although I did see an ad-

160

vertisement for an electric corset the other day, and wondered what it might do." She looked at Charlotte hopefully.

Charlotte had no idea; her mind had been on Theophilus and his unexpected death.

"I am sorry, Miss Worlingham, I did not see it. It sounds most uncomfortable — "

"Not to say dangerous," Grandmama snapped. She not only disapproved of electricity, she disapproved even more of being interrupted in what she considered to be her conversation. "And absurd," she added. "A bedpost and a maid with a good strong arm was sufficient for us — and we had waists a man could put his hands 'round — or at least could think of such a thing." She swiveled back to Celeste. "What a mercy her husband was not also killed," she said with a perfectly straight face, not even a flicker or a blush. "How did it happen?"

Caroline closed her eyes and Grandmama surreptitiously poked her with her stick to keep her from intervening.

Charlotte let out a sigh.

Celeste looked taken aback.

"He was out on a call," Angeline answered with total candor. "A confinement a little earlier than expected. He is a doctor, you know, in many ways a fine man, in spite of — " She stopped as abruptly as she had begun, a

161

tinge of pride creeping up her cheeks. "Oh dear, I do beg your pardon. One should not speak ill, our dear father was always saying that. Such a wonderful man!" She sighed and smiled, staring mistily into some distance within her mind. "It was such a privilege to have lived in the same house with him and been of service, caring for him, seeing that he was looked after as such a man should be."

Charlotte looked at the plump, fair figure with its benign face, a blurred echo of her sister's, softer, and more obviously vulnerable. She must have had suitors as a young woman. Surely she would rather have accepted one of them than spend her life ministering to her father's needs, had she been permitted the chance. There were parents who kept their daughters at home as permanent servants, unpaid but for their keep, unable to give notice because they had no other means of support, ever dutiful, obedient, ever loving — and at the same time hating, as all prisoners do — until it was too late to leave even when the doors were at last opened by death.

Was Angeline Worlingham one of these? Indeed, were they both?

"And your brother also." Grandmama was unstoppable; her beadlike eyes were bright and she sat upright with attention. "Another fine man. Tragic he should die so young. What was the cause?"

"Mama-in-law!" Caroline was aghast. "I really think we — Oh!" She gave a little squeal as the old lady's stick poked her leg with a sharp pain.

"Have you the hiccups?" Grandmama inquired blandly. "Take a little more of your tea." She returned to Celeste. "You were telling us of poor Theophilus's passing. What a loss!"

"We do not know the cause," Celeste said with chill. "It appears it may have been an apoplectic seizure of some sort, but we are not perfectly sure."

"It was poor Clemency who found him," Angeline added. "That is another thing for which I hold Stephen responsible. Sometimes he is a touch too free in his ideas. He expects too much."

"All men expect too much," Grandmama opined sententiously.

Angeline blushed furiously and looked at the floor; even Celeste looked uncomfortable.

This time Caroline ignored all strictures and spoke.

"That was a most unfortunate turn of phrase," she apologized. "I am sure that you meant it was unfair to expect Clemency to cope with the discovery of her father's death, especially when it was quite unexpected."

"Oh — of course." Angeline collected herself with a gasp of relief. "He had been ill for a few days, but we had not presumed it serious. Stephen paid scant regard to it. Of course" — she drew down her brows and lowered her voice confidentially — "they were not as close as they might have been, in spite of being father- and son-in-law. Theophilus disapproved of some of Stephen's ideas."

"We all disapprove of them," Celeste said with asperity. "But they were social and theological matters, not upon the subject of medicine. He is a very competent doctor. Everyone says so."

"Indeed, he has many patients," Angeline added eagerly, her plump hands fingering the beads at her bosom. "Young Miss Lutterworth would not go to anyone else."

"Flora Lutterworth is no better than she should be," Celeste said darkly. "She consults him at every fit and turn, and I have my own opinions that she would be a good deal less afflicted with whatever malady it is had Stephen a wart on the end of his nose, or a squint in one eye."

"Nobody knows what it is," Angeline whispered. "She looks as healthy as a horse to me. Of course they are very *nouveau riche*," she added, explaining to Caroline and Charlotte. "Working-class really, for all that money. Alfred Lutterworth made it in cotton mills in

Lancashire and only came down here when he sold them. He tries to act the gentleman, but of course everyone knows."

Charlotte was unreasonably irritated; after all, this was the world in which she had grown up, and at one time might have thought similarly herself.

"Knows what?" she inquired with an edge to her voice.

"Why, that he made his money in trade," Angeline said with surprise. "It is really quite obvious, my dear. He has brought up his daughter to sound like a lady, but speech is not all, is it?"

"Certainly not," Charlotte agreed dryly. "Many who sound like ladies are anything but."

Angeline took no double meaning and settled back in her seat with satisfaction, rearranging her skirts a trifle. "More tea?" she inquired, holding up the silver pot with its ornate, swan neck spout.

They were interrupted by the parlormaid's return to announce that the vicar and Mrs. Clitheridge had called.

Celeste glanced at Grandmama, and realized she had not the slightest intention of leaving.

"Please show them in," Celeste instructed with a lift of one of her heavy eyebrows. She did not glance at Angeline; humor was not something they were able to share, their perceptions were too different. "And bring more tea."

Hector Clitheridge was solid and bland, with the sort of face that in his youth had been handsome, but was now marred by constant anxiety and a nervousness which had scored lines in his cheeks and taken the ease and directness out of his eyes. He came forward now in a rush to express his condolences yet again, and then was startled to find an additional three women there whom he did not know.

His wife, on the other hand, was quite homely and probably even in her very best years could only have offered no more charms than a freshness of complexion and a good head of hair. But her back was straight, she could well have walked with a pile of books on her head without losing any, and her eye was calm, her manner composed. Her voice was unusually low and agreeable.

"My dear Celeste — Angeline. I know we have already expressed our sympathies and offered our services, but the vicar thought we should call again, merely to assure you that we are most sincere. So often people say these things as a matter of custom, and one does not care to take them up on it for precisely that reason. Some people avoid the bereaved, which is scarcely Christian."

"Quite," her husband agreed, relief flooding his face. "If there is anything we can do for you?" He looked from one to the other of them as if he awaited a suggestion.

Celeste introduced them to the company already present, and everyone exchanged greetings.

"How very kind," Clitheridge said, smiling at Grandmama. His hands fiddled with his badly tied tie, making it worse. "Surely a sign of true friendship when one comes in times of grief. Have you known the Misses Worlingham long? I do not recall having seen you here before."

"Forty years," Grandmama said promptly.

"Oh my goodness, how very fine. You must be exceedingly fond of each other."

"And it is thirty of them since we last saw you." Celeste finally lost her temper. It was apparent from her face that Grandmama mildly amused her, but the vicar's waving hands and bland words irritated her beyond bearing. "So kind of you to have come just now when we are suffering a dramatic loss."

Charlotte heard the sarcasm in her tone, and could see in the strong, intelligent face that none of the motives or excuses had passed her by.

Grandmama sniffed indignantly. "I told you, I did not read of poor Theophilus's death.

If I had I would surely have come then. It is the least one can do."

"And at Papa's death too, no doubt," Celeste said with a very slight smile. "Except perhaps you did not read of that either?"

"Oh, Celeste. Don't be ridiculous." Angeline's eyes were very wide. "Everyone heard of Papa's passing. He was a bishop, after all, and a most distinguished one. He was respected by absolutely everybody!"

Caroline attempted to rescue Grandmama.

"I think perhaps when someone passes in the fullness of their years, it is not quite the same grief as when a younger person is cut off," she offered.

Grandmama swung around and glared at her, and Caroline colored faintly, more with annoyance at herself than apology.

The vicar fidgeted from one foot to the other, opened his mouth to say something, then realized it was a family dispute, and retreated hastily.

Charlotte spoke at last.

"I came because I had heard of Mrs. Shaw's magnificent work attempting to improve the housing standards of the poor," she said into the silence. "I have several friends who held her in the very highest esteem, and feel her loss is one to the whole community. She was a very fine woman."

There was utter silence. The vicar cleared his throat nervously. Angeline gave a little gasp, then put her handkerchief to her mouth and stifled it. Grandmama swiveled around in her seat with a crackle of taffeta and glared at Charlotte.

"I beg your pardon?" Celeste said huskily.

Charlotte realized with a hollowness, and a rush of blood up her cheeks, that obviously Clemency's work was unknown to her family, and to her vicar. But it was impossible to retreat; she had left herself no room at all. There was nothing to do but advance and hope for the best.

"I said she was a very fine woman," she repeated with a rather forced smile. "Her efforts to improve the living standards of the poor were greatly admired."

"I fear you are laboring under a misapprehension, Mrs. . . . er — Pitt," Celeste replied, now that she had recovered her poise. "Clemency was not concerned in any such matter. She did her ordinary duties such as any Christian woman will do. She took soup and the like, preserves and so on, to the deserving poor about the neighborhood, but so do we all. No one does as much as Angeline. She is always busy with some such thing. Indeed, I serve on several committees to assist young women who have — er — fallen into difficult circumstances and lost their character. You appear to have poor Clemency confused with someone else — I have not the slightest idea who."

"Nor I," Angeline added.

"It sounds a very virtuous work," Mrs. Clitheridge put in tentatively. "And most courageous."

"Quite unsuitable, my dear." The vicar shook his head. "I am sure dear Clemency would not have done such a thing."

"So am I." Celeste finished the subject with a chilly stare at Charlotte, her rather heavy brows raised very slightly. "Nevertheless, it was gracious of you to call. I am sure your mistake was perfectly genuine."

"Perfectly," Charlotte assured her. "My informants were the daughter of a duke and a member of Parliament."

Celeste was taken aback. "Indeed? You have some notable acquaintances — "

"Thank you." Charlotte inclined her head as if accepting a compliment.

"There must be another lady by the same name," the vicar suggested soothingly. "It seems unlikely, and yet what other explanation is there?"

"You must be right, my dear." His wife touched his arm with approval. "It seems obvious now. Of course that is what has happened."

"It all seems to be quite unimportant." Grandmama reasserted her influence on the conversation. "My acquaintance is with you, and has been since our youth. I should like to pay my respects at the funeral, and should be greatly indebted if you would inform me as to when it is."

"Oh certainly," the vicar answered before either of the Misses Worlingham had time. "How kind of you. Yes — it is to be held in St. Anne's, next Thursday at two o'clock in the afternoon."

"I am obliged." Grandmama was suddenly very gracious.

The door opened again and the parlormaid announced Mr. and Mrs. Hatch, and was followed immediately by a woman of about the same height as Angeline, and with a considerable resemblance to her in feature. The nose was a trifle more pronounced, the eyes had not faded, nor the hair, and she was obviously a generation younger, yet there was much in the bearing that was like, and she too wore the total black of mourning.

Her husband, only a step behind her, was of medium height and extreme gravity. He reminded Charlotte quite strongly of pictures of Mr. Gladstone, the great Liberal prime minister, in his earlier years. There was the same dedicated purpose in his stare, the same look of total rectitude and certainty in his own convictions. His side whiskers were less bristling and his nose of less grand proportions; still, the impression was sharp.

"My dear Prudence." Celeste greeted Mrs. Hatch with outstretched hands.

"Aunt Celeste." Prudence went to her and they kissed each other lightly, then she moved to her Aunt Angeline, and was kissed more closely and held a moment longer.

Josiah was more formal, but his condolences seemed every bit as sincere. In fact he looked quite obviously distressed; his face was pale and there was a drawn appearance to the skin about his mouth. His emotions were apparently very deep and he kept them in control with some effort.

"The whole situation is quite dreadful," he said fixedly, looking at no one in particular. "Everywhere there is moral decline and decay. Young people in confusion, not knowing whom or what to admire anymore, women unprotected — " His voice was thick with distress. "Look at this unspeakable business in Whitechapel. Bestial — quite bestial. A sign of the chaos of our times — rising anarchy, the Queen closed up in Osborne ignoring us all, the Prince of Wales squandering his time and money in gambling and loose living, the Duke of Clarence worse." Still he looked at no one, his mind consumed with his inner vision. His body was motionless, but there was great strength in it, a feeling of waiting power. "The coarsest and most absurd ideas are being propagated and there is one tragedy after another. Everything has begun to slip ever since the dear bishop died. What a terrible loss that was." For a moment a look of sheer anguish crossed his features as if he gazed upon the end of a golden age, and all that followed must be darker and lonelier. His hands clenched in front of him, large knuckled and powerful. "And no one remotely near his stature has arisen to carry God's light for the rest of us."

"Theophilus . . ." Angeline said tentatively, then stopped. His look of contempt froze the words before they were formed.

"He was a good man," Prudence said loyally.

"Of course he was," her husband agreed. "But not his father's equal, not by a very long way. He was a pygmy in comparison." A strange mixture of grief and contempt crossed his face, then a zeal that had a wild beauty, almost visionary. "The bishop was a saint! He had wisdom incomparable with any of us. He understood the order of things as they should be, he had the insight into God's ways and how we should live His word." He smiled briefly. "How often I have heard him give counsel to men — and to women. Always his advice was wise and of spiritual and moral upliftment."

Angeline sighed gently and reached for her handkerchief, a wisp of cambric and lace.

"Men be upright," he continued. "Be utterly honest in your dealings, preside over your families, instruct your wives and children in the teachings of God. Women be obedient and virtuous, be diligent in your labors and they shall be your crown in heaven."

Charlotte shifted uncomfortably in her chair. The strength of his emotion was so obvious she could not dismiss it, but the sentiment was one she longed to quarrel with.

"Love your children and teach them by your example," Hatch went on, unaware of her, or anyone else. "Be chaste — and above all, be dutiful and be loyal to your family; therein lies your happiness and the happiness of the world."

"Amen," Angeline said with a sweet smile, her eyes raised as if in thought she could feel her father somewhere above her. "Thank you, Josiah, you have again reminded one of the purpose and reason for life. I don't know what we should do without you. I do not mean to speak slightly of Theophilus, but more than once I have thought you were Papa's true spiritual heir."

The color spread up his cheeks and for a moment there seemed to be tears in his eyes.

"Thank you, my dear Angeline. No man alive could wish for a finer compliment, and I swear to you, I shall endeavor to live worthily of it."

She beamed at him.

"The window?" Celeste said quietly, her face also softer and an expression of pleasure filling her eyes. "How is it progressing?"

"Very well," he answered after a sharp sniff and a shake of his head. "Very well indeed. It is most gratifying to see how everyone in Highgate, and far beyond, wishes to remember him and give all they can. I think they truly realize that these are dark times full of the doubts and misguided philosophies that these days pass as some kind of greater freedom. If we do not show very plainly what is the right way, God's way, then many souls will perish, and drag the innocent down with them."

"You are so very right, Josiah," Celeste put in.

"Indeed," Angeline nodded. "Indeed you are."

"And this window will be a powerful influence." He would not be cut off before he had spoken his mind, even by agreement. "People will look at it, and remember what a great man Bishop Worlingham was, and revere his teachings. It is one of the achievements of my life, if I may say so, to perpetuate his name and the good works that he performed in his mortal existence here."

"I'm sure we are all indebted to you," Angeline said heartily. "And Papa's work will not die as long as you are alive."

"Indeed we are most grateful," Celeste agreed. "I'm sure Theophilus would say so too, were he alive to do so."

"Such a loss," Clitheridge said awkwardly, two spots of pink coloring his cheeks.

His wife put her hand on his arm and her grip was surprisingly firm; Charlotte could see the white of her knuckles.

A pinched expression crossed Josiah Hatch's face, drawing tight the corners of his mouth, and he blinked several times. It seemed a mixture of sudden envy and disapproval.

"Ah — I — I would have expected Theophilus to initiate such a project himself," he said with wide eyes. "I am sometimes tempted to think, indeed I cannot avoid it, that Theophilus did not truly appreciate what an outstanding man his father was. Perhaps he was too close to him to realize how far above that of others were his thoughts and his ideals, how profound his perception."

It seemed no one had anything to add to

this, and there were several moments of uncomfortable silence.

"Ahem!" The vicar cleared his throat. "I think, if you will excuse me, we will leave you, and go and visit Mrs. Hardy. Such a sad case, so difficult to know what to say to be of comfort. Good day, ladies." He bowed rather generally in the visitors' direction. "Good day to you, Josiah. Come, Eulalia." And taking his wife by the arm he went rather hastily out into the hallway and they heard the front door open and close again.

"Such a kind man — so kind," Angeline said almost as if she were pronouncing an incantation. "And so is dear Lally, of course. Such a strength to him — and to us all."

Charlotte thought that perhaps without her the vicar would collapse into incomprehensibility, but she forbore from saying so.

"He preaches a very good sermon," Celeste said with faint surprise. "He is really very learned, you know. It doesn't come through in his conversation, but perhaps that is as well. It doesn't do to overwhelm people with more learning than they can understand. It offers neither comfort nor instruction."

"How very true," Prudence agreed. "In fact I admit at times I do not know what he is talking about. But Josiah assures me it is all extremely good sense, don't you, my dear?"

177

"So it is," he said decisively, nodding his head a little, but there was no warmth in his tone. "He is always up to date on what the learned doctors of theology have said, and frequently quotes their works; and he is always correct, because I have taken the liberty of checking." He glanced briefly at the three visitors. "I have a considerable library, you know. And I have made it my business to take such periodicals as are enlightening and enlarging to the mind."

"Very commendable." Grandmama was frustrated with her enforced silence for so long. "I presume Theophilus inherited the bishop's library?"

"He did not." Celeste corrected her instantly. "I did."

"Celeste wrote up all Papa's sermons and notes for him," Angeline explained. "And of course Theophilus was not interested in books," she went on, looking with a nervous glance at Prudence. "He preferred paintings. He had a great many very fine paintings, mostly landscapes, you know? Lots of cows and water and trees and things. Very restful."

"Charming," Caroline said, simply for something to add to the conversation. "Are they oils or watercolors?"

"Watercolors, I believe. His taste was excellent, so I am told. His collection is worth a great deal."

Charlotte was curious to know if Clemency had inherited it, or Prudence; but her family had already disgraced itself more than enough for one day. And she did not believe that the motive for Clemency's murder, which they had all skirted delicately around mentioning, was money. Far more likely was the dangerous and radical reform she so passionately worked for — and apparently so secretly. Why had she not told even her aunts and her sister? Surely it was something to be proud of, most particularly with such a history of service as her grandfather's?

Her speculation was cut short by the parlormaid arriving yet again to announce Dr. Stephen Shaw. And again, he was so hard on her heels that she almost bumped into him as she turned to leave. He was not above average height and of strong but not stocky build, but it was the vitality in his face that dominated everything else and made the others in the room seem composed of browns and grays. Even tragedy, which had left its mark on him in shadows around his eyes and more deeply scored lines around his mouth, did not drain from him the inner energy.

" 'Afternoon, Aunt Celeste, Aunt Angeline." His voice was excellent with a resonance and a diction full of character and yet in no way eccentric. "Josiah — Prudence." He gave her a light kiss on the cheek, more a gesture than anything else, but a shadow of irritation crossed Hatch's face. There was the bleakest flicker of amusement in Shaw's eyes as he turned to look at Grandmama, Caroline and Charlotte.

"Mrs. Ellison," Celeste explained, introducing Grandmama. "She was a friend of ours some forty years ago. She called to give us her condolences."

"Indeed." The shadow of a smile became more distinct around his mouth. "For the bishop, for Theophilus, or for Clemency?"

"Stephen — you should not speak flippantly of such matters," Celeste said sharply. "It is most unseemly. You will allow people to take the wrong notion."

Without waiting for invitation he sat down in the largest chair.

"My dear aunt, there is nothing in creation I can do to prevent people from taking the wrong notion, if that is what they wish to do." He swung around to face Grandmama. "Most civil of you. You must have a great deal of news to catch up on — after such a space."

Neither the implication nor his amusement were lost on Grandmama, but she refused to acknowledge them even by an excuse. "My daughter-in-law, Mrs. Caroline Ellison," she said coldly. "And my granddaughter, Mrs. Pitt."

"How do you do." Shaw inclined his head courteously to Caroline. Then as he looked at Charlotte, a flash of interest crossed his features, as though he saw in her face something unusual.

"How do you do, Mrs. Pitt. Surely you are not acquainted with the Misses Worlingham also?"

Hatch opened his mouth to say something, but Charlotte cut across him.

"Not until today; but of course the bishop was much admired by repute."

"How excellently you choose your words, Mrs. Pitt. I presume you did not know him personally either?"

"Of course she didn't!" Hatch snapped. "He has been gone about ten years — to our misfortune."

"Let us hope it was not to his." Shaw smiled at Charlotte with his back to his brother-in-law.

"How dare you!" Hatch was furious, spots of color mottling his cheeks. He was still standing and he glared down at Shaw. "We are all more than tired of hearing your irreverent and critical remarks. You may imagine some twisted modicum of what you are pleased to call humor excuses anything at all — but it does not. You make a mock of too much. You encourage people to be light-minded and jeer at the things they should most value. That you could not appreciate the virtue of Bishop Worlingham says more about your own shallowness and triviality than it does about the magnitide of his character!"

"I think you are being a trifle harsh, Josiah," his wife said soothingly. "I daresay Stephen did not mean anything by it."

"Of course he did." Hatch would not be placated. "He is always making derisory remarks which he imagines to be amusing." His voice rose and he looked at Celeste. "He did not even wish to donate to the window. Can you imagine? And he supports that wretched man Lindsay in his revolutionary paper which questions the very foundations of decent society."

"No it doesn't," Shaw said. "It merely puts out certain ideas on reform which would distribute wealth more equitably."

"More equitably than what?" Hatch demanded. "Our present system? That amounts to overthrow of the government — in fact, revolution, as I said."

"No it does not." Shaw was overtly annoyed now and he swung around in his chair to face Hatch. "They believe in a gradual change, through legislation, to a system of collectivist state ownership of the means of producing wealth, with workers' control — full employment and appropriation of unearned increment — "

"I don't know what you are talking about, Stephen," Angeline said with her face screwed up in concentration.

"Neither do I," Celeste agreed. "Are you speaking about George Bernard Shaw and those fearful Webbs?"

"He is talking about anarchy and the total change or loss of everything you know!" Hatch replied with very real anger.

This was far deeper than the reopening of an old family quarrel. They were profound issues of morality. And turning from him to Shaw, Charlotte believed that in his eyes also she saw a fire of seriousness beneath the perception of a very surface absurdity. Humor was always with him, it was deep in all the lines of his face, but it was only the outer garment of a passionate mind.

"People can get away with anything these days," Grandmama said unhelpfully. "In my youth, Bernard Shaw, Mr. Webb, and their like would have been put in prison before they were permitted to speak of such ideas — but today they are quite openly quoted. And of course Mrs. Webb is quite beyond the pale."

"Be quiet," Caroline said sharply. "You are

making bad into worse."

"It is already worse," the old lady retorted in a stage whisper audible to everyone in the room.

"Oh dear." Angeline wrung her hands nervously, looking from one to the other of her nephews-in-law.

Charlotte attempted to repair some of the damage.

"Mr. Hatch, do you not think that when people read the ideas proposed in these pamphlets they will consider them, and if they are truly evil or preposterous then they will see them for what they are, and reject them out of hand? After all, is it not better they should know what they stand for and so find them the more repellent and frightening, than merely by our recounting of them? Truth cannot but benefit from the comparison."

Hatch stopped with his breath drawn in and his mouth open. Her premise was one he could not possibly deny, and yet to do so would rob him of his argument against Shaw.

For seconds the silence hung. A carriage rattled past the street going up Highgate Hill. A snatch of song came from somewhere upstairs and was hushed instantly, presumably some young housemaid disciplined for levity.

"You are very young, Mrs. Pitt," Hatch said at last. "I fear you do not fully grasp the weakness of some people, how easily greed, ignorance and envy can draw them to espouse values that are quite obviously false to those of us who have had the advantage of a moral upbringing. Unfortunately there are an increasing number" — here he shot a bright, hard glance at Shaw — "who confuse freedom with license and thus behave completely irresponsibly. We have just such a person here, named John Dalgetty, who keeps a shop of sorts, selling books and pamphlets, some of which pander to the lowest possible tastes, some which excite flighty minds to dwell on subjects with which they are quite unable to deal, questions of philosophy disruptive both to the individual and to society."

"Josiah would have a censor to tell everyone what they may read and what they may not." Shaw turned to Charlotte, his arms wide, his eyebrows raised. "No one would have had a new idea, or questioned an old one, since Noah landed on Ararat. There would be no inventors, no explorations of the mind, nothing to challenge or excite, nothing to stretch the boundaries of thought. No one would do anything that hadn't been done before. There would certainly be no Empire."

"Balderdash," Charlotte said frankly, then blanched at her temerity. Aunt Vespasia might be able to get away with such candor, but she had neither the social status nor the beauty for it. But it was too late to withdraw it. "I mean, you will never stop people from having radical thoughts, or from speaking them — "

Shaw started to laugh. It was a rich, wonderful sound; even around all the black crepes and the somber faces, it was full of joy.

"How can I argue with you?" He controlled his mirth with difficulty. The room seemed alight with his presence. "You are the perfect argument for your case. Obviously not even Josiah's presence in person can stop you from saying precisely what comes into your mind."

"I apologize," she said, uncertain whether to be offended, embarrassed, or to laugh with him. Grandmama was outraged, probably because Charlotte was the center of attention; Caroline was mortified; and Angeline, Celeste and Prudence were struck dumb. Josiah Hatch struggled between conflicting emotions so powerful he dared not put them into speech. "I was extremely discourteous," she added. "Whatever my opinions, they were not asked for, and I should not have expressed them so forcefully."

"You should not have expressed them at all," Grandmama snapped, sitting bolt upright and glaring at her. "I always said your marriage would do you no good — and heaven knows you were wayward enough to begin with. Now you are a disaster. I should not have brought you."

Charlotte would have liked to retort that she should not have come herself — but it was not the time, and perhaps there was no such time.

Shaw came to Caroline's rescue.

"I am delighted that you did, Mrs. Ellison. I am exceedingly tired of the polite but meaningless conversation of people who wish to express their sympathy but endlessly repeat each other simply because there is nothing anyone can say that is deep enough." His face lightened. "Words do not encompass it, nor do they bridge the gap between those who grieve and those who do not. It is a relief to talk of something else."

Suddenly the memory of Somerset Carlisle and the sorrow in his face was as clear in Charlotte's mind as if he had been here in the room with them.

"May I speak privately with you, Dr. Shaw?"

"Really!" Prudence murmured in amazement.

"Well . . ." Angeline fluttered her hands as if to brush something away.

"Charlotte," Caroline said warningly.

The same smile touched Shaw's mouth with amusement.

"Certainly. We shall repair to the library." He glanced at Celeste. "And leave the door open," he added deliberately, and watched her scowl with irritation. A protest rose to her lips, and she abandoned it; the explanation of what she had not thought, or implied, was worse than its absence. She shot him a look of intense annoyance.

He held the door open for Charlotte and then as she swept out, chin high, he followed her and strode ahead. Since she had no idea where she was going, he led the way to the library, which turned out to be as impressive and pompous as the hall, with cases and cases of leather-bound books in brown and burgundy and dark green, all lettered with gold. Pious scripts were framed in mahogany on the free wall space, and there was a large picture of some high church dignitary above the mantelpiece, carved in marble and inset with quartz pillars supporting the shelf. Massive leather-covered chairs occupied much of the dark green carpet, giving the whole room a claustrophobic feeling. A large bronze statue of a lion ornamented the one table. The curtains, like those in the withdrawing room, were heavily fringed, tied back with fringed sashes, and splayed carefully over the floor at their base.

"Not a room to put you at your ease, is

it?" Shaw met her eyes very directly. "But then that was never the intention." A smile curled the corners of his mouth. "Are you impressed?"

"That was the intention?" She smiled back.

"Oh assuredly. And are you?"

"I'm impressed with how much money he must have had." She was perfectly frank without even considering it. He was a man whose honesty demanded from her exactly the same. "All these leather-bound books. There must be a hundred pounds' worth in every case. The contents of the whole room would keep an average family for at least two years — food, gaslight, a new outfit for every season, coal enough to keep them thoroughly warm, roast beef every Sunday and goose for Christmas, and pay a housemaid to boot."

"Indeed it is, but the good bishop did not see it that way. Books are not only the source of knowledge, but the display of them is the symbol of it." He made a slight gesture of distaste with his shoulders, and paced over to the mantel, and back again, straightening the bronze as he passed it.

"You were not fond of him," she said with a half smile.

Again his face was unwaveringly direct. In any other man she might have felt it bold, but it was so obviously part of his nature only the most conceited woman would have interpreted it so.

"I disagreed with him about almost everything." He waved his hands. "Not, of course, that that is the same thing. I do not mean to equivocate. I apologize. No, I was not fond of him. Some beliefs are fundamental, and color everything that a man is."

"Or a woman," she added.

His smile was sudden and illuminated his entire face. "Of course. Again, I apologize. It is very avant-garde to suppose that women think at all; I am surprised you mention it. You must keep most unusual company. Are you related to the policeman Pitt who is investigating the fire?"

She noticed that he did not say "Clemency's death," and the flicker of pain in his moment of hesitation was not lost on her. He might mask the hurt, but the second's glimpse of it showed a side of him that she liked even better.

"Yes — he is my husband." It was the only time she had admitted it when she was involving herself in a case. Every other time she had used her anonymity to gain an advantage. And also, the wives of policemen were not received in society, any more than would be the tradesmen's wives. Commerce was considered vulgar; trade was beneath mention. In fact the very necessity of earning money at all was not spoken of in the best circles. One simply presumed it came from lands or investments. Labor was honest and good for the soul, and the morals; but the more leisure one had, the greater status one possessed.

He stood perfectly still for a moment, and the very unnaturalness of it in him spoke a kind of pain.

"Is that why you came — to learn more information about us? And brought your mother and grandmother too!"

The only possible answer was the truth. Any alternatives, however laced with honesty, would jar on his ear and degrade them both.

"I think curiosity may well be why Grandmama came. Mama, I think, came with her to try to make it a little less — awful." She stood facing him across the table with its rampant bronze lion. "I came because I heard from Lady Vespasia Cumming-Gould, and Mr. Somerset Carlisle, that Mrs. Shaw was a most remarkable person who had given much time to fighting against the power of slum landlords, that she wished to change the law to make them more accessible to public awareness."

They were standing barely a yard from each other and she was acutely aware of his total attention.

"Mr. Carlisle said she had an unusual passion and unselfishness about it," she went on. "She was not looking for personal praise nor for a cause to occupy herself, but that she simply cared. I felt such a woman's death should not go unsolved, nor people who would murder her in order to protect their miserable money remain unexposed — and perhaps scandal of that might even further her work. But your aunts tell me she was not involved in anything of that kind. So it seems I have the wrong Clemency Shaw."

"No you have not." Now his voice was very quiet and he moved at last, turning a little away from her towards the mantelpiece and the fire. "She did not choose to tell anyone else what she was doing. She had her reasons."

"But you knew?"

"Oh yes. She trusted me. We had been" — he hesitated, choosing his word carefully — "friends . . . for a long time."

She wondered why he chose the term. Did it mean they had been more than merely lovers — or something less — or both?

He turned back and looked directly at her, without bothering to disguise the grief in his face, nor its nature. She thought he did mean "friends," and not more.

"She was a remarkable woman." He used

her own words. "I admired her very much. She had an extraordinary inner courage. She could know things, and face them squarely, that would have crushed most people." He drew in his breath and let it out slowly. "There is a terrible empty space where she used to be, a goodness no longer here."

She wanted to move forward and touch him, put her hand over his and convey her empathy in the simplest and most immediate way. But such a gesture would be bold, intrusively intimate between a man and a woman who had met only moments ago. All she could do was stand on the spot and repeat the words anyone would use.

"I'm sorry, truly I am sorry."

He swung his hands out wide, then started pacing the floor again. He did not bother to thank her; such trivialities could be taken for granted between them.

"I should be very glad if you learned anything." Quite automatically he adjusted the heavy curtains to remove a crooked fold, then swung back to face her. "If I can help, tell me how, and I shall do it."

"I will."

His smile returned for an instant, full of warmth.

"Thank you. Now let us return and see if Josiah and the aunts have been totally scandalized — unless, of course, there is something else you wish to say?"

"No — not at all. I simply desired to know if I was mistaken in my beliefs, or if there were two people with such an unusual name."

"Then we may leave the wild seductiveness of the bishop's library" — he glanced around it with a rueful smile — "and return to the propriety of the withdrawing room. Really, you know, Mrs. Pitt, we should have conducted this interview in the conservatory. They have a magnificent one here, full of wrought iron stands with palms and ferns and potted flowers. It would have given them so much more to be shocked about."

She regarded him with interest. "You enjoy shocking them, don't you?"

His expression was a curious mixture of impatience and pity.

"I am a doctor, Mrs. Pitt; I see a great deal of real suffering. I get impatient with the unnecessary pain imposed by hypocrisy and idle imaginations which have nothing better to do than speculate unkindly and create pain where there need be none. Yes, I hate idiotic pretense and I blow it away where I can."

"But what do your aunts know of your reality?"

"Nothing," he admitted, pulling his face into a rueful smile. "They grew up here. They have neither of them ever left this house except to make social calls or to attend suitable functions and charitable meetings which never see the objects of their efforts. The old bishop kept them here after his wife died; Celeste to write his letters, read to him, look up reference works for his sermons and discourses and to keep him company when he wished to talk. She also plays the piano, loudly when she is in a temper, and rather badly, but he couldn't tell. He liked the idea of music, but he was indifferent to its practice."

Even standing in the doorway his intense inner energy was such that he could not keep entirely still. "Angeline took care of all his domestic needs and ran the household, and read romantic novels in brown paper wrappers when no one was looking. They never kept a housekeeper. He considered it a woman's place and her fulfillment to keep a home for a man and make it a haven of peace and security." He waved his hands, strong and neat. "Free from all the evils and soil of the outer world with its vulgarity and greed. And Angeline has done precisely that — all her life. I suppose one should hardly blame her if she knows nothing else. I stand reproved. Neither her ignorance nor her sometime fatuity are her fault."

"They must have had suitors?" Charlotte

said before she thought.

He was tidying the curtains automatically and straightened up to look at her.

"Of course. But he saw them off in short shrift, and made sure the call of duty drowned out everything else."

Charlotte saw a world of disappointment and domestic details, suppressed and confused passions forever overlaid by pious words and the irresistible pressures of ignorance, fear and guilt; duty always winning in the end. Whatever the Worlingham sisters did to occupy their minds and justify the arid years of their lives was to be pitied, not added to further by blame.

"I don't think I would have cared for the bishop either," she said with a tight smile. "Although I suppose he is like a great many. They are certainly not the only daughters whose lives have been spent so, with father — or mother. I have known several."

"And I," he agreed.

Perhaps the conversation might have gone further had not Caroline and Grandmama appeared in the doorway of the withdrawing room across the hall and seen them.

"Ah, good," Caroline said immediately. "You are ready to leave. We were just saying good-bye to the Misses Worlingham. Mr. and Mrs. Hatch have already gone." She looked at Shaw. "May we extend our condolences to you, Dr. Shaw, and apologize for intruding upon a family occasion. You have been most courteous. Come, Charlotte."

"Good afternoon, Dr. Shaw." Charlotte held out her hand and he took it immediately, holding it till she felt the warmth of him through her gloves.

"Thank you for coming, Mrs. Pitt. I look forward to our meeting again. Good day to you."

"Perhaps I should — " Charlotte glanced towards the withdrawing room door.

"Nonsense!" Grandmama snapped. "We have said all that is necessary. It is time we left." And she marched out of the front door, held open for them by a footman; the parlormaid was presumably occupied in the kitchen.

"Well?" Grandmama demanded when they were seated in the carriage.

"I beg your pardon?" Charlotte pretended mystification.

"What did you ask Shaw, and what did he say, child?" Grandmama said impatiently. "Don't affect to be stupid with me. Awkward you may be, and certainly lacking in any degree of subtlety whatever, but you are not without native wit. What did that man say to you?"

"That Clemency was precisely what I had supposed her," Charlotte replied. "But that she preferred to keep her work for the poor a private matter, even from her family, and he would be most obliged if I learned anything about who murdered her."

"Indeed," Grandmama said dubiously. "He took an uncommonly long time to say so little. I shouldn't be the slightest bit surprised if he did it himself. There is a great deal of money in the Worlingham family, you know, and Theophilus's share, as the only son, passed to his daughters equally. Shaw stands to inherit everything poor Clemency had." She rearranged her skirts more carefully. "And according to Celeste, even that is not sufficient for him. He has set his cap on that young Flora Lutterworth, and she is little better than she should be, chasing after him, seeing him in private goodness knows how many times a month. Her father is furious. He has ambitions for her a great deal higher than a widowed doctor twice her age and of no particular background. Caroline, please move yourself farther to the left; you have not left me sufficient room. Thank you." She settled herself again. "They have quarreled over it quite obviously, to any discerning eye. And I daresay Mrs. Clitheridge has had a word with her, in a motherly sort of way. It is part of the vicar's duty to care for the moral welfare of his flock."

"What makes you think that?" Caroline said with a frown.

"For goodness sake, use your wits!" Grandmama glared at her. "You heard Angeline say Lally Clitheridge and Flora Lutterworth had had a heated and most unpleasant exchange, and were hardly on speaking terms with one another. No doubt that was what it was about — anyone could deduce that, without being a detective." She turned a malevolent eye on Charlotte. "No — your doctor friend had every reason to have done away with his wife — and no doubt he did. Mark my words."

CHAPTER FIVE

Charlotte dreaded Grandmama's attending the funeral of Clemency Shaw, but long as she considered the matter, she devised no way of preventing her. When she called upon them next she did suggest tentatively that perhaps in the tragic circumstances it would be better if the affair were as private as possible. The old lady gave that the contemptuous dismissal it deserved.

"Don't be absurd, child." She looked at Charlotte down her nose. This was an achievement in itself since she was considerably shorter than Charlotte, even when they were both seated, as they now were in the withdrawing room by the fire. "Sometimes I despair of your intelligence," she added for good measure. "You display absolutely not a jot at times. Everyone will be there. Do you really imagine people will pass up such an opportunity to gossip at domestic disaster and make distasteful speculations? It is just the time when your friends should show a bold face and make it apparent to everyone that they are with you and support you in your distress — and believe you perfectly innocent of — of anything at all."

It was such a ridiculous argument Charlotte did not bother to make a reply. It would change nothing except Grandmama's temper, and that for the worse.

Emily did not go, to her chagrin. But dearly as she would like to have, she acknowledged that her motive was purely curiosity, and she herself felt it would be indecent. The more she thought of Clemency Shaw, the more she became determined to do all she could that her work might continue, as the best tribute she could pay her, and she would not spoil it by an act of self-indulgence.

However she did offer to lend Charlotte a black dress. It was certainly a season old, but nonetheless extraordinarily handsome, cut in black velvet and stitched with an embroidery of leaves and ferns on the lapels of the jacket and around the hem of the skirt. Tacked in at the back was the name of the maker, Maison Worth, the most fashionable house in Europe.

Bless Emily!

And also offered was the use of her carriage so Charlotte would not be obliged either to hire one or to ride on the omnibus to Cater Street and go with Caroline and the old lady.

She had shared with Pitt both the few scraps

of definite information and the large and very general impressions she had gained.

He was sitting in the armchair beside the parlor fire, his feet stretched out on the fender, watching through half-closed eyes the flames jumping in the grate.

"I shall go to the funeral," she added in a tone that was only half a statement and left room for him to contradict if he wished — not because she thought he would, but as a matter of policy.

He looked up, and as far as she could judge in the firelight his eyes were bright, his expression one of tolerance, even a curious kind of conspiracy.

"I shall be in some respects in a better position than you to observe," she went on. "After all, to most of them I shall be another mourner and they will assume I am there to grieve — which the more I know of Clemency Shaw, the more truly I am. Whereas those who know you will think of the police, and remember that it was murder, and that there is so much more yet ahead of them that will be exceedingly unpleasant, if not actually tragic."

"You don't need to convince me," he said with a smile, and she realized he was very gently laughing at her.

She relaxed and leaned back in her chair,

reaching out her foot to touch his, toe to toe.

"Thank you."

"Be careful," he warned. "Remember, it is not just grief — it is murder."

"I will," she promised. "I'm going in Emily's carriage."

He grinned. "Of course."

Charlotte was not by any means the first to arrive. As she alighted with Emily's footman handing her down, she saw Josiah and Prudence Hatch ahead of her passing through the gate and up the path towards the vestry entrance. They were both dressed in black as one would expect, Josiah with his hat in his hand and the cold wind ruffling his hair. They walked side by side, staring straight in front of them, stiff backed. Even from behind, Charlotte could tell that they had quarreled over something and were each isolated in a cocoon of anger.

Ahead of them and passing through the doors as Charlotte crossed the pavement was Alfred Lutterworth, alone. Either Flora was not coming or she had accompanied someone else. It struck Charlotte as unusual. She would have to inquire, as discreetly as possible, after the cause.

She was welcomed at the door by a curate, probably in his late twenties, thin, rather homely of feature, but with such animation and concern in his expression that she warmed to him immediately.

"Good morning, ma'am." He spoke quietly but without the reverential singsong which she always felt to be more a matter of show than of sincerity. "Where would you care to sit? Are you alone, or expecting someone?"

A thought ran through Charlotte's mind to say she was alone, but she resisted the temptation. "I am expecting my mother and grandmother — "

He moved to go with her. "Then perhaps you would like the pew here to the right? Did you know Mrs. Shaw well?" The innocence of his manner and the traces of grief in his face robbed his question of any offense.

"No," she replied with complete honesty. "I knew her only by repute, but all I hear of her only quickens my admiration." She saw the puzzlement in his eyes and hastened to clarify to a degree which surprised her. "My husband is in charge of the investigation into the fire. I took an interest in it, and learned from a friend who is a member of Parliament about the work Mrs. Shaw did to fight against the exploitation of the poor. She was very modest about it, but she had both courage and compassion of a remarkable degree. I wish to be here to pay my respects — " She stopped abruptly, seeing the distress in his face. Indeed he seemed to be far more moved by grief than were either of Clemency's aunts, or her sister, when Charlotte had visited them two days before.

He mastered his feelings with difficulty, and did not apologize. She liked him the better for it. Why should one apologize for grief at a funeral? In silence he showed her to the pew, met her eyes once in a look for which words would have been unnecessary, then returned to the doorway, holding his head high.

He was just in time to greet Somerset Carlisle, looking thin and a trifle tired, and Great-Aunt Vespasia, wearing magnificent black with osprey feathers in her hat, sideswept at a marvelous angle, and a black gown of silk and barathea cut to exaggerate both her height and the elegance of her bearing. It was asymmetrical, as was the very ultimate in fashion. She carried an ebony stick with a silver handle, but refused to lean on it. She spoke very briefly to the curate, explained who she was, but not why she had chosen to come, and then walked past him with great dignity, took out her lorgnette and surveyed the body of the church. She saw Charlotte after only a moment, and lost further interest in anyone else. She took Somerset Carlisle's arm and instructed him to lead her to Charlotte's pew, thus making it impossible for Caroline or Grandmama to join her when they arrived a few moments later.

Charlotte did not attempt to explain. She simply smiled with great sweetness, then bent her head in an attitude of prayer — to conceal her smile.

After several minutes she raised her eyes again, and saw well in front of her the white head of Amos Lindsay, and beside him Stephen Shaw. She could only imagine the turmoil of emotions that must be in him as he saw the agitated figure of Hector Clitheridge flapping about like a wounded crow. His wife was in handsome and serviceable black in the front row, trying to reassure him, alternately smiling and looking appropriately somber. The organ was playing slowly, either because the organist considered it the correct tempo for a funeral or because she could not find the notes. The result was a sense of uncertainty and a loss of rhythm.

The pews were filling up. Quinton Pascoe passed up the aisle, finding himself a seat as far as possible from John Dalgetty and his wife. Nowhere among the forest of black hats of every shape and decoration could Charlotte see any that looked as if they might belong to Celeste or Angeline Worlingham.

The organ changed pitch abruptly and the service began. Clitheridge was intensely nervous; his voice cracked into falsetto and back again. Twice he lost his place in what must surely be long-familiar passages and fumbled to regain himself, only making his mistake the more obvious. Charlotte ached for him, and heard Aunt Vespasia beside her sigh with exasperation. Somerset Carlisle buried his face in his hands, but whether he was thinking of Clemency, or the vicar, she did not know.

Charlotte found her own attention wandering. It was probably the safest thing to do; Clitheridge was unbearable, and the young curate was so full of genuine distress she found it too harrowing to look at him. Instead her eyes roamed upward over and across traceries of stone, plaques of long-dead worthies, and eventually, with a jolt of returning memory, to the Worlingham window with its almost completed picture of the late bishop in the thin disguise of Jeremiah, surrounded by other patriarchs and topped by an angel. She recognized the bishop quite easily. The face was indistinct — the medium enforced it — but the thick curls of white hair, so like an aureole in the glass with the light shining through, was exactly like the portrait in the family hallway and it was unmistakable. It was a remarkably handsome memorial and must have cost a sizable sum. No wonder Josiah Hatch was proud of it.

At last the formal part of the service was

over and with immense relief the final amen was said, and the congregation rose to follow the coffin out into the graveyard, where they all stood huddled in a bitter west wind while the body was interred.

Charlotte shivered and moved a little closer to Aunt Vespasia, and behind her half a step, to shield her from the gusts, which if the sky had been less clear, would surely have carried snow. She stared across the open grave with Clitheridge standing at the edge, his cassock whipping around his ankles and his face strained with embarrassment and apprehension. A couple of yards away Alfred Lutterworth was planted squarely, ignoring the cold, his face somber in reflection, his thoughts unreadable. Next to him, but several feet away, Stephen Shaw was folded in a mixture of private anger and grief, the emotion so deep in his face only the crudest of strangers would have intruded. Amos Lindsay stood silently at his elbow.

Josiah Hatch was taking control of the pallbearers. He was a sidesman and used to some responsibility. His expression was grim, but he did his duty meticulously and not a word or a movement was omitted or performed without ceremony. It was done to an exactness that honored the dead and preserved the importance above all of the litany and tradition of the church.

Clitheridge was obviously relieved to allow someone else to take over, however pedantic. Only the curate seemed less than pleased. His bony features and wide mouth reflected some impatience that appeared to increase his grief.

Charlotte had been quite correct, there were about fifty people present, most of them men, and quite definitely neither Angeline nor Celeste Worlingham were among them; nor was Flora Lutterworth.

"Why are the Worlinghams not here?" she whispered to Aunt Vespasia as they turned at last, cold to the bone, and made their way back to the carriages for the short ride to the funeral supper. She had not been specifically invited, but she fully intended to go. They passed Pitt standing near the gate, so discreet as to be almost invisible. He might have been one of the pallbearers or an undertaker's assistant, except that his gloves were odd, there was a bulge in one pocket of his coat, and his boots were brown. She smiled at him quickly as they passed, and saw an answering warmth in his face, then continued on her way to the carriage.

"I daresay the bishop did not consider it suitable," Aunt Vespasia replied. "Many people don't. Quite idiotic, of course. Women are every bit as strong as men in coping with tragedy and the more distressing weaknesses of the flesh. In fact in many cases stronger — they have to be, or none of us would have more than one child, and certainly never care for the sick!"

"But the bishop is dead," Charlotte pointed out. "And has been for ten years."

"My dear, the bishop will never be dead as far as his daughters are concerned. They lived under his roof for over forty years of their lives, and obeyed every rule of conduct he set out for them. And I gather he had very precise opinions about everything. They are not likely to break the habit now, least of all in a time of bereavement when one most wishes to cling to the familiar."

"Oh — " Charlotte had not thought of that, but now some recollection returned to her of other families where it had been considered too much strain on delicate sensibilities. Fits of the vapors detracted rather seriously from the proper solemnity due to the dead. "Is that why Flora Lutterworth isn't here either?" That seemed dubious to her, but not impossible. Alfred Lutterworth apparently had great ambitions towards gentility, and all that might seem well-bred.

"I imagine so," Vespasia replied with the ghost of a smile. They were at the carriages. Caroline and Grandmama were somewhere behind them. Charlotte glanced over her shoulder and saw Caroline talking to Josiah Hatch with intense concentration, and Grandmama was staring at Charlotte with a look like thunder.

"Are you waiting?" Vespasia asked, her silver eyebrows raised.

"Certainly not!" Charlotte waved her arm imperiously and Emily's coachman moved his horses forward. "They have their own equipage." It gave her a childish satisfaction to say it aloud. "I shall follow you. I assume the Misses Worlingham will be up to the occasion of the funeral supper?"

"Of course." Now Vespasia's smile was undisguised. "That is the social event — this was merely the necessary preamble." And she accepted her footman's hand and mounted the step into her carriage, after handing to the crossing sweeper, a child of no more than ten or eleven years, a halfpenny, for which he thanked her loudly, and pushed his broom through another pile of manure. The door was closed behind her and a moment later it drew away.

Charlotte did the same, and was still behind her when they alighted outside the imposing and now familiar Worlingham house, all its blinds drawn and black crepe fluttering from the door. The roadway was liberally spread with straw to silence the horses' hooves, out of respect for the dead, and the wheels made barely a sound as the coachman drove away to wait.

Inside everything had been prepared to the last detail. The huge dining room was festooned with black crepe till it looked as if some enormous spider had been followed by a chimney fire and an extremely clumsy sweep. White lilies, which must have cost enough to feed an ordinary family for a week, were arranged with some artistry on the table, and in a porcelain vase on the jardiniere. The table itself was set with a magnificent array of baked meats, sandwiches, fruits and confectionary, bottles of wine in baskets, suitably dusty from the cellar and carrying labels to satisfy even the most discriminating connoisseur. Some of the Port was very old indeed. The bishop must have laid it down in his prime, and forgotten it.

Celeste and Angeline stood side by side, both dressed in black bombazine. Celeste's was stitched with jet beads and had a fall of velvet over the front and caught up in the bustle. It was a fraction tight at the bosom. Angeline's was draped over the shoulders with heavy black lace fastened with a jet pin set with tiny pearls, a very traditional mourning brooch. The lace was also echoed across the stomach and under the bombazine bustle; only the most discriminating would know it was last year's arrangement of folds. And it was even tighter around the bosom. Charlotte guessed they had performed the same service at Theophilus's funeral, and perhaps at the bishop's as well. A clever dressmaker could do a great deal, and from observation it seemed, like many wealthy people, the Worlingham sisters liked their economies.

Celeste greeted them with deep solemnity, as if she had been a duchess receiving callers, standing stiff-backed, inclining her head a fraction and repeating everyone's names as though they were of significant importance. Angeline kept a lace-edged handkerchief in her hand and dabbed at her cheek occasionally, echoing the last two words of everything Celeste said.

"Good afternoon, Mrs. Pitt." Celeste moved her hand an inch in recognition of a relative stranger of no discernible rank.

"Mrs. Pitt," Angeline repeated, smiling uncertainly.

"Gracious of you to come to express your condolences."

"Gracious." Angeline chose the first word this time.

"Lady Vespasia Cumming-Gould." Celeste was startled, and for once the fact that she was a bishop's daughter seemed unimpressive. "How — how generous of you to come. I am sure our late father would have been quite touched."

"Quite touched," Angeline added eagerly.

"There would be no reason for him to be," Vespasia said with a cool smile and very direct stare. "I came entirely on Clemency Shaw's behalf. She was a very fine woman of both courage and conscience — a rare-enough combination. I am truly grieved that she is gone."

Celeste was lost for words. She knew nothing of Clemency to warrant such an extraordinary tribute.

"Oh!" Angeline gave a little gasp and clutched the handkerchief more tightly, then dabbed at a tear that started down her pink cheek. "Poor Clemency," she whispered almost inaudibly.

Vespasia did not linger for any further trivialities that could only be painful, and led the way into the dining room. Somerset Carlisle, immediately behind her, was so used to speaking gently with the inarticulate he had no trouble murmuring something kind but meaningless and following them in.

There were some thirty people there already. Charlotte recognized several from her own previous brief meetings at the Worlinghams', others she deduced from Pitt's description as she had done in the church.

She looked at the table, pretending to be

engrossed in admiring it, as Caroline and Grandmama came in. Grandmama was scowling and waving her stick in front of her to the considerable peril of anyone within range. She did not particularly want Charlotte with her, but she was furious at being left behind. It lacked the respect due to her.

It was a gracious room, very large, with fine windows all ornately curtained, a dark marble fireplace, an oak sideboard and serving table and a dresser with a Crown Derby tea service set out for display, all reds, blues and golds.

The main table was exquisitely appointed, crystal with a coat of arms engraved on the side of each goblet, silver polished till it reflected every facet of the chandelier, also monogrammed with an ornate Gothic W, and linen embroidered in white with both crest and monogram. The porcelain serving platters were blue-and-gold-rimmed Minton; Charlotte remembered the pattern from the details of such knowledge her mother had taught her, in the days when she attended such functions where information of the sort was required in the would-be bride.

"They never put all this out for her when she was alive," Shaw said at her elbow. "But then I suppose, God help us, we never had the entire neighborhood in to dine, especially all at once."

"It often helps grief to do something with a special effort," Charlotte answered him quietly. "Perhaps even a trifle to excess. We do not all cope with our losses in the same way."

"What a very charitable view," he said gloomily. "If I had not already met you before, and heard you be most excruciatingly candid, I would suspect you of hypocrisy."

"Then you would do me an injustice," she said quickly. "I meant what I said. If I wished to be critical I could think of several things to comment on, but that is not one of them."

"Oh!" His fair eyebrows rose. "What would you choose?" The faintest smile lit his eyes. "If, of course, you wished to be critical."

"Should I wish to be, and you are still interested, I shall let you know," she replied without the slightest rancor. Then remembering that it was his bereavement more than anyone else's, and not wishing to seem to cut him, even in so small a way, she leaned a little closer and whispered, "Celeste's gown is a trifle tight, and should have been let out under the arms. The gentleman I take to be Mr. Dalgetty needs a haircut, and Mrs. Hatch has odd gloves, which is probably why she has taken one off and is carrying it."

His smile was immediate and filled with warmth.

"What acute observation! Did you learn it being married to the police, or is it a natural gift?"

"I think it comes from being a woman," she replied. "When I was single I had so little to do that observation of other people formed a very large part of the day. It is more entertaining than embroidery and painting bad watercolors."

"I thought women spent their time gossiping and doing good works," he whispered back, the humor still in his eyes, not masking the pain but contrasting with it so he seemed alive and intensely vulnerable.

"We do," she assured him. "But you have to have something to gossip about, if it is to be any fun at all. And doing good work is deadly, because one does it with such an air of condescension it is more to justify oneself than to benefit anyone else. I should have to be very desperate indeed before a visit from a society lady bringing me a jar of honey would do more than make me want to spit at her — which of course I could not afford to do at all." She was exaggerating, but his smile was ample reward, and she was perfectly sure he knew the truth was both homelier and kinder, at least much of the time.

Before he could reply their attention was drawn to Celeste a few feet away from them, still playing the duchess. Alfred Lutterworth was standing in front of her with Flora by his side, and Celeste had just cut them dead, meeting their eyes and then moving on as if they were servants and not to be spoken to. The color flared up Lutterworth's cheeks and Flora looked for a moment as if she would weep.

"Damn her!" Shaw said savagely under his breath, then added a simile from the farmyard that was extremely unkind, and unfair to the animal in question. Without excusing himself to Charlotte he walked forward, treading on a thin woman's dress and ignoring her.

"Good afternoon, Lutterworth," he said loudly. "Good of you to come. I appreciate it. Good afternoon, Miss Lutterworth. Thank you for being here — not the sort of thing one would choose, except in friendship."

Flora smiled uncertainly, then saw the candor in his eyes and regained her composure.

"We would hardly do less, Dr. Shaw. We feel for you very much."

Shaw indicated Charlotte. "Do you know Mrs. Pitt?" He introduced them and they all made formal acknowledgment of each other. The tension evaporated, but Celeste, who could not have failed to hear the exchange, as must everyone else in their half of the room, was stiff-faced and tight-lipped. Shaw ignored her and continued a loud, inconsequential conversation, drawing in Charlotte as an ally, willingly or not.

Ten minutes later both the group and the conversation had changed. Caroline and Grandmama had joined them, and Charlotte was listening to an extremely handsome woman in her middle forties with shining hair piled most fashionably high, magnificent dark eyes, and a black hat which would have been daring two years ago. Her face was beginning to lose the bloom of youth, but there was still enough beauty to cause several people to look at her more than once, albeit a type of beauty more characteristic of hotter climates than the restrained English rose — especially those bred in the genteel gardens of Highgate. She had been introduced as Maude Dalgetty, and Charlotte liked her more the longer she spoke. She seemed a woman too contented within herself to bear any malice towards others, and there were none of the small barbs of callousness or idleness in her comments.

Charlotte was surprised when Josiah Hatch joined them, and it was immediately apparent from the softening of his grim expression that he held her in considerable esteem. He looked at Charlotte with little interest and even that was prepared to be critical. He already suspected she had come either out of curiosity, which he considered intolerable, or because she was a friend of Shaw's of whom he would be bound to disapprove. However, when he turned to Maude Dalgetty the angle of his body eased, even the rigidity of his collar seemed less constricting.

"Mrs. Dalgetty, I'm so pleased you were able to come." He sought for something else to add, perhaps more personal, and failed to find it.

"Of course, Mr. Hatch." She smiled at him and he unbent even more, finding a very small smile himself. "I was very fond of Clemency; I think she was one of the best women I knew."

Hatch paled again, the blood leaving his cheeks. "Indeed," he said huskily, then cleared his throat with a rasping breath. "There was very much in her to praise — a virtuous woman, neither immodest nor unmindful of all her duties, and yet with good humor at all times. It is a great tragedy her life — was — " His face hardened again and he shot a glance across the table to where Shaw's fair head could be seen bending a little to listen to a stout woman wearing a tiny hat. "Was in so many ways wasted. She could have had so much more." He left it hanging in the air, ambiguous as to whether he was referring to Shaw or Clemency's longevity.

Maude Dalgetty chose to interpret it as the latter.

"Indeed it is," she agreed with a sad shake of her head. "Poor Dr. Shaw. This must be appalling for him, and yet I can think of nothing at all that one could do to help. It is a miserable feeling to see grief and be unable even to reach it, let alone offer anything of comfort."

"Your compassion does you credit," he said quickly. "But do not distress yourself too deeply on his behalf; he is unworthy of it." All the tightness returned to his body, his shoulders cramped in the black fabric of his coat seemed to strain at the seams. "He has characteristics it would be inappropriate I should mention in front of you, dear lady, but I assure you I speak from knowledge." His voice shook a little, whether from weariness or emotion it was impossible to say. "He treats with mockery and insult all that is worthiest of reverence in our society. Indeed he would spread slander about the finest of us, did not some of us, your husband among them, prevent him."

He looked at Maude intently. "I disagree with all your husband's principles as far as publishing is concerned, as you well know; but I stand by him in the defense of a lady's good name — "

Maude Dalgetty's fine arched brows rose in surprise and interest.

"A lady's good name! Good gracious, was Dr. Shaw speaking ill of someone? You surprise me."

"That is because you do not know him." Hatch was warming to the subject. "And your mind is too fine to imagine ill of people unless it is proved right before you." His cheeks were quite pink. "But I soon put him in his place, and your husband added to my words, most eloquently, although I flatter myself that what I said to him was sufficient."

"John did?" Her husky voice lifted in surprise. "How very unusual. You almost make me think it was me Dr. Shaw spoke ill of."

Hatch colored furiously and his breath quickened; his large hands were clenched by his sides.

Standing well within earshot, Charlotte was certain that it had indeed been Maude Dalgetty Shaw had spoken ill of, truly or not, and she wished intensely there were some way to learn what he had said, and why.

Hatch moved a little, turning his back half towards Charlotte. Since she did not wish to be conspicuous in her interest, she allowed herself to be excluded, and drifted towards Lally Clitheridge and Celeste. But before she reached them they separated and Lally accosted Flora Lutterworth, circumspectly but very definitely.

"How good of you to come, my dear Flora." Her tone was at once warm and acutely condescending, like a duchess interviewing a prospective daughter-in-law. "You are charmingly softhearted — a nice virtue in a girl, if not carried to indiscretion."

Flora stared at her, opened her mouth to reply, and was lost for any words that would express her feelings.

"And modesty as well," Lally continued. "I am so glad you do not argue, my dear. Indiscretion can be the ruin of a girl, indeed has been of many. But I am sure your father will have told you that."

Flora blushed. Obviously the quarrel had not yet been healed.

"You must heed him, you know." Lally was equally perceptive, and placed her arm in Flora's as if in confidence. "He has your very best interest at heart. You are very young, and inexperienced in society and the ways in which people assess each other. An unwise act now, and you may well be considered a girl of less than complete virtue — which would ruin all the excellent chances you have for a fine future." She nodded very slightly. "I hope you understand me, my dear."

Flora stared at her. "No — I don't think

I do," she said coolly, but her face was very tight and her knuckles were white where she clasped her handkerchief.

"Then I must explain." Lally leaned a little closer. "Dr. Shaw is a very charming man, but at times rather too outspoken in his opinions and rash in his respect for other people's judgment. Such things are acceptable in a man, especially a professional man — "

"I find Dr. Shaw perfectly agreeable." Flora defended him hotly. "I have received nothing but kindness at his hands. If you disagree with his opinions, that is your affair, Mrs. Clitheridge. You must tell him so. Pray do not concern me with the matter."

"You misunderstand me." Lally was plainly annoyed. "I am concerned for your reputation, my dear — which is frankly in some need of repair."

"Then your quarrel is with those who speak ill of me," Flora retorted. "I have done nothing to warrant it."

"Of course not!" Lally said sharply. "I know that. It is not what you have done, it is your indiscretion in appearance. I warn you as your vicar's wife. He finds the matter difficult to discuss with a young lady, but he is concerned for your welfare."

"Then please thank him for me." Flora looked at her very directly, her cheeks pink, her eyes blazing. "And assure him that neither my body nor my soul are in any jeopardy. You may consider your duty well acquitted." And with a tight little smile she inclined her head politely and walked away, leaving Lally standing in the center of the room, her mouth in a thin line of anger.

Charlotte moved backward hastily in case Lally should realize she had been listening. As she swung around, she came face-to-face with Great-Aunt Vespasia, who had been waiting until she had her attention, her eyebrows raised in curiosity, her mouth touched with humor.

"Eavesdropping?" she said under her breath.

"Yes," Charlotte admitted. "Most interesting. Flora Lutterworth and the vicar's wife, having a spat over Dr. Shaw."

"Indeed? Who is for him and who against?"

"Oh, both for him — very much. I rather think that is the trouble."

Vespasia's smile widened, but it was not without pity. "How very interesting — and wildly unsuitable. Poor Mrs. Clitheridge, she seems worthy of better stuff than the vicar. I am hardly surprised she is drawn elsewhere, even if her virtue forbids she follow." She took Charlotte by the arm and moved away from the two women now close behind them. She was able to resume a normal speaking voice.

"Do you think you have learned anything else? I do not find it easy to believe the vicar's wife set fire to the house out of unrequited love for the doctor — although it is not impossible."

"Or Flora Lutterworth, for that matter," Charlotte added. "And perhaps it is not unrequited. Flora will have a great deal of money when her father dies."

"And you think the Worlingham money is not sufficient for Dr. Shaw, and he has eyes on Lutterworth's as well?" Vespasia asked.

Charlotte thought of her conversation with Stephen Shaw, of the energy in him, the humor, the intense feeling of inner honesty that still lingered with her. It was a painful idea. And she did not wish to think Clemency Shaw had spent her life married to such a man. And surely she would have known.

"No," she said aloud. "I believe it may all have to do with Clemency's work against slum owners. But Thomas thinks it is here in Highgate, and that really it was Dr. Shaw himself who was the intended victim. So naturally I shall observe all I can, and tell him of it, whether I can see any sense in it or not."

"Very proper of you." Now Vespasia did not even attempt to hide her amusement. "Perhaps it was Shaw himself who killed his wife — I imagine Thomas has thought of that, even if you have not."

"Why should I not think of it also?" Charlotte said briskly, but under her breath.

"Because you like him, my dear; and I believe your feeling is more than returned. Good afternoon, Dr. Shaw." As she spoke Shaw had come back and was standing in front of them, courteous to Vespasia, but his attention principally upon Charlotte.

Aware of Vespasia's remarks, Charlotte found herself coloring, her cheeks hot.

"Lady Cumming-Gould." He inclined his head politely. "I appreciate your coming. I'm sure Clemency would have been pleased." He winced as if saying her name aloud had touched a nerve. "You are one of the few here who have not come out of curiosity, the social desire to be seen, or sheer greed for the best repast the Worlinghams have laid out since Theophilus died."

Amos Lindsay materialized at Shaw's elbow. "Really, Stephen, sometimes you do yourself less than justice in expressing your thoughts. A great many people are here for more commendable reasons." His words were directed not to curbing Shaw but to excusing him to Vespasia and Charlotte.

"Nevertheless we must eat," Shaw said rather ungraciously. "Mrs. Pitt — may I offer you a slice of pheasant in aspic? It looks repulsive, but I am assured it is delicious."

"No thank you," Charlotte declined rather crisply. "I do not feel any compulsion to eat, or indeed any desire."

"I apologize," he said immediately, and his smile was so unforced she found her anger evaporated. She felt for his distress, whatever the nature of his love for Clemency. This was a time of grief for him when he would probably far rather have been alone than standing being polite to a crowd of people of widely varying emotions from family bereavement, in Prudence, right to social obligation like Alfred Lutterworth, or even vulgar curiosity, as was ill-hidden on the faces of several people whose names Charlotte did not know. And it was even possible one of them might be Clemency's murderer.

"There is no need," she said, answering his smile. "You have every cause to find us intrusive and extremely trying. It is we who should apologize."

He reached out his hand as if he would have touched her, so much more immediate a communication than words. Then he remembered at the last moment that it was inappropriate, and withdrew, but she felt almost as if he had, the desire was so plain in his eyes. It was a gesture of both gratitude and understanding. For an instant he had not been alone.

"You are very gracious, Mrs. Pitt," he said aloud. "Lady Cumming-Gould, may I offer you anything, or are you also less than hungry?"

Vespasia gave him her goblet. "You may bring me another glass of claret," she answered graciously. "I imagine it has been in the cellar since the bishop's time. It is excellent."

"With pleasure." He took the goblet and withdrew.

He was replaced within moments by Celeste and Angeline, still presiding over the gathering like a duchess and her lady-in-waiting. Prudence Hatch brought up the rear, her face very pale and her eyes pink rimmed. Charlotte remembered with a sharp pang of pity that Clemency had been her sister. Were it Emily who had been burned to death, she did not think she could be here with any composure at all; in fact she would probably be at home unable to stop weeping, and the idea of being civil to a lot of comparative strangers would be unbearable. She smiled at Prudence with all the gentleness she could convey, and met only a numb and confused stare. Perhaps shock was still anesthetizing at least some of the pain? The reality of it would come later in the days of loneliness, the mornings when she woke and remembered.

But Celeste was busy being the bishop's

daughter and conducting the funeral supper as it should be done. The conversation should be elevated and suitable to the occasion. Maude Dalgetty had mentioned a romantic novel of no literary pretension at all, and must be put in her place.

"I don't mind the servants reading that sort of thing, as long as their work is satisfactory of course; but such books really have no merit at all."

Beside her a curious mixture of expressions crossed Prudence's face: first alarm, then embarrassment, then a kind of obscure satisfaction.

"And a lady of any breeding is far better without them," Celeste went on. "They really are totally trivial and encourage the most superficial of emotions."

Angeline became very pink. "I think you are too critical, Celeste. Not all romances are as shallow as you suggest. I recently — I mean, I learned of one entitled *Lady Pamela's Secret*, which was very moving and most sensitively written."

"You what?" Celeste's eyebrows rose in utter contempt.

"Some of them reflect what many people feel . . ." Angeline began, then tailed off under Celeste's icy stare.

"I'm sure I don't know any women who

feel anything of the sort." Celeste was not prepared to let it go. "Such fancies are entirely spurious." She turned to Maude, apparently oblivious of Prudence's scarlet face and wide eyes. "Mrs. Dalgetty, I am sure with your literary background, your husband's tastes, that you found it so? Girls like Flora Lutterworth, for example . . . But then her status in Highgate is very recent; her background is in trade, poor girl — which of course she cannot help, but neither can she change it."

Maude Dalgetty met Celeste's gaze with complete candor. "Actually it makes me think of my own youth, Miss Worlingham, and I thoroughly enjoyed *Lady Pamela's Secret*. Also I considered it quite well written — without pretensions and with a considerable sensitivity."

Prudence blushed painfully and stared at the carpet.

"Good gracious," Celeste replied flatly, making it very obvious she was thinking something far less civil. "Dear me."

Shaw had returned with Vespasia's glass of claret and she took it from him with a nod of thanks. He looked from one to another of them and noticed Prudence's high color.

"Are you all right, Prudence?" he asked with more solicitude than tact.

"Ah!" She jumped nervously and met his concerned expression with alarm, and colored even more deeply.

"Are you all right?" he repeated. "Would you like to retire for a while, perhaps lie down?"

"No. No, I am perfectly — oh — " She sniffed fiercely. "Oh dear — "

Amos Lindsay came up behind her, glanced at Shaw, then took her by the elbow. "Come, my dear," he said gently. "Perhaps a little air. Please allow me to help you." And without waiting for her to make up her mind, he assisted her away from the crush and out of the door towards some private part of the house.

"Poor soul," Angeline said softly. "She and Clemency were very fond of each other."

"We were all fond of her," Celeste added, and for a moment she too looked into some distance far away, or within her memory, and her face reflected sadness and hurt. Charlotte wondered how much her managerial attitude and abrasively condescending manner were her way of coping with loss, not only of a niece but perhaps of all the opportunities for affection she had missed, or forfeited, over the years. She had probably loved her father at the time, admired him, been grateful for the ample provision of home, gowns, servants, social position; and also hated him for all the things her duty had cost her.

"I mean the family," Celeste added, looking

232

at Shaw with sudden distaste. "There are ties of blood which no one else can understand — particularly in a family with a heritage like ours." Shaw winced but she ignored him. "I never cease to be grateful for our blessings, nor to realize the responsibility they carry. Our dear father, Clemency's grandfather, was one of the world's great men. I think outside those of us of his blood, only Josiah truly appreciates what a marvelous man he was."

"You are quite right," Shaw said abruptly. "I certainly didn't and don't now. . . . I think he was an opinionated, domineering, sententious and thoroughly selfish old hypocrite — "

"How dare you!" Celeste was furious. Her face purpled and her whole body shook, the jet beads on her bosom scintillating in the light of the chandeliers. "If you do not apologize this instant I shall demand you leave this house."

"Oh, Stephen, really." Angeline moved from one foot to the other nervously. "You go too far, you know. That is unforgivable. Papa was a veritable saint."

Charlotte struggled for something to say, anything that would retrieve an awful situation. Privately she thought Shaw might well be right, but he had no business to say so here, or now. She was still searching her brain wildly when Aunt Vespasia came to the rescue.

"Saints are seldom easy to live with," she said in the appalled silence. "Least of all by those who are obliged to put up with them every day. Not that I am granting that the late Bishop Worlingham was necessarily a saint," she added as Shaw's face darkened. She held up her hand elegantly and her expression was enough to freeze the rebuttal on his lips. "But no doubt he was a man of decided opinions — and such people always arouse controversy, thank heaven. Who wills a nation of sheep who bleat agreement to everything that is said to them?"

Shaw's temper subsided, and both Celeste and Angeline seemed to feel that honor had been served. Charlotte grabbed for some harmless subject, and heard herself complimenting Celeste on the lilies displayed on the table, rather as if laid out above a coffin.

"Beautiful," she repeated fatuously. "Where did you find such perfect blooms?"

"Oh, we grow them," Angeline put in, gushing with relief. "In our conservatory, you know. They require a lot of attention — " She told them all at some length exactly how they were planted, fertilized and cared for. They all listened in sheer gratitude for the respite from unpleasantness.

When Angeline finally ran out of anything to add, they murmured politely and drifted

234

away, pretending to have caught the eye of another acquaintance. Charlotte found herself with Maude Dalgetty again, and then when she went to see if Prudence was recovered, with John Dalgetty, listening to him expound on the latest article he had reviewed, on the subject of liberty of expression.

"One of the sacred principles of civilized men, Mrs. Pitt," he said, leaning towards her, his face intent. "The tragedy is that there are so many well-meaning but ignorant and frightened people who would bind us in the chains of old ideas. Take Quinton Pascoe." He nodded towards Pascoe very slightly, to be sure Charlotte knew to whom he was referring. "A good man, in his own way, but terrified of a new thought." He waved his arm. "Which wouldn't matter if he were only limiting himself, but he wants to imprison all our minds in what he believes to be best for us." His voice rose in outrage at the very conception.

Charlotte felt a strong sympathy with him. She could clearly recall her indignation when her father had forbidden her the newspaper, as he had all his daughters, and she felt as if all the interest and excitement in the world were passing her by and she was shut out from it. She had bribed the butler to pass her the political pages, without her parents' knowledge, and pored over them, reading every word and visualizing the people and events in minute detail. To have robbed her of it would have been like shutting all the windows in the house and drawing the curtains.

"I quite agree with you," she said with feeling. "Thought should never be imprisoned nor anyone told they may not believe as they choose."

"How right you are, Mrs. Pitt! Unfortunately, not everyone is able to see it as you do. Pascoe, and those like him, would set themselves up to decide what people may learn, and what they may not. He is not personally an unpleasant man — far from it, you would find him charming — yet the arrogance of the man is beyond belief."

Apparently Pascoe had heard his name mentioned. He pushed his way between two men discussing finance and faced Dalgetty, his eyes hot with anger.

"It is not arrogance, Dalgetty." His voice was low but only just in control. "It is a sense of responsibility. To publish every single thing that comes into your hand, regardless of what it is or whom it may hurt, is not freedom; it is an abuse of the art of printing. It is no better than a fool who stands on the corner of the street and shouts out whatever enters his thoughts — be it true or false — "

"And who is to judge whether it is true or false?" Dalgetty demanded. "You? Are you to be the final arbiter of what the world shall believe? Who are you to judge what we may hope for or aspire to? How dare you?" His eyes blazed with the sheer monstrosity of any mere human limiting the dreams of mankind.

Pascoe was equally enraged. His whole body quivered with frustrated fury at Dalgetty's obtuseness and willful failure to grasp the real meaning.

"You are utterly wrong!" he shouted, his skin suffusing with color. "It has nothing whatsoever to do with limiting aspiration or dreams — as well you know. But it does have to do with not creating nightmares." He swung his arms wildly, catching the top of a nearby woman's feathered hat and knocking it over her eye, and quite oblivious of it. "What you do not have the right to do is topple the dreams of others by making mock of them — yes — it is you who are arrogant, not I."

"You pygmy!" Dalgetty shouted back. "You nincompoop. You are talking complete balderdash — which perfectly reflects your muddled thinking. It is an impossibility to build a new idea except at the expense of part of the old — by the very fact that it *is* new."

"And what if your new idea is ugly and dangerous?" Pascoe demanded furiously, his hand chopping the air. "And adds nothing to human knowledge or happiness? Ah? Nincompoop. You are an intellectual child — and a spiritual and moral vandal. You are — "

At this point the heated voices had drawn everyone's attention, all other conversation had ceased and Hector Clitheridge was wading towards them in extreme agitation, his clothes flapping, his arms waving in the air and his face expressing extreme embarrassment and a kind of desperate confusion.

"Mr. Pascoe! Please!" he implored. "Gentlemen!" he turned to Dalgetty. "Please remember poor Dr. Shaw — "

That was the last thing he should have said. The very name was as a red rag to a bull for Pascoe.

"A perfect case in point," he said triumphantly. "A very precise example! He rushes in — "

"Exactly!" Dalgetty chopped the air with his hands in excitement. "He is an honest man who abhors idolatry. Especially the worship of the unworthy, the dishonorable, the valueless — "

"Who says it is valueless?" Pascoe jumped up and down on the spot, his voice rising to falsetto in triumph. "Do you set yourself up to decide what may be kept, and what destroyed? Eh?"

Now Dalgetty lost his temper completely. "You incompetent!" he shouted, scarlet-cheeked. "You double-dyed ass! You — "

"Mr. Dalgetty!" Clitheridge pleaded futilely. "Mr. — "

Eulalia came to the rescue, her face set in firm lines of disapproval. For an instant she reminded Charlotte of a particularly strict nanny. She ignored Dalgetty except for one glare. "Mr. Pascoe." Her voice was determined and under perfect control. "You are behaving disgracefully. This is a funeral supper — have you completely forgotten yourself? You are not usually without any sense of what is fitting, or of how much distress you may be causing to innocent people, already injured by circumstance."

Pascoe's bearing changed. He looked crest-fallen and thoroughly abashed. But she had no intention of leaving any blow unstruck.

"Imagine how poor Prudence feels. Is one tragedy not enough?"

"Oh, I am sorry." Pascoe was shocked at himself and his penitence was transparently sincere. Dalgetty no longer entered even the edge of his thoughts. "I am mortified that I should have been so utterly thoughtless. How can I apologize?"

"You can't." Eulalia was relentless. "But you should try." She turned to Dalgetty, who was looking decidedly apprehensive. "You, of course, I do not expect to have any sensitivity towards the feelings of others. Liberty is your god, and I sometimes think you are prepared to sacrifice anyone at all on its shrine."

"That is unfair." He was sincerely aggrieved. "Quite unfair. I desire to liberate, not to injure — I wish only to do good."

"Indeed?" Her eyebrows shot up. "Then you are singularly unsuccessful. You should most seriously reconsider your assumptions — and your resulting behavior. You are a foolish man." And having delivered herself of her most formidable tirade to date, she was flushed, and handsomer than at any time since she was a bride. She was also rather alarmed at what she had dared to say, and the fact that she had rescued the whole assembly from a miserable and acutely embarrassing situation was only just becoming apparent to her. She blushed as she saw every eye on her, and retreated hastily. For once it would be ridiculous to pretend she had merely been helping her husband. He was standing with his hands in the air and his mouth open, but intensely relieved, and also alarmed and a little resentful.

"Bravo, Lally," Shaw said quietly. "You are quite magnificent. We are all duly chastened." He bowed very slightly in a small, quaintly courteous gesture, then moved to stand beside Charlotte.

Again Eulalia colored hotly. This time it was obviously with pleasure, but so acute and unaccustomed it was painful to see.

"Really — " Clitheridge protested. No one heard what he was going to say next, if indeed he knew himself. He was interrupted by Shaw.

"You make me feel as if we are all in the nursery again. Perhaps that is where we should be." He looked at Dalgetty and Pascoe and there was humor in his face rather than anger. If he resented Clemency's funeral being interrupted by such a scene there was no trace of it in his expression. In fact Charlotte thought it might even have been a relief to him from the pain of the reality. He looked set now to prolong the tension and make matters worse.

"I think it is long past time we all grew out of it," she said briskly, taking Shaw by the arm. "Don't you, Dr. Shaw? Squabbling is quite fun at times, but this is a selfish and totally inappropriate place for it. We should be adult enough to think of others, as well as ourselves. I am sure you agree?" She was not sure at all, but she did not intend to allow him the opportunity to say so. "You have already told me about the magnificent conservatory the Misses Worlingham have, and I have seen the lilies on the table. Perhaps you would be generous enough to show it to me now?"

"I should be delighted," he said with enthusiasm. "I cannot think of anything I should rather do." And he took her hand in his and placed it on his arm, leading her through the room to the far side. She glanced backwards only once, and saw a look of fury and dislike on Lally Clitheridge's face so intense the memory of it remained with her the rest of the day. It was still powerful in her mind when she finally returned home to Bloomsbury, and gave Pitt her account of the day, and her impressions of it.

CHAPTER SIX

Pitt woke in the middle of the night to hear a loud, repeated banging which through the unraveling layers of sleep he realized was at the front door. He climbed out of bed, feeling Charlotte stirring beside him.

"Door," he mumbled, reaching for his clothes. There was no point in hoping it was simply a matter of information he could accept, then go back to the warm oblivion of sleep. Anyone banging so fiercely and repeatedly wanted his presence. He pulled on trousers and socks; his boots were in front of the kitchen stove. He attempted to tuck in his shirttails, and lost them. He padded downstairs, turned up the gas on the lamp in the hall, and unbolted the front door.

The chill of the damp night air made him shiver, but it was a small discomfort compared with the sight of Murdo's ashen face and the bull's-eye lantern high in his hand, which threw its yellow light on the paving stones and into the mist around him. It picked out the dark shape of a hansom cab waiting at the curb beyond, the horse's flanks steaming, the cabby shrouded in his cloak.

Before he could ask, Murdo blurted it out, his voice cracking a little.

"There's another fire!" He forgot the "sir." He looked very young, the freckles standing out on his fair skin in its unnatural pallor. "Amos Lindsay's house."

"Bad?" Pitt asked, although he knew.

"Terrible." Murdo kept his voice under control with difficulty. "I never saw anything like it — you can feel the heat a hundred yards up the road; fair hurts your eye to look at it. God — how can anyone do that?"

"Come in," Pitt said quickly. The night air was cold.

Murdo hesitated.

"My boots are in the kitchen." Pitt turned and left him to do as he pleased. He heard the latch close and Murdo tiptoeing heavily after him.

In the kitchen he put up the gas and sat on the hard-backed chair, reaching for his boots and then lacing them tightly. Murdo came in as far as the stove, relishing the warmth. His eyes went over the clean wood, the china gleaming on the dresser, and he caught the smell of laundry drying on the airing rail winched up towards the ceiling above them. Unconsciously the lines in his young face were already less desperate.

Charlotte appeared in the doorway in her nightgown, her bare feet having made no sound on the linoleum.

Pitt smiled at her bleakly.

"What is it?" she asked, glancing at Murdo and back at Pitt.

"Fire," he said simply.

"Where?"

"Amos Lindsay's. Go back to bed," he said gently. "You'll get cold."

She stood white-faced. Her hair was dark over her shoulders, copper where the gaslight caught it.

"Who was in the house?" she asked Murdo.

"I dunno, ma'am. We aren't sure. They was trying to get the servants out, but the heat was terrible, scorch the hair off — " He stopped, realizing he was speaking to a woman and probably should not be saying such things.

"What?" she demanded.

He looked miserable and guilty for his clumsiness. He stared at Pitt, who was now ready to go.

"Eyebrows, ma'am," he answered miserably, and she knew he was too shocked to equivocate.

Pitt kissed Charlotte quickly on the cheek and pushed her back. "Go to bed," he said again. "Standing here catching a chill won't help anyone."

"Can you tell me if — " Then she realized what she was asking. To dispatch someone with a message, simply to allay her fears, or confirm them, would be a ridiculous waste of manpower, when there were urgent things to be done, injured and perhaps bereaved people to help. "I'm sorry."

He smiled, an instant of understanding, then turned and went out with Murdo and pulled the front door closed behind him.

"What about Shaw?" he asked as they climbed up into the cab and it started forward immediately. It was obviously quite unnecessary to tell the cabby where they were going. Within moments the horse had broken from a trot into a canter and its hooves rang on the stones as the cab swayed and turned, throwing them from one wall to the other, and against each other, with some violence.

"I don't know, sir, impossible to tell. The place is an inferno. We 'aven't seen 'im — it looks bad."

"Lindsay?"

"Nor 'im neither."

"Dear God, what a mess!" Pitt said under his breath as the cab lurched around a corner, the wheels lifting for an instant and landing hard on the cobbles again with a jar that shook his bones.

It was a long, wretched ride to Highgate and they neither of them spoke again. There was nothing to say; each was consumed in his own imagination of the furnace they were racing towards, and the memory of Clemency Shaw's charred body removed from another ruin so shortly before.

The red glow was visible through the cab window as soon as they turned the last corner of Kentish Town Road onto Highgate Road. In Highgate Rise the horse jerked to a halt and the cabby leaped down and threw the door open.

"I can't take yer no further!"

Pitt climbed out and the heat hit him, enveloping him in stinging, acrid, smut-filled, roaring chaos. The whole sky seemed red with the towering brilliance of it. Showers of sparks exploded in the air, white and yellow, flying hundreds of feet up, then falling in dying cinders. The street was congested with fire engines, horses plunging and crying out in terror as debris fell around them. Men clung onto them, trying to steady them amid the confusion. There were hoses connected up to the Highgate Ponds, and men struggled with leather buckets, passing them from hand to hand, but all they were doing was protecting the nearest other houses. Nothing could save Lindsay's house now. Even as Pitt and Murdo

247

stood in the road a great section of the top story collapsed, the beams exploded and fell in rapid succession and a huge gout of flame fifty feet high went soaring upwards, the heat of it driving them back to the far pavement and behind the hedge, even as far as they were from the house.

One of the fire engine horses screamed as a length of wood fell across its back and the smell of burning hair and flesh filled the immediate air. It plunged forward, tearing its reins out of the fireman's hands. Another man, almost too quick for thought, caught up a bucket of water and threw it over the beast, quenching in one act both the heat and the pain.

Pitt ran forward and caught the animal, throwing all his weight against its charge, and it shuddered to a halt. Murdo, who had grown up on a farm, took off his jacket, squashed it into another bucket of water, then slapped it onto the beast's back and held it.

The chief fireman was coming towards Pitt, his face a mask of smoke stains. Only the eyes showed through, red-rimmed and desperate. His eyebrows were singed and there were angry red weals under the blackened grime. His clothes were torn and soiled almost beyond recognition by water and the charring of heat and debris.

"We've got the servants out!" he shouted, then spluttered into coughing and controlled himself with difficulty. He waved them farther back and they followed him to where there was a faint touch of coolness of night air softening the heat and the stench, and the roaring and crashing of masonry and the explosion of wood were less deafening. His face was haggard, not only with sorrow but with his own failure. "But we didn't get either of the two gentlemen." It was unnecessary to add that it was now beyond hope, it was apparent to anyone at all. Nothing could be alive in that conflagration.

Pitt had known it, yet to hear it from someone else who spoke from years of such hope and struggle gave him a sudden gaping emptiness inside that took him by surprise. He realized only now how much he had been drawn to Shaw, even though he accepted that he might have murdered Clemency. Or perhaps it was only his brain that accepted it, his inner judgment always denied it. And with Amos Lindsay there had been no suspicion, only interest, and a little blossom of warmth because he had known Nobby Gunne. Now there was only a sense of sharp pain for the destruction. Anger would come later when the wound was less consuming.

He turned to Murdo and saw the shock and

misery in his face. He was young and very new to murder and its sudden, violent loss. Pitt took him by the arm.

"Come on," he said quietly. "We failed to prevent this, but we've got to get him before he does any more. Or her," he added. "It could be a woman."

Murdo was still stunned. "What woman would ever do that?" He jerked his hand back, but he did not turn.

"Women are just as capable of passion and hatred as men," Pitt replied. "And of violence, given the means."

"Oh no, sir — " Murdo began instinctively, the argument born of his own memories. Sharp tongues, yes; and a box on the ears; certainly greed at times, and coldness; nagging, bossiness and a great deal of criticism; and mind-staggering, speech-robbing unfairness. But not violence like this —

Memory returned, crowding in on Pitt, and he spoke with surprise.

"Some of the most gruesome murders I've ever worked on were committed by women, Murdo. And some of them I understood very well — when I knew why — and pitied. We know so little about this case — none of the real passions underneath it — "

"We know the Worlinghams have a great deal of money, and so does old Lutterworth."

Murdo struggled to gather everything in his mind. "We know — we know Pascoe and Dalgetty hate each other, although what that has to do with Mrs. Shaw. . ." He trailed off, searching for something more relevant. "We know Lindsay wrote pro-Fabian essays — although that has nothing to do with Mrs. Shaw either — but the doctor approved it."

"That's hardly a passion to kindle a funeral pyre like that," Pitt said bitterly. "No, Murdo. We don't know very much. But dear God — we're going to find out." He swung around and walked back towards the fire chief, who was now directing his men to saving the houses in the immediate vicinity.

"Have you any idea if it was set the same way?" Pitt shouted.

The fire chief turned a filthy, miserable face to him.

"Probably. It went up very quick. Two people called us — one saw it from the street at the front, towards the town, the other down towards Holly Village and half at the back. That's at least two places. From the speed of it I daresay there was more."

"But you got the servants out? How? Why not Lindsay and Shaw? Were the fires all in the main house?"

"Looks like it. Although by the time we got here it was spread pretty well all over.

Got one man badly burned and another with a broken leg getting the servants out."

"Where are they now?"

"Dunno. Some feller in a nightshirt and cassock was running 'round trying to help, and getting in the way. Good-hearted, I suppose — but a damn nuisance. Woman with 'im 'ad more sense. 'Nother couple over off to the side, looked white as ghosts — woman weeping — but they brought blankets. 'Bin too busy to watch 'em when they're safe out. Now, I'll answer your questions tomorrer — "

"Did you get the horse out?" Pitt did not know why he asked it, except some dim memory of terrified animals in another fire long ago in his youth.

"Horse?" The fire chief frowned. "What horse?"

"The doctor's horse — for his trap."

"Charlie!" the fire chief yelled at a soaked and filthy man who was walking a few yards away, limping badly. "Charlie!"

"Sir?" Charlie stopped and came over towards them, his eyebrows scorched, his eyes red-rimmed and exhausted.

"You were 'round the back — did you get the horse?"

"Weren't no 'orse, sir. I looked special. Can't bear a good animal burnt."

"Yes there was," Pitt argued. "Dr. Shaw

252

has a trap, for his calls — "

"No trap neither, sir." Charlie was adamant. "Stable was still standing when I got there. No 'orse and no trap. Either they was kept somewhere else — or they're out."

Out! Was it possible Shaw was not here at all, that once again the fire had not caught him? In all this fearful pyre could only Amos Lindsay be dead?

Who would know? Who could he ask? He turned around in the red night, still loud with the crackling of sparks and the roar and boom of flame. He could see at the far edge of the tangle of engines, horses, water buckets, ladders, and weary and injured men, the two black figures of Josiah and Prudence Hatch, a little apart from each other, huddled in a private and separate misery. The cassocked figure of Clitheridge was striding along, skirts flying, a flask in his outstretched hand, and Lally was rewrapping a blanket around the shoulders of a tiny kitchen girl who was shuddering so violently Pitt could see it even through the smoke and the melee. Lindsay's manservant with the polished hair stood alone, stupefied, like a person upright in his sleep.

Pitt skirted around the horses and buckets and the men still working, and started towards the far side. He was off the opposite pavement and in the middle of the road when he heard the clatter of hooves and looked automatically up the street towards Highgate center to see who it was. There was no purpose in more fire engines now — and anyway there was no sound of bells.

It was a trap, horse almost at a gallop, wheels racing and jumping in their speed and recklessness. Pitt knew long before he saw him that it was Shaw, and he felt an intense relief, followed the instant after by a new darkness. If Shaw was alive, then it was still possible he had set both fires, first to kill Clemency, now to kill Lindsay. Why Lindsay? Perhaps in the few days he had stayed with Lindsay, Shaw had betrayed himself by a word, an expression, even something unsaid when it should have been? It was a sickening thought, and yet honesty could not dismiss it.

"Pitt!" Shaw almost fell off the step of the trap and took no trouble even to tie the rein, leaving the horse to go where it would. He grabbed Pitt by the arm, almost swinging him off his feet. "Pitt! For God's sake, what's happened? Where's Amos? Where are the staff?" His face was so gaunt with horror it was impossible not to be moved by it.

Pitt put out his hand to steady him. "The servants are all right, but I'm afraid Lindsay was not brought out. I'm sorry."

"No! No!" The cry was torn from Shaw

and he plunged forward, bumping into people, knocking them aside in his headlong race towards the flames.

After a moment's stupefaction Pitt ran after him, leaping a water hose and accidentally sending a fireman flying. He caught Shaw so close to the building the heat was immense and the roaring of the flames seemed almost around them. He brought him to the ground, driving the wind out of him.

"You can't do anything!" he shouted above the din. "You'll only get killed yourself!"

Shaw coughed and struggled to get up. "Amos is in there!" His voice was close to hysteria. "I've got to — " Then he stopped, on his hands and knees facing the blaze, and realization came to him at last that it was utterly futile. Something inside him collapsed and he made no resistance when Pitt pulled him to his feet.

"Come back, or you'll get burned," Pitt said gently.

"What?" Shaw was still staring at the violence of the flames. They were so close the heat was hurting their skin, and the brightness made him screw up his eyes, but he seemed only peripherally aware of it.

"Come back!" Pitt shouted as a beam fell in with a crash and an explosion of sparks. Without thinking he took Shaw by the arms

255

and pulled him as if he had been a frightened animal. For a moment he was afraid Shaw was going to fall over, then at last he obeyed, stumbling a little, careless if he hurt himself.

Pitt wanted to say something of comfort, but what was there? Amos Lindsay was dead, the one man who had seemed to understand Shaw and not be offended by his abrasiveness, who saw beyond the words to the mind and its intent. It was Shaw's second terrible bereavement in less than two weeks. There was nothing to say that would not be fatuous and offensive, only betraying a complete failure to understand anything of his true pain. Silence at least did not intrude, but it left Pitt feeling helpless and inadequate.

Clitheridge was floundering over towards them, a look of dedication and terror on his face. He obviously had not the faintest idea what to say or do, except that he was determined not to flinch from his duty. At the last moment he was saved by events. The horse in the trap took flight as a piece of burning debris shot past it and it reared up and twisted around.

That at least was something Clitheridge understood. He abandoned Shaw, for whom he could do nothing and whose grief appalled and embarrassed him, and reached instead for the horse, holding the rein close to its head and throwing all his considerable weight against the momentum of its lunge.

"Whoa! Steady — steady now. It's all right — steady, girl. Hold hard!" And miraculously for once he was completely successful. The animal stopped and stood still, shuddering and rolling its eyes. "Steady," he said again, full of relief, and began to lead it across the road, away from the roar and heat, and away from Shaw.

"The servants." At last Shaw spoke. He twisted around on one foot and swayed a little. "What about the servants? Where are they? Are they hurt?"

"Not seriously," Pitt replied. "They'll be all right."

Clitheridge was still across the street with the horse and trap, leading it away, but Oliphant the curate was coming towards them, his thin face lit by the glare from the flames, his figure gawky in a coat whose shoulders were too big. He stopped in front of them and his voice was quiet and certain.

"Dr. Shaw; I lodge with Mrs. Turner up on West Hill. She has other rooms and you'd be welcome to stay there as long as you choose. There is nothing you can do here, and I think a strong cup of tea, some hot water to wash in, and then sleep would help you to face tomorrow."

Shaw opened his mouth to argue, then realized that Oliphant had not offered facile words of comfort. He had offered practical help and reminded him that there was another day ahead, and regardless of pain or shock, there would be duties, things to do that would be useful and have meaning.

"I — " He struggled for the practical. "I have no — nothing — it is all gone — again — "

"Of course," Oliphant agreed. "I have an extra nightshirt you are welcome to, and a razor, soap, a clean shirt. Anything I have is yours."

Shaw tried to cling to the moment, as if something could still be retrieved, some horror undone that would become fixed if he were to leave. It was as though accepting it made it true. Pitt knew the feeling, irrational and yet so strong it held one to the scene of tragedy because to move was to acknowledge it and allow it to be real.

"The servants," Shaw said again. "What about them? Where are they to sleep? I must — " He turned one way and another, frantic for some action to help, and saw none.

Oliphant nodded, his face red in the flames' reflection, his voice level. "Mary and Mrs. Wiggins will stay with Mr. and Mrs. Hatch, and Jones will stay with Mr. Clitheridge."

Shaw stared at him. Two firemen went past

supporting a third between them.

"We shall begin to search for new positions for them in the morning." Oliphant held out his hand. "There are plenty of people who want good, reliable help that has been well trained. Don't worry about it. They are frightened, but not hurt. They need sleep and the assurance that they will not be put on the street."

Shaw looked at him incredulously.

"Come," Oliphant repeated. "You cannot help here — "

"I can't just — just walk away!" Shaw protested. "My friend is in that — " He stared helplessly at the blaze, now redder and sinking as the last of the wood crumbled away inside and the masonry collapsed inward. He searched for words to explain the tumult of emotions inside him, and failed. There were tears in the grime on his face. His hands clenched at his sides and jerked as if he still longed to move violently, and had no idea where or how.

"Yes you can leave it," Oliphant insisted. "There is no one left here; but tomorrow there will be people who need you — sick, frightened people who trust you to be there and use the knowledge you have to help them."

Shaw stared at him, horror in his face turning to a slow amazement. Then finally, without speaking, he followed him obediently, his shoulders sagging, his feet slow, as if he were bruised, and intensely, painfully tired.

Pitt watched him go and felt a racking mixture of emotions inside himself; pity for Shaw's grief and the stunning pain he obviously felt, fury at the fearful waste of it, and a kind of anger because he did not know who to blame for it all, who to cherish and who to want to hunt and see punished. It was like having a dam pent up inside him and the pressure of confusion ached to burst in some easy and total action, and yet there was none.

The building crashed in sparks again as another wall subsided. Two firemen were shouting at each other.

Finally he left them and retraced his own steps to look for Murdo and begin the miserable task of questioning the closest neighbors to see if any of them had seen or heard anything before the fire, anyone close to Lindsay's house, any light, any movement.

Murdo was amazed by how tumultuous were his feelings about accompanying Pitt to the Lutterworths'. Away from the immediate heat of the fire his face hurt where the skin was a little scorched, his eyes stung and watered from the smoke, even his throat ached from it, and there was a large and painful blister forming on his hand where he had been struck by a flying cinder. But his body was chilled, and inside the coat Oliphant had found for him, he was shivering and clenched with cold.

He thought of the huge, dark house of the Lutterworths, of the splendor inside it, carpets, pictures, velvet curtains bound with sashes and splayed on the floor like overlong skirts. He had only ever seen such luxury at the Worlinghams' themselves, and theirs was a lot older, and worn in one or two places. The Lutterworths' was all new.

But far sharper in his mind, and making him clench his sore hands before he remembered the blister, was the memory of Flora Lutterworth with her wide, dark eyes, so very direct, the proud way she carried her head, chin high. He had noticed her hands especially; he always remarked hands, and hers were the most beautiful he had ever seen, slender, with tapering fingers and perfect nails, not plump and useless like those of so many ladies of quality — like the Misses Worlingham, for example.

The more he thought of Flora the lighter his feet were on the frosty pavement, and the more wildly his stomach lurched at the prospect of Pitt knocking on the front door with its brass lion's head, until he disturbed the entire household and brought the footman to let them in, furious and full of contempt, so they could stand dripping and filthy on the clean carpet till Lutterworth himself was roused and came down. Then Pitt would ask him a lot of intrusive questions that would all be pointless in the end, and could have waited until morning anyway.

They were actually on the step when he finally spoke.

"Wouldn't it be better to wait until morning?" he said breathlessly. He was still very wary of Pitt. At times he admired him, at others he was torn by old loyalties, parochial and deep rooted, understanding his colleagues' resentment and sense of having been undervalued and passed by. But most often he was lost in his own eagerness to solve the case and he thought of nothing but how could he help, what could he contribute to their knowledge. He was gaining a measure of respect for Pitt's patience and his observation of people. Some of his conclusions had escaped Murdo. He had had no notion how Pitt knew of some of the exchanges between Pascoe and Dalgetty — until Pitt had quite openly recounted how Mrs. Pitt had attended the funeral supper and repeated back to him all her impressions. In that moment Murdo had ceased to dislike Pitt; it was impossible to dislike a man who was so candid about his deductions. He could easily have pretended a superior ability, and Murdo knew a good many who would have.

Pitt's reply was unnecessary, both because Murdo knew perfectly well what it would be, and because the front door swung open the moment after Pitt knocked and Alfred Lutterworth himself stood in the lighted hall, hastily but fully dressed. Only his neck without a tie and his ill-matched coat and trousers betrayed that he had already been up. Perhaps he had been one of the many who had crowded around the edge of the fire, anxious, curious, concerned, some offering help — or to see the job done to its bitter conclusion.

"Lindsay's 'ouse." He made it a statement rather than a question. "Poor devil. 'E was a good man. What about Shaw — did they get 'im this time?"

"You believe it was Shaw they were after, sir?" Pitt stepped in and Murdo followed him nervously.

Lutterworth closed the door behind them. "Do you take me for a fool, man? Who else would they be after, first 'is own 'ouse, and now Lindsay's? Don't stand there. You'd best come in, although there's nowt I can tell yer." His northern accent was more pronounced in his emotion. "If I'd seen anyone you'd not 'ave 'ad to come seekin' me, I'd'a gone seekin' you."

Pitt followed him and Murdo came a step behind. The withdrawing room was cold, the ashes of the fire already dark, but Flora was standing beside it. She was also fully dressed, in a gray, winter gown, her face pale and her hair tied back with a silk kerchief. Murdo felt himself suddenly excruciatingly awkward, not knowing what to do with his feet, where to put his painful, dirty hands.

"Good evening, Inspector." She looked at Pitt courteously, then at Murdo with something he thought was a smile. "Good evening, Constable Murdo."

She had remembered his name. His heart lurched. It had been a smile — hadn't it?

"Good evening, Miss Lutterworth." His voice sounded husky and ended in a squeak.

"Can we help, Inspector?" She turned to Pitt again. "Does anyone . . . need shelter?" Her eyes pleaded with him to tell her the answer to the question she had not asked.

Murdo drew breath to tell her, but Pitt cut across him and he was left openmouthed.

"Your father thinks the fire was deliberately set, in order to kill Dr. Shaw." Pitt was watching her, waiting for reaction.

Murdo was furious. He saw the last trace of color leave her face and he would have rushed forward to save her from collapsing, had he dared. In that instant he loathed Pitt for his brutality, and Lutterworth himself for not having protected her, he whose duty and privilege it was.

She bit her lip to stop it trembling and her eyes filled with tears. She turned away to hide them.

"No need to cry for 'im, girl," Lutterworth said gently. " 'E was no use to you, nor to 'is poor wife neither. 'E was a greedy man, with no sense o' right nor wrong. Save your tears for poor Amos Lindsay. 'E was a good-enough chap, in 'is own way. A bit blunt, but none the worse for that. Don't take on." Then he swung around to Pitt. "Mind you could'a chosen your time and your words better! Clumsy great fool!"

Murdo was in an agony of indecision. Should he offer her his handkerchief? It had been clean this morning, as it was every morning, but it must smell terrible with smoke now; and anyway, wouldn't she think him impertinent, overfamiliar?

Her shoulders were trembling and she sobbed without sound. She looked so hurt, like a woman and a child at once.

He could bear it no longer. He pulled the handkerchief out of his pocket, dropping keys and a pencil along with it, and went forward to give it to her, arm outstretched. He no longer cared what Pitt thought, or what detective strategy he might be using. He also hated Shaw, with an utterly new emotion that had never touched him before, because Flora wept for him with such heartbreak.

"He in't dead, miss," he said bluntly. "He was out on a call somewhere an' 'e's terrible upset — but he in't even hurt. Mr. Oliphant, the curate, took him back to his lodgings for the night. Please don't cry like that — "

Lutterworth's face was dark. "You said he was dead." He swung around, accusing Pitt.

"No, Mr. Lutterworth," Pitt contradicted. "You assumed it. I am deeply sorry to say that Mr. Lindsay is dead. But Dr. Shaw is perfectly well."

"Out again?" Lutterworth was staring at Flora now, his brows drawn down, his mouth tight. "I'll lay odds that bounder struck the match 'imself."

Flora jerked up, her face tearstained, Murdo's handkerchief clasped in her fingers, but now her eyes were wide with fury.

"That's a terrible thing to say, and you have no right even to think it, let alone to put it into words! It is completely irresponsible!"

"Oh, and you know all about responsibility, of course, girl," Lutterworth retorted, by now regardless of Pitt or Murdo. His face was suffused with color and his voice thick in his emotion. "Creepin' in and out at all hours to see 'im — imagining I don't know. For heaven's sake, 'alf Highgate knows! And talk about it over the teacups, like you were some common whore — "

Murdo gasped as if the word had struck him physically. He would rather have sustained a dozen blows from a thief or a drunkard than have such a term used of Flora. Were it any other man he would have knocked him to the ground — but he was helpless.

" — and I've nothing with which to call them liars!" Lutterworth was anguished with impotent fury himself, and anyone but Murdo would have pitied him. "Dear God — if your mother were alive she'd weep 'erself sick to see you. First time since she died I 'aven't grieved she weren't 'ere with me — the very first time . . ."

Flora stared at him and stood even straighter. She drew a breath to defend herself, her cheeks scarlet, her eyes burning. Then her face filled with misery and she remained silent.

"Nothing to say?" he demanded. "No excuses? No — what a fine man he is, if only I knew 'im like you do, eh?"

"You do me an injustice, Papa," she said stiffly. "And yourself also. I am sorry you think so ill of me, but you must believe what you will."

"Don't you come high and mighty with

267

me, girl." Lutterworth's face was torn between anger and pain. Had she been looking at him more closely she might have seen the pride as he gazed at her, and the shattered hope. But his words were unfortunate. "I'm your father, not some tomfool lad following after you. You're not too big to send to your room, if I have to. An' I'll approve any man that sets 'is cap at you, or you'll not so much as give 'im the time o' day. Do you hear me, girl?"

She was trembling. "I'm sure everyone in the house hears you, Papa, including the tweeny in the attic — "

His face flushed purple with anger.

" — but if anyone does me the honor of courting me," she went on before he had mustered the words, "I shall most certainly seek your approval. But if I love him, I'll marry him whether you like him or not." She turned to Murdo, and with a barely shaking voice thanked him for informing her that Dr. Shaw was alive and well. Then, still clutching his handkerchief, she swept out and they heard her footsteps go across the hall and up the stairs.

Lutterworth was too wretched and too embarrassed to apologize or seek polite excuses for such a scene.

"I can't tell you anything you don't know

for yourselves," he said brusquely when the silence returned. "I 'eard the alarm and went out to see, same as 'alf the street, but I didn't see nor 'ear anything before that. Now I'll be going back to my bed and you'd best get about your business. Good night to you."

"Good night sir," they replied quietly, and found their own way to the door.

It was not the only quarrel they witnessed that night.

Pascoe was too distressed to see them, and his servant refused on his behalf. They trudged in silence and little expectation of learning anything useful, first to the Hatches' house to question Lindsay's maid, who was bundled up in blankets and shaking so violently she could not hold a cup steady in her hand. She could tell them nothing except that she had woken to the sound of fire bells and had been so terrified she did not know what to do. A fireman had come to the window and carried her out, across the roof of the house and down a long ladder to the garden, where she had been soaked with water from a hose, no doubt by accident.

At this point her teeth were chattering on the edge of the cup and Pitt recognized that she was unlikely to know anything useful, and was beyond being able to tell him anyway.

Not even the prospect of a clue towards who had burned two houses to the ground, with their occupants inside, prompted him to press her any further.

When she had been escorted upstairs to bed, he turned to Josiah Hatch, who was gaunt faced, eyes fixed in horror at the vision within his mind.

Pitt watched him anxiously, he seemed so close to retreating into himself with shock. Perhaps to be forced to speak and think of and answer questions of fact would be less of a torture than one might suppose. It would draw him from the contemplation of the enormity of destruction, and from the flicker in the muscles in his eyelids and the corners of his mouth, the fear of the evil which now was so obviously still in their midst.

"What time did you retire this evening, Mr. Hatch?" he began.

"Ugh?" Hatch recalled himself to the present with difficulty. "Oh — late — I did not look at the clock. I was in deep contemplation of what I had been reading."

"I heard you come up the stairs at about quarter to two," Prudence put in very quietly, looking first at her husband and then at Pitt.

He turned a blank face towards her. "I disturbed you? I'm sorry, that was the last thing I intended."

"Oh no, my dear! I had been roused by one of the children. Elizabeth had a nightmare. I had merely not yet gone back to sleep."

"Is she well this morning?"

Prudence's face relaxed into the ghost of a smile. "Of course. It was simply an ill dream. Children do have them, you know — quite often. All she required was a little reassurance."

"Could not one of the older children have given her that without disturbing you?" He frowned, seizing on the matter as if it were important. "Nan is fifteen! In another few years she may have children of her own."

"There is a world of difference between fifteen and twenty, Josiah. I can remember when I was fifteen." The tiny smile returned again, soft and sad. "I knew nothing — and I imagined I knew everything. There were entire regions — continents of experience of which I had not the faintest conception."

Pitt wondered what particular ignorances were in her mind. He thought perhaps those of marriage, the responsibility after the romance had cooled, the obedience, and perhaps the bearing of children — but he could have been wrong. It might have been worldly things, quite outside the home, other struggles or tragedies she had seen and coped with.

Hatch apparently did not know what she

referred to either. He frowned at her in incomprehension for a few moments longer, then turned to Pitt again.

"I saw nothing of any import." He answered the question before it was asked. "I was in my study, reading from the work of St. Augustine." The muscles in his jaw and neck tightened and some inner dream took hold of him. "The words of men who have sought after God in other ages are a great enlightenment to us — and comfort. There has always been powerful evil in the world, and will be as long as the soul of man is as weak and beset by temptations as it is." He looked at Pitt again. "But I am afraid I can be of no assistance to you. My mind and my senses were totally absorbed in contemplation and study."

"How terrible," Prudence said to no one in particular, "that you were awake in your study, reading of the very essence of the conflict between good and evil." She shivered and held her arms close around herself. "And only a few hundred yards away, someone was setting a fire that murdered poor Mr. Lindsay — and but for a stroke of good fortune, would have murdered poor Stephen as well."

"There are mighty forces of evil here in Highgate." He stared straight ahead of him again, as if he could see the pattern in the

272

space between the jardiniere with its gold chrysanthemums and the stitched sampler on the wall with the words of the Twenty-third Psalm. "Wickedness has been entertained, and invited to take up its abode with us," he went on.

"Do you know by whom, Mr. Hatch?" It was surely a futile question, and yet Pitt felt impelled to ask it. Murdo behind him, silent until now, shifted uncomfortably from one foot to the other.

Hatch looked around in surprise. "God forgive him and give him peace, by Lindsay himself. He spread dark ideas of revolution and anarchy, overthrow of the order of things as they are. He wanted some new society where individual ownership of property was done away and men were no longer rewarded according to their ability and effort but given a common wage regardless. It would do away with self-reliance, diligence, industry and responsibility — all the virtues which have made the Empire great and the nation the envy of all the Christian world." His face was pinched with anger at the distortion, and grief for all that would be lost. "And John Dalgetty published them — to his dishonor — but he is a foolish man forever pursuing what he imagines is justice and a kind of freedom of the mind that has become all important to him, consuming all his better judgment. In his frenzy he deludes others."

He looked at Pitt. "Poor Pascoe has done all he can to dissuade him, and then to prevent him by public opinion, and even the law; but he is puny against the tide of inquisitiveness and disobedience in mankind and the passion for novelty — always novelty." His body was clenched under his clothes, aching with tension. "Novelty at any price! New sciences, a new social order, new art — we are insatiable. The minute we have seen a thing, we want to cast it aside and find something else. We worship freedom as if it were some infinite good. But you cannot escape morality — freedom from the consequence of your acts is the great delusion at the core of all this" — he flung his hand out — "this frenzy for newness — and for irresponsibility. We have been from the first a race that hungers for forbidden knowledge and would eat the fruit of sin and death. God commanded our first parents to abstain, and they would not. What chance has poor Quinton Pascoe?"

His face tightened and a look of defeat washed his whole countenance with pain. "And Stephen in his arrogance upheld Dalgetty and made mock of Pascoe and his attempts to protect the weak and the sensitive from the cruder expressions of ideas that could

274

only injure and frighten at best — and at worst deprave. Mockery of the truth, of all man's past aspirations to higher good, is one of the Evil One's most fearsome weapons, and God help him, Stephen has been more than willing to use it."

"Josiah — I think you speak too harshly," Prudence protested. "I know Stephen speaks foolishly at times, but there is no cruelty in him — "

He turned around to her, his face grim, his eyes burning. "You know him very little, my dear. You see only the best. That is to your credit — and it is what I intend shall continue, but be counseled by me: I have heard him say much that I shall never repeat to you, which has been both cruel and degraded. He has a contempt for the virtues which you most admire."

"Oh, Josiah, are you sure? Could you not perhaps have misunderstood him? He has an unfortunate sense of humor at times — and — "

"I could not!" He was absolute. "I am perfectly capable of telling when he is attempting to be amusing and when he means what he says, however superficially he covers it with lightness. The essence of mockery, Prudence, is that it should make good people laugh at what they would otherwise have taken seriously and loved — to make moral purity, labor, hope, and belief in people, seem ridiculous to them — things of jest to be derided."

Prudence opened her mouth to refute what he was saying; then recalling some other knowledge, some fact until then secondary, she colored with embarrassment and looked down at the floor. Pitt was aware of her misery as if she had touched him, but he had no idea what caused it. She wanted to defend Shaw, but why? Affection, simple compassion because she believed his suffering to be genuine, or some other reason unguessed by him yet? And what held her back?

"I regret we cannot help you," Hatch said civilly, but he could not mask the exhaustion in his voice, nor the shock in his eyes. He was on the point of collapse, and it was nearly four in the morning.

Pitt gave up. "Thank you for your time now, and your courtesy. We will not keep you up longer. Good night, sir — Mrs. Hatch."

Outside the night was black and the wind whined in the darkness, glaring red over towards the ruins of Amos Lindsay's house. The street was still full of fire engines, and firemen were walking the horses up and down to keep them from chilling.

"Go home," Pitt said to Murdo, stamping his feet on the ice around the pavement. "Get a few hours' sleep and I'll see you at the station at ten."

"Yes sir. Do you think Shaw did it himself, sir? To cover the murder of his wife?"

Pitt looked at Murdo's scorched and miserable face. He knew what he was thinking.

"Over Flora Lutterworth? Possibly. She's a handsome girl, and can expect a lot of money. But I doubt Flora had any part in it. Now go home and sleep — and get that hand attended to. If that blister breaks and you get it dirty, God knows what infection you could get. Good night, Murdo."

"Good night, sir." And Murdo turned and made his way hastily across the road and past the firemen up towards Highgate.

It took Pitt nearly half an hour to find a cab, and then he only succeeded because some late-night junketer had failed to pay his fare and the cabby was standing on the pavement calling after him instead of making a hasty return to his own bed. He grumbled, and asked for extra, but since Bloomsbury was more or less on his way, he weighed exhaustion against profit and came out on the side of profit.

Charlotte came flying down the stairs almost before Pitt had the door shut, a shawl caught half around her shoulders and no slippers on. She stared at him, waiting for the answer.

"Amos Lindsay's dead," he said, taking off his boots and moving frozen toes inside his socks. Really he ought to put his socks in the kitchen to dry out. "Shaw was out on a call again. He got back soon after we arrived." His coat fell off the hook behind him and landed in a heap on the floor. He was too tired to care. "The servants are all right."

She hesitated only a moment, absorbing the knowledge. Then she came down the rest of the stairs and put her arms around him, her head against his shoulder. There was no need to talk now; all she could think of was relief, and how cold he was, and dirty, and tired. She wanted to hold him and ease out the horror, make him warm again and let him sleep, as if he had been a child.

"The bed's warm," she said at last.

"I'm covered in smut and the smell of smoke," he answered, stroking her hair.

"I'll wash the sheets," she said without moving.

"You'll have to soak them," he warned.

"I know. What time do you have to go back?"

"I told Murdo ten o'clock."

"Then don't stand here shivering." She stood back and held out her hand.

Silently he followed her upstairs and as soon as his outer clothes were off, fell gratefully

278

into the warm sheets and held her close to him. Within minutes he was asleep.

Pitt slept late and when he woke Charlotte was already up. He dressed quickly and was downstairs for hot water to shave within five minutes and at the breakfast table in ten to share the meal with his children. This was a rare pleasure, since he was too often gone when they ate.

"Good morning, Jemima," he said formally. "Good morning, Daniel."

"Good morning, Papa," they replied as he sat down. Daniel stopped eating his porridge, spoon in the air, a drop of milk on his chin. His face was soft and the features still barely formed. His baby teeth were even and perfectly formed. He had Pitt's dark curls — unlike Jemima, two years older, who had her mother's auburn coloring, but her hair had to be tied in rags all night if it were to curl.

"Eat your porridge," Jemima ordered him, taking another spoonful of her own. She was inquisitive, bossy, fiercely protective of him, and seldom stopped talking. "You'll get cold in school if you don't!"

Pitt hid a smile, wondering where she had picked up that piece of information.

Daniel obeyed. He had learned in his four years of life that it was a lot easier in the long run than arguing, and his nature was not quarrelsome or assertive, except over issues that mattered, like who had how much pudding, or that the wooden fire engine was his, not hers, and that since he was the boy he had the right to walk on the outside. And the hoop was also his — and the stick that went with it.

She was agreeable to most of these, except walking on the outside — she was older, and taller, and therefore it only made sense that she should.

"Are you working on a very important case, Papa?" Jemima asked, her eyes wide. She was very proud of her father, and everything he did was important.

He smiled at her. Sometimes she looked so like Charlotte must have at the same age, the same soft little mouth, stubborn chin and demanding eyes.

"Yes — away up in Highgate."

"Somebody dead?" she asked. She had very little idea what "dead" meant, but she had heard the word many times, and she and Charlotte and Daniel had buried several dead birds in the garden. But she could not remember all that Charlotte had told her, except it was all right and something to do with heaven.

Pitt met Charlotte's eyes over Jemima's head. She nodded.

"Yes," he replied.

"Are you going to solve it?" Jemima continued.

"I hope so."

"I'm going to be a detective when I grow up," she said, taking another spoonful of her porridge. "I shall solve cases as well."

"So shall I," Daniel added.

Charlotte passed Pitt his porridge and they continued in gentle conversation until it was time for him to leave. He kissed the children — Daniel was still just young enough not to object — kissed Charlotte, who definitely did not object, and put on his boots, which she had remembered to bring in this morning to warm, and took his leave.

Outside it was one of those crisp autumn mornings when the air is cold, tingling in the nostrils, but the sky is blue and the crackle of frost under the feet is a sharp, pleasing sound.

He went first to Bow Street to report to Micah Drummond.

"Another fire?" Drummond frowned, standing by his window looking over the wet rooftops towards the river. The morning sunlight made everything gleam in gray and silver and there was mist only over the water itself. "Still they didn't get Shaw?" He turned back and met Pitt's eyes. "Makes one think."

"He was very distressed." Pitt remembered the night before with an ache of pity.

Drummond did not answer that. He knew Pitt felt it unarguably and they both knew all the possibilities that rose from it.

"I suppose the Highgate police are looking into all the known arsonists in the area, methods and patterns and so on? Made a note of all the people who turned out to watch, in case it's a pyromaniac who just lights them for the love of it?"

"Very keen," Pitt said ruefully.

"But you think it's a deliberate murder?" Drummond eyed him curiously.

"I think so."

"Bit of pressure to get this cleared up." Drummond was at his desk now, and his long fingers played idly with the copper-handled paper knife. "Need you back here. They've taken half a dozen men for this Whitechapel business. I suppose you've seen the newspapers?"

"I saw the letter to Mr. Lusk," Pitt said grimly. "With the human kidney in it, and purported to come 'from hell.' I should think he may be right. Anyone who can kill and mutilate repeatedly like this must live in hell, and carry it with him."

"Pity aside," Drummond said very seriously, "people are beginning to panic. Whitechapel is deserted as soon as it's dusk, people are calling for the commissioner to resign,

282

the newspapers are getting more and more sensational. One woman died from a heart attack with the latest edition in her hand." Drummond sighed in a twisted unhappiness, his eyes on Pitt's. "They don't joke about it in the music halls, you know. People usually make jokes about what frightens them most — it's a way of defusing it. But this is too bad even for that."

"Don't they?" Curiously, that meant more to Pitt than all the sensational press and posters. It was an indication of the depth of fear in the ordinary people. He smiled lopsidedly. "Haven't had much time to go to the halls lately."

Drummond acknowledged the jibe with the good nature with which it was intended.

"Do what you can with this Highgate business, Pitt, and keep me informed."

"Yes sir."

This time instead of taking a hansom, Pitt walked briskly down to the Embankment and caught a train. He got off at the Highgate Road station, putting the few pence difference aside towards Charlotte's holiday. It was a beginning. He walked up Highgate Rise to the police station.

He was greeted with very guarded civility.

"Mornin' sir." Their faces were grave and

resentful, and yet there was a certain satisfaction in them.

"Good morning," he replied, waiting for the explanation. "Discovered something?"

"Yes sir. We got an arsonist who done this kind o' thing before. Never killed anyone, but reckon that was more luck than anything. Method's the same — fuel oil. Done it over Kentish Town way up 'til now, but that's only a step away. Got too 'ot for 'im there an' 'e moved north, I reckon."

Pitt was startled and he tried without success to keep the disbelief out of his face. "Have you arrested him?"

"Not yet, but we will. We know 'is name an' where 'e lodges. Only a matter of time." The man smiled and met Pitt's eyes. "Seems like they didn't need to send a top officer from Bow Street to 'elp us. We done it ourselves: just solid police work — checkin' an' knowin' our area. Mebbe you'd best go an' give them an 'and in Whitechapel — seems this Jack the Ripper's got the 'ole city in a state o' terror."

"Takin' photographs o' the dead women's eyes," another constable added unhelpfully. " 'Cause they reckon that the last thing a person sees is there at the back o' their eyes, if you can just get it. But we got no corpses worth mentioning — poor devils."

"And we've got no murderer worth mentioning yet either," Pitt added. He remembered to exercise some tact just in time. He still had to work with these men. "I expect you are already looking into who owned the other property this arsonist burned? In case there is insurance fraud."

The officer blushed and lied. "Yes sir, seein' into that today."

"I thought so." Pitt looked back at him without a flicker. "Arsonists sometimes have a reason beyond just watching the flames and feeling their own power. Meanwhile I'll get on with the other possibilities. Where's Murdo?"

"In the duty room, sir."

"Thank you."

Pitt found Murdo waiting for him just inside the door of the duty room. He looked tired and had his hand bandaged and held stiffly at his side. He still looked uncertain whether to like Pitt or resent him, and he had not forgotten Pitt's treatment of Flora Lutterworth, nor his own inability to prevent it. All his emotions were bare in his face, and Pitt was reminded again how young he was.

"Anything new, apart from the arsonist?" he asked automatically.

"No sir, except the fire chief says this was just like the last one — but I reckon you know that."

"Fuel oil?"

"Yes sir, most likely — and started in at least three places."

"Then we'll go and see if Pascoe is fit to talk to this morning."

"Yes sir."

Quinton Pascoe was up and dressed, sitting beside a roaring fire in his withdrawing room, but he still looked cold, possibly from tiredness. There were dark circles under his eyes and his hands were knotted in his lap. He seemed older than Pitt had thought when they last met, and for all his stocky body, less robust.

"Come in, Inspector, Constable," he said without rising. "I am sorry I was not able to see you last night, but I really cannot tell you anything anyway. I took a little laudanum — I have been most distressed over the turn of events lately, and I wished to get a good night of rest." He looked at Pitt hopefully, searching to see if he understood. "So much ugliness," he said with a shake of his head. "I seem to be losing all the time. It puts me in mind of the end of King Arthur's table, when the knights go out one by one to seek the Holy Grail, and all the honor and companionship begins to crumble apart. Loyalties were ended. It seems to me that a certain kind of nobility died with the end of chivalry, and courage for its own sake, the idealism that believes in true virtue and is prepared to fight and to die to preserve it, and counts the privilege of battle the only reward."

Murdo looked nonplussed.

Pitt struggled with memory of *Morte d'Arthur* and *Idylls of the King,* and thought perhaps he saw a shred of what Pascoe meant.

"Was your distress due to Mrs. Shaw's death?" Pitt asked. "Or other concerns as well? You spoke of evil — a general sense — "

"That was quite appalling." Pascoe's face looked drained, as if he were totally confused and overcome by events. "But there are other things as well." He shook his head a little and frowned. "I know I keep returning to John Dalgetty, but his attitude towards deriding the old values and breaking them down in order to build new . . ." He looked at Pitt. "I don't condemn all new ideas, not at all. But so many of the things he advocates are destructive."

Pitt did not reply, knowing there was no good response and choosing to listen.

Pascoe's eyes wrinkled up. "He questions all the foundations we have built up over centuries, he casts doubt on the very origin of man and God, he makes the young believe they are invulnerable to the evil of false ideals, the corrosion of cynicism and irresponsibility — and at the same time strips them of the armor of faith. They want to break up and change things without thought. They think they can have things without laboring for them." He bit his lip and scowled. "What can we do, Mr. Pitt? I have lain awake in the night and wrestled with it, and I know less now than when I started."

He stood up and walked towards the window, then swung around and came back again.

"I have been to him, of course, pleaded with him to withhold some of the publications he sells, asked him not to praise some of the works he does, especially this Fabian political philosophy. But to no avail." He waved his hands. "All he says is that information is sacred and all men must have the right to hear and judge for themselves what they believe — and similarly, everyone must be free to put forward any ideas they please, be they true or false, good or evil, creative or destructive. And nothing I say dissuades him. And of course Shaw encourages him with his ideas of what is humorous, when it is really at other people's expense."

Murdo was unused to such passion over ideas. He shifted uncomfortably from one foot to the other.

"The thing is," Pascoe continued intently, "people do not always know when he is joking. Take that wretched business of Lindsay. I am profoundly grieved he is dead — and I did not dislike him personally, you understand — but I felt he was deeply wrong to have written that monograph. There are foolish people, you know" — he searched Pitt's face — "who believe this new nonsense about a political order which promises justice by taking away private property and paying everyone the same, regardless of how clever or how diligent they are. I don't suppose you've read this miserable Irishman, George Bernard Shaw? He writes so divisively, as if he were trying to stir up contention and make people dissatisfied. He talks of people with large appetites and no dinner at one end, and at the other, people with large dinners and no appetites. And of course he is all for freedom of speech." He laughed sharply. "He would be, wouldn't he? He wants to be able to say anything he pleases himself. And Lindsay reported him."

He stopped suddenly. "I'm sorry. I know nothing that can be of help to you, and I do not wish to speak ill of others when such an issue is at stake, especially the dead. I slept deeply until I was awoken by the fire bells, and poor Lindsay's house was a bonfire in the sky."

Pitt and Murdo left, each in his own thoughts as they stepped out of the shelter of the porch into the icy wind. All through an unfruitful visit to the Clitheridges they said nothing to each other. Lindsay's manservant could give them no help as to the origin of the fire, only that he had woken when the smell of smoke had penetrated his quarters, at the back of the house, by which time the main building was burning fiercely and his attempts to rescue his master were hopeless. He had opened the connecting door to be met by a wall of flame, and even as he sat hunched in Clitheridge's armchair, his face bore mute witness to the dedication of his efforts. His skin was red and wealed with blisters, his hands were bound in thin gauze and linen, and were useless to him.

"Dr. Shaw was 'round here early this morning to put balm on them and bind them for him," Lally said with shining admiration in her eyes. "I don't know how he can find the strength, after this new tragedy. He was so fond of Amos Lindsay, you know, apart from the sheer horror of it. I think he must be the strongest man I know."

There had been a bleak look of defeat in Clitheridge's face for an instant as she spoke, and Pitt had imagined a world of frustration, petty inadequacies and fear of other people's raw emotion that must have been the vicar's lot. He was not a man to whom passion came easily; rather the slow-burning, inner turmoil of repressed feelings, too much thought and too much uncertainty. In that instant he felt an overwhelming pity for him; and then turning and seeing Lally's eager, self-critical face, for her also. She was drawn to Shaw in spite of herself, trying to explain it in acceptable terms of admiration for his virtues, and knowing it was immeasurably deeper than that and quite different.

They left having learned nothing that seemed of use, except Oliphant's address, where they discovered that Shaw was out on a call.

At the Red Lion public house they ate hot steak and kidney pudding with a rich suet crust which was light as foam, and green vegetables, then a thick fruit pie and a glass of cider.

Murdo leaned back in his chair, his face flushed with physical well-being.

Pitt rose to his feet, to Murdo's chagrin.

"The Misses Worlingham," he announced. "By the way, do we know who reported the fire? It seems no one we know saw it till the engines were here, except Lindsay's manservant, and he was too busy trying to get Lindsay out."

"Yes sir, a man over in Holly Village was away from home in Holloway." He flushed faintly as he searched for the right word. "An assignation. He saw the glow, and being in mind of the first fire he knew what it was and called the engine." Reluctantly he followed Pitt out into the wind again. "Sir, what do you expect to learn from the Misses Worlingham?"

"I don't know. Something about Shaw and Clemency, perhaps; or Theophilus's death."

"Do you think Theophilus was murdered?" Murdo's voice changed and he faltered in his stride as the thought occurred to him. "Do you think Shaw killed him so his wife would inherit sooner? Then he killed his wife? That's dreadful. But why Lindsay, sir? What had he to gain from that? Surely he wouldn't have done it as a blind, just because it was — pointless." The enormity of it made him shudder and nearly miss his footstep on the path.

"I doubt it," Pitt replied, stretching his pace to keep warm and pulling his muffler tighter around his neck. It was cold enough to snow. "But he's stayed with Lindsay for several days. Lindsay's no fool. If Shaw made a mistake, betrayed himself in some way by a word, or an omission, Lindsay would have seen it and understood what it meant. He may have said nothing at the time, but Shaw, knowing his own guilt and fearing discovery, may have been frightened by the smallest thing, and acted immediately to protect himself."

Murdo hunched his shoulders and his face tightened as the ugliness of the thought caught hold of his mind. He looked cold and miserable in spite of his burned face.

"Do you think so, sir?"

"I don't know, but it's possible. We can't ignore it."

"It's brutal."

"Burning people to death is brutal." Pitt clenched his teeth against the wind stinging the flesh and creeping into every ill-covered corner of neck and wrist and ankle. "We're not looking for a moderate or squeamish man — or woman."

Murdo looked away, refusing to meet Pitt's eyes or even guess his thoughts when he spoke of women and these crimes. "There must be other motives," he said doggedly. "Shaw's a doctor. He could have treated all kinds of diseases, deaths that someone wants hidden — or at least the way of it. What if someone else murdered Theophilus Worlingham?"

"Who?" Pitt asked.

"Mrs. Shaw? She would inherit."

"And then burned herself to death — and Lindsay?" Pitt said sarcastically.

Murdo restrained an angry answer with difficulty. Pitt was his superior and he dared not be openly rude, but the unhappiness inside him wanted to lash out. Every time Pitt mentioned motive Flora's face came back to his mind, flushed with anger, lovely, full of fire to defend Shaw.

Pitt's voice broke through his thoughts.

"But you are right; there is a whole area of motive we haven't even begun to uncover. God knows what ugly or tragic secrets. We've got to get Shaw to tell us."

They were almost at the Worlinghams' house and nothing more was said until they were in the morning room by the fire. Angeline was sitting upright in the large armchair and Celeste was standing behind her.

"I'm sure I don't know what we can tell you, Mr. Pitt," Celeste said quietly. She looked older than the last time he had seen her; there were lines of strain around her eyes and mouth and her hair was pulled back more severely in an unflattering fashion. But it made the strength of her face more apparent. Angeline, on the other hand, looked pale and puffy, and the softer shape of her jaw, sagging a little, showed her irresolution. There were signs of weeping in the redness of her eyelids, and she looked tremulous enough to weep again now.

"We were asleep," Angeline added. "This is terrible! What is happening to us? Who would do these things?"

"Perhaps if we learn why, we will also

know who." Pitt guided them towards the subject he wanted.

"Why?" Angeline blinked. "We don't know!"

"You may, Miss Worlingham — without realizing it. There is money involved, inheritances . . ."

"Our money?" Celeste said the word unconsciously.

"Your brother Theophilus's money, to be exact," Pitt corrected her. "But yes, Worlingham money. I know it is intrusive, but it is necessary that we know; can you tell us all you remember of your brother's death, Miss Worlingham?" He looked from one to the other of them, making sure they knew he included them both.

"It was very sudden," Celeste's features hardened, her mouth forming a thin, judgmental line. "I am afraid I agree with Angeline: Stephen did not care for him as we would have wished. Theophilus was in the most excellent health."

"If you had known him," Angeline added, "you would have been as shocked as we were. He was such a — " She searched her memory for the vision of him as he had been. "He was so vigorous." She smiled tearfully. "He was so alive. He always knew what to do. He was so decisive, you know, a natural leader, like Papa. He believed in health in the mind and a lot of exercise and fresh air for the body — for men, of course. Not ladies. Theophilus always knew the right answer, and what one should believe. He was not Papa's equal, of course, but still I never knew him when he was mistaken about anything that mattered." She sniffed hard and reached for a wholly inadequate wisp of a handkerchief. "We always doubted the manner of his death, one may as well say so now. It was not natural, not for Theophilus."

"What was the cause, Miss Worlingham?"

"Stephen said it was apoplexy," Celeste answered coldly. "But of course we have only his word for that."

"Who found him?" Pitt pressed, although he already knew.

"Clemency." Celeste's eyes opened wide. "Do you believe Stephen killed him, and then when he realized that Clemency knew what he had done, he killed her also? And then poor Mr. Lindsay. Dear heaven." She shivered convulsively. "How evil — how monstrously evil. He shall not come into this house again — not set foot over the step!"

"Of course not, dear." Angeline sniffed noisily. "Mr. Pitt will arrest him, and he will be put in prison."

"Hanged," Celeste corrected grimly.

"Oh dear." Angeline was horrified. "How dreadful — thank heaven Papa did not live to see it. Someone in our family hanged." She began to weep, her shoulders bent, her body huddled in frightened misery.

"Stephen Shaw is not in our family!" Celeste snapped. "He is not and never was a Worlingham. It is Clemency's misfortune that she married him, but she became a Shaw — he is not one of us."

"It is still dreadful. We have never had such shame anywhere near us, even by marriage," Angeline protested. "The name of Worlingham has been synonymous with honor and dignity of the highest order. Just imagine what poor Papa would have felt if the slightest spot of dishonor had touched his name. He never did anything in his entire life to merit an ugly word. And now his son has been murdered — and his granddaughter — and her husband will be hanged. He would have died of shame."

Pitt let her continue because he was curious to see how easily and completely they both accepted that Shaw was guilty. Now he must impress on them that it was only one of several possibilities.

"There is no need to distress yourself yet, Miss Worlingham. Your brother's death may well have been apoplexy, just as Dr. Shaw said, and we do not know that he is guilty of anything yet. It may have nothing to do with money. It may well be that he has treated some medical case which he realized involved a crime, or some disease that the sufferer would kill to keep secret."

Angeline looked up sharply. "You mean insanity? Someone is mad, and Stephen knows about it? Then why doesn't he say? They ought to be locked up in Bedlam, with other lunatics. He shouldn't allow them to go around free — where they can burn people to death."

Pitt opened his mouth to explain to her that perhaps the person only thought Shaw knew. Then he looked at the mounting hysteria in her, and at Celeste's tense eyes, and decided it would be a waste of time.

"It is only a possibility," he said levelly. "It may be someone's death was not natural, and Dr. Shaw knew of it, or suspected it. There are many other motives, perhaps even some we have not yet thought of."

"You are frightening me," Angeline said in a small, shaky voice. "I am very confused. Did Stephen kill anyone, or not?"

"No one knows," Celeste answered her. "It is the police's job to find out."

Pitt asked them several more questions, indirectly about Shaw or Theophilus, but learned nothing more. When they left, the sky had cleared and the wind was even colder. Pitt and Murdo walked side by side in silence till they reached Oliphant's lodging house and at last found Shaw sitting in the front parlor by the fire writing up notes at a rolltop desk. He looked tired, his eyes ringed around with dark hollows and his skin pale, almost papery in quality. There was grief in the sag of his shoulders and the nervous energy in him was transmuted into tension, and jumpiness of his hands.

"There is no point in asking me who I treated or for what ailment," he said tersely as soon as he saw Pitt. "Even if I knew of some disease that would prompt someone to kill me, there is certainly nothing that would cause anyone to harm poor Amos. But then I suppose he died because I was in his house." His voice broke; he found the words so hard to say. "First Clemency — and now Amos. Yes, I suppose you are right; if I really knew who it was, I would do something about it — I don't know what. Perhaps not tell you — but something."

Pitt sat down in the chair nearest him without being asked, and Murdo stood discreetly by the door.

"Think, Dr. Shaw," he said quietly, looking at the exhausted figure opposite him and hating the need to remind him of his role in the tragedy. "Please think of anything you and Amos Lindsay discussed while you were in his house. It is possible that you were aware of some fact that, had you understood it, would have told you who set the first fire."

Shaw looked up, a spark of interest in his eyes for the first time since they had entered the room. "And you think perhaps Amos understood it — and the murderer knew?"

"It's possible," Pitt replied carefully. "You knew him well, didn't you? Was he the sort of man who might have gone to them himself — perhaps seeking proof?"

Suddenly Shaw's eyes brimmed with tears and he turned away, his voice thick with emotion. "Yes," he said so quietly Pitt barely heard him. "Yes — he was. And God help me, I've no idea who he saw or where he went when I was there. I was so wrapped up in my own grief and anger I didn't see and I didn't ask."

"Then please think now, Dr. Shaw." Pitt rose to his feet, moved more by pity not to intrude on a very obvious distress than the sort of impersonal curiosity his profession dictated. "And if you remember anything at all, come and tell me — no one else."

"I will." Shaw seemed sunk within himself again, almost as if Pitt and Murdo had already left.

Outside in the late-afternoon sun, pale and already touched with the dying fire of autumn, Murdo looked at Pitt, his eyes narrowed against the cold.

"Do you think that's what happened, sir: Mr. Lindsay realized who did it — and went looking for proof?"

"God knows," Pitt replied. "What did he see that we haven't?"

Murdo shook his head and together, hands deep in pockets, they trudged back along the footpath towards the Highgate police station.

CHAPTER SEVEN

Charlotte was deeply distressed that Lindsay had died in the second fire. Her relief that Shaw had escaped was like a healing on the surface of the first fear, but underneath that skin of sudden ease there ached the loss of a man she had seen and liked so very shortly since. She had noticed his kindness, especially to Shaw at his most abrasive. Perhaps he was the only one who understood his grief for Clemency, and the biting knowledge that she might have died in his place; that some enmity he had earned, incited, somehow induced, had sparked that inferno.

And now Amos Lindsay was gone too, burned beyond recognition.

How must Shaw be feeling this morning? Grieved — bewildered — guilty that yet another had suffered a death meant for him — frightened in case this was not the end? Would there go on being fires, more and more deaths until his own? Did he look at everyone and wonder? Was he even now searching his memory, his records, to guess whose secret was so devastating they would murder to keep it? Or did he already know — but feel bound by some professional ethic to guard it even at this price?

She felt the need for more furious action while the questions raced through her thoughts. She stripped the beds and threw the sheets and pillowcases down the stairs, adding nightshirts for all the family, and towels; then followed them down, carrying armfuls into the scullery, off the kitchen, where she filled both tubs with water and added soap to one, screwed the mangle between them, and began the laundry. She was in one of her oldest dresses, sleeves rolled up and a pinafore around her waist, scrubbing fiercely, and she let her mind return to the problem again.

For all the possible motives to murder Shaw, including money, love, hate and revenge (if indeed someone believed him guilty of medical neglect, Theophilus Worlingham or anyone else), her thoughts still returned to Clemency and her battle against slum profiteers.

She was up to her elbows in suds, her pinafore soaked, and her hair falling out of its pins, when the front doorbell rang. Fishmonger's boy, she thought. Gracie will get it.

A moment later Gracie came flying back up the corridor, her feet clattering on the linoleum. She swung around the kitchen doorway, breathless, her eyes wide with amazement, awe and horror as she saw her mistress.

"Lady Vespasia Cumming-Gould!" she said squeakily. "She's right 'ere be'ind me, ma'am! I couldn't put 'er in the parlor, ma'am; she wouldn't stay!"

And indeed Great-Aunt Vespasia was on Gracie's heels, elegant and very upright in a dark teal gown embroidered in silver on the lapels, and carrying a silver-topped cane. These days she was seldom without it. Her eyes took in the kitchen, scrubbed table, newly blacked range, rows of blue-and-white china on the dresser, earthenware polished brown and cream, steaming tubs in the scullery beyond, and Charlotte like a particularly harassed and untidy laundrymaid.

Charlotte froze. Gracie was already transfixed to the spot as Vespasia swept past her.

Vespasia regarded the mangle with curiosity.

"What in heaven's name is that contraption?" she inquired with her eyebrows raised. "It looks like something that should have belonged to the Spanish Inquisition."

"A mangle," Charlotte replied, brushing her hair back with her arm. "You push the clothes through it and it squeezes out the soap and water."

"I am greatly relieved to hear it." Vespasia sat down at the table, unconsciously arranging her skirts with one hand. She looked at the mangle again. "Very commendable. But what are you going to do about this second fire in Highgate? I presume you are going to do something? Whatever the reasons for it, it does not alter the fact that Clemency Shaw is dead, and deserves a better epitaph than that she was murdered in error for her husband."

Charlotte wiped her hands and came to the table, ignoring the sheets still soaking in the tub. "I am not sure that she was. Would you like a cup of tea?"

"I would. What makes you believe that? Why should anyone murder poor Amos Lindsay, if not in an attempt to get rid of Shaw more successfully than last time?"

Charlotte glanced at Gracie, who at last moved from the doorway and reached for the kettle.

"Maybe they were afraid Shaw had realized who they were, or that he might realize?" she suggested, sitting down opposite Vespasia. "He may well have all the information, if he knew how to add it up and see the pattern. After all, he knew what Clemency was doing; she may have left papers which he had seen. In fact, that may be why they chose fire. To destroy not only Clemency but all the evidence she had collected."

Vespasia straightened a little. "Indeed, that

is something I had not considered. It is foolish, because it makes no difference to her, poor creature, but I should prefer not to believe she did not even die in her own right. If Shaw knows already who it is, why does he not say so? Surely he has not yet worked it out, and certainly has no proof. You do not suggest he is in any kind of collusion with them?"

"No — "

Behind Charlotte, Gracie was rather nervously heating the teapot and spooning in tea from the caddie. She had never prepared anything for someone of Great-Aunt Vespasia's importance before. She wished to make it exactly right, and she did not know what exactly right might be. Also she was listening to everything that was said. She was horrified by and very proud of Pitt's occupation, and of Charlotte's occasional involvement.

"I assume Thomas has already thought of everything that we have," Vespasia continued. "Therefore for us to pursue that line would be fruitless — "

Gracie brought the tea, set it on the table, the cup rattling and slopping in her shaking hands. She made a half curtsey to Vespasia.

"Thank you." Vespasia acknowledged it graciously. She was not in the habit of thanking servants, but this was obviously different. The child was in a state of nervous awe.

306

Gracie blushed and withdrew to take up the laundry where Charlotte had left off. Vespasia wiped out her saucer with the napkin Charlotte handed her.

Charlotte made her decision.

"I shall learn what I can about Clemency's work, who she met, what course she followed from the time she began to care so much, and somewhere I shall cross the path of whoever caused these fires."

Vespasia sipped her tea. "And how do you intend to do it so you survive to share your discoveries with the rest of us?"

"By saying nothing whatever about reform," Charlotte replied, her plan very imperfectly formed. "I shall begin with the local parish — " Her mind went back to her youth, when she and her sisters had trailed dutifully behind Caroline doing "good works," visiting the sick or elderly, offering soup and preserves and kind words. It was part of a gentlewoman's life. In all probability Clemency had done the same, and then seen a deeper pain and not turned away from it with complacency or resignation, but questioned and began the fight.

Vespasia was looking at her critically. "Do you imagine that will be sufficient to safeguard you?"

"If he murders every woman who is involved in visiting or inquiring after the parish poor, he will need a bigger conflagration than the great fire of London," Charlotte replied with decision. "Anyway," she added rather more practically, "I shall be a long way from the kind of person who owns the properties. I shall simply start where Clemency started. Long before I discover whatever someone murdered to keep, I shall draw other people in, you and Emily — and of course Thomas." Then suddenly she thought she might be being presumptuous. Vespasia had not said she wished to be involved in such a way. Charlotte looked at her anxiously.

Vespasia sipped her tea again and her eyes were bright over the rim of her cup.

"Emily and I already have plans," she said, setting the cup down in its saucer and looking over Charlotte's shoulder at Gracie, who was self-consciously scrubbing at the washboard, her shoulders hunched. "If you think it advisable not to go alone, leave the children with your mother for a few days and take your maid with you."

Gracie stopped in mid-motion, laundry dripping in the sink, her back bent, her hands in the air. She let out a long sigh of exquisite anticipation. She was going to detect — with the mistress! It would be the biggest adventure of her entire life!

Charlotte was incredulous. "Gracie!"

"And why not?" Vespasia inquired. "It would appear quite natural. I shall lend you my second carriage and Percival to drive it for you. There is no point in doing it if you do not do it as well as possible. I am concerned in the matter. My admiration for Clemency Shaw is considerable. I shall require you to inform me of your findings, if any. Naturally you will also tell Thomas. I have no intention of allowing the whole thing to be swallowed up in public assumption that the intended victim was Stephen Shaw, and Clemency's death can be dismissed as an error, however tragic. Oh!" Her face fell with sudden awful comprehension. "Do you think it is conceivable that that is why poor Lindsay was murdered? So we might well assume Clemency's death was unintended? How cold-bloodedly deliberate."

"I am going to find out," Charlotte said quietly with a little shiver. "As soon as Percival arrives with the carriage, I shall take the children to Mama's, and we shall begin."

"Fetch what they require," Vespasia commanded. "And I shall take them with me on my return. I have no errands until this evening when the House rises."

Charlotte got to her feet. "Somerset Carlisle?"

"Just so. If we are to fight against the slum

profiteers, we require to know the exact state of the law, and what it is most reasonable to expect we may achieve. One may assume that Clemency did much the same, and discovered some weakness in their position. We need to know what it was."

Gracie was scrubbing so hard the board was rattling in the tub.

"Stop that now, child!" Vespasia ordered. "I can hardly hear myself think! Put it through that contraption and hang it up. I am sure it is clean enough. For goodness sake, they are only bed sheets! Then when you have done that, go and tidy yourself up and put on a coat, and a hat if you have one. Your mistress will require you to accompany her to Highgate."

"Yes ma'am!" Gracie heaved the entire lot of linen up, standing on tiptoe to get it clear of the water, dropped it in the clean water in the opposite tub, pulled the plug, then began to pay it through the mangle, winding like fury in her excitement.

Vespasia seemed completely unaware that she had just given a complete hour's instructions to someone else's servant. It seemed common sense, and that was sufficient to justify it.

"Go upstairs to the nursery and pack whatever is necessary," she continued, speaking to

Charlotte in almost the same tone of voice. "For several days. You do not want to be anxious for them while you are endeavoring to unravel this matter."

Charlotte obeyed with a very slight smile. She did not resent being ordered around; it was what she would have done anyway, and the familiarity with which Vespasia did it was a kind of affection, also an unspoken trust that they were involved in the affair together and desired the same end.

Upstairs she found Jemima solemnly practicing her writing. She had progressed from the stage of rather carefully drawing letters and now she did them with some abandon, confident she was making words, and of their meaning. Sums she was considerably less fond of.

Daniel was still struggling, and with immeasurable superiority now and again Jemima gave him assistance, explaining carefully precisely what he must do, and why. He bore it with placid good nature, imitating her round script and concealing both his ignorance and his admiration behind a frown of attention. It can be very difficult being four and having a sister two years older.

"You are going to stay with Grandmama for a few days," Charlotte informed them with a bright smile. "You will enjoy it very much.

You can take your lessons with you if you wish, but you don't have to do them more than an hour or two in the mornings. I shall explain why you are not at school. If you are good, Grandmama might take you for a carriage ride, to the zoo perhaps?"

She had their immediate cooperation, as she had intended. "You will be going with Great-Aunt Vespasia, who is ready to take you as soon as you are packed. She is a very important lady indeed, and you must do everything exactly as she tells you."

"Who is Great Vepsia?" Daniel asked curiously, his face puckered up trying to remember. "I only 'member Aunt Emily."

"She is Aunt Emily's aunt," Charlotte simplified for the sake of clarity, and to avoid mentioning George, whom Jemima at least could recall quite clearly. She did not understand death, except in relation to small animals, but she knew loss.

Daniel seemed satisfied, and rapidly Charlotte set about putting into a Gladstone bag everything they would require. When it was fastened she made sure they were clean and wrapped up in coats and that their gloves were attached to their cuffs, their shoes buttoned, their hair brushed and their scarves tied. Then she took them downstairs to where Vespasia was waiting, still seated in the kitchen chair.

They greeted her very formally, Daniel half a step behind Jemima, but as she took out her lorgnette to regard them, they were so fascinated by it they forgot to be shy. Charlotte had no qualms as she watched them mount into the carriage, with considerable assistance from the footman, and depart along the street.

Gracie was so excited she could hardly hold her comb in her hand to tidy her hair, and her fingers slipped and made a knot in the strings of her bonnet which she would probably have to cut with scissors ever to get it off again. But what did it matter? She was going with the mistress to help her detect! She had very little clear idea of what it would involve, but it would absolutely without question be marvelously interesting and very important. She might learn secrets and make discoveries concerning issues of such magnitude that people were prepared to commit murder in their cause. And possibly it would even be dangerous.

Of course she would walk a couple of steps behind, and only speak when she was invited to; but she would watch and listen all the time, and notice everything that anyone said or did, even the way their faces looked. Maybe she would notice something vital that no one else did.

It was some two hours later when Charlotte and Gracie descended from the second carriage. They were handed down by Percival, to Gracie's intense delight; she had never ridden in a proper carriage before, still less been assisted by another servant. They walked up the path to St. Anne's Church side by side at Charlotte's insistence, in hope of finding someone there who might guide them in matters of parish relief, and thus to a more precise knowledge of Clemency Shaw's interest in housing.

Charlotte had given the matter a good deal of thought. She did not wish to be open about her intentions and it had been necessary to construct a believable story. She had tussled with the problem without success until Gracie, biting her lip and not wishing to be impertinent, had suggested they inquire about a relative who had been thrown on the parish as a result of widowhood, which they had just heard about and were anxious to help.

Charlotte had thought this so unlikely to be true that even Hector Clitheridge would doubt it, but then Gracie had pointed out that her Aunt Bertha had been in just such a predicament, and Gracie had indeed heard about it only two weeks ago. Then Charlotte realized what she meant, and seized upon the idea instantly.

"O' course me Aunt Bertha din't live in 'Ighgate," Gracie said honestly. "She lived in Clerkenwell — but then they dunno that."

And so after learning that there was no one in at the parsonage, they repaired to the church of St. Anne's itself, and found Lally Clitheridge arranging flowers in the vestry. She turned at the sound of the door opening, a look of welcome on her face. Then she recognized Charlotte and the smile froze. She kept the Michaelmas daisy in her hand and did not move from the bench.

"Good afternoon, Mrs. Pitt. Are you looking for someone?"

"I expect you could help me, if you would be so kind," Charlotte answered, forcing a warmth into her voice which did not come naturally in the face of Lally's chill gaze.

"Indeed?" Lally looked beyond her at Gracie with slightly raised brows. "Is this lady with you?"

"She is my maid." Charlotte was conscious as she said it of sounding a trifle pompous, but there was no other reasonable answer.

"Good gracious!" Lally's eyebrows shot up. "Are you unwell?"

"I am perfectly well, thank you." It was becoming harder and harder to keep an amiability in her tone. She wanted to tell Lally she owed her no account of her arrangements and would give none, but that would defeat her purpose. She needed at the least an ally, better still a friend. "It is on Gracie's behalf we are here," she continued her civil tone with an effort. "She has just heard that her uncle has died and left her aunt in very poor circumstances, most probably a charge on the parish. Perhaps you would be kind enough to tell me which of the ladies in the neighborhood have been most involved in charitable works and might know of her whereabouts."

Lally was quite obviously torn between her dislike for Charlotte and her compassion for Gracie, who was staring at her belligerently, but Lally apparently took it for well-controlled grief.

"You do not know her address?" She looked past Charlotte as if she had not been there. It was an excellent compromise.

Gracie's mind was quick. "I know 'er old 'ouse, ma'am; but I'm afraid wot wif poor Uncle Albert bein' took so sudden, and not much put by, that they might'a bin put out on the street. They'd 'ave no one to turn to, 'ceptin the parish."

Lally's face softened. "There's been no Albert buried in this parish, child; not in more than a year. And believe me, I mark every burial. It is part of my Christian duty, as well as my wish. Are you sure it is here in Highgate?"

Gracie did not look at Charlotte, but she was acutely conscious of her a foot or two away.

"Oh, yes ma'am," she replied earnestly. "I'm sure that's wot they said. Per'aps if you would just tell us the names o' the other ladies as 'elps them as is in trouble, we could ask an' mebbe they'd know, like?" She smiled appealingly, putting to the front of her mind their purpose in having come; it was, after all, the greater loyalty. This must be what detecting involved, learning facts people were reluctant to tell you.

Lally was won over, in spite of herself. Still ignoring Charlotte she directed her answer to Gracie.

"Of course. Mrs. Hatch may be able to assist you, or Mrs. Dalgetty, or Mrs. Simpson, Mrs. Braithwaite or Miss Crombie. Would you like their addresses?"

"Oh, yes ma'am, if you'd be so good?"

"Of course." Lally fished in her reticule for a piece of paper, and failed to find a pencil.

Charlotte produced one and handed it to her. She took it in silence, wrote for several moments, then gave the slip to Gracie, who took it, still without looking at Charlotte, and held on to it tightly. She thanked Lally with a slight curtsey. "That's ever so kind of you, ma'am."

"Not at all," Lally said generously. Then her expression clouded over again and she looked at Charlotte. "Good day, Mrs. Pitt. I hope you are successful." She passed back the pencil. "Now if you will excuse me I have several vases of flowers to finish and then some calls to make." And she turned her back on them and began furiously poking daisies into the rolled-up wire mesh in the vase, sticking them in at all angles.

Side by side Charlotte and Gracie left, eyes downcast until they were outside. Then immediately Gracie pushed the paper at Charlotte with a glow of triumph.

Charlotte took it and read it. "You did expertly, Gracie," she said sincerely. "I couldn't have managed without you!"

Gracie flushed with pleasure. "What does it say, ma'am? I carsn't read that kind o' writin'."

Charlotte looked at the sprawling cursive script. "It is exactly what we want," she answered approvingly. "The names and addresses of several of the women who might know where Clemency Shaw began her work. We shall start immediately with Maude Dalgetty. I rather liked her manner at the funeral. I think she may be a sensible woman and generous spirited. She was a friend of Clemency's and so, I expect, inclined to help us."

★ ★ ★

And so it proved. Maude Dalgetty was both sensible and desirous to help. She welcomed them into a withdrawing room full of sunlight and bowls of late roses. The room had a graciousness of proportion and was elegantly furnished, although many of the pieces were beginning to show wear. There were little knots and gaps in some of the fringes around lamps and the sashes on the curtains, and some of the crystals were missing from the chandelier. But the warmth was unmistakable. The books were used — here was one open on the side table. There was a large sewing basket with mending and embroidery clearly visible. The painting above the mantelpiece was a portrait of Maude herself, probably done a dozen years earlier, sitting in a garden on a summer day, the light on her skin and hair. She certainly had been a remarkable beauty, and much of it was left, even if a little more amply proportioned.

Two cats lay curled up together in a single ball of fur by the fire, sound asleep.

"How may I help you?" Maude said as soon as they were in. She paid no less attention to Gracie than to Charlotte. "Would you like a cup of tea?"

It was, strictly speaking, too early for such a thing, but Charlotte judged it was sincerely offered and since she was thirsty and had eaten no lunch, and she imagined Gracie was the same, she accepted.

Maude ordered it from the maid, then inquired again how she might help.

Charlotte hesitated. Sitting in this warm room looking at Maude's intelligent face she was uncertain whether to risk telling her the truth rather than a concocted lie, however plausible. Then she recalled Clemency's death, and Lindsay's so soon after, and changed her mind. Wherever the heart of the murders lay, there were tentacles of it here. An unwitting word by even an innocent person might provoke more violence. It was one of the ugliest changes in the aftermath of murder that instinctive trusts disappeared. One looked for betrayal and suspected every answer of being a lie, every careless or angry word of hiding greed or hatred, every guarded comment of concealing envy.

"Gracie has recently heard that an aunt of hers in this locality has been widowed," she explained. "She fears she may be in straitened circumstances, perhaps even to the degree of being put out on the street."

Maude's face showed immediate concern but she did not interrupt.

"If she has fallen on the care of the parish then perhaps you know what has become of her?" Charlotte tried to put the urgency into her voice that she would have felt had it been true, and saw the compassion in Maude's eyes, and hated herself for the duplicity. She hurried on to cover it in speech. "And if you do not, then someone else may? I believe that the late Mrs. Shaw concerned herself greatly with such cases?" She felt her cheeks burn. This was the kind of deception she most despised.

Maude tightened her lips and blinked several times to control the very obvious grief that flooded her face.

"Indeed she did," she said gently. "But if she had any record of whom she helped it will have been destroyed when the house was burned." She turned to Gracie, since it was Gracie whose aunt they were speaking of. "The only other person likely to know would be the curate, Matthew Oliphant. I think she confided in him and he gave her counsel, and possibly even help. She spoke very little of her work, but I know she felt more deeply about it as time passed. Most of it was not within the parish, you know? I am not at all sure she would have been directly involved with a local loss. You might be better advised to ask Mrs. Hatch, or perhaps Mrs. Wetherell."

The maid returned with tea and the most delicious sandwiches, made with the thinnest of bread and tomato cut into minute cubes so there was nothing squashy in them and no stringy skins to embarrass the eater. For several minutes Charlotte abandoned the purpose of her visit and simply enjoyed them. Gracie, who had never even seen anything so fine, let alone tasted it, was absolutely spellbound.

It was early afternoon and becoming overcast when Percival drew up the carriage outside the lodging house where Matthew Oliphant lived. He handed down Charlotte, and then Gracie, and watched them walk up the path and knock on the door before he returned to the carriage seat and prepared to wait.

The door was opened by a maid who advised them that Mr. Oliphant was in the sitting room and would no doubt receive them, since he seemed to receive everyone.

They reached the sitting room, an impersonal place furnished with extreme conservatism, armchairs with antimacassars, a portrait of the Queen over the mantel and one of Mr. Gladstone on the far wall, several samplers of religious texts, three stuffed birds under glass, an arrangement of dried flowers, a stuffed weasel in a case, and two aspidistras. They reminded Charlotte immediately of the sort of things that had been left over after everyone else had taken what they liked. She could not imagine the person who would willingly have selected these. Certainly not Matthew Oliphant, with his humorous, imaginative face, rising in his chair to greet them, leaving his Bible open on the table; nor Stephen Shaw, busy writing at the rolltop desk by the window. He stood up also when he saw Charlotte, surprise and pleasure in his face.

"Mrs. Pitt, how charming to see you." He came towards her, his hand extended. He glanced at Gracie, who was standing well back, smitten with shyness now they were dealing with gentlemen.

"Good afternoon, Dr. Shaw," Charlotte replied, hastily concealing her chagrin. How could she question the curate with Shaw himself present? Her whole plan of action would have to be changed. "This is Gracie, my maid — " She could think of no explanation for her presence, so she did not try. "Good afternoon, Mr. Oliphant."

"Good afternoon, Mrs. Pitt. If — if you wish to be alone with the doctor, I can quite easily excuse myself. My room is not cold; I can pursue my studies there."

Charlotte knew from the temperature of the hallway that that was almost certainly a fiction.

"Not at all, Mr. Oliphant. Please remain.

This is your home and I should be most uncomfortable to have driven you away from the fire."

"What may I do for you, Mrs. Pitt?" Shaw asked, frowning at her in grave concern. "I hope you are as well as you seem? And your maid?"

"We are very well, thank you. Our visit has nothing to do with your profession, Dr. Shaw." There was now no purpose whatsoever in continuing with the tale of Gracie's uncle. He would see through it and despise them both, not only for the lie, but for the inadequacy of it. "I did not come about myself." She faced him boldly, meeting his eyes and being considerably disconcerted by the acute intelligence in them, and the directness of his gaze back at her. She took a deep breath and plunged on. "I have determined to pursue the work that your late wife was involved in regarding the housing of the poor, and their conditions. I would like to learn where she began, so I may begin in the same place."

There was a full minute's total silence. Matthew Oliphant stood by the fire with the Bible in his hand, his knuckles white where he grasped it, his face pale, then flushed. Gracie was rooted to the spot. Shaw's expression flashed from amazement to disbelief, and then suspicion.

"Why?" he said guardedly. "If you have

some passion to work with the poor or the dispossessed what is wrong with those in your own neighborhood?" His voice hovered on the edge of sarcasm. "Surely there are some? London is teeming with poor. Do you live in some area so select you have to come to Highgate to find anyone in need?"

Charlotte could think of no answer. "You are being unnecessarily rude, Dr. Shaw." She heard herself mimicking Aunt Vespasia's tone, and thought for an awful moment that she sounded ridiculous. Then she saw Shaw's face and the sudden color of shame in his cheeks.

"I apologize, Mrs. Pitt. Of course I am." He was contrite. "Please forgive me." He did not mention either his bereavement or the loss of his friend; as an excuse it would have been cheap and beneath him.

She smiled at him with all the warmth and deep empathy that she felt for him, and the very considerable liking. "The matter is forgotten." She dismissed it charmingly. "Can you help me? I should be so obliged. Her crusade is one in which I should like to become involved myself, and draw others. It would be foolish not to profit from what she has already done. She has earned much admiration."

Very slowly, wordlessly, Matthew Oliphant sat down again and opened his Bible, upside down.

"Do you?" Shaw frowned in some inner concentration. "I cannot see that it will be much advantage to you. She worked alone, so far as I know. She certainly did not work with the parish ladies, or the vicar." He sighed. "Not that poor old Clitheridge could fight his way out of a wet paper bag!" He looked at her gravely, a kind of laughing admiration in his eyes she found a trifle discomfitting. One or two rather absurd thoughts flashed through her mind, and she dismissed them hastily, a flush in her cheeks.

"Nevertheless I should like to try," she insisted.

"Mrs. Pitt," he said gently. "I can tell you almost nothing, only that Clemency cared very much about reforming the laws. In fact I think she cared more about them than almost anything else." His face pinched a little. "But if, as I suspect, what you are really seeking is to discover who set fire to my house, you will not accomplish it this way. It is I who was meant to die in that fire, as it was when poor Amos died."

She was at once fiercely sorry for him and extraordinarily angry.

"Indeed?" Her eyebrows shot up. "How arrogant of you! Do you assume that no one else could possibly be important enough in the scheme of things, and only you arouse enough passion or fear to be murdered?"

It was one sting too much. His temper exploded.

"Clemency was one of the finest women alive. If you had known her, instead of arriving the moment she was dead, you wouldn't have to be told." He was leaning forward a little, his shoulders tight and hunched. "She did nothing to incur the kind of insane hatred that burns down houses and risks the lives of everyone in them. For heaven's sake if you must meddle — at least do it efficiently!"

"I am trying to!" she shouted back. "But you are determined to obstruct me. One would almost think you did not want it solved." She pointed at him sharply. "You won't help. You won't tell the police anything. You stick to your wretched confidences as if they were secrets of state. What do you imagine that we are going to do with them, except catch a murderer?"

He jerked very upright, back straight. "I don't know any secrets that will catch anyone but a few unfortunate devils who would rather keep their diseases private than have them spread 'round the neighborhood for every able and nosy busybody to turn over and speculate on," he shouted back. "Dear God — don't you think I want him caught — whoever he is? He murdered my wife and my best

327

friend — and I may be next."

"Don't give yourself airs," she said coldly, because suddenly her anger had evaporated and she was feeling guilty for being so ruthless, but she did not know how to get out of the situation she had created. "Unless you know who it is, as it appears poor Mr. Lindsay did, you are probably not in danger at all."

He threw an ashtray into the corner of the room, where it splintered and lay in pieces, then he walked out, slamming the door.

Gracie was still standing on the spot, her eyes like saucers.

Oliphant looked up from his Bible and at last realized it was upside down. He closed it quickly and stood up.

"Mrs. Pitt," he said very softly. "I know where Mrs. Shaw began, and some of where it led her. If you wish, I will take you."

Charlotte looked at his bony, agreeable face, and the quiet pain in it, and felt ashamed of her outburst for its noise and self-indulgence.

"Thank you, Mr. Oliphant, I should be very grateful."

Percival drove them; it was well beyond the area of Highgate and into Upper Holloway. They stopped at a narrow street and alighted from the carriage, once again leaving it to wait. Charlotte looked around. The houses were cheek by jowl, one room upstairs and one down, to judge by the width, but there may have been more at the back beyond view. The doors were all closed and the steps scrubbed and whitestoned. It was not appreciably poorer than the street on which she and Pitt had lived when they were first married.

"Come." Oliphant set out along the pavement and almost immediately turned in along an alley that Charlotte had not observed before. Here it was dank and a chill draft blew on their faces, carrying the smell of raw sewage and drains.

Charlotte coughed and reached for her handkerchief — even Gracie put her hand up to her face — but they hurried after him till he emerged in a small, dim courtyard and crossed it, warning them to step over the open gutters. At the far side he knocked on a paint-peeled door and waited.

After several minutes it was opened by a girl of fourteen or fifteen with a gray-white face and fair hair greasy with dirt. Her eyes were pink-rimmed and there was a flicker of fear in the defiance with which she spoke.

"Yeah? 'Oo are yer?"

"Is Mrs. Bradley at home?" he asked quietly, opening his coat a fraction to show his clerical collar.

Her face softened in relief. "Yeah, Ma's in

bed. She took poorly again. The doc were 'ere yest'dy an' 'e give 'er some med'cine, but it don't do no good."

"May I come in and see her?" Oliphant requested.

"Yeah, I s'pose. But don' wake 'er if she's sleepin'."

"I won't," he promised, and held the door wide for Charlotte and Gracie to enter.

Inside the narrow room was cold. Damp seeped through wallpaper, staining it with mold, and the air had an odor that was sour and clung in the back of the throat. There was no tap or standpipe, and a bucket in the corner covered with a makeshift lid served the purposes of nature. Rickety stairs led upwards through a gap in the ceiling and Oliphant went up first, cautioning Charlotte and Gracie to wait their turn in case the weight of more than one person should collapse them.

Charlotte emerged into a bedroom with two wooden cots, both heaped with blankets. In one lay a woman who at a glance might have been Charlotte's mother's age. Her face was gaunt, her skin withered and papery, and her eyes so hollow the bones of her brow seemed almost skull-like.

Then as Charlotte moved closer she saw the fair hair and the skin of her neck above the patched nightshirt, and realized she was probably no more than thirty. There was a handkerchief with blood on it grasped loosely in the thin hand.

The three of them stood in silence for several minutes, staring at the sleeping woman, each racked with silent, impotent pity.

Downstairs again, Charlotte turned to Oliphant and the girl.

"We must do something! Who owns this — this heap of timber? It's not fit for horses, let alone women to live in. He should be prosecuted. We will begin straightaway. Who collects the rent?"

The girl was as white as flour; her whole body shook.

"Don't do that, please miss! I beg yer, don't turn us aht. Me ma'll die if yer put 'er in the street — and me an' Alice and Becky'll 'ave ter go inter the poor 'ouse. Please don't. We 'aven't done nuthin' wrong, honest we 'aven't. We paid the rent — I swear."

"I don't want to put you out." Charlotte was aghast. "I want to force whoever owns this place to make it fit to live in."

The girl looked at her with disbelief.

"Wotcher mean? If we makes a fuss 'e'll 'ave us aht. There's plenty more as'd be glad ter 'ave it — an' we'll 'ave ter go souf into — w'ere it'll be worse. Please miss, don't do it!"

331

"Worse?" Charlotte said slowly. "But he should make this — this fit to live in. You should have water at least, and drainage. No wonder your mother is ill — "

"She'll get better — jus' let 'er sleep a bit. We're all right, miss. Just leave us be."

"But if — "

"That's wot 'appened ter Bessie Jones. She complained, an' now she's gorn ter live in St. Giles, an' she ain't got no more'n a corner o' the room to 'erself. You let be — please miss."

Her fear was so palpable that Charlotte could do no more than promise to say nothing, to swear it in front of Matthew Oliphant, and leave shivering and by now aware of a rising nausea in her stomach, and an anger so tight it made all the muscles in her body ache.

"Tomorrow I'll take you to St. Giles," Oliphant said quietly when they were out in the main street again. "If you want to go."

"I want to go." Charlotte said the words without hesitation — if she had thought for even a moment she might have lost her resolve.

"Did you go there with Clemency also?" she asked more gently, trying to imagine the journey she was copying, thinking of Clemency's distress as she must have seen sights just like these. "I expect she was very moved?"

He turned to her. His face was curiously luminous with memory that for all its bleakness held some beauty for him that still shone in his mind and warmed him till he was temporarily oblivious of the street or the cold.

"Yes — we came here," he answered with sweetness in his voice. "And then to St. Giles, and from there eastwards into Mile End and Whitechapel — " He might have been speaking of the pillared ruins of Isfahan, or the Golden Road to Samarkand, so did his tongue caress the words.

Charlotte hesitated only a moment before plunging on, ignoring what was suddenly so obvious to her.

"Then could you tell me where she went last?"

"If I could, Mrs. Pitt, I would have offered," he said gravely, his cheeks pink. "I only knew the general direction, because I was not with her when she found Bessie Jones. I only know that she did, because she told me afterwards. Would to God I had been." He strove to master his anguish, and almost succeeded. "Maybe I could have saved her." His voice cracked and finished husky and almost inaudible.

Charlotte could not argue, although perhaps by then Clemency had already frightened those landlords and owners whose greed had eaten into them until they had destroyed her.

Oliphant turned away, struggling for control. "But if you wish to go there, I shall try to take you — as long as you understand the risk. If we find the same place, then — " He stopped; the conclusion was not needed.

"You are not afraid?" she asked, not as a challenge but because she was certain that he was not. He was harrowed by feelings, almost laid naked by them, and yet fear was not among them — anger, pity, indignation, loss, but not fear.

He turned back to her, his face for a moment almost beautiful with the power of his caring.

"You wish to continue Clemency's work, Mrs. Pitt — and I think perhaps even more than that, you wish to learn who killed her, and expose them. So do I."

She did not answer; it was hardly necessary. She caught a sudden glimpse of how much he had cared for Clemency. He would never have spoken; she was a married woman, older than he and of higher social station. Anything more than friendship was impossible. But that had not altered his feeling, nor taken anything from his loss.

She smiled at him, politely, as if she had seen no more than anyone else, and thanked him for his help. She and Gracie would be most obliged.

Naturally she explained to Pitt what she

was doing, and to what end. She might have evaded it had not Vespasia taken the children to Caroline, but their absence had to be explained and she was in no mood to equivocate.

She did not tell him what manner of place she would be going to because nothing in her experience could have foreseen where the following two days would take her. She, Oliphant and Gracie were driven by Percival from street to street, forever narrower, darker and more foul, following the decline of the unfortunate Bessie Jones. Gracie was of inestimable help because she had seen such places before and she understood the desperation that makes men and women accept such treatment rather than lose their frail hold on space and shelter, however poor, and be driven out into the streets to be huddled in doorways shuddering with cold, exposed to the rain and casual violence.

Finally in the later afternoon of the third day they found Bessie Jones, as Clemency Shaw had done before them. It was in the heart of Mile End, off the Whitechapel Road. There seemed to be an unusual number of police around.

Bessie was crouching in the corner of a room no more than twelve feet by sixteen, and occupied by three families, one in each corner.

There were about sixteen people in all, including two babies in arms, which cried constantly. There was a blackened potbellied stove against one wall, but it was barely alight. There were buckets for the necessities of nature, but no drain to empty either that or any other waste, except the one in the courtyard, which overflowed and the stench filled the air, catching in the throat, soiling the clothes, the hair and the skin. There was no running water. For washing, cooking, drinking, it all had to be fetched in a pail from a standpipe three hundred yards away along the street.

There was no furniture except one broken wooden chair. People slept in what scraps of rag and blanket they could gather together for warmth; men, women and children, with nothing between them and the boards of the floor but more rags and loose ends of oakum, and the dross of the cloth industry too wretched even to remake into drab for the workhouse.

Above the crying of children, the snoring of an old man asleep under the broken window, boarded with a loose piece of linoleum, was the constant squeaking and scuttling of rats. On the floor below were the raucous sounds of a gin mill and the shouts of drunkards as they fought, swore and sang snatches of bawdy songs. Two women lay senseless in the gutter and a sailor relieved himself against the wall.

Below street level, in ill-lit cellars, ninety-eight women and girls sat shoulder to shoulder in a sweatshop stitching shirts for a few pence a day. It was better than the match factory with its phosphorous poisoning.

Upstairs a brothel prepared for the evening trade. Twenty yards away rows of men lay in bunks, their bodies rotting, their minds adrift in the sweet dreams of opium.

Bessie Jones was worn out, exhausted by the fruitless fight, and glad now at least to be under shelter from the rain and to have a stove to creep close to in the night, and two slices of bread to eat.

Charlotte emptied her purse and felt it a gross and futile thing to have done, but the money burned her hand.

In all of it she had followed the path that Clemency Shaw had taken, and she had felt as she must have felt, but she had learned nothing as to who might have killed her, although why was only too apparent. If the ownership of such places was accredited publicly there would be some who would not care, they had no reputation or status to lose. But there were surely those who drew their money from such abysmal suffering, and who would pay dearly to keep it secret, and call it by some other name. To say one owned property implied estates somewhere in the shires; farmlands might be envisioned, rich earth yielding food, cattle, timber — not the misery, crime and disease Charlotte and Gracie had seen these few days.

When she reached home she stripped off all her clothes, even her shift and pantaloons, and put them all in the wash, and told Gracie to do the same. She could not imagine any soap that would cleanse them of the odor of filth — her imagination would always furnish it as long as the memory lasted — but the sheer act of boiling and scrubbing would help.

"What are you going ter do, ma'am?" Gracie asked, wide-eyed and husky. Even she had never seen such wretchedness.

"We are going to discover who owns these abominable places," Charlotte replied grimly.

"An' one of 'em murdered Miss Clemency," Gracie added, passing over her clothes and wrapping herself in Charlotte's old gown. The waist of it was around her hips and the skirt trailed on the floor. She looked such a child Charlotte had a moment of guilt for involving her in this fearful pursuit.

"I believe so. Are you afraid?"

"Yes ma'am." Gracie's thin little face hardened. "But I in't stoppin' 'ere. I'm goin' ter 'elp yer, never doubt that, an' nob'dy in't goin' ter stop me. Nor I in't goin' ter let yer go there on yer own, neither."

Charlotte gave her a great hug, taking her utterly by surprise so she blushed fiercely with pleasure.

"I wouldn't dream of going without you," Charlotte said candidly.

While Charlotte and Gracie were following the path of Clemency Shaw, Jack Radley looked up one of his less reputable friends from his gambling days, before he had met Emily, and persuaded him that it would be both interesting and profitable to take a turn around some of the worst rented accommodation in London. Anton was very dubious about the interest it would afford, but since Jack promised him his silver cigar cutter — he had given up the habit anyway — he understood the profit readily enough, and agreed to do it.

Jack absolutely forbade Emily to go with them, and for the first time in their relationship he brooked no argument whatsoever.

"You may not come," he said with a charming smile and completely steady eyes.

"But — " she began, smiling back at him, searching for a lightness in him, a softness in his expression which would allow her to win him over. To her surprise she found none.

"But — " she began again, looking for an argument in her favor.

"You may not come, Emily." There was not a flicker in his eyes and no yielding in his mouth. "It will be dangerous, if we have any success, and you would be in the way. Remember the reason we are doing this, and don't argue the toss. It is a waste of time, because whatever you say, you are not coming."

She drew in a deep breath. "Very well," she conceded with as much grace as she could muster. "If that is what you wish."

"It is better than that, my love," he said with the first edge of a smile. "It is an order."

When he and Anton had departed, leaving her on the doorstep, she felt completely betrayed. Then as she gave the matter more reasoned consideration, she realized that he had done it to protect her from both the unpleasantness of the journey and the distress of what she would inevitably see; and she was pleased that he showed such concern. She had no desire to be taken for granted. And while she did not like being denied or countermanded, she also did not like being able to prevail over his wishes. Getting your own way too often can be singularly unsatisfying.

With an idle afternoon on her hands, and a mind teeming with questions, she ordered the other carriage. After dressing extremely carefully in a new gown from Salon Worth in Paris, a deep thunder blue which flattered her fair coloring, and embroidered lavishly in blouse front and around the hem, she set out to visit a certain lady whose wealth and family interests were greater than her scruples. This she knew from high society friends she had met in the past, at places where breeding and money were of far more account than personal affection or any form of regard.

Emily alighted and climbed the steps at the Park Lane address. When the door was opened, she presented her card and stood her ground while a slightly disconcerted parlormaid read it. It was one of Emily's old ones from before her remarriage, and still read "The Viscountess Ashworth," which was very much more impressive than "Mrs. Jack Radley."

Normally a lady would have left her card so the lady of the house might in turn leave hers and they would agree on a future time to meet, but Emily was clearly not going to depart. The parlormaid was obliged either to ask her to go or to invite her in. The title left her only one choice.

"Please come in, my lady, and I will see if Lady Priscilla will receive you."

Emily accepted graciously, and head high, walked through the large hallway decked with family portraits, even a suit of armor on a stand. She took her place in the morning room in front of the fire, until the maid returned and ushered her upstairs into the first-story boudoir, the sitting room specially reserved for ladies.

It was an exquisite room, decorated in the Oriental style, which had become popular lately, and full of chinoiserie of every sort: lacquer boxes, an embroidered silk screen, landscape paintings where mountains floated above mists and waterfalls and tiny figures like black dots traveled on interminable roads. There was a glass-shelved cupboard containing at least twenty jade and ivory figures, and two carved ivory fans like frozen white lace.

Lady Priscilla herself was perhaps fifty, thin and with black hair of an unnatural depth that only her fondest friends imagined to be her own. She was wearing magenta and rose, also embroidered, but perfectly symmetrical. She knew it was a mistake as soon as she saw Emily.

"Lady Ashworth!" she exclaimed with courteous surprise. "How charming of you to have called upon me — and how unexpected."

Emily knew perfectly well she meant "how uncouth and without the appropriate warning," but she had come with a highly practical purpose in mind, and had no intention of jeopardizing it with impulsive words.

"I wished to find you alone," Emily replied with a slight inclining of her head. "I would like some confidential advice, and it suddenly occurred to me that no one in London would be better able to give it than you."

"Good gracious. How you flatter me!" Lady Priscilla exclaimed, but her overriding expression was not vain so much as curious. "Whatever do I know that you do not know quite as well yourself?" She smiled. "A little scandal, perhaps — but surely you have not come alone at this time of day for that."

"I am not averse to it." Emily sat down on the chair indicated. "But that is not why I am here. It is counsel I want, in certain matters in which I now have the freedom to be my own mistress — " She let it hang in the air, and saw Priscilla's sharp face quicken with interest.

"Your own mistress? Of course I heard of Lord Ashworth's death — " She composed her features to the appropriate solicitude. "My dear, how awful. I am so sorry."

"It was some time ago now." Emily brushed it aside. "I have remarried, you know — "

"But your card."

"Oh — did I give you one of the old ones? How careless of me. I do apologize. I am getting so shortsighted these days."

It was on Priscilla's tongue to say "A small pair of spectacles, perhaps?" but she did not wish to be too offensive in case she did not learn the cause for Emily's consulting her, and then how could she relate it to others?

"It is of no consequence," she murmured.

Emily smiled dazzlingly. "How gracious of you."

"If I can help?" Priscilla offered intently.

"Oh I'm sure." Emily settled a little farther into her seat. This could have been quite entertaining, but she must not lose sight of her reason for coming. Clemency Shaw's death was enough to sober any amusement. "I have a certain amount of money at my disposal, and I should like to invest it profitably, and if possible where it is both safe and reasonably discreet."

"Oh — " Priscilla let out her breath slowly, a dawn of comprehension in her face. "You would like it to return you some profit, but be inaccessible to your family. And you are married again?"

"I am." Silently Emily thought of Jack, and apologized to him. "Hence the need for the utmost . . . discretion."

"Absolute secrecy," Priscilla assured her, her eyes alight. "I can advise you very well; you certainly came to the right person."

"I knew it," Emily said with triumph in

her voice, not for investment, but because she was on the brink of discovering exactly what she sought. "I knew you were the very best person. What should I do with it? I have quite a substantial amount, you understand?"

"Property," Priscilla replied without hesitation.

Emily schooled her face very carefully into disappointment.

"Property? But then anyone who wished could ascertain exactly what I owned, and what income it brought me — which is precisely what I wish to avoid!"

"Oh my dear — don't be naive!" Priscilla waved her hands, dismissing the very idea. "I don't mean domestic residences in Primrose Hill. I mean two or three blocks of old tenements in Mile End or Wapping, or St. Giles."

"Wapping?" Emily said with careful incredulity. "What on earth would that be worth to me?"

"A fortune," Priscilla replied. "Place it in the hands of a good business manager, who will see that it is let advantageously, and that the rent is collected every week or month, and it will double your outlay in no time."

Emily frowned. "Really? How on earth would rent for places like that amount to much? Only the poorest people live in such areas, don't they? They could hardly pay the kind of rents I should wish."

"Oh yes they can," Priscilla assured her. "If there are enough of them, it will be most profitable, I promise you."

"Enough?"

"Certainly. Ask no questions as to what people do, and what profit they in turn can make, then you can let every room in the building to a dozen people, and they will sublet it, and so on. There is always someone who will pay more, believe me."

"I am not sure I should care to be associated with such a place," Emily demurred. "It is not — something — "

"Ha!" Priscilla laughed aloud. "Who would? That is why you do it through a business manager, and a solicitor, and his employees, and a rent collector, and so on. No one will ever know it is you who owns it, except your own man of affairs, and he will certainly never tell anyone. That is his purpose."

"Are you sure?" Emily widened her eyes. "Does anyone else do such a thing?"

"Of course. Dozens of people."

"Who — for instance?"

"My dear, don't be so indiscreet. You will make yourself highly unpopular if you ask such questions. They are protected, just as you will be. I promise you, no one will know."

"It is only a matter of — " Emily shrugged

her shoulders high and opened her eyes innocently. "Really — people might not understand. There is nothing illegal, I presume?"

"Of course not. Apart from having no desire to break the law" — Priscilla smiled and pursed her lips — "these are all highly respectable people with positions to maintain — it also would be very foolish." She spread elegant hands wide, palms upwards, her rings momentarily hidden. "Anyway, it is quite unnecessary. There is no law to prevent your doing everything I suggest. And believe me, my dear, the profits are exceedingly good."

"Is there any risk?" Emily said lightly. "I mean — there are people agitating for reforms of one sort or another. Might one end up losing it all — or on the other hand being exposed to public dislike, if — "

"None at all," Priscilla said with a laugh. "I don't know what reformers you have heard of, but they have not even a ghost of a chance of bringing about any real changes — not in the areas I propose. New houses will be built here and there, in manufacturing towns, but it will not affect the properties we are concerned with. There will always be slums, my dear, and there will always be people with nowhere else to live."

Emily felt such a passion of revulsion she found it almost impossible to hide it. She looked down to conceal her face, and searched in her reticule for a handkerchief, then blew her nose a good deal less delicately than was ladylike. Then she felt sufficiently composed to meet Priscilla's eyes again and try to make the loathing in her own look like anxiety.

"I thought it was such slums that reformers were involved in?"

Now the contempt in Priscilla's face was easily readable.

"You are being timid for no reason, Emily." The use of her name added an infinite condescension to Priscilla's words. "There are very powerful people involved. It would not only be quite pointless trying to ruin them, it would be extremely dangerous. No one will cause more than a little inconvenience, I promise, and that will be dealt with without your needing even to know about it, much less involve yourself."

Emily leaned back and forced a smile to her face, although it felt more like the baring of teeth. She met Priscilla's gaze without a flicker though inside she was burning with a hatred that made her want to react with physical violence.

"You have told me precisely what I wished to know. And I am sure you are totally reliable and unquestionably are fully aware what you are dealing with. No doubt we will meet again on the matter, or at least you will hear from me. Thank you so much for sparing me your time."

Priscilla smiled more widely as Emily rose to her feet. "I am always happy to be of assistance to a friend. When you have realized your assets and decided what you would like to invest, come back and I shall put you in touch with the best person to help you, and to be utterly discreet."

Money was not mentioned, but Emily knew perfectly well it was understood, and she was equally sure Priscilla herself took a proportion for her services.

"Of course." Emily inclined her head very slightly. "You have been most gracious; I shall not forget it." And she took her leave and went out of the house into the cold air of the street where even the manure on the cobbles could not spoil its comparative sweetness to her.

"Take me home," she told the coachman as he handed her up. "Immediately."

When Jack returned tired and dirty, his face ashen, she was waiting for him. He was just as somber, with an underlying anger equal to hers.

He stopped in the hallway where she had come from the withdrawing room to meet him. She still found his step on the black-and-white flagstones quickened her heart and the sound of his voice as the footman took his coat made her smile. She looked at him and searched his dark gray eyes, with the curling lashes she had marveled at — and envied — when they first met. She had considered him far too conscious of his own charm. Now that she knew him better, she still found him just as engaging, but knew the man behind the manners and liked him immensely. He was an excellent friend, and she knew the supreme value of that.

"Was it very bad?" She did not waste words in foolish questions like "How are you?" She could see in his face how he was, that he had been exhausted and hurt and was as violently angry as she, and as impotent to change or destroy the offenders or to help the victims.

"Beyond anything I can convey in words," he replied. "I'll be lucky if I can get the smell out of my clothes or the taste out of my throat. And I don't think I'll ever completely lose the picture of their misery. I can see their faces every time I close my eyes as if they were painted on the inside of my eyelids." He looked around the huge hallway with its flagged floor, oak-paneled walls, the sweeping staircase up to a gallery, the paintings, the vases laden with flowers two and three feet tall, the huge carved furniture with gleaming wood and the umbrella stand with five silver- and horn-handled sticks.

Emily knew what he was thinking; the same thoughts had passed through her head more than once. But it was George's house, Ashworth heritage, and belonged to her son Edward, not to her except as a trust until he was of age. Jack knew that too, but they both still felt a taste of guilt that they enjoyed its luxury as easily as if it had been theirs, which in all practical ways it was.

"Come into the withdrawing room and sit down," she said gently. "Albert can draw you a bath. Tell me what you learned."

Taking her arm he went with her and in a quiet, very grave voice he described where Anton had taken him. He chose few words, not wanting to harass her nor to relive the horror and the helpless pity he had felt himself, not the nauseating disgust. He told her of rat-and-lice-infected tenements where the walls dripped and hung with mold, of open sewers and drains and piles of refuse. Many rooms were occupied by fifteen or twenty people, all ages and both sexes, without privacy or sanitation of any kind, without water or drainage. In some the roofs or windows were in such disrepair the rain came in; and yet the rent was collected every week without fail.

Some desperate people sublet even the few square yards they had, in order to maintain their own payments.

He forbore from describing the conditions in the sweatshops where women and girls worked beneath street level, by gaslight or candlelight and without ventilation, eighteen hours a day stitching shirts or gloves or dresses for people who inhabited another world.

He did not go into any detail about the brothels, the gin mills and the narrow, fetid rooms where men found oblivion in opium; he simply stated their existence. By the time he had said all he needed to, to share the burden and feel her understanding, her anguish at the same things, her equal sense of outrage and helplessness, Albert had been twice to say his bath was getting cold, and had finally come a third time to say that a fresh bath had been drawn.

They were in bed, close together and almost ready for sleep, when she finally told him what she had done, where she had been, and what she had learned.

Vespasia took the questions to Somerset Carlisle, when the parliamentary business of the day was done. It was after eleven in the evening chill with a rising fog when she finally reached her home. She was tired, but too filled with concern to sleep. Part of her thoughts were turned towards the matters she had raised with him, but a good deal of her anxiety was for Charlotte. It was not untouched with guilt, lest by suggestion, the offer of Percival and the carriage, and the ready ease with which she had taken the children to Caroline Ellison, that she had enabled Charlotte to embark on a course which might become personally dangerous. At the time she had simply thought of Clemency Shaw and the appalling injustice of her death. For once she had allowed anger to outweigh judgment, and had sent the woman she was most fond of into considerable risk. It was true; she cared for Charlotte as much as anyone, now her own daughter was dead. And more than that; she liked her — enjoyed her company, her humor, her courage. It was not only rash, it was completely irresponsible. She had not even consulted Thomas, and he of all people had a right to know.

But it was not her nature to spend time over what could not be undone. She must bear it — and take the blame should there be any. There was no purpose to be served in speaking or writing to Thomas now; Charlotte would tell him, or not, as she wished; and he would prevent her from continuing, or not, as he was able. Vespasia's meddling now would only compound the error.

But she found it hard to sleep.

The following evening they met at Vespasia's house for dinner, and to compare notes upon what they had learned, but primarily to hear from Somerset Carlisle the state of the law they must fight, deal with, and change if possible.

Emily and Jack arrived early. Emily was less glamorously dressed than Vespasia could remember her being since she had ceased mourning for George. Jack looked tired; there were lines of strain on his normally handsome face and the humor was absent from his eyes. He was courteous, from habit, but even the usual compliments were not on his lips.

Charlotte was late, and Vespasia was beginning to feel anxious, her mind wandering from the trivial conversation they maintained until the business of the evening could be shared.

Somerset Carlisle came in, grim-faced. He glanced at Vespasia, then Emily and Jack, and forbore from asking where Charlotte was.

But Charlotte finally arrived, brought by Percival and the returned carriage. She was breathless, tired, and her hair markedly less well done than customarily. Vespasia was so overwhelmingly relieved to see her all she could do was criticize her for being late. She dared not to show her emotions; it would have been most unseemly.

They repaired to the dining room and dinner was served.

Each reported what he or she had seen and done, cursorily and with no unnecessary description; the facts were fearful enough. They did not speak as if they had been tired, sickened or endangered themselves. What they had seen dwarfed self-pity or praise.

When the last was finished they turned as one to Somerset Carlisle.

Pale-faced, weary of heart, he explained the law to them as he had ascertained it. He confirmed what they already knew: that is was almost impossible to discover who owned property if the owner wished to remain anonymous, and that the law required nothing to assist the tenant or shield him. There were no basic requirements of fitness for habitation concerning water, sewage, shelter or any other facility. There were no means of redress regarding payment of rents or freedom from eviction.

"Then we must change the law," Vespasia said when he had finished. "We will continue where Clemency Shaw was cut off by her murderers."

"It may be dangerous," Somerset Carlisle

warned. "We will be disturbing powerful people. The little I have learned so far indicates there are members of great families who come by at least part of their income that way, some industrialists with vast fortunes reinvested. It has not failed to touch others of ambition and greed, men who can be tempted and who have favors to sell — members of the House, judges of court. It will be a very hard struggle — and with no easy victories."

"That is a pity," Vespasia said without even consulting the others by so much as a glance. "But it is irrelevant."

"We need more people in power." Carlisle glanced at Jack. "More men in Parliament prepared to risk a comfortable seat by fighting against the vested interests."

Jack did not reply, but he spoke little the rest of the evening, and all the way home he was deep in thought.

CHAPTER
EIGHT

Pitt and Murdo were working from early in the morning until long after dark pursuing every scrap of material evidence until there was nothing else to learn. The Highgate police themselves were still searching for the arsonist they were convinced was guilty, but as yet they had not found him, although they felt that every day's inquiry brought them closer. There had been other fires started in similar manner: an empty house in Kentish Town, a stable in Hampstead, a small villa to the north in Crouch End. They questioned every source of fuel oil within a three-mile radius of Highgate, but discovered no purchases other than those which were accounted for by normal household needs. They asked every medical practitioner if they had treated burns not explained to their certain knowledge. They counseled with neighboring police and fire forces on the name, present whereabouts, past history and methods of every other person known to have committed arson in the last ten years, and

357

learned nothing of use.

Pitt and Murdo also delved into the value, insurance and ownership of all the houses that had been burned, and found nothing in common. Then they asked into the dispositions in wills and testaments of Clemency Shaw and Amos Lindsay. Clemency bequeathed everything of which she died possessed to her husband, Stephen Robert Shaw, with the solitary exception of a few personal items to friends; and Amos Lindsay left his works of art, his books and the mementos of his travels also to Stephen Shaw, and the house itself most surprisingly to Matthew Oliphant, a startling and unexplained gift of which Pitt entirely approved. It was just one more evidence of a kind and most unconventional man.

He knew that Charlotte was busy, but since she was traveling in Great-Aunt Vespasia's carriage, and with her footman in attendance, he was satisfied there was no danger involved. He thought there was also little profit, since she had told him she was pursuing Clemency Shaw's last known journeys, and he was quite sure, since Lindsay's death, that Clemency had been killed by chance and the true intended victim was Stephen Shaw.

So the morning after the dinner at Vespasia's house in which they had learned the extent and nature of the law, Charlotte dressed herself in tidy but unremarkable clothes. This was not in the least difficult, since that description encompassed the greater part of her wardrobe. She then waited for Emily and Jack to arrive.

They came surprisingly early. She had not honestly thought Emily rose at an hour to make this possible, but Emily was at the door before nine, looking her usual fashionable self, with Jack only a pace behind her, dressed in plain, undistinguished browns.

"It won't do," Charlotte said immediately.

"I am quite aware that it won't." Emily came in, gave her a quick peck on the cheek and made her way to the kitchen. "I am only half awake. For pity's sake have Gracie put on the kettle. I shall have to borrow something of yours. Everything of mine looks as if it cost at least as much as it did — which of course was the intention. Have you got a brown dress? I look terrible in brown."

"No I haven't," Charlotte said a little stiffly. "But I have two dark plum-colored ones, and you would look just as terrible in either of them."

Emily broke into laughter, her face lighting up and some of the tiredness vanishing.

"Thank you, my dear. How charming of you. Do they both fit you, or might one of them be small enough for me?"

"No." Charlotte joined in the mood, her

eyes wide, preventing herself from smiling back with difficulty. "They will be excellent 'round the waist, but too big in the bosom!"

"Liar!" Emily shot back. "They will bag around the waist, and I shall trip over the skirts. Either will do excellently. I shall go and change while you make the tea. Are we taking Gracie as well? It will hardly be a pleasant adventure for her."

"Please ma'am?" Gracie said urgently. She had tasted the excitement of the chase, of being included, and was bold enough to plead her own cause. "I can 'elp. I unnerstand them people."

"Of course," Charlotte said quickly. "If you wish. But you must stay close to us at all times. If you don't there is no accounting for what may happen to you."

"Oh I will, ma'am," she promised, her sober little face as grave as if she were swearing an oath. "An' I'll watch an' listen. Sometimes I knows w'en people is tellin' lies."

Half an hour later the four of them set out in Emily's second carriage on the journey to Mile End to trace the ownership of the tenement house to which Charlotte had followed the trail of Clemency Shaw. Their first intent was to discover the rent collector and learn from him for whom he did this miserable duty. She had made note of the exact location.

Even so it took them some time to find it again; the streets were narrow and took careful negotiation through the moil of costers' barrows, old clothes carts, peddlers, vegetable wagons and clusters of people buying, selling and begging. So many of the byways looked alike; pavements wide enough to allow the passage of only one person; the cobbled centers, often with open gutters meandering through them filled with the night's waste; the jettied houses leaning far out over the street, some so close at the top as to block out most of the daylight. One could imagine people in the upper stories being able to all but shake hands across the divide, if they leaned out far enough, and were minded to do so.

The wood was pitted where sections were rotten and had fallen away, the plaster was dark with stains of old leakage and rising dampness from the stones, and here and there ancient pargetting made half-broken patterns or insignia.

People stood in doorways, dark forms huddled together, faces catching the light now and then as one or another moved.

Emily reached out and took Jack's hand. The teeming, fathomless despair of it frightened her. She had never felt quite this kind of inadequacy. There were so many. There was a child running along beside them, begging. He was no older than her own son sitting at home in his schoolroom struggling with learning his multiplication tables and looking forward to luncheon, apart from the obligatory rice pudding which he loathed, and the afternoon, when he could play.

Jack fished in his pockets for a coin and threw it for the boy. The child dived on it as it rolled almost under the carriage wheels and for a sickening moment Emily thought he would be crushed. But he emerged an instant later, jubilant, clutching the coin in a filthy hand and biting his teeth on it to check its metal.

Within moments a dozen more urchins were close around them, calling out, stretching their hands, fighting each other to reach them first. Older men appeared. There were catcalls, jeers, threats; and all the time the crowd closing in till the horses could barely make their way forward and the coachman was afraid to urge them in case he crushed the weight of yelling, writhing, shoving humanity.

"Oh my God!" Jack looked ashen, realizing suddenly what he had done. Frantically he turned out his pockets for more.

Emily was thoroughly frightened. She hunched down on the seat, closer to his side. There seemed to be clamoring, reaching people all around them, hands grasping, faces contorted with hunger and hatred.

Gracie was wrapped with her shawl around her, wide-eyed, frozen.

Charlotte did not know what Jack intended that would help, but she emptied out her own few coins to add to his.

He took them without hesitation and forcing the window open flung them as far behind the coach as he could.

Instantly the crowd parted and dived where the coins had fallen. The coachman urged the horses forward and they were free, clattering down the road, wheels hissing on the damp surface.

Jack fell back on the seat, still pale, but the beginning of a smile on his lips.

Emily straightened up and turned to look at him, her eyes very bright and her color returned. Now as well as pity and fear, there was a new, sharp admiration.

Charlotte too felt a very pleasant respect which had not been there before.

When they reached the tenement it was decided Charlotte and Gracie should go in, since they were familiar to the occupants. To send more might appear like a show of force and produce quite the opposite effect from the one they wished.

"Mr. Thickett?" A small group of drab

women looked from one to another. "Dunno w'ere 'e comes from. 'E jus' comes every week and takes the money."

"Is it his house?" Charlotte asked.

" 'Ow the 'ell der we know?" a toothless woman said angrily. "An' why der you care, eh? Wot's it ter you? 'Oo are yer any'ow, comin' 'ere arskin' questions?"

"We pays our rent an' we don' make no trouble," another added, folding fat arms over an even fatter bosom. It was a vaguely threatening stance, although she held no weapon nor had any within reach. It was the way she rocked very slightly on her feet and stared fiercely at Charlotte's face. She was a woman with little left to lose, and she knew it.

"We wanna rent," Gracie said quickly. "We've bin put aht o' our own place, an' we gotta find summink else quick. We can't wait till rent day; we gotta find it now."

"Oh — why dincher say so?" The woman looked at Charlotte with a mixture of pity and exasperation. "Proud, are yer? Stupid, more like. Fallen on 'ard times, 'ave yer, livin' too 'igh on the 'og — an' now yer gotta come down in the world? 'Appens to lots of folk. Well, Thickett don't come today, but fer a consideration I'll tell yer w'ere ter find 'im — "

"We're on 'ard times," Gracie said plaintively.

"Yeah? Well your 'ard times in't the same as my 'ard times." The woman's pale mouth twisted into a sneer. "I in't arskin' money. O' course you in't got no money, or yer wouldn't be 'ere — but I'll 'ave yer 'at." She looked at Charlotte, then at her hands and saw their size, and looked instead at Gracie's brown woollen shawl. "An' 'er shawl. Then I'll tell yer w'ere ter go."

"You can have the hat now." Charlotte took it off as she spoke. "And the shawl if we find Thickett where you say. If we don't — " She hesitated, a threat on her lips, then looked at the hard disillusioned face and knew its futility. "Then you'll do without," she ended.

"Yeah?" The woman's voice was steeped in years of experience. "An' w'en yer've got Thickett yer goin' ter come back 'ere ter give me yer shawl. Wotcher take me for, eh? Shawl now, or no Thickett."

"Garn," Gracie said with withering scorn. "Take the 'at and be 'appy. No Thickett, no 'at. She may look like gentry, but she's mean w'en she's crossed — an' she's crossed right now! Wotsa matter wiv yer — yer stupid or suffink? Take the 'at and give us Thickett." Her little face was tight with disgust and concentration. She was on an adventure and prepared to risk everything to win.

The woman saw her different mettle, heard

the familiar vowels in her voice and knew she was dealing with one more her own kind. She dropped the bluff, shrugging her heavy shoulders. It had been a reasonable attempt, and you could not blame one for trying.

"Yer'll find Thickett in Sceptre Street, big 'ouse on the corner o' Usk. Go ter ve back an' ask fer Tom Thickett, an' say it's ter give 'im rent. They'll let yer in, an' if yer says aught abaht money e'll listen ter yer." She snatched the hat out of Charlotte's hands and ran her fingers over it appreciatively, her lips pursed in concentration. "If yer on 'ard times, 'ock a few o' these and yer'll 'ave enough ter eat for days. 'Ard times. Yer don' know 'ard times from nuffin'."

No one argued with her. They knew their poverty was affected for the occasion and a lie excusable only by its brevity, and their own flicker of knowledge as to what its reality would be.

Back in the carriage, huddled against the chill, they rode still slowly to Sceptre Street as the woman had told them. The thoroughfare was wider, the houses on each side broader fronted and not jettied across the roadway, but the gutters still rolled with waste and smelled raw and sour, and Charlotte wondered if she would ever be able to get the stains out of the bottom of her skirts. Emily would probably throw hers away. She would have to make some recompense to Gracie for this. She looked across at her thin body, as upright as Aunt Vespasia, in her own way, but a full head shorter. Her face, with its still childish softness of skin, was more alive with excitement than she had ever seen it before.

They stepped down at the designated corner and crossed the footpath, wider here, and knocked on the door. When a tousle-headed maid answered they asked for Mr. Thickett, stating very clearly that it was a matter of money, and some urgency to it, Gracie putting in a dramatic sniff. They were permitted to enter and led to a chilly room apparently used for storing furniture and for such occasional meetings as this. Several chests and old chairs were piled recklessly on top of each other, and there was a table missing a leg and a bundle of curtains which seemed to have rotted in places with damp. The whole smelled musty and Emily pulled a face as soon as they were inside.

There was no place to sit down, and she remembered with a jolt that they were supplicants now, seeking a favor of this man and in no position to be anything but crawlingly civil. Only the remembrance of Clemency Shaw's death, the charred corpse in her imagination, enabled her to do it.

"He won't tell us the owner," she whispered quickly. "He thinks he has the whip hand of us if we are here to beg half a room from him."

"You're right, m'lady," Gracie whispered back, unable to forget the title even here. "If 'e's a rent collector 'e'll be a bully — they always is — an' like as not big wif it. 'E won't do nuffin' fer nobody less'n 'e 'as ter."

For a moment they were all caught in confusion. The first story would no longer serve. Then Jack smiled just as they heard heavy footsteps along the passageway and the door opened to show a big man, barrel-chested, with a hatchet face, jutting nose and small, round, clever eyes. He hooked his thumbs in his waistcoat, which was once beige but was now mottled and faded with years of misuse.

"Well?" He surveyed them with mild curiosity. He had only one yardstick by which he measured people. Could they pay the rent, either by means already in their possession or by some they could earn, steal or sublet to obtain. He looked at the women also, not as possessors of money or labor force worth considering, but to see if they were handsome or young enough to earn their livings on the street. He judged them all handsome enough, but only Gracie to have the necessary realism. The other two, and it showed plainly in his face, would have to come down a good deal further in the world before they were accommodating enough to please a paying customer. However, a friendliness made up for a lot of flaws, in fact almost anything except age.

On the other hand, Jack looked like a dandy, in spite of his rather well-worn clothes. They might be old, but that did not disguise the flair with which he tied his cravat, or the good cut of the shoulders and the lie of the lapels. No, here was a man who knew and liked the good things. If he was on hard times he would make no worker: his hands, smooth, well-manicured and gloveless, attested to that. But then he did look shrewd, and there was an air about him of easiness, a charm. He might make an excellent trickster, well able to live on his arts. And he would not be the first gentleman to do that — by a long way.

"So yer want a room?" he said mildly. "I daresay as I can find yer one. Mebbe if yer can pay fer it, one all ter yerselves, like. 'Ow abaht five shillin's a week?"

Jack's lip curled with distaste and he reached out and put his hand on Emily's arm. "Actually you mistake our purpose," he said very frankly, looking at Thickett with hard eyes. "I represent Smurfitt, Taylor and Mordue, Solicitors. My name is John Consterdine." He saw Thickett's face tighten in a mixture of anger and caution. "There is a suit due to be heard regarding property upon which there have been acts of negligence which bear responsibility for considerable loss. Since you collect the rents for this property, we assume you own it, and therefore are liable — "

"No I don't!" Thickett's eyes narrowed and he tightened his body defensively. "I collect rents, that's all. Just collect. That's an honest job and yer got no business wi' me. I can't 'elp yer."

"I am not in need of help, Mr. Thickett," Jack said with considerable aplomb. "It is you, if you own the property, who will shortly be in prison for undischarged debt — "

"Oh no I won't. I don't own nuffin but this 'ouse, which in't 'ad nuffin wrong wif it fer years. Anyway" — he screwed up his face in new appraisal, his native common sense returning, now the first alarm had worn off — "if yer a lawyer, 'oo are they? Lawyers' clerks, eh?" He jabbed a powerful finger towards Emily, Charlotte and Gracie.

Jack answered with transparent honesty.

"This is my wife, this is my sister-in-law, and this is her maid. I brought them because I knew you would be little likely to see me alone, having a good idea who I was and why I came. And circumstances proved me right.

You took us for a family on hard fortune and needing to rent your rooms. The law requires that I serve papers on you — " He made as if to reach into his inside pocket.

"No it don't," Thickett said rapidly. "I don't own no buildings; like I said, I just collect the rents — "

"And put them in your pocket," Jack finished for him. "Good. You'll likely have a nice fund somewhere to pay the costs — "

"All I 'ave is me wage wot I'm paid for it. I give all the rest, ceptin' my bit, over."

"Oh yes?" Jack's eyebrows went up disbelievingly. "To whom?"

"Ter ve manager, o' course. Ter 'im wot manages the business fer 'o'ever owns all them buildings along Lisbon Street."

"Indeed? And who is he?" The disbelief was still there.

"I dunno. W'ere the 'ell are you from? D'yer think people 'oo 'as places like vat puts their names on the door? Yer daft, or suffink?"

"The manager," Jack backtracked adeptly. "Of course the owner wouldn't tell the likes of you, if you don't report to him — who is the manager? I'm going to serve these papers on someone."

"Mr. Buffery, Fred Buffery. Yer'll find 'im at Nicholas Street, over be'ind the brewery, vat's w'ere 'e does business. Yer go an' serve

371

yer papers on 'im. It in't nuffink ter do wi' me. I just take the rents. It's a job — like yours."

Jack did not bother to dispute it with him. They had what they wanted and he had no desire to remain. Without expressing any civilities he opened the door and they all left, finding the carriage a few houses away, and proceeding to the next address.

Here they were informed that Mr. Buffery was taking luncheon at the neighboring public house, the Goat and Compasses, and they decided it would be an excellent time to do the same. Emily particularly was fascinated. She had never been inside such an establishment before, and Charlotte had only in more salubrious neighborhoods, and that on infrequent occasions.

Inside was noisy with laughter, voices in excited and often bawdy conversation, and the clink of glasses and crockery. It smelled of ale, sweat, sawdust, vinegar and boiled vegetables.

Jack hesitated. This was not a suitable place for ladies, the thought was as plain on his face as if he had spoken it.

"Nonsense," Emily said fiercely just behind him. "We are all extremely hungry. Are you going to refuse to get us luncheon?"

"Yes I am — in this place," he said firmly.

"We'll find something better, even if it's a pie stall. We can get Mr. Buffery when he returns to his office."

"I'm staying here," Emily retorted. "I want to see — it's all part of what we are doing."

"No it isn't." He took her arm. "We need Buffery to tell us who he manages the building for; we don't need this place. I'm not going to argue about it, Emily. You are coming out."

"But Jack — "

Before the altercation could proceed any further Gracie slid forward and grasped the bartender waiting on the next table, pulling his sleeve till he turned to see what was upsetting his balance.

"Please mister," she appealed to him with wide eyes. "Is Mr. Buffery in 'ere? I can't 'ear 'is voice, an' I don't see too well. 'E's me uncle an' I got a message fer 'im."

"Give it ter me, girl, an' I'll give it 'im," the bartender said not unkindly.

"Oh I carsn't do that, mister, it'd be more 'n me life's worf. Me pa'd tan me summink wicked."

" 'Ere, I'll take yer. 'E's over 'ere in the corner. Don't you bovver 'im now, mind. I'll not 'ave me customers bovvered. You give yer message, then scarper, right?"

"Yes mister. Thank yer, mister." And she allowed him to lead her over to the far corner, where a man with a red face and golden red hair was seated behind a small table and a plate generously spread with succulent pie and crisp pickles and a large slice of ripe cheese. Two tankards of ale stood a hand's reach away.

"Uncle Fred?" she began, for the bartender's benefit, hoping fervently at least Charlotte, if not all of them, were immediately behind her.

Buffery looked at her with irritation.

"I in't yer uncle. Go and bother someone else. I in't interested in your sort. If I want a woman I'll find me own, a lot sassier than you — and I don't give ter beggars."

" 'Ere!" the bartender said angrily. "You said as 'e were yer uncle."

"So 'e is," Gracie said desperately. "Me pa said as ter tell 'im me gramma's took bad, an' we need money fer 'elp for 'er. She's that cold."

"That right?" the bartender demanded, turning to Buffery. "You runnin' out on yer own ma?"

By this time Charlotte, Emily and Jack were all behind Gracie. She felt the warmth of relief flood through her. She sniffed fiercely, half afraid, half determined to play this for all it was worth.

"Yer got all them 'ouses, Uncle Fred, all Lisbon Street mostly. You can find Gramma a nice place w'ere she can be warm. She's real bad. Ma'll look after 'er, if'n yer just find a better place. We got water on all the walls an' it's cold summink awful."

"I in't yer Uncle Fred," Buffery said furiously. "I in't never seen yer before. Git out of 'ere. 'Ere — take this!" He thrust a sixpence at her. "Now get out of 'ere."

Gracie ignored the sixpence, with difficulty, and burst into tears — with ease.

"That won't buy more'n one night. Then wot'll we do? Yer got all the 'ouses on Lisbon Street. Why can't yer get Ma and Pa a room in one of 'em, so we can keep dry? I'll work, honest I will. We'll pay yer."

"They in't my 'ouses, yer little fool!" Buffery was embarrassed now as other diners turned to look at the spectacle. "D'yer think I'd be 'ere eatin' cold pie and drinkin' ale if I got the rents fer that lot? I jus' manages the bus'ness of 'em. Now get aht an' leave me alone, yer little bleeder. I in't never seen yer an' I got no ma wot's sick."

Gracie was saved further dramatic effort by Jack stepping forward and pretending to be a lawyer's clerk again, entirely unconnected with Gracie, and offering his services to dispatch her on her way. Buffery accepted eagerly, very aware now of his associates and neighbors staring at him. His discomfort offered a better sideshow than many of the running patterers who sang ballads of the latest news or scandal. This was immediate and the afflicted one was known to them.

When Buffery had identified himself, Jack told Gracie to leave, which she did rapidly and with deep gratitude, after picking up the sixpence. Jack then proceeded to threaten him with lawsuits as accessory to fraud, and Buffery was ready to swear blind that he did not own the buildings in Lisbon Street, and prove it if necessary before the lawyer who took the rent money from him every month, less his own miserable pittance for the service he performed.

After a brief luncheon, early afternoon found them in the offices on Bethnal Green Road of Fulsom and Son, Penrose and Fulsom, a small room up narrow stairs where Jack insisted on going alone. He returned after a chilly half hour. Emily and Charlotte and Gracie were wrapped in carriage rugs, Gracie still glowing from her triumph in the public house, and the subsequent praise she had received.

They spent until dark trying to track down the property management company whose name Jack had elicited, by a mixture of lies and trickery from the seedy little Mr. Penrose, but eventually were obliged to return home unsuccessful.

Charlotte intended to recount the day's events to Pitt, but when he arrived home late, lines of weariness deep in his face, and in his eyes a mixture of eagerness and total bafflement, she set aside her own news and asked after his.

He sat down at the kitchen table and picked up the mug of tea she had automatically put before him, but instead of drinking it he simply warmed his hands holding it, and began to talk.

"We went to Shaw's solicitors today and read Clemency's will. The estate was left to Shaw, as we had been told, all except a few personal items to friends. The most remarkable was her Bible, which she left to Matthew Oliphant, the curate."

Charlotte could see nothing very odd in this. One might well leave a Bible to one's minister, especially if he were as sincere and thoughtful as Oliphant. She could almost certainly have had no idea of his feelings for her; they had been so desperately private. She recalled his bony, vulnerable face as clearly as if she had seen it a few moments ago.

Why was Pitt so concerned? It seemed ordinary enough. She looked at him, waiting.

"Of course the Bible was destroyed in the

fire." He leaned forward a little, elbows on the table, his face puckered in concentration. "But the solicitor had seen it — it was an extraordinary thing, leather bound, tooled in gold and with a hasp and lock on it which he thought must be brass, but he wasn't sure." His eyes were bright with the recollection. "And inside every initial letter of a chapter was illuminated in color and gold leaf with the most exquisite tiny paintings." He smiled slowly. "As if one glimpsed a vision of heaven or hell through lighted keyholes. She showed it to him just once, so he would know what item he was dealing with and there could be no mistake. It had been her grandfather's." His face shadowed for a moment with distaste. "Not Worlingham, on the other side." Then the awareness of the present returned and with it the waste and the destruction. His face was suddenly blank and the light died out of it. "It must have been marvelous, and worth a great deal. But of course it's gone with everything else."

He looked at her, puzzled and anxious. "But why on earth should she leave it to Oliphant? He's not even the vicar, he's only a curate. He almost certainly won't stay there in Highgate. If he gets a living it will be elsewhere — possibly even in a different county."

Charlotte knew the answer immediately and

without any effort of reasoning. It was as obvious to her as to any woman who had loved and not dared to show it, as she had once, ages ago, before Pitt. She had been infatuated with Dominic Corde, her eldest sister's husband, when Sarah was alive and they all lived in Cater Street. Of course that had died as delusion became reality and impossible, agonizing love resolved into a fairly simple friendship. But she thought that for Clemency Shaw it had remained achingly real. Matthew Oliphant's character was not a sham she had painted on by dream, as Charlotte had with Dominic. He was not handsome, dashing, there at every turn in her life; he was at least fifteen years her junior, a struggling curate with barely the means of subsistence, and to the kindest eye he was a little plain and far from graceful.

And yet a spirit burned inside him. In the face of other people's agony Clitheridge was totally inadequate, graceless, inarticulate and left on the outside untouched. Oliphant's compassion robbed him of awkwardness because he felt the pain as if it were his own and pity taught his tongue.

The answer was clear. Clemency had loved him just as much as he had loved her, and been equally unable to show it even in the slightest way, except when she was dead to leave him something of infinite value to her, and yet which would not seem so very remarkable that it would hurt his reputation. A Bible, not a painting or an ornament or some other article which would betray an unseemly emotion, just a Bible — to the curate. Only those who had seen it would know — and perhaps that would be the solicitor — and Stephen Shaw.

Pitt was staring at her across the table. "Charlotte?"

She looked up at him, smiling a very little, suddenly a tightness in her throat.

"He loved her too, you know," she said, swallowing hard. "I realized that when he was helping me to follow Bessie Jones and those awful houses. He knew the way she went."

Pitt put the cup down and reached to take her hands, gently, holding them and touching her fingers one by one. There was no need to say anything else, and he did not wish to.

In fact it was the following morning, just before he left, that he told her the other thing that had so troubled him. He was tying up his boots at the front door and she was holding his coat.

"The lawyers have sorted the estate already. It's quite simple. There is no money — only a couple of hundred pounds left."

"What?" She felt she must have misunderstood him.

He straightened up and she helped him on with the coat.

"There is no money left," he repeated. "All the Worlingham money she inherited is gone, except about two hundred and fourteen pounds and fifteen shillings."

"But I thought there was a lot — I mean, wasn't Theophilus rich?"

"Extremely. And all of it went to his two daughters, Prudence Hatch and Clemency Shaw. But Clemency has none left."

There was one ugly thought which she had to speak because it would haunt her mind anyway. "Did Shaw spend it?"

"No — the solicitor says definitely not. Clemency herself paid huge drafts to all kinds of people — individuals and societies."

"Whatever for?" said Charlotte, although the beginning of an idea was plain in her mind, as she could see that it was in his also. "Housing reform?"

"Yes — most of it that the solicitor knew about, but there is a great deal he cannot trace — to individuals he has never heard of."

"Are you going to find them?"

"Of course. Although I don't think it has anything to do with the fire. I still believe that was intended for Shaw, although I haven't

381

even the beginning of proof as to why."

"And Amos Lindsay?"

He shrugged. "Because he knew, or guessed, who was responsible; perhaps from something Shaw said, without realizing its significance himself. Or even uglier and perhaps more likely, whoever it is is still after Shaw, and that fire was a failed attempt to kill him also." He pulled his muffler off the hook and put it around his neck, the ends hanging loosely. "And of course it is still not impossible Shaw set them himself: the first to kill Clemency, the second to kill Lindsay because in some way he had betrayed himself to him — or feared he had."

"That's vile!" she said fiercely. "After Lindsay had been his closest friend. And why? Why should Shaw murder Clemency? You just said there was no money to inherit."

He hated saying it, and the revulsion showed in his face as he formed the words. "Precisely because there is no money. If it was all gone, and he needed more, then Flora Lutterworth was young, very pretty and the sole heiress to the biggest fortune in Highgate. And she is certainly very fond of him — to the point where it is the cause of local gossip."

"Oh," she said very quietly, unable to find anything to refute what he said, although she refused to believe it unless there was

382

inescapable proof.

He kissed her very gently, and she knew he understood what she felt, and shared it. Then he left, and she turned immediately and went upstairs to dress for the day's journey with Emily, Jack and Gracie.

It took all morning to trace the management company, and a mixture of evasions and trickery to elicit from them the name of the solicitors, this time a highly reputable firm in the City which took care of the affairs of the company which actually owned the properties in Lisbon Street, and also several others.

At two o'clock they were all seated in the warm and extremely comfortable offices of Messrs Warburg, Warburg, Boddy and Boddy, awaiting Mr. Boddy Senior's return from an extended luncheon with a client. Grave young clerks perched on stools writing in perfect copperplate script on documents of vellum, which had scarlet seals dangling from them. Errand boys scurried on silent feet, discreet and obedient, and a wrinkled man in a stiff, winged collar kept a careful eye on them, never moving from his wooden chair behind the desk. Gracie, who had never been in an office of any sort before, was fascinated and her eyes followed every movement.

Eventually Mr. Boddy returned, he was

silver-haired, smooth-faced, impeccably bland in voice and manner. He disregarded the women and addressed himself solely to Jack. It seemed he had not moved with the times and recognized that women now had a legal entity. To him they were still appendages to a man's property: his pleasure possibly, his responsibility certainly, but not to be informed or consulted.

Charlotte bristled and Emily took a step forward, but Jack's hand stayed her and as a matter of tactics she obeyed. In the last two days she had learned a quite new respect for his ability to read character and to obtain information.

But Mr. Boddy was of an entirely different mettle than those they had dealt with to date. He was smooth, quite certain of his own safety from suit of any kind, and his calm, unctuous face did not flicker when he explained with barely civil condescension that yes, he handled affairs of property and rent for certain clients but he was not at liberty to name them nor give any particulars whatsoever. Yes, most certainly Mrs. Shaw had called upon him with similar questions, and he had been equally unable to answer her. He was profoundly grieved that she should have met so tragic a fate — his eyes remained chill and expressionless — please accept his sincerest condolences, but the facts remained.

This was a murder inquiry, Jack explained. He was acting on behalf of persons, whom he also was unable to name, and would Mr. Boddy prefer it if the police came and asked these questions?

Mr. Boddy did not take kindly to threats. Was Jack aware that the persons who owned these properties were among the most powerful in the City, and had friends they could call upon, if need be, to protect their interests? Some of these said people had high positions and were able to give, or to withhold, favors, which might make a considerable difference to the agreeability of one's life and the prospect of one's future advancement in profession, finance or society.

Jack raised his eyebrows and asked with very slight surprise if Mr. Boddy was telling him that these people to whom he was referring were so embarrassed by their ownership of the property in question that they were prepared to damage the reputation or interests of anyone who might inquire.

"You must assume whatever you will, Mr. Radley," Boddy replied with a tight smile. "I am not answerable for your situation, I have discharged my duty towards you. Now I have further clients to see. Good day to you."

And with that they were obliged to depart

with no more than the company name, which they had already gleaned from the management. No names were given and no principals — the matter was not described in any way, except by the rather amorphous threat.

"Odious little person," Aunt Vespasia replied when they told her. "But what we might have expected. If he were to repeat names to any Tom, Dick and Harry who came to the door, he would not have lasted long as lawyer to the kind of people who own such properties." She had already ordered tea and they were sitting around the fire in her withdrawing room, thawing out from the chill both of the weather outside and of their disappointment at having met, at least for the time being, what seemed to be a dead end. Even Gracie was permitted, on this occasion, to sit with them and to take tea, but she said nothing at all. Instead she stared with huge eyes at the paintings on the walls, the delicate furniture with its satin-smooth surfaces, and when she dared, at Vespasia herself, who was sitting upright, her silver hair coiled immaculately on the crown of her head, great pearl drops in her ears, ecru-colored French lace at her throat and in long ruffles over her thin, tapered hands, bright with diamonds. Gracie had never seen anyone so splendid in all her life, and to be sitting in her house taking tea with her was probably the most memorable thing she would ever do.

"But he did say he'd seen Clemency," Charlotte pointed out. "He didn't make the slightest attempt to conceal it. He was as bold as brass, and twice as smooth. He probably told whoever owns it that she had been there, and what she meant to do. I would dearly like to have hit him as hard as I could."

"Impractical," Emily said, biting her lip. "But so would I, preferably with an exceedingly sharp umbrella point. But how can we find who owns this company? Surely there must be a way?"

"Perhaps Thomas could," Vespasia suggested, frowning slightly. "Commerce is not something with which I have any familiarity. It is at times like these I regret my lack of knowledge of certain aspects of society. Charlotte?"

"I don't know whether he could." She was sharply reminded of the previous evening. "But he doesn't think there is any purpose. He is quite convinced that Dr. Shaw is the intended victim, not Clemency."

"He may well be right," Vespasia conceded. "It does not alter the fact that Clemency was fighting a battle in which we believe intensely, and that since she is dead there is no one else, so far as we know. The abuse is intolerable, for the wretchedness of its victims, and for the abysmal humbug. Nothing irks my temper like hypocrisy. I should like to rip the masks off these sanctimonious faces, for the sheer pleasure of doing it."

"We are with you," Jack said instantly. "I didn't know I had it in me to be so angry, but at the moment I find it hard to think of much else."

A very slight smile touched Vespasia's lips and she regarded him with considerable approval. He seemed unaware of it, but it gave Emily a feeling of warmth that startled her, and she realized how much it mattered to her that Vespasia should think well of him. She found herself smiling back.

Charlotte thought of Pitt still struggling with Shaw's patients, seeking for the one piece of knowledge that was so hideous it had led to two murders, and might lead to more, until Shaw himself was dead. But she still felt it was Clemency that had been meant to die in that first fire, and the second was merely to cover it. The murderer in act might be any one of dozens of arsonists for hire, but the murderer in spirit was whoever owned those fearful, rotting, teeming tenements in Lisbon Street, and was afraid of the public embarrassment Clemency would expose him to when she succeeded in her quest.

"We don't know how to find who owns a company." She set her cup down and stared at Vespasia. "But surely Mr. Carlisle will — or he will know someone else who does. If necessary we must hire someone."

"I will speak to him," Vespasia agreed. "I think he will see that the matter is of some urgency. He may be persuaded to set aside other tasks and pursue this."

And so he did, and the following evening reported to them, again in Vespasia's withdrawing room. He looked startled and a little confused when he was shown in by the footman. His usual wry humor was sharp in his eyes, but there was a smoothness in his face as if surprise had ironed out the customary lines deep around his mouth.

He gave the greetings of courtesy briefly and accepted Vespasia's offer of a seat. They all stared at him, aware that he bore extraordinary news, but they could only guess at its nature.

Vespasia's silver-gray eyes dared him to indulge in histrionics. Words of caution were superfluous.

"You may begin," she informed him.

"The company which owns the buildings is in turn owned by another company." He told the story without embroidery, just the bare details that were required in order for it to make sense, looking from one to another of them, including Gracie, so that she might feel equally involved. "I called upon certain people who owe me favors, or will wish for my goodwill in the future, and managed to learn the names of the holders of stock in this second company. There is only one of them still alive — in fact only one has been alive for several years. Even when the company was formed in 1873, from the remnants of another similar company, and that apparently in the same way from an even earlier one, even in 1873 the other holders of stock were either absent from the country indefinitely or of such age and state of health as to be incapable of active interest."

Vespasia fixed him firmly with her level, penetrating gaze, but he had no guilt of unnecessary drama, and he continued in his own pace.

"This one person who was active and who signed all necessary documents I succeeded in visiting. She is an elderly lady, unmarried, and therefore always mistress of her own property, such as it is, and only acts as go-between, holding shares in name but hardly in any act. Her income is sufficient to keep her in some form of comfort, but certainly not luxury. It was obvious as soon as I was through the door that the bulk of the money, which will amount to several thousands each year, was going somewhere else."

Jack shifted in his chair and Emily drew in her breath expectantly.

"I told her who I was." Carlisle blushed faintly. "She was extremely impressed. The government, especially when expressed as Her Majesty's instrument for ruling her people, and the church, are the two fixed and immutable forces for good in this lady's world."

Charlotte made a leap of imagination. "You are not saying that the person for whom she acts is a member of Parliament, are you?"

Vespasia stiffened.

Emily leaned forward, waiting.

Jack drew in his breath, and Charlotte had her hands clenched in her lap.

Carlisle smiled broadly, showing excellent teeth. "No, but you are almost right. He is — or was — a most distinguished member of the church — in fact, Bishop Augustus Worlingham!"

Emily gasped. Even Vespasia gave a little squeak of amazement.

"What?" Charlotte was incredulous, then she began to laugh a little hysterically, wild, absurd humor welling up inside her, black as the charred ruins of Shaw's house. She could scarcely grasp the horror Clemency must have felt when she came this far. And surely she had? She had found this innocent, befuddled old lady who had funneled the slum rents, the waves of misery and sin, into her own family coffers to make the bishop's house warm and rich, and to buy the roasts and wine she and her sister ate, to clothe them in silk and be waited upon by servants.

No wonder Clemency spent all her inheritance, hundreds of pounds at a time, uncounted, to right his wrongs.

Had Theophilus known? What about Angeline and Celeste? Did they know where the family money came from, even while they sought donations from the people of Highgate to build a stained-glass window to their bishop's memory?

She imagined what Shaw would make of this when he knew. And surely one day he would? It would become public knowledge when Clemency's murderer was tried — then she stopped. But if the owner were Bishop Worlingham — he was long dead, ten years ago — and Theophilus too. The income was Clemency's — and for Prudence, Angeline and Celeste. Would they really murder their sister and niece to protect their family money? Surely Clemency would not have revealed the truth? Would she?

Or would she? Had they had a fearful quarrel and she had told them precisely the cost of their comfort, and that she meant to fight for a law to expose all such men as the bishop to the public obloquy and disgust they deserved?

Yes — it was not inconceivable Celeste at least might kill to prevent that. Her whole life had been used up caring for the bishop. She had denied herself husband and children in order to stay at his side and obey his every command, write out his letters and sermons, look up his references, play the piano for his relaxation, read aloud to him when his eyes were tired, always his gracious and unpaid servant. It was a total sacrifice of her own will, all her choices eaten up in his. She must justify it — he must remain worthy of such a gift, or her life became ridiculous, a thing thrown away for no cause.

Perhaps Pitt was right, and it was close to home, the heart as well as the act in Highgate all the time.

They were all watching her, seeing in her eyes her racing thoughts and in the shadows across her face the plunges from anger to pity to dawning realization.

"Bishop Augustus Worlingham," Somerset Carlisle repeated, letting each syllable fall with full value. "The whole of Lisbon Street was owned, very tortuously and with extreme secrecy, by the 'good' bishop, and when he died, inherited by Theophilus, Celeste and Angeline. I presume he provided for his daughters so generously because they had spent their lives as his servants, and certainly they would have no other means of support and it would be beyond any expectation, reasonable or unreasonable, that they might marry at that point — or would wish to by then. I looked up his will, by the way. Two thirds went to Theophilus, the other third, plus the house, which is worth a great deal of course, to the sisters. That would be more than enough to keep them in better than comfort for the rest of their lives."

"Then Theophilus must have had a fortune," Emily said with surprise.

"He inherited one," Carlisle agreed. "But he lived extremely well, according to what I heard; ate well, had one of the finest cellars in London, and collected paintings, some of which he donated to local museums and other institutions. All the same, he left a very handsome sum indeed to each of his daughters when he died unexpectedly."

"So Clemency had a great deal of money," Vespasia said, almost to herself. "Until she began to give it away. Do we know when that was?" She looked at Jack, then at Carlisle.

"The lawyer would not say when she was there," Jack replied, his lips tightening at remembrance of his frustration and the lawyer's bland, supercilious face.

"Her fight to get some alteration in the disclosure of ownership began about six months ago," Carlisle said somberly. "And she made her first large donation to a charitable shelter for the poor at about the same time. I would hazard a guess that that is when she discovered her grandfather was the owner she had sought."

"Poor Clemency." Charlotte remembered the sad trail of sick women and children, gaunt and hopeless men which she herself had followed from Shaw's patient list in Highgate, down through worse and worse houses and tenements till she at last found Bessie Jones huddled in one corner of an overcrowded and filthy room. Clemency had followed the same course, seen the same wretched faces, the illness and the resignation. And then she had started upwards towards the owners, as they had done.

"We must not let the fight die with her," Jack said, sitting a little more upright in his chair. "Worlingham may be dead, but there are scores, perhaps hundreds of others. She knew that, and she would have given her life to exposing them — " He stopped. "And I

395

still think she may have died because of it. We were warned specifically that there are powerful people who could make us, if we are discreet and withdraw, or break us if we persist. Obviously Worlingham himself did not kill her, but one of the other owners may well have. They have a great deal to lose — and I don't imagine Clemency paid any heed to threats. There was too much passion in her, and revulsion for her own inheritance. Nothing but death would have stopped her."

"What can we do?" Emily looked at Vespasia, then at Carlisle.

Carlisle's face was very grave and he drew his brows down in thought.

"I'm not sure. The forces against it are very large; they are vested interests, a great deal of money. Lots of powerful families may not be sure where all their income originates. Nor will they be in any haste to embarrass their friends."

"We need a voice in Parliament," Vespasia said with decision. "I know we have one." She glanced at Carlisle. "We need more. We need someone new, who will address this matter in particular. Jack — you are doing nothing whatever but enjoying yourself. Your honeymoon is over. It is time you were useful."

Jack stared at her as if she had risen out of the ground in front of him. Their eyes met, hers steady silver-gray and absolutely un-flinching, his dark gray-blue, long-lashed and wide in total incredulity. Then gradually the amazement passed into the beginning of an idea. His hands tightened on the arm of his chair. Still his gaze never left hers, nor did hers waver for a second.

No one else moved or made the tiniest sound. Emily all but held her breath.

"Yes," Jack said at last. "What an excellent idea. Where do I begin?"

CHAPTER NINE

Charlotte had recounted to Pitt at least the salient points of her experiences searching for the ownership of the buildings in Lisbon Street, and when she made the shattering discovery not only that it was the Worlingham family themselves, but that Clemency had learned it several months before she died, she poured it all out to him the moment she arrived home. She saw his coat in the hall and without even taking off her hat she raced down the corridor to the kitchen.

"Thomas. Thomas — Lisbon Street was owned by Bishop Worlingham himself! Now the family takes all the rents. Clemency discovered it. She knew!"

"What?" He stared at her, half turned in his seat, his eyes wide.

"Bishop Worlingham owned Lisbon Street," she said again. "All those slums and gin houses were his! Now they belong to the rest of the family — and Clemency discovered it. That's why she felt so awful." She sat down in a heap in the chair opposite him, skirts awry, and leaned across the table towards him. "That's probably why she worked so hard at undoing it all. Just think how she must have felt." She closed her eyes and put her head in her hands, elbows on the table. "Oh!"

"Poor Clemency," Pitt said very quietly. "What a very remarkable woman. I wish I could have known her."

"So do I," Charlotte agreed through her fingers. "Why do we so often get to know about people only when it's too late?"

It was a question to which she expected no answer. They both knew that they would have had no occasion to know of Clemency Shaw had she not been murdered, and it required no words to convey their understanding.

It was another half hour before she even remembered to tell him that Jack was seriously considering standing for Parliament.

"Really?" His voice rose in surprise and he looked at her carefully to make sure she was not making some obscure joke.

"Oh yes — I think it's excellent. He ought to do something or they'll both be bored to pieces." She grinned. "We cannot meddle in all your cases."

He let out a snort and refrained from comment. But there was a sense of deep comfort in him, experiences and emotions shared, horror, exultation, pity, anger, at times fear, all the multitude of feelings that are roused by terrible events, common purpose, and the unique bond that comes of sharing.

Consequently, when he joined Murdo at the Highgate Police Station the next day there were several things he had to tell him, most of which only added to Murdo's growing anxiety about Flora Lutterworth. He thought of their few brief and rather stilted conversations, the hot silences, the clumsiness he felt standing there in her magnificent house, his boots shining like huge wedges of coal, his uniform buttons so obviously marking him out as a policeman, an intruder of the most unwelcome sort. And always her face came back burning across his mind, wide-eyed, fair-skinned with that wonderful color in her cheeks, so proud and full of courage. Surely she must be one of the most beautiful women he could ever see? But there was far more than beauty to her; there was spirit and gentleness. She was so very alive, it was as if she could smell winds and flowers he only imagined, see beyond his everyday horizons into a brighter, more important world, hear melodies of which he only knew the beat.

And yet he also knew she was afraid. He longed to protect her, and was agonizingly aware than he could not. He did not understand the nature of what threatened her, only that it was connected with Clemency Shaw's death, and now with Lindsay's as well.

And with a part of him he refused even to listen to, in spite of its still, cold voice in his brain, he was also aware that her role in it might not be entirely innocent. He would not even think that she was personally involved, perhaps actually to blame. But he had heard the rumors, seen the looks and blushes and the secrecy; he knew there was a special relationship between Flora and Stephen Shaw, one so definite that her father was furious about it, yet she felt it so precious to her she was prepared to brave his anger and defy him.

Murdo was confused. He had never felt jealousy of this muddled nature before, at once so sure she had done nothing shameful, and yet unable to deny to himself that there was a real and deep emotion inside her towards Shaw.

And of course the alternative fear was large; perhaps it was its very size which blocked out the other even more hideous thought — that Alfred Lutterworth was responsible for the attempts on Shaw's life. There were two possible reasons for this, both quite believable, and both ruinous.

The one he refused to think was that Shaw had dishonored Flora, or even knew of some fearful shame in her life, perhaps an illegitimate child, or worse, an abortion; and Lutterworth had tried to kill him when somehow he had learned of it — to keep him silent. He could hardly hope for a fine marriage for her if such a thing were known — in fact no marriage at all would be possible. She would grow old alone, rich, excluded, whispered about and forever an object of pity or contempt.

At the thought of it Murdo was ready to kill Shaw himself. His fists were clenched so tight his nails, short as they were, bit into the flesh of his palms. That thought must be cast out, obliterated from his mind. What betrayal that he would let it enter — even for an instant.

He hated himself even for having thought it. Shaw was pestering her; she was young and very lovely. He lusted after her, and she was too innocent to see how vile he was. That was far more like it. And of course there was her father's money. Shaw had already spent all his wife's money — and there was extraordinary evidence for that. Inspector Pitt had found out just yesterday that Clemency Shaw's money was all gone. Yes — that made perfect sense — Shaw was after Flora's money!

And Alfred Lutterworth had a great deal of money. That thought was also wretched. Murdo was a constable, and likely to remain so for a long time; he was only twenty-four. He earned enough to keep himself in something like decency, he ate three times a day and had a pleasant room and clean clothes, but it was as far from the splendor of Alfred Lutterworth's house as Lutterworth's was in turn from what Murdo imagined of the Queen's castle at Windsor. And Lutterworth might as well cast eyes upon one of the princesses as Murdo upon Flora.

It was with a finality of despair that he forced the last thought, the one prompted by Inspector Pitt's wife's discovery of the ownership of some of the worst slum tenements by old Bishop Worlingham. Murdo was not so very amazed. He had long known that some outwardly respectable people could have very ugly secrets, especially where money was concerned. But what Pitt had not mentioned was that if Mrs. Shaw, poor lady, had discovered who owned those particular houses, she might also have discovered who owned several others. Pitt had mentioned members of Parliament, titled families, even justices of the courts. Had he not also thought of retired industrialists who wanted to enter society and needed a good continuing income, and might not be too particular as to where their money was invested?

Alfred Lutterworth might well have been

in every bit as much danger from Clemency Shaw as the Worlinghams were — in fact more. Clemency might protect her own — it appeared she had. But why should she protect Lutterworth? He had every reason to kill her — and if Lindsay had guessed this, to kill him too.

That is, if he owned slum property too. And how could they ever find that out? They could hardly trace the ownership of every piece of rotten plaster and sagging timber in London, every blind alley, open drain and crumbling pile of masonry, every wretched home of cold and frightened people. He knew because he had tried. He blushed hot at the memory of it; it was a kind of betrayal that he had let the thought take root in his mind and had asked questions about Lutterworth's finances, the source of his income and if it could involve rents. But it was not as easy as he had imagined. Money came from companies, but what did those companies do? Time had been short, and he had no official instructions to give his questions the force of law.

Nothing had been resolved; he was simply uncertain and appallingly conscious of his guilt. Nothing he could even imagine doing would remove the ache of fear and imagination at the back of his mind.

He saw Flora's face in his heart's eye and

all the pain and the shame she would feel burned through him till he could hardly bear it. He was even glad to hear Pitt's footsteps return and to be told their duty for the morning. Part of him was still outraged that they sent an outsider — did they think Highgate's own men were incompetent? And part of him was immensely grateful that the responsibility was not theirs. This was a very ugly case, and the resolution seemed as far off now as it had when they were standing in the wet street staring at the smoldering remains of Shaw's house, long before the taper was struck to set Lindsay's alight.

"Yes sir?" he said automatically as Pitt came around the corner and into the foyer where he was standing. "Where to, sir?"

"Mr. Alfred Lutterworth's, I think," Pitt barely hesitated on his way out. He had been to the local superintendent, as a matter of courtesy, and on the small chance that something had occurred that Murdo did not know about, some thread worth following.

But the superintendent had looked at him with his habitual disfavor and reported with some satisfaction another fire, in Kentish Town, a possible lead on the arsonist he personally was sure was the guilty party in all cases, and rather a negative report on house insurance and the unlikelihood of either Shaw or Lindsay being involved in fire for the purposes of fraud.

"Well I hardly imagined Lindsay burned himself to death to claim the insurance!" Pitt had snapped back.

"No sir," the superintendent had said coldly, his eyes wide. "Neither did we. But then we are confident the fires were all set by the arsonist in Kentish Town — sir."

"Indeed." Pitt had been noncommittal. "Odd there were only two houses that were occupied."

"Well he didn't know Shaw's was — did he?" the superintendent had said irritably. "Shaw was out, and everyone thought Mrs. Shaw was too. She only canceled at the last minute."

"The only people who thought Mrs. Shaw was out were the people who knew her," Pitt had said with satisfaction.

The superintendent had glared at him and returned to his desk, leaving Pitt to go out of the door in silence.

Now he was ready to go and probe and watch and listen to people, where his true art lay. He had days ago given up expecting things to tell him anything. Murdo's heart sank, but there was no escaping duty. He followed Pitt and caught up with him, and together they walked along the damp, leaf-scattered foot-

406

path towards the Lutterworths' house.

They were admitted by the maid and shown into the morning room, where there was a brisk fire burning and a bowl of tawny chrysanthemums on the heavy Tudor dresser. Neither of them sat, although it was nearly quarter of an hour before Lutterworth appeared, closely followed by Flora, dressed in a dark blue stuff gown and looking pale but composed. She glanced at Murdo only once, and her eyes flickered away immediately, a faint, self-conscious flush on her cheeks.

Murdo remained in a bitterly painful silence. He longed to help her; he wanted to hit out at someone — Shaw, Lutterworth for allowing all this to happen and not protecting her, and Pitt for forging blindly ahead with his duty, regardless of the chaos it caused.

For an instant he hated Pitt for not hurting as much as he did, as if he were oblivious of pain; then he looked sideways for just a moment at him, and realized his error. Pitt's face was tense; there were shadows under his eyes and the fine lines in his skin were all weary and conscious of realms of suffering past and to come, and of his inability to heal it.

Murdo let out his breath in a sigh, and kept silent.

Lutterworth faced them across the expensive Turkish carpet. None of them sat.

"Well, what is it now?" he demanded. "I know nowt I 'aven't told you. I've no idea why anyone killed poor old Lindsay, unless it was Shaw, because the old man saw through 'im and 'ad to be silenced. Or it were that daft Pascoe, because 'e thought as Lindsay were an anarchist.

"Take that 'orse." He pointed to a fine figurine on the mantel shelf. "Bought that wi' me first big year's profit, when the mill started to do well. Got a fine consignment o' cloth and sold it ourselves — in the Cape. Turned a pretty penny, did that. Got the 'orse to remind me o' me early days when me and Ellen, that's Flora's mother" — he took a deep breath and let it out slowly to give himself time to regain his composure — "when me and Ellen went courtin'. Didn't 'ave no carriage. We used to ride an 'orse like that — 'er up in front o' me, an me be'ind wi' me arms 'round 'er. Them was good days. Every time I look at that 'orse I think o' them — like I could still see the sunlight through the trees on the dry earth and smell the 'orse's warm body and the 'ay in the wind, an' see the blossom in the 'edges like fallen snow, sweet as 'oney, and my Ellen's 'air brighter'n a peeled chestnut — an' 'ear 'er laugh."

He stood motionless, enveloped in the past. No one wanted to be the first to invade with the ugliness and immediacy of the present.

It was Pitt who broke the spell, and with words Murdo had not foreseen.

"What past do you think Mr. Lindsay recalled in his African artifacts, Mr. Lutterworth?"

"I don't know." Lutterworth smiled ruefully. " 'Is wife, mebbe. That's what most men remember."

"His wife!" Pitt was startled. "I didn't know Lindsay was married."

"No — well, no reason why you should." Lutterworth looked faintly sorry. " 'E didn't tell everyone. She died a long time ago — twenty years or more. Reckon as that's why 'e came 'ome. Not that 'e said so, mind."

"Were there any children?"

"Several, I think."

"Where are they? They've not come forward. His will didn't mention any."

"It wouldn't. They're in Africa."

"That wouldn't stop them inheriting."

"What — an 'ouse in 'Ighgate and a few books and mementos of Africa!" Lutterworth was smiling at some deep inner satisfaction.

"Why not?" Pitt demanded. "There were a great many books, some on anthropology must be worth a great deal."

"Not to them." Lutterworth's lips smiled grimly.

"Why not? And there's the house!"

"Not much use to a black man who lives in a jungle." Lutterworth looked at Pitt with dour satisfaction, savoring the surprise on his face. "That's it — Lindsay's wife was African, beautiful woman, black as your 'at. I saw a picture of 'er once. He showed me. I was talking about my Ellen, an' 'e showed me. Never saw a gentler face in me life. Couldn't pronounce 'er name, even when 'e said it slow, but 'e told me it meant some kind o' river bird."

"Did anyone else know about her?"

"No idea. He may have told Shaw. I suppose you 'aven't arrested him yet?"

"Papa!" Flora spoke for the first time, a cry of protest torn out in spite of herself.

"An' I'll not 'ave a word about it from you, my girl," Lutterworth said fiercely. " 'E's done enough damage to you already. Your name's a byword 'round 'ere, runnin' after 'im like a lovesick parlormaid."

Flora blushed scarlet and fumbled for words to defend herself and found none.

Murdo was in an agony of impotence. Had Lutterworth glanced at him he would have been startled by the fury in his eyes, but he was occupied with the irresponsibility he saw in his daughter.

"Well what do you want wi' me?" he snapped

at Pitt. "Not to hear about Amos Lindsay's dead wife — poor devil."

"No," Pitt agreed. "Actually I came to ask you about what properties you own in the city."

"What?" Lutterworth was so utterly taken aback it was hard not to believe he was as startled as he seemed. "What in heaven's name are you talking about, man? What property?"

"Housing, to be exact." Pitt was watching him closely, but even Murdo who cared more intensely about this case than about anything else he could remember, did not see a flicker of fear or comprehension in Lutterworth's face.

"I own this 'ouse, lock, stock and barrel, and the ground it stands on." Lutterworth unconsciously stiffened a fraction and pulled his shoulders straighter. "And I own a couple o' rows o' terraced 'ouses outside o' Manchester. Built 'em for my workers, I did. And good 'ouses they are, solid as the earth beneath 'em. Don't let water, chimneys don't smoke, privies in every back garden, an' a standpipe to every one of 'em. Can't say fairer than that."

"And that's all the property you own, Mr. Lutterworth?" Pitt's voice was lighter, a thread of relief in it already. "Could you prove that?"

"I could if I were minded to." Lutterworth was eyeing him curiously, his hands pushed deep into his pockets. "But why should I?"

"Because the cause of Mrs. Shaw's murder, and Mr. Lindsay's, may lie in the ownership of property in London," Pitt replied, glancing for less than a second at Flora, and away again.

"Balderdash!" Lutterworth said briskly. "If you ask me, Shaw killed 'is wife so 'e could be free to come after my Flora, and then 'e killed Lindsay because Lindsay knew what 'e was up to. Give 'imself away somehow — bragging, I shouldn't wonder, and went too far. Well 'e'll damn well not marry Flora — for my money, or anything else. I won't let 'er — and 'e'll not wait till I'm gone for 'er, I'll be bound."

"Papa!" Flora would not be hushed anymore, by discretion or filial duty or even the embarrassment which flamed scarlet up her cheeks now. "You are saying wicked things which are quite untrue."

"I'll not have argument." He rounded on her, his own color high. "Can you tell me you haven't been seeing 'im, sneaking in and out of his 'ouse when you thought no one was looking?"

She was on the verge of tears and Murdo tensed as if to step forward, but Pitt shot him a stony glare, his face tight.

Murdo longed to save her so desperately his body ached with the fierceness of his ef-

412

fort to control himself, but he had no idea what to say or do. It all had a dreadful inevitability, like a stone that has already started falling and must complete its journey.

"It was not illicit." She chose her words carefully, doing her best to ignore Pitt and Murdo standing like intrusive furniture in the room, and all her attention was focused on her father. "It was . . . was just — private."

Lutterworth's face was distorted with pain as well as fury. She was the one person left in the world he loved, and she had betrayed herself, and so wounded him where he could not bear it.

"Secret!" he shouted, pounding his fist on the back of the armchair beside him. "Decent women don't creep in the back door o' men's houses to see them in secret. Was Mrs. Shaw there? Was she? And don't lie to me, girl. Was she in the room with you — all the time?"

Flora's voice was a whisper, so strained it was barely heard.

"No."

"O' course she wasn't!" He threw out the words in a mixture of anguish because they were true and a desperate kind of triumph that at least she had not lied. "I know that. I know she'd gone out because half Highgate knows it. But I'll tell you this, my girl — I don't care what Highgate says, or all London society either — they can call you anything they can lay their tongues to. I'll not let you marry Shaw — and that's final."

"I don't want to marry him!" The tears were running down her face now. Her hand flew to her mouth and she bit her teeth on her finger as if the physical pain relieved her distress. "He's my doctor!"

"He's my doctor too." Lutterworth had not yet understood the change in her. "I don't go creeping in at the back door after him. I go to him openly, like an honest man."

"You don't have the same complaint as I do." Her voice was choked with tears and she refused to look at any of them, least of all Murdo. "He allowed me to go whenever I was in pain — and he — "

"Pain?" Lutterworth was horrified, all his anger drained away, leaving him pale and frightened. "What sort of pain? What's wrong with you?" Already he moved towards her as if she were about to collapse. "Flora? Flora, what is it? We'll get the best doctors in England. Why didn't you tell me, girl?"

She turned away from him, hunching her shoulders. "It's not an illness. It's just — please let me be! Leave me a little decency. Do I have to detail my most private discomforts in front of policemen?"

Lutterworth had forgotten Pitt and Murdo.

Now he swung around, ready to attack them for their crassness, then only just in time remembered that it was he who had demanded the explanation of her, not they.

"I have no property in London, Mr. Pitt, and if you want me to prove it to you I daresay I can." His face set hard and he balanced squarely on his feet. "My finances are open to you whenever you care to look at them. My daughter has nothing to tell you about her relationship with her doctor. It is a perfectly correct matter, but it is private, and is privileged to remain so. It is only decent." He met Pitt's eyes defiantly. "I am sure you would not wish your wife's medical condition to be the subject of other men's conversation. I know nothing further with which I can help you. I wish you good day." And he stepped over and rang the bell to have the maid show them out.

Pitt dispatched Murdo to question Shaw's previous servants again. The butler was recovering slowly and so was able to speak more lucidly. He might recall some details which he had been too shocked and in too much pain to think of before. Also Lindsay's manservant might be more forthcoming on a second or third attempt. Pitt most especially wanted to know what the man knew of Lindsay's last two days before the fire. Something, a word or an act, must have precipitated it. All the pieces gathered from one place and another might point to an answer.

Pitt himself returned to the boardinghouse, where he intended to wait for Shaw as long as might be necessary, and question the man until he learned some answers, however long that took, and however brutal it required him to be.

The landlady was getting used to people coming to the door and asking for Dr. Shaw, and to several of them requesting to sit in the parlor and wait for him to return. She treated Pitt with sympathy, having forgotten who he was, and regarding him as one of the doctor's patients, in need of a gentle word and a hot cup of tea.

He accepted both with a slight twinge of conscience, and warmed himself in front of the fire for twenty minutes until Shaw came in in a whirl of activity, setting his bag down on the chair by the desk, his stick up against the wall, having forgotten to put it in the hall stand, his hat on top of the desk and his coat where the landlady was waiting to take it from him. She picked up the rest of his apparel, scarf, gloves, hat and stick, and took them all out as if it were her custom and her pleasure. It seemed she had already developed a certain fondness for him even in these few days.

Shaw faced Pitt with some surprise, a guardedness in his eyes, but no dislike.

" 'Morning Pitt, what is it now? Have you discovered something?" He stood near the center of the room, hands in his pockets, and yet giving the appearance of being so balanced on his feet that he was ready for some intense action, only waiting to know what it might be. "Well, what is it, man? What have you learned?"

Pitt wished he had something to tell him, for Shaw's own sake, and because he felt so inadequate that he still had almost no idea who had started the fires or why, or even beyond question whether it was Shaw who was the intended victim or Clemency. He had begun by being sure it was Shaw; now with Charlotte's conviction that it was Clemency's activities to expose slum profiteers which had provoked it, his own certainty was shaken. But there was no point in lying; it was shabby and they both deserved better.

"I'm afraid I don't know anything further." He saw Shaw's face tighten and a keenness die from his eyes. "I'm sorry," he added unhappily. "The forensic evidence tells me nothing except that the fire was started in four separate places in your house and three in Mr.

Lindsay's, with some kind of fuel oil, probably ordinary lamp oil, poured onto the curtains in the downstairs rooms where it would catch quickly, climb upwards taking the whole window embrasure, and then any wooden furniture."

Shaw frowned. "How did they get in? We'd have heard breaking glass. And I certainly didn't leave any downstairs windows open."

"It isn't very difficult to cut glass," Pitt pointed out. "You can do it silently if you stick a piece of paper over it with a little glue. In the criminal fraternity they call it 'star glazing.' Of course they use it to reach in and undo the catch rather than to pour in oil and drop a taper."

"You think it was an ordinary thief turned assassin?" Shaw's brows rose in incredulity. "Why, for heaven's sake? It doesn't make any sense!" There was disappointment in his face, primarily in Pitt for having thought of nothing better than this.

Pitt was stung. Even though Shaw might be the murderer himself, and he hated to acknowledge that thought, he still respected the man and wanted his good opinion in return.

"I don't think it was an ordinary thief at all," he said quickly. "I am simply saying that there is a very ordinary method of cutting glass without making a noise. Unfortunately, in the mass of shattered glass, bricks, rubble and timbers around it was impossible to say whether that was done or not. Everything was trodden on by the firemen or broken by falling masonry. If there was any cut glass rather than broken it was long since destroyed. Not that it would have told us anything, except that he came prepared in skills as well as materials — which is fairly obvious anyway."

"So?" Shaw stared at him across the expanse of the worn, homely carpet and the comfortable chairs. "If you know nothing more, what are you here for? You haven't come simply to tell me that."

Pitt kept his temper with an effort and tried to order his thoughts.

"Something precipitated the fire in Amos Lindsay's house," he began levelly, fixing his eyes on Shaw's, at the same time sitting down in one of the big easy chairs, letting Shaw know that he intended the discussion to be a long and detailed one. "You were staying with him for the few days preceding; whatever happened you may have noticed, something which you could now recall, if you tried."

The skepticism vanished out of Shaw's face and was replaced by thought, which quickly deepened into concentration. He sat down in the opposite chair and crossed his legs, regarding Pitt through narrowed eyes.

"You think it was Lindsay they meant to kill?" A flicker of emotion crossed his face with peculiar pain, half hope and a release from guilt, half a new darkness of unknown violence and forces not guessed at yet. "Not me?"

"I don't know." Pitt pulled his mouth into a grimace that had been intended as a wry smile but died before humor touched it. "There are several possibilities." He took the wild risk of being honest. It crossed his mind to wonder what good an attempt at deception would do anyway. Shaw was neither gullible nor innocent enough to be taken in. "Possibly the first fire was meant for Mrs. Shaw, and the second was because either you or Lindsay had discovered who it was — or they feared you had — "

"I certainly haven't!" Shaw interrupted. "If I had I'd have told you. For heaven's sake, man, what do you — Oh!" His whole body sagged in the chair. "Of course — you have to suspect me. You'd be incompetent not to." He said it as if he could not believe it himself, as if he were repeating a rather bad joke. "But why should I kill poor Amos? He was about the best friend I had." Suddenly his voice faltered and he looked away to hide the emotion that filled his face. If he was acting, he was superb. But Pitt had known men before who killed someone they loved to save their own lives. He could not afford to spare Shaw the only answer that made sense.

"Because during the time you stayed with him you said or did something that betrayed yourself to him," he replied. "And when you knew that he understood, you had to kill him because you could not trust him to keep silent — not forever, when it meant the noose for you."

Shaw opened his mouth to protest, then the color drained from his skin as he realized how terribly rational it was. He could not sweep it away as preposterous, and the words fled before he began.

"Or the other possibilities," Pitt continued, "are that you said something which led him to learn, or deduce, who it was — without his mentioning it to you. That person became aware that Lindsay knew — perhaps he made further inquiries, or even faced them with it — and to preserve themselves, they killed him."

"What? For heaven's sake." Shaw sat upright, staring at Pitt. "If I had said anything at all that threw any light on it, he would have said so to me at the time, and then we should have reported it to you."

"Would you." Pitt said it with such heavy doubt that it was not a question. "Even if it concerned one of your patients? Or someone you had thought to be a close friend — or even family?" He did not need to add that Shaw was related in one degree or another to all the Worlinghams.

Shaw shifted his position in the chair, his strong, neat hands lying on the arms. Neither of them spoke, but remained staring at each other. Past conversations were recalled like living entities between them: Pitt's struggle to get Shaw to reveal any medical knowledge that might point to motive; Shaw's steady and unswerving refusal.

Finally Shaw spoke slowly, his voice soft and very carefully controlled.

"Do you think I could have told Amos anything I would not tell you?"

"I doubt you would tell him anything you considered a confidence," Pitt answered frankly. "But you could have spoken to him far more than to me, you were a guest in his house, and you were friends." He saw the pain flash across Shaw's face again and found it hard to imagine it was not real. But emotions are very complex, and sometimes survival can cut across others that are very deep, the wrenching of which never ceases to hurt. "In ordinary speech, a word dropped in passing in the course of your day, an expression of success over a patient recovered, or relapsed, and then at another time mention of where you had been — any number of things, which added together gave him some insight. Perhaps it was not total, merely something he wanted to pursue — and in doing so forewarned the murderer that he knew."

Shaw shivered and a spasm of distaste crossed his features.

"I think I liked Amos Lindsay as much as any man alive," he said very quietly. "If I knew who had burned him to death, I should expose them to every punishment the law allows." He looked away, as if to conceal the tenderness in his face. "He was a good man; wise, patient, honest not only with others but with himself, which is far rarer, generous in his means and his judgments. I never heard him make a hasty or ill-natured assessment of another man. And there wasn't a shred of hypocrisy in him."

He looked back at Pitt, his eyes direct and urgent. "He hated cant, and wasn't afraid to show it for what it was. Dear God, how I'm going to miss him. He was the only man around here I could talk to for hours on end about any subject under the sun — new ideas in medicine, old ideas in art, political theory, social order and change." He smiled suddenly, a luminous expression full of joy as fragile as sunlight. "A good wine or cheese, a beautiful woman, the opera, even a good horse — other religions, other people's customs — and not be afraid to say exactly what I thought."

He slid down a little in his chair and put his hands together, fingertips to fingertips. "Couldn't do that with anyone else here. Clitheridge is such a complete fool he can't express an opinion on anything." He let his breath out in a snort. "He's terrified of offending. Josiah has opinions on everything, mostly old Bishop Worlingham's. He wanted to take the cloth, you know." He looked at Pitt quizzically, to see what he made of the idea, whether he understood. "Studied under the old bastard, took everything he said as holy writ, adopted his entire philosophy, like a suit of clothes ready-made. I must say it fitted him to the quarter inch." He pulled a face. "But he was the only son, and his father had a flourishing business and he demanded poor Josiah take it over when he fell ill. The mother and sisters were dependent; there was nothing else he could do."

He sighed, still watching Pitt. "But he never lost the passion for the church. When he dies his ghost will come back to haunt us dressed in miter and robes, or perhaps a Dominican habit. He considers all argument heresy.

"Pascoe's a nice enough old fossil, but his ideas are wrapped in the romance of the Middle Ages, or more accurately the age of King Arthur, Lancelot, the Song of Roland, and other beautiful but unlikely epics. Dalgetty's full of ideas, but such a crusader for liberality of thought I find myself taking the opposing view simply to bring him back to some sort of moderation. Maude has more sense. Have you met her? Excellent woman." His mouth twitched at the corners as if at last he had found something that truly pleased him, something without shadow. "She used to be an artist's model, you know — in her youth. Magnificent body, and not coy about it. That was all before she met Dalgetty and became respectable — which I think her soul always was. But she's never lost her sense of proportion or humor, or turned her nose up at her old friends. She still goes back to Mile End now and again, taking them gifts."

Pitt was stunned, not only at the fact, but that Shaw should know, and now be telling him.

Shaw was watching him, laughing inwardly at the surprise in his face.

"Does Dalgetty know?" Pitt asked after a moment or two.

"Oh certainly. And he doesn't care in the slightest, to his eternal credit. Of course he couldn't spread it around, for her sake. She very much wants to be the respectable woman she appears. And if Highgate society knew they'd crucify her. Which would be their loss. She's worth any ten of them. Funnily enough, Josiah, for all his narrow limits, knows that. He admires her as if she were a plaster saint. Some part of his judgment must be good after all."

"And how did you find out about her modeling?" Pitt asked, his mind scrambling after explanations, trying to fit this new piece in to make sense of all the rest, and failing. Was it conceivable Dalgetty had tried to kill Shaw to keep this secret? He hardly seemed like a man who cared so desperately for social status — he did enough to jeopardize it quite deliberately with his liberal reviews. And yet that was fashionable in certain literary quarters — not the same thing as posing naked for young men to paint, and all the world to see. Could he love his wife so much he would murder to keep the respectability she enjoyed?

"By accident." Shaw was watching him with bright, amused eyes. "I was making a medical call on an artist on hard times, and he tried to pay me with a painting of Maude. I didn't take it, but I would like to have. Apart from the irony of it, it was damned good — but someone would have seen it. My heaven, she was a handsome woman. Still is, for that matter."

"Does Dalgetty know that you know this?" Pitt was curious whether he would believe the answer, either way.

"I've no idea," Shaw replied with apparent candor. "Maude does — I told her."

"And was she distressed?"

"A trifle embarrassed at first; then she saw the humor of it, and knew that I'd not tell anyone."

"You told me," Pitt pointed out.

"You are hardly Highgate society." Shaw was equally blunt, but there was no cruelty in his face. Highgate society was not something he admired, nor did he consider exclusion from it to be any disadvantage. "And I judge you not to be a man who would ruin her reputation for no reason but malice — or a loose tongue."

Pitt smiled in spite of himself. "Thank you, Doctor," he said with undisguised irony. "Now if you would turn your attention to the few days you were staying at Mr. Lindsay's house, especially the last forty-eight hours before the fire. Can you remember any conversations you had with him about the first fire, about Mrs. Shaw, or about anyone who could possibly be connected with a reason to kill her, or you?"

Shaw pulled a bleak face and the humor died from his eyes.

"That covers just about everyone, since I haven't any idea why anyone should hate me enough to burn me to death. Of course I've quarreled with people now and again — who hasn't? But no sane person bears grudges over a difference of opinion."

"I don't mean a general philosophy, Doctor." Pitt held him to the point. The answer might lie in his memory. Something had triggered in a murderer's mind the need to protect himself — or herself — so violently that the person had risked exposure by killing again. "Recall which patients you saw those last few days; you must have notes if you can't remember. What times did you come and go, when did you eat? What did you say to each other at table? Think!"

Shaw slumped in his chair and his face became lost in an effort of concentration. Pitt did not interrupt or prompt him.

"I remember Clitheridge came on the Thursday," Shaw said at last. "Early in the evening, just as we were about to dine. I had been out to see a man with stones. He was in great pain. I knew they would pass in time, but I wished there was more I could do to ease him. I came home very tired — the last thing I wanted was a lot of platitudes from the vicar. I'm afraid I was rude to him. He intends well, but he never gets to the point; he goes 'round and 'round things without saying what he means. I've begun to wonder if he really does mean anything, or if he thinks in the same idiotic homilies he speaks. Perhaps he's empty, and there's no one inside?" He sniffed. "Poor Lally."

Pitt allowed him to resume in his own time.

"Amos was civil to him." Shaw continued after a moment. "I suppose he picked up my errors and omissions rather often, especially in the last few weeks." Again the deep pain suffused his face, and Pitt felt like an intruder sitting so close to him. Shaw drew a deep breath. "Clitheridge went off as soon as he had satisfied his duty. I don't remember that we talked about anything in particular. I wasn't really listening. But I do remember the next day, the day before the fire, that both Pascoe and Dalgetty called, because Amos told me about it over dinner. It was about that damn monograph, of course. Dalgetty wanted him to do another, longer one on the new social order, all wrapped 'round in the essential message that freedom to explore the mind is the most sacred thing of all, and knowledge itself is the holiest thing, and every man's God-given right." He leaned forward a little again, his eyes searching Pitt's face, trying to deduce his reaction. Apparently he saw nothing but interest, and continued more quietly.

"Of course Pascoe told him he was irresponsible, that he was undermining the fabric of Christianity and feeding dangerous and

429

frightening ideas to people who did not want them and would not know what to do with them. He seemed to have got the idea that Amos was propagating seeds of revolution and anarchy. Which had an element of truth. I think Dalgetty was interested in the Fabian Society and its ideas on public ownership of the means of production, and more or less equal remuneration for all work" — he laughed sharply —"with the exception of unique minds, of course — by which I gather they mean philosophers and artists."

Pitt was compelled to smile as well. "Was Lindsay interested in such ideas?" he asked.

"Interested, yes — in agreement, I doubt. But he did approve of their beliefs in appropriation of capital wealth that perpetuates the extreme differences between the propertied classes and the workers."

"Did he quarrel with Pascoe?" It seemed a remote motive, but he could not leave it unmentioned.

"Yes — but I think it was more flash than heat. Pascoe is a born crusader; he's always tilting at something — mostly windmills. If it hadn't been poor Amos, it would have been someone else."

The faint flicker of motive receded. "Were there any other callers, so far as you know?"

"Only Oliphant, the curate. He came to see

me. He made it seem like a general call out of concern for my welfare, and I expect it was. He's a decent chap; I find myself liking him more each time I see him. Never really noticed him before this, but most of the parishioners speak well of him."

" 'He made it seem,' " Pitt prompted.

"Oh — well, he asked several questions about Clemency and her charity work on slum ownership. He wanted to know if she'd said anything to me about what she'd accomplished. Well of course she did. Not every day, just now and again. Actually she managed very little. There are some extremely powerful people who own most of the worst — and most profitable — streets. Financiers, industrialists, members of society, old families — "

"Did she mention any to you that you might have repeated to Oliphant, and thus Lindsay?" Pitt jumped at the thought, slender as it was, and Charlotte's face came to his mind, eyes bright, chin determined as she set out to trace Clemency's steps.

Shaw smiled bleakly. "I honestly don't remember, I'm sorry. I wasn't paying much attention. I tried to be civil because he was so earnest and he obviously cared, but I thought he was wasting his time — and mine." He drew his brows together. "Do you really think

Clemency was actually a threat to someone? She hadn't a dog in hell's chance of getting a law passed to disclose who profited out of slum tenements, you know. The worst she could have done would be to get herself sued for slander by some outraged industrialist — "

"Which you would not have liked," Pitt pointed out quietly. "It would have cost you all you possess, including your reputation, and presumably your livelihood."

Shaw laughed harshly. "Touché, Inspector. That may look like a perfect motive for me — but if you think she'd have done that, and left me exposed, you didn't know Clem. She wasn't a foolish woman and she understood money and reputation." His eyes were bright with a sad humor close to tears. "Far better than anyone will know now. You won't understand how much I miss her — and why should I try to explain? I stopped being in love with her long ago — but I think I liked Clem better than anyone else I've ever known — even Amos. She and Maude were good friends. She knew all about the modeling — and didn't give a damn." He stood up slowly, as if his body ached.

"I'm sorry, Pitt. I have no idea who killed Clem — or Amos, but if I did I should tell you immediately — in the middle of the night, if that's when it occurred to me. Now get out of here and go and dig somewhere else. I've got to eat something, and then go out on more calls. The sick can't wait."

The following morning Pitt was disturbed by a loud banging on his front door so urgent he dropped his toast and marmalade and swung up from the kitchen chair and along the hallway in half a dozen strides. In his mind the horror of fire was already gaping at him, nightmarish, and he had a sick premonition that this time it would be the lodging house, and the gentle curate, who found the right words to touch grief, would be in the ashes. It hurt him almost intolerably.

He yanked the door open and saw Murdo standing on the step, damp and miserable in the predawn light. The gas lamp a little beyond him to the left gave him the remnants of a halo in the mist.

"I'm sorry sir, but I thought I should tell you — just in case it has to do with it — sir," he said wretchedly. His words were unexplained, but apparently made sense to him.

"What are you talking about?" Pitt demanded, beginning to hope it was not fire after all.

"The fight, sir." Murdo shifted from one foot to the other, patently wishing he had not come. What had begun as a good idea now seemed a very bad one. "Mr. Pascoe and Mr. Dalgetty. Mrs. Dalgetty told the station sergeant last night, but I only just learned of it half an hour ago. Seems they didn't take it serious — "

"What fight?" Pitt pulled his coat off the hook by the door. "If they fought last night couldn't it have waited till after breakfast?" He scowled. "What do you mean, fight? Did they hurt each other?" He found the idea absurd and faintly amusing. "Does it really matter? They are always quarreling — it seems to be part of their way of life. It seems to give them a kind of validity."

"No sir." Murdo looked even more miserable. "They're planning to fight this morning — at dawn, sir."

"Don't be ridiculous!" Pitt snapped. "Who on earth is going to get out of a warm bed at dawn and plan to have a quarrel? Somebody's having a very ill considered joke at your expense." He turned to hang up his coat again.

"No sir," Murdo said stolidly. "They already had the quarrel, yesterday. The fight is this morning at sunrise — in the field between Highgate Road and the cemetery — with swords."

Pitt grasped for one more wild instant at the concept of a joke, saw in Murdo's face that it was not, and lost his temper.

"Hell's teeth!" he said furiously. "We've got two houses in ruins, charred bodies of two brave, kind people — others injured and terrified — and two bloody idiots want to fight a duel over some damnable piece of paper." He snatched the coat back again and pushed Murdo off the step onto the pavement, slamming the door. The cab Murdo had come in was only a few yards away. "Come on!" Pitt yanked the door open and climbed in. "Highgate Road!" he shouted. "I'll show these two prancing fools what a real fight is! I'll arrest them for disturbing the Queen's peace!"

Murdo scrambled in beside him, falling sideways as the cab jerked into motion and only just catching the door as it swung away. "I don't suppose they'll hurt each other," he said lamely.

"Pity." Pitt was totally without sympathy. "Serve them both right if they were skewered like puddings!" And he rode the rest of the way in furious silence, Murdo not daring to make any further suggestions.

Eventually the cab came to an abrupt halt and Pitt threw open the door and jumped out, leaving the fare to Murdo to pay, and set off across the path through the field, Highgate Road to his left and the wall of the magnificent cemetery to his right. Three hundred yards ahead of him, paced out on the grass, their figures squat in the distance, were five people.

The solid figure of Quinton Pascoe was standing, feet a little apart, a cape slung over one shoulder, the cold, early sun, clear as springwater, on his shock of white hair. In front of him the dew was heavy on the bent heads of the grass, giving the leaves a strange hint of turquoise as the light refracted.

No more than half a dozen yards away, John Dalgetty, dark-headed, his back to the sun, the shadow masking his face, stood with one arm thrown back and a long object raised as if he were about to charge. Pitt thought at first it was a walking stick. The whole thing was palpably ridiculous. He started to run towards them as fast as his long legs would carry him.

Standing well back were two gentlemen in black frock coats, a little apart from each other. Presumably they were acting as seconds. Another man, who had taken his coat off — for no apparent reason, it was a distinctly chilly morning — was standing in shirtsleeves and shouting first at Pascoe, then at Dalgetty. His voice came to Pitt across the distance, but not his words.

With a flourish Pascoe swung his cloak around his arm and threw it onto the ground in a heap, regardless of the damp. His second rushed to pick it up and held it in front of him, rather like a shield.

Dalgetty, who had no cloak, chose to keep his coat on. He flourished the stick, or whatever it was, again, and let out a cry of "Liberty!" and lunged forward at a run.

"Honor!" Pascoe shouted back, and brandishing something long and pale in his hand, ran forward as well. They met with a clash in the middle and Dalgetty slipped as his polished boots failed to take purchase on the wet grass.

Pascoe turned swiftly and only just missed spearing him through the chest. Instead he succeeded in tearing a long piece from Dalgetty's jacket and thoroughly enraging him. Dalgetty wielded what Pitt could now see was a sword stick, and dealt Pascoe a nasty blow across the shoulders.

"Stop it!" Pitt bellowed as loudly as his lungs would bear. He was running towards them, but he was still a hundred and fifty yards away, and no one paid him the slightest attention. "Stop it at once!"

Pascoe was startled, not by Pitt but by the blow, which must have hurt considerably. He stepped back a pace, shouted, "In the name of chivalry!" and swiped sideways with his ancient and very blunt sword, possibly an ill-cared-for relic of Waterloo, or some such battle.

Dalgetty, with a modern sword stick, sharp as a needle, parried the blow so fiercely the neglected metal broke off halfway up and flew in an arc, catching him across the cheek and opening up a scarlet weal which spurted blood down his coat front.

"You antiquated old fool!" he spluttered, startled and extremely angry. "You fossilized bigot! No man stands in the path of progress! A medieval mind like you won't stop one single good idea whose time has come! Think you can imprison the imagination of man in your old-fashioned ideas! Rubbish!" He swung his broken sword high in the air so wildly the singing sound of it was audible to Pitt even above the rasping of his own breath and the thud of his feet. It missed Pascoe by an inch, and clipped a tuft off the top of his silver head and sent it flying like thistledown.

Pitt tore off his coat and threw it over Dalgetty.

"Stop it!" he roared, and caught him across the chest with his shoulder, sending them both to the ground. The broken sword stick went flying bright in the sun to fall, end down, quivering in the ground a dozen yards away.

Pitt picked himself up and disregarded Dalgetty totally. He did not bother to straighten his clothes and dust off the earth and grass. He faced a shaken, weaponless and very startled Pascoe.

By this time Murdo had dealt with the cab driver and run across the field to join them. He stood aghast at the spectacle, helpless to know what do to.

Pitt glared at Pascoe.

"What on earth do you think you're doing?" he demanded at the top of his voice. "Two people are dead already, God knows who did it, or why — and you are out here trying to murder each other over some idiotic monograph that nobody will read anyway! I should charge you both with assault with a deadly weapon!"

Pascoe was deeply affronted. Blood was seeping through the tear across the shoulder of his shirt and he was clearly in some pain.

"You cannot possibly do that!" his voice was high and loud. "It was a gentleman's difference of opinion!" He jerked his hand up wildly. "Dalgetty is a desecrator of values, a man without judgment or discretion. He propagates the vulgar and destructive and what he imagines to be the cause of freedom, but which is actually license, indiscipline and the victory of the ugly and the dangerous." He waved both arms, nearly decapitating Murdo, who had moved closer. "But I do not lay any charge against him. He attacked me with my full permission — so you cannot arrest him." He stopped with some triumph and stared at Pitt out of bright round eyes.

Dalgetty climbed awkwardly to his feet, fighting his way out of Pitt's coat, his cheek streaming blood.

"Neither do I lay charge against Mr. Pascoe," he said, reaching for a handkerchief. "He is a misguided and ignorant old fool who wants to ban any idea that didn't begin in the Middle Ages. He will stop any freedom of ideas, any flight of the imagination, any discovery of anything new whatsoever. He would keep us believing the earth is flat and the sun revolves around it. But I do not charge him with attacking me — we attacked each other. You are merely a bystander who chose to interfere in something which is none of your affair. You owe us an apology, sir!"

Pitt was livid. But he knew that without a complaint he could not make an arrest that would be prosecuted.

"On the contrary," he said with sudden freezing contempt. "You owe me a considerable gratitude that I prevented you from injuring each other seriously, even fatally. If you can scramble your wits together long enough, think what that would have done to your cause — not to mention your lives from now on."

The possibility, which clearly had not occurred to either of them, stopped the next outburst before it began, and when one of the seconds stepped forward nervously, Pitt opened his mouth to round on him for his utter irresponsibility.

But before he could continue on his tirade the other second shouted out and swung around, pointing where across the field from the Highgate direction were rapidly advancing five figures, strung out a dozen yards from each other. The first was obviously, even at that distance, the vigorous, arm-swinging Stephen Shaw, black bag in his hand, coattails flying. Behind him loped the ungainly but surprisingly rapid figure of Hector Clitheridge, and running after him, waving and calling out, his wife, Eulalia. Separated by a slightly longer space was a grim figure with scarf and hat which Pitt guessed to be Josiah Hatch, but he was too distant to distinguish features. And presumably the woman behind him, just breaking into a run, was Prudence.

"Thank God," one of the seconds gasped. "The doctor — "

"And why in God's name didn't you call him before you began, you incompetent ass?" Pitt shouted at him. "If you are going to second in a duel, at least do it properly! It could have meant the difference between a man living or dying!"

The man was stung at last by the injustice of it, and the thoroughgoing fear that Pitt was right.

"Because my principal forbade me," he retaliated, pulling himself up very straight.

"I'll wager he did," Pitt agreed, looking at Dalgetty, now dripping blood freely and very pasty-faced; then at Pascoe holding his arm limply and beginning to shake from cold and shock. "Knew damned well he'd prevent this piece of idiocy!"

As he spoke Shaw came to a halt beside them, staring from one to the other of the two injured men, then at Pitt.

"Is there a crime?" he said briskly. "Is any of this palaver" — he waved his hands, dropping the bag to the ground — "needed for evidence?"

"Not unless they want to sue each other," Pitt said disgustedly. He could not even charge them with disturbing the peace, since they were out in the middle of a field and no one else was even aware of their having left their beds. The rest of Highgate was presumably taking its breakfast quietly in its dining rooms, pouring its tea, reading the morning papers and totally unaffected.

Shaw looked at the two participants and made the instant decision that Dalgetty was in the more urgent need of help, since he seemed to be suffering from shock whereas

Pascoe was merely in pain, and accordingly began his work. He had done no more than open his bag when Clitheridge arrived, acutely distressed and embarrassed.

"What on earth has happened?" he demanded. "Is somebody hurt?"

"Of course somebody's hurt, you fool!" Shaw said furiously. "Here, hold him up." He gestured at Dalgetty, who was covered in blood and was beginning to look as if he might buckle at the knees.

Clitheridge obeyed gladly, his face flooding with relief at some definite task he could turn himself to. He grasped Dalgetty, who rather awkwardly leaned against him.

"What happened?" Clitheridge made one more effort to understand, because it was his spiritual duty. "Has there been an accident?"

Lally had reached them now and her mind seized the situation immediately.

"Oh, how stupid," she said in exasperation. "I never thought you'd be so very childish — and now you've really hurt each other. And does that prove which of you is right? It only proves you are both extremely stubborn. Which all Highgate knew anyway." She swung around to Shaw, her face very slightly flushed. "What can I do to be of assistance, Doctor?" By that time Josiah Hatch had also reached them, but she disregarded him. "Do you need linen?" She peered in his bag, then at the extent of the bloodstains, which were increasing with every minute. "How about water? Brandy?"

"Nobody's going to pass out," he said sharply, glaring at Dalgetty. "For heaven's sake put him down!" he ordered Clitheridge, who was bearing most of Dalgetty's weight now. "Yes, please, Lally — get some more linen. I'd better tie some of this up before we move them. I've got enough alcohol to disinfect."

Prudence Hatch arrived breathlessly, gasping as she came to a halt. "This is awful! What on earth possessed you?" she demanded. "As if we haven't enough grief."

"A man who believes in his principles is sometimes obliged to fight in order to preserve them," Josiah said grimly. "The price of virtue is eternal vigilance."

"That is freedom," his wife corrected him.

"What?" he demanded, his brows drawing down sharply.

"The price of *freedom* is eternal vigilance," she replied. "You said virtue." Without being told she was taking a piece of clean cloth out of Shaw's bag, unfolding it and soaking it in clean spirit from one of his bottles. "Sit down!" she commanded Pascoe smartly, and as soon as he did, she began to clean away

444

the torn outer clothing and then the blood till she could see the ragged tear in the flesh. Then she held the pad of cloth to it and pushed firmly.

He winced and let out a squeak as the spirit hit the open wound, but no one took any notice of him.

"Freedom and virtue are not the same thing at all," Hatch argued with profound feeling, his face intent, his eyes alight. To him the issue obviously far outweighed the ephemeral abrasions of the encounter. "That is precisely what Mr. Pascoe risked his life to defend!"

"Balderdash!" Shaw snapped. "Virtue isn't in any danger — and prancing about on the heath with swords certainly isn't going to defend anything at all."

"There is no legal way to prevent the pernicious views and the dangerous and degrading ideas he propagates," Pascoe shouted across Prudence's instructions, his lips white with pain.

Lally was already setting off again towards the road on her errand. Her upright figure, shoulders back, was well on its way.

"There should be." Hatch shook his head. "It is part of our modern sickness that we admire everything new, regardless of its merit." His voice rose a little and he chopped his hands in the air. "We get hold of any new thought, rush to print any idea that overturns and makes mock of the past, the values that have served our forefathers and upon which we have built our nation and carried the faith of Christ to other lands and peoples." His shoulders were hunched with the intensity of his emotion. "Mr. Pascoe is one of the few men in our time who has the courage and the vision to fight, however futilely, against the tide of man's own intellectual arrogance, his indiscriminate greed for everything new without thought as to its value, or the result of our espousing it."

"This is not the place for a sermon, Josiah." Shaw was busy working on Dalgetty's cheek and did not even look up at him. Murdo was assisting him with considerable competence. "Especially the arrant rubbish you're talking," he went on. "Half these old ideas you're rehearsing are fossilized walls of cant and hypocrisy protecting a lot of rogues from the light of day. It's long past time a few questions were asked and a few shoddy pretenses shown for what they are."

Hatch was so pale he might have been the one wounded. He looked at Shaw's back with a loathing so intense it was unnerving that Shaw was oblivious of it.

"You would have every beautiful and virtuous thing stripped naked and paraded for the lewd and the ignorant to soil — and yet at the same time you would not protect the innocent from the mockery and the godless innovations of those who have no values, but constant titillation and endless lust of the mind. You are a destroyer, Stephen, a man whose eyes see only the futile and whose hand holds only the worthless."

Shaw's fingers stopped, the swab motionless, a white blob half soaked with scarlet. Dalgetty was still shaking. Maude Dalgetty had appeared from somewhere while no one was watching the path across the field.

Shaw faced Hatch. There was dangerous temper in every line of his face and the energy built up in the muscles of his body till he seemed ready to break into some violent motion.

"It would give me great pleasure," he said almost between his teeth, "to meet you here myself, tomorrow at dawn, and knock you senseless. But I don't settle my arguments that way. It decides nothing. I shall show you what a fool you are by stripping away the layers of pretense, the lies and the illusions — "

Pitt was aware of Prudence, frozen, her face ashen pale, her eyes fixed on Shaw's lips as if he were about to pronounce the name of some mortal illness whose diagnosis she had long dreaded.

447

Maude Dalgetty, on the other hand, looked only a little impatient. There was no fear in her at all. And John Dalgetty, half lying on the ground, looked aware only of his own pain and the predicament he had got himself into. He looked at his wife with a definite anxiety, but it was obvious he was nervous of her anger, not for her safety or for Shaw in temper ruining her long-woven reputation.

Pitt had seen all he needed. Dalgetty had no fear of Shaw — Prudence was terrified.

"The whited sepulchers — " Shaw said viciously, two spots of color high on his cheeks. "The — "

"This is not the time," Pitt interrupted, putting himself physically between them. "There's more than enough blood spilled already — and enough pain. Doctor, get on with treating your patients. Mr. Hatch, perhaps you would be good enough to go back to the street and fetch some conveyance so we can carry Mr. Pascoe and Mr. Dalgetty back to their respective homes. If you want to pursue the quarrel on the merits or necessities for censorship, then do it at a more fortunate time — and in a more civilized manner."

For a moment he thought neither of them was going to take any notice of him. They stood glaring at each other with the violence of feeling as ugly as that between Pascoe and

Dalgetty. Then slowly Shaw relaxed, and as if Hatch had suddenly ceased to be of any importance, turned his back on him and bent down to Dalgetty's wound again.

Hatch, his face like gray granite, his eyes blazing, swiveled on his heel, tearing up the grass, and marched along the footpath back towards the road.

Maude Dalgetty went, not to her husband, with whom she was obviously out of patience, but to Prudence Hatch, and gently put her arm around her.

CHAPTER TEN

"I suppose we should have expected it — had we bothered to take the matter seriously at all," Aunt Vespasia said when Charlotte told her about the duel in the field. "One might have hoped they would have more sense, but had they any proportion in things in the first place, they would not have become involved in such extremes of opinion. Some men lose track of reality so easily."

"Thomas said they were both injured," Charlotte went on. "Quite unpleasantly. I knew they said a great deal about the subject of freedom of expression, and the need to censor certain ideas in the public interest, but I did not expect it to come to actual physical harm. Thomas was very angry indeed — it all seems so farcical, in the face of real tragedy."

Vespasia sat very upright and her concentration seemed to be entirely inward, as if she did not see the graciousness of the room around her, or the gentle movement of the bronzing beech leaves outside the window, dappling the light.

450

"Failure, disillusion and love rejected can all make us behave in ways that seem absurd, my dear — perhaps loneliness most of all. It does not lessen the pain in the slightest, even if you are one who is able to laugh while you weep. I have thought at times that laughter is man's greatest salvation — and at other times that it is what damns him beneath the animals. Beasts may kill one another, they may ignore the sick or distressed — but they never mock. Blasphemy is a peculiarly human ability."

Charlotte was confused for a moment. Vespasia had taken the thought much further than anything she had intended. Perhaps she had overdramatized the scene.

"The whole quarrel was about the rights of censorship," she said, starting to explain herself. "That wretched monograph of Amos Lindsay's, which is academic now, since the poor man is dead anyway."

Vespasia stood up and walked over towards the window.

"I thought it was the question as to whether some men have the right to make mock of other men's gods, because they believe them to be either vicious or absurd — or simply irrelevant."

"One has the right to question them," Charlotte said with irritation. "One must, or there will be no progress of ideas, no reforming. The most senseless ideologies could be taught, and if we cannot challenge them, how are we to know whether they are good or evil? How can we test our ideas except by thinking — and talking?"

"We cannot," Vespasia replied. "But there are many ways of doing it. And we must take responsibility for what we destroy, as well as for what we create. Now tell me, what was it Thomas said about Prudence Hatch being so mesmerized with fright? Did she imagine Shaw was going to let slip some appalling secret?"

"That is what Thomas thought — but he has never persuaded Shaw to tell him anything at all that would indicate any secret he knows worth killing to hide."

Vespasia turned to face Charlotte.

"You have met the man — is he a fool?"

Charlotte thought for several seconds, visualizing Shaw's dynamic face with its quick, clear eyes, the power in him, the vitality that almost overflowed.

"He's extremely intelligent," she replied frankly.

"I daresay," Vespasia agreed dryly. "That is not the same thing. Many people have high intelligence and no wisdom at all. You have not answered me."

Charlotte smiled very slightly. "No, Aunt Vespasia, I am not sure that I can. I don't think I know."

"Then perhaps you had better find out." Vespasia arched her brows very gently but her eyes were unwavering.

Very reluctantly Charlotte rose to her feet, a quiver of excitement inside her, and a very real sense of fear which was getting larger with every moment. This time she could not hide behind a play of innocence as she had done so often in the past when meddling in Pitt's cases. Nor would she go with some slight disguise as she had often done, the pretense of being some gentlewoman of no account, up from the country, and insinuate herself into a situation, then observe. Shaw clearly knew exactly who she was and the precise nature of her interest. To try to deceive him would be ridiculous and demean them both.

She must go, if she went at all, quite openly as herself, frank about her reasons, asking questions without opportunity of camouflage or retreat. How could she possibly behave in such a way that it would be anything but intrusive and impertinent — and hideously insensitive?

It was on the edge of her tongue to make an excuse, simply say all that was in her mind; then she saw Vespasia's slender shoulders stiff as a general commanding a charge to battle, and her eyes as steady as a governess controlling a nursery. Insubordination was not even to be considered. Vespasia had already understood all her arguments, and would accept none of them.

" 'England expects that every man will do his duty,' " Charlotte said with a ghost of a smile.

A spark of laughter lit Vespasia's eyes.

"Quite," she agreed relentlessly. "You may take my carriage."

"Thank you, Aunt Vespasia."

Charlotte arrived at the lodging house where Shaw was temporarily resident exactly as the landlady was serving luncheon. This was ill-mannered in the extreme, but most practical. It was probably the only time when she could have found him present and not either in the act of repacking his bag to leave again or trying to catch up with his notes and messages.

He was obviously surprised to see her, when the landlady showed her in, but the expression on his face showed far more pleasure than irritation. If he minded being interrupted in his meal he hid it with great skill.

"Mrs. Pitt. How very agreeable to see you." He rose, setting his napkin aside, and came around to greet her, holding out his hand and taking hers in a strong, warm grip.

"I apologize for calling at such an inconvenient time." She was embarrassed already, and she had not yet even begun. "Please do not allow me to spoil your luncheon." It was a fatuous remark. She had already done so by her mere presence. Whatever she said, he would not allow her to wait in the parlor while he ate in the dining room, and even if he were to, it could hardly be a comfortable repast in such circumstances. She felt her face coloring with awareness of the clumsy way she had begun. How could she possibly ask him all the intimate and personal questions she wished? Whether she ever learned if he was a fool — in Aunt Vespasia's terms of reference — she herself most certainly was.

"Have you eaten?" he asked, still holding her hand.

She seized the opportunity he offered.

"No — no, I have somehow mislaid time this morning, and it is much later than I had realized." It was a lie, but a very convenient one.

"Then Mrs. Turner will fetch you something, if you care to join me." He indicated the table set for one. Whatever other lodgers there were resident, they appeared to take their midday meal elsewhere.

"I would not dream of inconveniencing Mrs.

Turner." She had only one answer open to her. She cooked herself; she knew perfectly well any woman with the slightest economy in mind did not prepare more than she knew would be required. "She cannot have been expecting me. But I should be most happy to take a cup of tea, and perhaps a few slices of bread and butter — if she would be so good. I had a late breakfast, and do not wish for a full meal." That was not true either, but it would serve. She had eaten a considerable number of tomato sandwiches at Aunt Vespasia's.

He swung his arms wide in an expansive gesture and walked over to the bell, pulling it sharply.

"Excellent," he agreed, smiling because he knew as well as she did that they were reaching a compromise of courtesy and truth. "Mrs. Turner!" His voice rang through the room and must have been clearly audible to her long before she had even entered the hall, let alone the dining room.

"Yes, Dr. Shaw?" she said patiently as she opened the door.

"Ah! Mrs. Turner, can you bring a pot of tea for Mrs. Pitt — and perhaps a few slices of bread and butter. She is not in need of luncheon, but some slight refreshment would be most welcome."

Mrs. Turner shook her head in a mixture of doubt and acceptance, glanced once at Charlotte, then hurried away to do as she was requested.

"Sit down, sit down," Shaw offered, drawing out a chair for her and holding it while she made herself comfortable.

"Please continue with your meal." She meant it as more than good manners. She knew he worked hard, and hated to think of him obliged to eat his boiled mutton, potatoes, vegetables and caper sauce cold.

He returned to his own seat and began to eat again with considerable appetite.

"What can I do for you, Mrs. Pitt?" It was a simple question and no more than courtesy dictated. Yet meeting his eyes across the polished wood set with dried flowers, a silver cruet stand and assorted handmade doilies, she knew any evasion would meet his immediate knowledge, and contempt.

She did not want to make a fool of herself in his estimation. She was surprised how painful the idea was. And yet she must say something quickly. He was watching her and waiting. His expression had a remarkable warmth; he was not seeking to find the slightest fault with her, and her sudden realization of that only made it worse. Old memories of other men who had admired her, more than

457

admired, came back with a peculiar sharpness, and a sense of guilt which she had thought forgotten.

She found herself telling the truth because it was the only thing that was tolerable.

"I followed Mrs. Shaw's work," she said slowly. "I began with the parish council, where I learned very little."

"You would," he agreed, his eyes puzzled. "She started from my patients. There was one in particular who did not get better, regardless of my treatment of her. Clemency was concerned, and when she visited her she began to realize it was the condition of the house, the damp, the cold, the lack of clean water and any sanitation. She never would recover as long as she lived there. I could have told her that, but I didn't because I knew there was nothing that could be done to better it, and it would only cause her distress. Clem felt people's misery very much. She was a remarkable woman."

"Yes I know," Charlotte said quickly. "I went to those same houses — and I asked the same questions she had. I have learned why they didn't complain to the landlord — and what happened to those who did."

Mrs. Turner knocked briskly on the door, opened it and brought in a tray with teapot, cup and saucer and a plate of thin bread and butter. She put it down on the table, was thanked, and departed.

Charlotte poured herself a cup of tea, and Shaw resumed his meal.

"They got evicted and had to seek accommodation even less clean or warm," Charlotte continued. "I followed them down the scale from one slum to another, until I saw what I think may be the worst there is, short of sleeping in doorways and gutters. I was going to say I don't know how people survive — but of course they don't. The weak die."

He said nothing, but she knew from his face that he understood it even better than she did, and felt the same helplessness, the anger that it should be, the desire to lash out at someone — preferably the clean and comfortable who chose to laugh and look the other way — and the same pity that haunted both of them whenever the eyes closed and the mind relaxed vigilance, when the hollow faces came back, dull with hunger and dirt and weariness.

"I followed her all the way to one particular street she went where the houses were so crammed with people old and young, men and women, children and even babies, all together without privacy or sanitation, twenty or thirty in a room." She ate a piece of bread and butter because it had been provided — memory robbed her of appetite. "Along the corridor and up the stairs was a brothel. Down two doors was a gin mill with drunken women rolling about on the steps and in the gutter. In the basement was a sweatshop where women worked eighteen hours a day without daylight or air — " She stopped, but again she saw in his eyes that he knew these places; if not this particular one, then a dozen others like it.

"I discovered how hard it is to find out who owns such buildings," she continued. "They are hidden by rent collectors, companies, managers, lawyers' offices, and more companies. At the very end there are powerful people. I was warned that I would make enemies, people who could make life most unpleasant for me, if I persisted in trying to embarrass them."

He smiled bleakly, but still did not interrupt. She knew without question that he believed her. Perhaps Clemency had shared the same discoveries and the same feelings with him.

"Did they threaten her also?" she asked. "Do you know how close she came to learning names of people who might have been afraid she would make their ownership public?"

He had stopped eating altogether, and now he looked down at his plate, his face shadowed, a painful mixture of emotions conflicting within him.

"You think it was Clem they meant to kill in the fire, don't you?"

"I did," she admitted, and saw him stiffen. His eyes lifted instantly and met hers, searching, startled. "Now I'm not sure," she finished. "Why should anyone wish to kill you? And please don't give me an evasive answer. This is too serious to play games with words. Clemency and Amos Lindsay are dead already. Are you sure there will be no more? What about Mrs. Turner and Mr. Oliphant?"

He winced as if she had struck him, and the pain in his eyes was dark, the tightening of his lips undisguised. The knife and fork slid from his hands.

"Do you imagine I haven't thought? I've been through every case I have treated in the last five years. There isn't a single one that it would be even sane to suspect of murder, let alone anything one would pursue."

There was no point in turning back now, even though no doubt Thomas had already asked exactly the same questions.

"Every death?" she said quietly. "Are you sure absolutely every death was natural? Couldn't one of them, somewhere, be murder?"

A half-unbelieving smile curled the corners of his lips.

"And you think whoever did it may fear

461

I knew — or may come to realize that — and is trying to kill me to keep me silent?" He was not accepting the idea, simply turning over the possibility of it and finding it hard to fit into the medicine he knew, the ordinary domestic release or tragedy of death.

"Couldn't it be so?" she asked, trying to keep the urgency out of her voice. "Aren't there any deaths which could have been profitable to someone?"

He said nothing, and she knew he was remembering, and each one had its own pain. Each patient who had died had been some kind of failure for him, small or great, inevitable or shocking.

A new thought occurred to her. "Perhaps it was an accident and they covered it up, and they are afraid you realized the truth, and then they became afraid you would suspect them of having done it intentionally."

"You have a melodramatic idea of death, Mrs. Pitt," he said softly. "Usually it is simple: a fever that does not break but exhausts the body and burns it out; or a hacking cough that ends in hemorrhage and greater and greater weakness until there is no strength left. Sometimes it is a child, or a young person, perhaps a woman worn down by work and too many childbirths, or a man who has labored in the cold and the wet till his lungs are wasted. Sometimes it's a fat man with apoplexy, or a baby that was never strong enough to live. Surprisingly often in the very end it is peaceful."

She looked at his face, the memories so plain in his eyes, the grief not for the dead but for the confusion, anger and pain of those left behind; his inability to help them, even to touch the loneliness of that sudden, awful void when the soul of someone you love leaves the shell and gradually even the echo of life goes and it becomes only clay in the form of a person but without the substance — like a cold hearth when the fire is gone.

"But not always," she said with regret, hating to have to pursue it. "Some people fight all the way, and some relatives don't accept. Might there not be someone who felt you did not do all you could? Perhaps not from malice, simply neglect, or ignorance?" She said it with a small, sad smile, and so gently he could not think that she believed it herself.

A pucker formed between his brows and he met her eyes with a mild amusement.

"No one has ever showed anything beyond a natural distress. People are often angry, if death is unexpected; angry because fate has robbed them and they have to have something to blame, but it passes; and to be honest no one has suggested I could have done more."

"No one?" She looked at him very carefully, but there was no evasion in his eyes, no faint color of deceit in his cheeks. "Not even the Misses Worlingham — over Theophilus's death?"

"Oh — " He let out his breath in a sigh. "But that is just their way. They are among those who find it hard to accept that someone as . . . as full of opinion and as sound as Theophilus could die. He was always so much in evidence. If there was any subject under discussion, Theophilus would express his views, with lots of words and with great certainty that he was right."

"And of course Angeline and Celeste agreed with him — " she prompted.

He laughed sharply. "Of course. Unless he was out of sympathy with his father. The late bishop's opinions took precedence over everyone else's."

"And did they disagree overmuch?"

"Very little. Only things of no importance, like tastes and pastimes — whether to collect books or paintings; whether to wear brown or gray; whether to serve claret or burgundy, mutton or pork, fish or game; whether chinoiserie was good taste — or bad. Nothing that mattered. They were in perfect accord on moral duties, the place and virtue of women, and the manner in which society should be governed, and by whom."

"I don't think I should have cared for Theophilus much," she said without thinking first and recalling that he had been Shaw's father-in-law. The description of him sounded so much like Uncle Eustace March, and her memories of him were touched with conflicting emotions, all of them shades of dislike.

He smiled at her broadly, for a moment all thought of death banished, and nothing there but his intense pleasure in her company.

"You would have loathed him," he assured her. "I did."

An element in her wanted to laugh, to see only the easy and absurd in it; but she could not forget the virulence in Celeste's face as she had spoken of her brother's death, and the way Angeline had echoed it with equal sincerity.

"What did he die of, and why was it so sudden?"

"A seizure of the brain," he replied, this time looking up and meeting her eyes with complete candor. "He suffered occasional severe headaches, great heat of the blood, dizziness and once or twice apoplectic fits. And of course now and again gout. A week before he died he had a spasm of temporary blindness. It only lasted a day, but it frightened him profoundly. I think he looked on it as a presage of death — "

"He was right." She bit her lip, trying to find the words to ask without implying blame. It was difficult. "Did you know that at the time?"

"I thought it was possible. I didn't expect it so soon. Why?"

"Could you have prevented it — if you had been sure?"

"No. No doctor knows how to prevent a seizure of the brain. Of course not all seizures are fatal. Very often a patient loses the use of one side of his body — or perhaps his speech, or his sight — but will live on for years. Some people have several seizures before the one that kills them. Some lie paralyzed and unable to speak for years — but as far as one can tell, perfectly conscious and aware of what is going on around them."

"How terrible — like death, but without its peace." She shivered. "Could that have happened to Theophilus?"

"It could. But he went with the first seizure. Perhaps that was not so unlucky."

"Did you tell Angeline and Celeste that?"

His brows rose in slight surprise, perhaps at his own omission.

"No — no, I didn't." He pulled a face. "I suppose it is a trifle late now. They would think I was making excuses."

"Yes," she agreed. "They blame you — but how bitterly I don't know."

"For heaven's sake!" He exploded, amazement filling his eyes. "You don't imagine Angeline and Celeste crept around in the dark and set fire to my house hoping to burn me to death because they think I could have saved Theophilus? That's preposterous!"

"Someone did."

The hilarity vanished and left only the hurt.

"I know — but not over Theophilus."

"Are you absolutely positive? Is it not possible that his death was murder — and someone is afraid you may realize it, and then know who killed him? After all, the circumstances were extraordinary."

He looked at her with disbelief which was almost comic, his eyes wide, his mouth open. Then gradually the thought became less absurd and he realized the darkness of it. He picked up his knife and fork again and began to eat automatically, thinking.

"No," he said at last. "If it was murder, which I don't believe, then it was perfect. I never suspected a thing — and I still don't. And who would want to kill him anyway? He was insufferable, but then so are a lot of people. And neither Prudence nor Clemency wanted his money."

"Are you sure?" she said gently.

His hand came up; he stopped eating and smiled at her with sudden charm, a light of sheer pleasure in his eyes.

"Certainly. Clemency was giving her money away as fast as she could — and Prudence has quite sufficient from her books."

"Books?" Charlotte was totally confused. "What books?"

"Well, *Lady Pamela's Secret* for one," he said, now grinning broadly. "She writes romances — oh, under another name, of course. But she is really very successful. Josiah would have apoplexy if he knew. So would Celeste — for utterly different reasons."

"Are you sure?" Charlotte was delighted, and incredulous.

"Of course I'm sure. Clemency managed the business for her — to keep it out of Josiah's knowledge. I suppose I shall have to now."

"Good gracious." She wanted to giggle, it was all so richly absurd, but there was too much else pressing in on both of them.

"All right." She sobered herself with an effort. "If it was not over Theophilus, either personally or his money, over what then?"

"I don't know. I've racked my brain, gone over and over everything I can think of, real or imaginary, that could cause anyone to hate or fear me enough to take the awful step of murder. Even the risk — " He stopped

468

and a shred of the old irony came back. "Not that it has proved to be much of a risk. The police don't seem to have any more idea who it was now than they did the first night."

She defended Pitt in a moment of instinct, and then regretted it.

"You mean they have not told you of anything? That does not mean they don't know — "

His head jerked up, his eyes wide.

"Nor have they told me," she said quickly.

But he had understood the difference.

"Of course. I was too hasty. They seem so candid, but then they would hardly tell me. I must be one of their chief suspects — which is absurd to me, but I suppose quite reasonable to them."

There was nothing else for her to say to him, no other questions she could think of to ask. And yet she could not answer Aunt Vespasia's question yet. Was he a fool, in her sense — blind to some emotional value that any woman would have seen?

"Thank you for sparing me so much time, Dr. Shaw." She rose from the table. "I realize my questions are impertinent." She smiled in apology and saw the quick response in his face. "I asked them only because having followed Clemency's path I have such a respect for her that I care very much that whoever killed her should be found — and I intend to see that her work is continued. My brother-in-law is actually considering standing for Parliament — he and my sister were so moved by what they learned, I think they will not rest until they are engaged in doing what they can to have such a law passed as she suggested."

He stood also, as a matter of courtesy, and came around to pull her chair back so she might move the more easily.

"You are wasting your time, Mrs. Pitt," he said very quietly. It was not in the tone of a criticism, but rather of regret, as if he had said exactly the same words before, for the same reasons — and not been believed then either. It was as if Clemency were in the room with them, a benign ghost whom they both liked. There was no sense of intrusion, simply a treasured presence who did not resent their moments of friendship, not even the warmth in the touch of his hand on Charlotte's arm, his closeness to her as he bade her good-bye, nor the quick, soft brightness of his eyes as he watched her departing figure down the front steps and up into the carriage, helped by Vespasia's footman. He remained in the hallway, straight-backed, long after the carriage had turned the corner before eventually he closed the door and returned to the dining room.

★ ★ ★

Charlotte had instructed the coachman to drive to the Worlingham house. It did sound unlikely that either Celeste or Angeline would have attempted to kill Shaw, however derelict they believed him to have been in the matter of Theophilus's death. And yet Clemency, and thus Shaw, had inherited a great deal of money because of it. It was a motive which could not be disregarded. And the more she thought of it, the more did it seem the only sensible alternative if it were not some powerful owner of tenements who feared the exposure she might bring. Was that realistic? Who else's name had she uncovered, apart from her own grandfather's?

In the search surely she must have found others, if not before Worlingham's, then afterwards? That had been the beginning of her total commitment to change the law, which would mean highly unwelcome attention to quite a number of people. Somerset Carlisle had mentioned aristocratic families, bankers, judges, diplomats, men in public life who could ill afford such a source of income to be common knowledge. And the lawyer with the smug face had been so sure his clients would exercise violence of their own sort to keep themselves anonymous he had been prepared to use threats.

But who had gone so far out of the ordinary social or financial avenues of power as to commit murder? Was there any way whatsoever they could learn? Visions floated into her mind of searching the figures of the criminal world for the arsonist, and trying to force him to confess his employer. It would be hopeless, but for a wild element of luck.

How would they ever know? Had Clemency been rash enough to confront him? Surely not. What would be the purpose?

And she had not exposed the Worlinghams, that much was certain. They could hardly be building the magnificent memorial window to him, and having the Archbishop of York dedicate it, were there the slightest breath of scandal around his name.

Had Theophilus known? Certainly Clemency had not told him because he had died long before she came anywhere near her conclusion, in fact before she became closely involved in the matter at all. Had he ever questioned where the family money came from, or had he simply been happy to accept its lavish bounty, smile, and leave everything well covered?

And Angeline and Celeste?

The carriage was already drawing up at the magnificent entrance. In a moment the footman would be opening the door and she would climb out and ascend the steps. She would have to have some excuse for calling. It was early; it would be unlikely for anyone else to be there. She was hardly a friend, merely the granddaughter of a past acquaintance, and an unfortunate reminder of murder and the police, and other such terrible secret evils.

The front door swung wide and the parlormaid looked at her with polite and chilly inquiry.

Charlotte did not even have a card to present!

She smiled charmingly.

"Good afternoon. I am continuing some of the work of the late Mrs. Shaw, and I should so much like to tell the Misses Worlingham how much I admired her. Are they receiving this afternoon?"

The parlormaid was too well trained to turn away someone who might present an oasis of interest in two extremely monotonous lives. The Misses Worlingham hardly ever went out, except to church. What they saw of the world was what came to their door.

Since there was no card, the parlormaid put down the silver card tray on the hall table and stepped back to allow Charlotte inside.

"If you would care to wait, ma'am, I shall inquire. Who shall I say is calling?"

"Mrs. Pitt. The Misses Worlingham are

acquainted with my grandmother, Mrs. Ellison. We are all admirers of the family." That was stretching the truth a great deal — the only one Charlotte admired in the slightest was Clemency — but that was indeed enough if spread fine to cover them all.

She was shown into the hall, with its marvelous tessellated floor and its dominating picture of the bishop, his pink face supremely confident, beaming with almost luminous satisfaction down at all who crossed his threshold. The other portraits receded into obscurity, acolytes, a congregation, not principals. Pity there was no portrait of Theophilus; she would like to have seen his face, made some judgment of him, the mouth, the eyes, seen some link between the bishop and his daughters. She imagined him as utterly unlike Shaw as possible, two men unintelligible to each other by the very cast of their natures.

The parlormaid returned and told Charlotte that she would be received — a shade coolly, from her demeanor.

Angeline and Celeste were in the withdrawing room in very much the same postures as they had been when she had called with Caroline and Grandmama. They were wearing afternoon gowns in black similar to the ones they had worn then, good quality, a little strained at the seams, decorated with beads and, in Angeline's case, black feathers also, very discreetly. Celeste wore jet earrings and a necklace, very long, dangling over her rather handsome bosom and winking in the light, its facets turning as she breathed.

"Good afternoon, Mrs. Pitt," she said with a formal nod of her head. "It is kind of you to come to tell us how much you admired poor Clemency. But I thought you expressed yourself very fully on the subject when you were here before. And I may remind you, you were under some misapprehension as to her work for the less fortunate."

"I am sure it was a mistake, dear," Angeline put in hastily. "Mrs Pitt will not have meant to distress us or cause anxiety." She smiled at Charlotte. "Will you?"

"There is nothing I have learned of Mrs. Shaw which could make you anything but profoundly proud of her," Charlotte replied, looking very levelly at Angeline and watching her face for the slightest flicker of knowledge.

"Learned?" Angeline was confused, but that was the only emotion Charlotte could identify in her bland features.

"Oh yes," she answered, accepting the seat which was only half offered, and sitting herself down comfortably well in the back of the lush, tasseled and brocaded cushions. She had no intention of leaving until she had said all she

475

could think of and watched their reactions minutely. This house had been bought and furnished with agony. The old bishop had known it; had Theophilus? And far more recently and more to the point, had these two innocent-looking sisters? Was it conceivable Clemency had come home in her desperate distress when she first learned beyond doubt where her inheritance had been made, and faced them with it? And if she had, what would they have done?

Perhaps fire, secretly and in the night, burning to its terrible conclusion, when they were safely back in their own beds, was just the weapon they might choose. It was horrible to think of, close, like suffocation, and terrifying as the change from mildness to hatred in a face you have known all your life.

Had these women, who had given the whole of their lives, wasted their youth and their mature womanhood pandering to their father, killed to protect that same reputation — and their own comfort in a community they had led for over half a century? It was not inconceivable.

"I heard so well of her from other people," Charlotte went on, her voice sounding gushing in her ears, artificial and a little too highly pitched. Was she foolish to have come here alone? No — that was stupid. It was the middle of the day, and Aunt Vespasia's coachman and footman were outside.

But did they know that?

Yes of course they did. They would hardly imagine she had walked here.

But she might have come on the public omnibus. She frequently traveled on it.

"Which other people?" Celeste said with raised eyebrows. "I hardly thought poor Clemency was known outside the parish."

"Oh indeed she was." Charlotte swallowed the lump in her throat and tried to sound normal. Her hands were shaking, so she clasped them together, digging her nails into her palms. "Mr. Somerset Carlisle spoke of her in the highest terms possible — he is a noted member of Parliament, you know. And Lady Vespasia Cumming-Gould also. In fact I was speaking to her only this morning, telling her I should call upon you this afternoon, and she lent me her carriage, for my convenience. She is determined that Mrs. Shaw shall not be forgotten, nor her work perish." She saw Celeste's heavy face darken. "And of course there are others," she plowed on. "But she was so discreet, perhaps she was too modest to tell you much herself?"

"She told us nothing," Celeste replied. "Because I believe, Mrs. Pitt, that there was nothing to tell. Clemency did the sort of kindnesses among the poor that all the women of our family have always done." She lifted her chin a fraction and her tone became more condescending. "We were raised in a very Christian household, as I daresay you are aware. We were taught as children to care for those less fortunate, whether through their own indigence or not. Our father told us not to judge, merely to serve."

Charlotte found it hard to hold her tongue. She ached to tell them precisely what she thought of the bishop's charity.

"Modesty is one of the most attractive of all the virtues," she said aloud, gritting her teeth. "It seems that she said nothing to you of her work to have the laws changed with regard to the ownership of the very worst of slum properties."

There was nothing at all in either of their faces that looked like even comprehension, let alone fear.

"Slum properities?" Angeline was utterly confused.

"The ownership of them," Charlotte continued, her voice sounding dry and very forced. "At present it is almost impossible to discern who is the true owner."

"Why should anyone wish to know?" Angeline asked. "It seems an extraordinary and purposeless piece of knowledge."

"Because the conditions are appalling."

Charlotte murmured her answer and tried to make it as gentle as was appropriate to two elderly women who knew nothing of the world beyond their house, the church and a few of the people in the parish. It would be grossly unfair now to blame them for an ignorance of which it was far too late for them to remedy. The whole pattern of their lives, which had been set for them by others, had never been questioned or disturbed.

"Of course we know that the poor suffer," Angeline said with a frown. "But that has always been so, and is surely inevitable. That is the purpose of charity — to relieve suffering as much as we can."

"A good deal of it could be prevented, if other people did not exercise their greed at the expense of the poor." Charlotte sought for words they would understand to explain the devastating poverty she had seen. She looked at the total lack of comprehension on their faces. "When people are poor already, they are much more prone to illness, which makes them unable to work, and they become poorer still. The are evicted from decent housing and have to seek whatever they can get." She was simplifying drastically, but a long explanation of circumstances they had never imagined would only lose their emotion. "Landlords know their plight and offer them room without light or air, without running water or any sanitary facilities — "

"Then why do they take them?" Angeline opened her eyes wide in inquiry. "Perhaps they do not want such things, as we would?"

"They want the best they can get," Charlotte said simply. "And very often that is merely a place where they can shelter and lie down — and perhaps, if they are lucky, share a stove with others so they can cook."

"That doesn't sound too bad," Celeste replied. "If that is all they can afford."

Charlotte put forward the one fact she knew would reach the bishop's daughters.

"Men, women and children all in the same room?" She stared straight into Celeste's strong, clever face. "With no lavatory but a bucket in the corner — for all of them — and nowhere to change clothes in privacy, or to wash — and no way of sleeping alone?"

Charlotte saw all the horror she could have wished.

"Oh, my dear! You don't mean that?" Angeline was shocked. "That is — quite uncivilized . . . and certainly unchristian!"

"Of course it is," Charlotte agreed. "But they have no alternative, except the street, which would be even worse."

Celeste looked distressed. It was not beyond her imagination to think of such conditions and feel at least a shadow of their wretchedness, but she was still at a loss to see what purpose could be served by making the owners known.

"The owners cannot make more space," she said slowly. "Nor solve the problems of poverty. Why should you wish to discover who they are?"

"Because the owners are making a very large profit indeed," Charlotte replied. "And if their names were public, they might be shamed into maintaining the buildings so they are at least clean and dry, instead of having mold on the walls and timbers rotting."

It was beyond the experience of either Celeste or Angeline. They had spent all their lives in this gracious house with every comfort that money and status could supply. They had never seen rot, never smelled it, had no conception of a running gutter or open sewerage.

Charlotte drew breath to try to depict it in words, and was prevented from beginning by the parlormaid returning to announce the arrival of Prudence Hatch and Mrs. Clitheridge.

They came in together, Prudence looking a little strained and unable to stand or to sit with any repose. Lally Clitheridge was charming to Celeste, full of smiles to Angeline; and then when she turned to where Charlotte had risen to her feet, recognizing her before introductions were made, her face froze and she became icily polite, her eyes hard and a brittle timbre to her voice.

"Good afternoon, Mrs. Pitt. How surprising to see you here again so soon. I had not thought you such a personal friend."

Celeste invited them to be seated, and they all obeyed, rearranging skirts.

"She came to express her admiration for Clemency," Angeline said with a slight nervous cough. "It seems Clemency really did look into the question of people making extreme profits out of the wretchedness of some of the poor. We really had no idea. She was so very modest about it."

"Indeed?" Lally raised her eyebrows and looked at Charlotte with frank disbelief. "I had not realized you were acquainted with Clemency at all — let alone to the degree where you know more of her than her family."

Charlotte was stung by the manner more than the words. Lally Clitheridge was regarding her with the air one might show a rival who had tricked one out of a deserved advantage.

"I did not know her, Mrs. Clitheridge. But I know those who did. And why she chose to share her concern with them and not with her family and neighbors I am unaware — but possibly it was because they were almost as concerned as she and they understood and respected her feelings."

"Good gracious." Lally's voice rose in amazement and offense. "Your intrusion knows no bounds. Now you suggest she did not trust her own family — but chose instead these friends of yours, whom you have been careful not to name."

"Really, Lally," Prudence said gently, knotting her hands together in her lap. "You are distressing yourself unnecessarily. You have allowed Flora Lutterworth to upset you too much." She glanced at Charlotte. "We have had a rather distasteful encounter, and I am afraid hasty words were said. That young woman's behavior is quite shameless where poor Stephen is concerned. She is obsessed with him, and does not seem able to comport herself with any restraint at all — even now."

"Oh dear — that again." Angeline sighed and shook her head. "Well of course she has no breeding, poor soul, what can you expect? And raised virtually without a mother. I dare say there is no one to instruct her how to behave. Her father is in trade, after all and he's from the north; you could hardly expect him to have the least idea."

"No amount of money in the world makes up for lack of breeding," Celeste agreed. "But people will insist upon trying."

"Exactly," Charlotte said with a voice that cut like acid. "People with breeding can lie, cheat, steal or sell their daughters to obtain money, but people who only have money can never acquire breeding, no matter what they do."

There was a silence that was like thunder, prickling the air and touching the skin in a cold sweat.

Charlotte looked at their faces one by one. She was quite sure, although there was no proof whatever, that neither Celeste nor Angeline had even the shadow of an idea where their family money came from. Nor did she believe that money was at the root of Prudence's fear. She looked aghast now, but not for herself; her hands were quite still, even loose in her lap. She was staring at Charlotte in total incomprehension, for her devastating rudeness, not because she was afraid of her.

Lally Clitheridge was dumbfounded.

"I thought Stephen Shaw was the rudest person I had ever met," she said with a tremor in her voice. "But you leave him standing. You are totally extraordinary."

There was only one possible thing to say.

"Thank you." Charlotte did not flinch in the slightest. "Next time I see him I shall tell him of your words. I am sure he will be most comforted."

Lally's face tightened, almost as if she had been struck — and quite suddenly and ridiculously Charlotte realized the root of her enmity. She was intensely jealous. She might regard Shaw as verbally reckless, full of dangerous and unwelcome ideas, but she was also fascinated by him, drawn from her pedestrian and dutiful life with the vicar towards something that promised excitement, danger, and a vitality and confidence that must be like elixir in the desert of her days.

Now the whole charade not only made Charlotte angry but stirred her to pity for its futility and the pointless courage of Lally's crusade to make Clitheridge into something he was not, to do his duty when he was swamped by it, constantly to push him, support him, tell him what to say. And for her daydreams of a man so much more alive, the vigor that horrified and enchanted her, and the hatred she felt for Charlotte because Shaw was drawn to her, as easily and hopelessly as Lally was to Shaw.

It was all so futile.

And yet she could hardly take the words back, that would only make it worse by allowing everyone to see that she understood. The only possible thing now was to leave. Accordingly she rose to her feet.

"Thank you, Miss Worlingham, for permitting me to express my admiration for Clemency's work, and to assure you that despite any dangers, or any threats that may be made, I will continue with every effort at my command. It did not die with her, nor will it ever. Miss Angeline." She withdrew her hand, clutched her reticule a trifle more closely, and turned to leave.

"What do you mean, Mrs. Pitt?" Prudence stood up and came forward. "Are you saying that you believe Clemency was murdered by someone who — who objected to this work you say she was doing?"

"It seems very likely, Mrs. Hatch."

"Stuff and nonsense," Celeste said sharply. "Or are you suggesting that Amos Lindsay was involved in it as well?"

"Not so far as I know — " Charlotte began, and was cut off instantly.

"Of course not," Celeste agreed, rising to her feet also. Her skirt was puckered but she was unaware of it in her annoyance. "Mr. Lindsay was no doubt murdered for his radical political views, this Fabian Society and all these dreadful pamphlets he writes and supports." She glared at Charlotte. "He associated with people who have all sorts of wild ideas: socialism, anarchy, even revolution. There are some very sinister plots being laid in our times. There is murder far more abominable than the fires here in Highgate, fearful as they were. One does not read the newspapers, of course. But one cannot help but be aware of what is going on — people talk about it, even here. Some madman is loose in Whitechapel ripping women apart and disfiguring them in the most fearful way — and the police seem powerless either to catch him or prevent him." Her face was white as she spoke and no one could fail to feel her horror rippling out in the room like coldness from a door opened on ice.

"I am sure you are right, Celeste." Angeline seemed to withdraw into herself as if she would retreat from these new and terrible forces that threatened them all. "The world is changing. People are thinking quite new and very dangerous ideas. It sometimes seems to me as if everything we have is threatened." She shook her head and pulled at her black shawl to put it more closely around her shoulders, as if it could protect her. "And I really believe from the way Stephen speaks that he quite admires this talk of overthrowing the old order and setting up those Fabian ideas."

"Oh, I'm sure he doesn't," Lally contradicted strongly, her face pink and her eyes very bright. "I know he liked Mr. Lindsay, but he certainly never agreed with his ideas. They are quite revolutionary. Mr. Lindsay was reading some of the essays and pamphlets and things by that fearful Mrs. Bezant who helped to put the match girls up to refusing to work. You remember that in April — or was it May? I mean, if people refuse to work, where will we all be?"

Charlotte was powerfully tempted to put forward her own political views, in favor of Mrs. Bezant and explaining the plight of the match girls, their physical suffering, the necrosis of the facial bones from breathing the phosphorus; but this was neither the time nor were these the people. Instead she turned to Lally with interest.

"Do you believe they were political murders, Mrs. Clitheridge? That poor Mrs. Shaw was killed because of her agitation for slum reform? You know I think you may well be correct. In fact it is what I believe myself, and have been saying so for some time."

Lally was very much put out of composure by having to agree with Charlotte, but she could not backtrack now.

"I would not have put it quite in those terms," she said, bridling. "But I suppose that is what I think. After all, it makes by far the most sense out of things. What other reason could there be?"

"Well there are others who have suggested more personal forms of passion," Prudence pointed out, frowning at Charlotte. "Perhaps Mr. Lutterworth, because of Dr. Shaw's involvement with Flora — if, of course, it was Stephen he meant to kill, not poor Clemency."

"Then why would he kill Mr. Lindsay?" Angeline shook her head. "Mr. Lindsay certainly never did her any harm."

"Because he knew something, of course." Prudence's face tightened in impatience. "That does not take a great deal of guessing."

They were all standing close together near the door, the sunlight slanting between the curtains and the blinds making a bright patch behind them and causing the black crepes to look faintly dusty.

"I am surprised the police have not worked it out yet," Lally added, glancing at Charlotte. "But then I suppose they are not a very superior class of person — or they would not be employed in such work. I mean, if they were clever enough to do something better — they would, wouldn't they?"

Charlotte could accommodate a certain amount of insult to herself and keep her temper, but insult to Pitt was different. Again her anger slipped out of control.

"There are only a certain number of people who are willing to spend their time, and sometimes to risk their lives, digging into the sin and tragedy of other people's affairs and uncovering the violence in them," she said acidly, staring at Lally, her eyes wide. "So many people who look the picture of rectitude on the outside and pretend to civic virtue have inner lives that are thoroughly sordid, greedy and full of lies." She looked from one to another of them, and was satisfied to see alarm, even fear in some of their faces, most especially Prudence's. And seeing it she instantly relented and was ashamed. It was not Prudence she had intended to hurt.

But again there was no verbal retreat, only physical, and this time she excused herself, bade them farewell and swept out, head high, twitching her skirts smartly over the step. A few moments later she was back in Aunt Vespasia's carriage and once again going towards Stephen Shaw's lodgings. There were now far more questions she wished to ask him. Perhaps it really was all to do with radical political ideas, not merely Clemency's slum profiteers, but Lindsay's socialist beliefs as well. She had never asked him if Lindsay knew about Clemency's work, or if it had taken her to the new Fabian Society; it simply had not occurred to her.

Mrs. Turner admitted her again with no surprise, and told her that the doctor was out on a call but she expected him back shortly, and if Charlotte cared to wait in the parlor she was welcome. She was brought yet another pot of tea, set out on a brand-new Japanese lacquer tray.

She poured herself a cup of tea and sat sipping it. Could Shaw really know anything that someone would kill to keep secret? Pitt had said little to her about the other patients he had investigated. Shaw seemed so certain all the deaths he had attended were natural — but then if he were in conspiracy with someone, he would say that. Was it possible he had helped someone to murder, either by actually providing the means, or simply by concealing it afterwards? Would he?

She recalled his face to mind easily, the strength in him, and the conviction. Yes — if he believed it to be right, she had no doubt he would. He was quite capable of exercising his powers. If ever a man had the courage of his convictions it was Stephen Shaw.

But did he believe it was right — or could ever be? No, surely not. Not even a violent or insane person? Or someone with a painful and incurable disease?

She had no idea if he was treating such a person. Pitt must have thought of all this too — surely?

She had resolved nothing when some thirty minutes later Shaw burst in, half throwing his case into the corner and flinging his jacket over the back of the chair. He swung around, startled to see her, but his expression lit with delight and he made no pretense of indifference.

"Mrs. Pitt! What fortune brings you back here again so soon? Have you discovered something?" There was humor in his eyes, and a little anxiety, but nothing disguised his liking for her.

"I have just been visiting the Misses Worlingham," she answered, and saw the instant appreciation of all that that meant in his face. "I was not especially welcome," she said in answer to his unspoken question. "In fact Mrs. Clitheridge, who called at the same time, has taken a strong dislike to me. But as a result of certain conversation that took place, several other thoughts come to my mind."

"Indeed? And what are they? I see Mrs. Turner gave you some tea. Is there any left? I am as dry as one of poor Amos's wooden gods." He reached for the pot and lifted it experimentally. It was obvious from the weight that there was considerable liquid left in it. "Ah — good." He poured out her used cup in the slop bowl, rinsed it from the hot water jug, and proceeded to pour himself some tea. "What did Celeste and Angeline say that sparked these new ideas? I must admit, the thought intrigues me."

"Well, there is always money," she began slowly. "The Worlinghams have a great deal of money, which Clemency must have inherited, along with Prudence, when Theophilus died."

He met her eyes with total candor, even a black laughter without a shred of rancor at her for the suggestion.

"And you think I might have murdered poor Clem to get my hands on it?" he asked. "I assure you, there isn't a penny left — she gave it all away." He moved restlessly around the room, poking at a cushion, setting a book straight on a shelf so it did not stand out from the rest. "When her will is probated you will see that for the last few months she had been obliged to me even for a dress allowance. I promise you, Mrs. Pitt, I shall inherit nothing from the Worlingham estate except a couple of dressmakers' bills and a milliner's account. Which I shall be happy to settle."

"Given it all away?" Charlotte affected surprise. Pitt had already told her that Clemency had given her money away.

"All of it," he repeated. "Mostly to societies for slum clearance, help to the extremely poor, housing improvement, sanitation, and of course the battle to get the law changed to make ownership easily traceable. She went through thirty thousand pounds in less than a year. She just gave it away until there was no more." His face was illuminated with a kind of pride and a fierce gentleness.

Charlotte asked the next question without even stopping to weigh it. She had to know, and it seemed so easy and natural to ask.

"Did she tell you why? I mean, did she tell you where the Worlingham money came from?"

His mouth curled downward and his eyes were full of bitter laughter.

"Where the old bastard got it from? Oh, yes — when she discovered it she was devastated." He walked over and stood with his back to the mantel. "I remember the night she came home after she found out. She was so pale I thought she would pass out, but she was white with fury, and shame." He looked at Charlotte, his eyes very steady on hers. "All evening she paced the floor back and forth, talking about it, and nothing I could say could take away the guilt from her. She was distraught. She must have been up half the night — " He bit his lip and looked downwards. "And I'm ashamed to say I was so tired from being up the night before that I slept. But I knew in the morning she had been weeping. All I could do was tell her that whatever her decision, I would support her. She took two more days to decide that she would not face

Celeste and Angeline with it."

He jerked up again, his foot kicking against the brass fender around the hearth. "What good would it do? They had no responsibility for it. They gave their whole lives to looking after and pandering to that old swine. They couldn't bear it now to think it had all been a farce, all the goodness they thought was there a whited sepulcher if ever there was one!"

"But she told Prudence," Charlotte said quietly, remembering the haunting fear and the guilt in Prudence's eyes.

He frowned at her, his expression clouded where she had expected to see something a little like relief.

"No." He was quite definite. "No, she certainly didn't tell Prudence. What could she do, except be plagued with shame too?"

"But she is," Charlotte said, still gently. She was filled with sorrow, catching some glimpse of how it would torment Prudence, when her husband admired the bishop almost to hero worship. What a terrible burden to live with, and never to let slip, even by hint or implication. Prudence must be a very strong woman with deep loyalty to keep such a secret. "She must find it almost unendurable," she added.

"She doesn't know!" he insisted. "Clem never told her — just because it would be, as you say, unendurable. Old Josiah thinks the bishop was the next thing to a saint — God help him. The bloody window was all his idea — "

"Yes, she does," Charlotte argued, leaning a little forward. "I saw it in her eyes looking at Angeline and Celeste. She's terrified of it coming out, and she's desperately ashamed of it."

They sat across the table staring at each other, equally determined they were in the right, until slowly Shaw's face cleared and understanding was so plain in him she spoke automatically.

"What? What have you realized?"

"Prudence doesn't know anything about the Worlingham money. That's not what she is afraid of — the stupid woman — "

"Then what?" She resented his calling her stupid, but this was not the time to take it up. "What is she afraid of?"

"Josiah — and her family's contempt and indignation — "

"For what?" she interrupted him again. "What is it?"

"Prudence has six children." He smiled ruefully, full of pity. "Her confinements were very hard. The first time she was in pain for twenty-three hours before the child was delivered. The second time looked like being similar, so I offered her anesthetic — and she took it."

"Anesthetic — " Suddenly she too began to see what terrified Prudence. She remembered Josiah Hatch's remarks about women and the travail of childbirth, and it being God's will. He would, like many men, consider it an evasion of Christian responsibility to dull the pain with medical anesthesia. Most doctors would not even offer it. And Shaw had allowed Prudence her choice, without asking or telling her husband — and she was living in mortal fear now that he might break his silence and betray her to her husband.

"I see," she said with a sigh. "How tragic — and absurd." She could recall her own pain of childbirth only dimly. Nature is merciful in expunging the recollection in all save a small corner of the mind, and hers had not been harsh, compared with many. "Poor Prudence. You would never tell him — would you?" She knew as she said it that the question was unnecessary. In fact, she was grateful he was not angry even that she asked.

He smiled and did not answer.

She changed the subject.

"Do you think it would be acceptable for me to come to Amos Lindsay's funeral? I liked him, even though I knew him for so short a while."

His face softened again, and for a moment the full magnitude of his hurt was naked.

"I should like it very much if you did. I shall speak the eulogy. The whole affair will be awful — Clitheridge will behave like a fool, he always does when anything real is involved. Lally will probably have to pick up the pieces. Oliphant will be as good as he is allowed to be, and Josiah will be the same pompous, blind ass he always is. I shall loathe every moment of it. I will almost certainly quarrel with Josiah because I can't help it. The more sycophantic he is about the damn bishop the angrier I shall be, and the more I shall want to shout from the pulpit what an obscene old sinner he was — and not even decent sins of passion or appetite — just cold, complacent greed and the love of dominion over other people."

Without thinking she put out her hand and touched his arm.

"But you won't."

He smiled reluctantly and stood immobile lest she move.

"I shall try to behave like the model mourner and friend — even if it chokes me. Josiah and I have had enough quarreling — but he does tempt me sorely. He lives in a totally spurious world and I can't bear his cant! I know better, Charlotte. I hate lies; they rob us of the real good by covering it over with so many coats

498

of sickening excuses and evasions until what was really beautiful, brave, or clean, is distorted and devalued." His voice shook with the intensity of his feeling. "I hate hypocrites! And the church seems to spawn them like abscesses, eating away at real virtue — like Matthew Oliphant's."

She was a little embarrassed; his emotion was so transparent and she could feel the vitality of him under her hand as if he filled the room.

She moved away carefully, not to break the moment.

"Then I shall see you at the funeral tomorrow. We shall both behave properly — however hard it is for us. I shall not quarrel with Mrs. Clitheridge, although I should dearly like to, and you will not tell Josiah what you think of the bishop. We shall simply mourn a good friend who died before his time." And without looking at him again she walked very straight-backed and very gracefully to the parlor door, and out into the hallway.

CHAPTER ELEVEN

It had taken Murdo two days of anxiety and doubt, lurching hope and black despair before he found an excuse to call on Flora Lutterworth. And it took him at least half an hour to wash, shave and dress himself in immaculately clean clothes, pressed to perfection, his buttons polished — he hated his buttons because they made his rank so obvious, but since they were inescapable, they had better be clean and bright.

He had thought of going quite frankly to express his admiration for her, then blushed scarlet as he imagined how she would laugh at him for his presumption. And then she would be thoroughly annoyed that a policeman, of all the miserable trades — and not even a senior one — should dare to think of such a thing, let alone express it. He had lain awake burning with shame over that.

No, the only way was to find some professional excuse, and then in the course of speaking to her, slip in that she had his deepest admiration, and then retreat with as much grace as possible.

So at twenty-five minutes past nine he knocked on the door of the Lutterworth house. When the maid answered, he asked if he might see Miss Flora Lutterworth, to seek her aid in an official matter.

He tripped over the step on the way in, and was sure the maid was giggling at his clumsiness. He was angry and blushing at the same time and already wished he had not come. It was doomed to failure. He was making a fool of himself and she would only despise him.

"If you'll wait in the morning room, I'll see if Miss Lutterworth'll see you," the maid said, smoothing her white starched apron over her hips. She thought he was very agreeable, nice eyes and very clean-looking, not like some she could name, but she wasn't for having him get above himself. But when he had finished with Miss Flora, she would make sure it was she who showed him out. She wouldn't mind if he asked her to take a walk in the park on her half day off.

"Thank you." He stood in the middle of the carpet, twisting his helmet in his hands, and waited while she went. For a wild moment he thought of simply leaving, but his feet stayed leadenly on the floor and while his mind took flight and was halfway back to the station, his body remained, one moment hot, the next cold, in the Lutterworths' elegant morning room.

Flora came in looking flushed and devastatingly pretty, her eyes shining. She was dressed in a deep rose-pink which was quite the most distinguished and becoming gown he had ever seen. His heart beat so hard he felt sure the shaking of his body must be visible to her, and his mouth was completely dry.

"Good morning, Constable Murdo," she said sweetly.

"G — good morning, ma'am." His voice croaked and squeaked alternatively. She must think him a complete fool. He drew in a deep breath, and then let it out without speaking.

"What can I do for you, Constable?" She sat down in the largest chair and her skirts billowed around her. She gazed at him most disconcertingly.

"Ah — " He found it easier to look away. "Er, ma'am — " He fixed his eyes on the carpet and the prepared words came out in a rush. "Is it possible, ma'am, that some young gentleman, who admired you very much, might have misunderstood your visits to Dr. Shaw, and become very jealous — ma'am?" He dared not look up at her. She must see through this ruse, which had sounded so plausible alone in his room. Now it was horribly transparent.

"I don't think so, Constable Murdo," she said after considering it for a moment. "I really don't know of any young gentlemen who have such powerful feelings about me that they would entertain such . . . jealousy. It doesn't seem likely."

Without thinking he looked up at her and spoke. "Oh yes, ma'am — if a gentleman had kept your company, socially of course, and met you a number of times, he might well be moved to — to such passions — that — " He felt himself blushing furiously, but unable to move his eyes from hers.

"Do you think so?" she said innocently. She lowered her eyes demurely. "That would suppose him to be in love with me, Constable — to quite an intense degree. Surely you don't believe that is so?"

He plunged in — he would never in his wildest dreams have a better opportunity. "I don't know whether it is, ma'am — but it would be very easy to believe. If it is not so now, it will be — There are bound to be many gentlemen who would give everything they possessed to have the chance to earn your affections. I mean — er — " She was looking at him with a most curious smile, half interested and half amused. He knew he had betrayed himself and felt as if there were nothing in the world he wanted so much as to run away, and yet his feet were rooted to the floor.

Her smiled widened. "How very charming of you, Constable," she said softly. "You say it as if you really believed I were quite beautiful and exciting. It is certainly the nicest thing anyone has told me for as long as I can remember."

He had no idea what to say, no idea at all. He simply smiled back at her and felt happy and ridiculous.

"I cannot think of anyone who might entertain such emotions that they could have harmed Dr. Shaw on my account," she went on, sitting up very straight. "I am sure I have not encouraged anyone. But of course the matter is very serious, I know. I promise you I shall think about it hard, and then I shall tell you."

"May I call in a few days' time to learn what you have to say?" he asked.

The corners of her mouth curled up in a tiny smile.

"I think, if you don't mind, Constable, I would rather discuss it somewhere where Papa will not overhear us. He does tend to misunderstand me at times — only in my best interest, of course. Perhaps you would be good enough to take a short walk with me along

Bromwich Walk? The weather is still most pleasant and it would not be disagreeable. If you would meet me at the parsonage end, the day after tomorrow, we might walk up to Highgate, and perhaps find a lemonade stall to refresh ourselves?"

"I — " His voice would hardly obey him, his heart was so high in his throat and there was a curious, singing happiness all through his veins. "I'm sure that would be most — " He wanted to say "marvelous" but it was much too forward. "Most satisfactory, ma'am." He should get that silly smile off his face, but it would not go.

"I'm so glad," she said, rising to her feet and passing so close to him he could smell the scent of flowers and hear the soft rustle of the fabric of her skirts. "Good day, Constable Murdo."

He gulped and swallowed hard. "G-good day, Miss Lutterworth."

"An artists' model?" Micah Drummond's eyes widened and there was laughter in them, and a wry appreciation. "Maude Dalgetty was that Maude!"

Now it was Pitt's turn to be startled. "You know of her?"

"Certainly." Drummond was standing by the window in his office, the autumn sunlight

505

streaming in, making bright patterns on the carpet. "She was one of the great beauties — of a certain sort, of course." His smile widened. "Perhaps not quite your generation, Pitt. But believe me, any young gentleman who attended the music halls and bought the odd artistic postcard knew the face — and other attributes — of Maude Racine. She was more than just handsome; there was a kind of generosity in her, a warmth. I'm delighted to hear she married someone who loves her and found a respectable domestic life. I imagine it was what she always wanted, after the fun was over and it came time to leave the boards."

Pitt found himself smiling too. He had liked Maude Dalgetty, and she had been a friend of Clemency Shaw.

"And you have ruled her out?" Drummond pursued. "Not that I can imagine Maude caring passionately enough about her reputation to kill anyone to preserve it. There was never anything of the hypocrite in her in the old days. Are you equally sure about the husband — John Dalgetty? No evasions, Pitt!"

Pitt leaned against the mantel shelf and faced Drummond squarely.

"Absolutely," he said without a flicker. "Dalgetty believes passionately in total freedom of speech. That is what the idiotic affair

506

in the field was about. No censorship, everything open and public, say and write what you please, all the new and daring ideas you can think of. The people who matter most to him wouldn't cut him because his wife was on the stage and posed for pictures without certain of her clothes."

"But she would care," Drummond argued. "Didn't you say she works in the parish, attends church and is part of an extremely respectable community?"

"Yes I did." Pitt put his hands in his pockets. One of Emily's silk handkerchiefs was in his breast pocket and he had folded it to show slightly. Drummond's eyes had caught it, and it gave him a slow satisfaction which more than made up for the cold, early ride on the public omnibus, so he could add a few more pence to the economy for Charlotte's holiday.

"But the only person who knew," he went on, "so far as I am aware, was Shaw — and, I presume, Clemency. And Clemency was her friend — and Shaw wouldn't tell anyone." Then a flash of memory returned. "Except in a fit of anger because Josiah Hatch thinks Maude is the finest woman he's ever met." His eyes widened. "And he's such a rigid creature — with all the old bishop's ideas about the purity and virtue of women, and of course their duties as the guardians of the sanctity of the home as an island from the vile realities of the outer world. I can well imagine Shaw giving the lie to that, as a piece of cant he couldn't abide. But I still think he wouldn't actually betray her — simply tell."

"I'm inclined to agree with you." Drummond pursed his lips. "No reason to suspect Pascoe — no motive we know of. You've ruled out Prudence Hatch, because Shaw would never betray her medical secrets." Drummond's eyes were bright. "Please convey my compliments to Charlotte." He slid down a little in his chair and rested his feet on the desk. "The vicar is an ass, you say, but you know of no quarrel with Shaw, except that his wife is titillated by the man's virility — hardly enough to drive a clergyman to multiple arson and murder. You don't think Mrs. Clitheridge could be so besotted with Shaw, and have been rejected, to the point where she tried to murder him in fury?" He was watching Pitt's expression as he spoke. "All right — no. Nor, I assume, would she have killed Mrs. Shaw in jealousy. No — I thought not. What about Lutterworth, over his daughter?"

"Possible," Pitt conceded doubtfully. Lutterworth's broad, powerful face came back to his mind, and the expression of rage in it when he mentioned Shaw's name, and Flora's.

There was no question he loved his daughter profoundly, and had the depth of emotion and the determination of character to carry through such an act, if he thought there were justification. "Yes, he is possible. Or he was — I think he knows now that Flora's connection with the doctor was purely a medical one."

"Then why the sneaking in and out instead of going to the usual surgery?" Drummond persisted.

"Because of the nature of her complaint. It is personal, and she is highly sensitive about it, didn't want anyone else to know. Not difficult to understand."

Drummond, who had a wife and daughters himself, did not need to make further comment.

"Who does that leave?"

"Hatch — but he and Shaw have quarreled over one thing or another for years, and you don't kill someone suddenly over a basic difference in temperament and philosophy. Or the elderly Worlingham sisters — if they really believed that he was responsible for Theophilus's death — "

"And do they?" Drummond only half believed it, and it was obvious in his face. "Would they really feel so strongly about it? Seems more likely to me they might have killed him to keep him quiet over the real source of the Worlingham money. That I could believe."

"Shaw says Clemency didn't tell them," Pitt replied, although it seemed far more likely to him also. "But perhaps he didn't know she had. She might have done it the night before she died. I need to find what precipitated the first murder. Something happened that day — or the day immediately before — that frightened or angered someone beyond enduring. Something changed the situation so drastically that what had been at the worst difficult, but maybe not even that, suddenly became so threatening or so intolerably unjust to them, they exploded into murder — "

"What did happen that day?" Drummond was watching him closely.

"I don't know," Pitt confessed. "I've been concentrating on Shaw, and he won't tell me anything. Of course, it is still possible he killed Clemency himself, set the fire before he left, and killed Amos Lindsay because somehow he had betrayed himself by a word, or an omission, and Lindsay knew what he'd done. They were friends — but I don't believe Lindsay would have kept silent once he was sure Shaw was guilty." It was a peculiarly repugnant thought, but honesty compelled that he allow it.

Drummond saw the reluctance in him.

"Not the first time you've liked a murderer, Pitt — nor I, for that matter. Life would be a great deal easier at times, if we could like all the heroes and dislike all the villains. Or personally I'd settle for simply not pitying the villains as much as I do the victims half the time."

"I can't always tell the difference." Pitt smiled sadly. "I've known murderers I've felt were victims as much as anyone in the whole affair. And if it turns out to be Angeline and Celeste I may well this time too. The old bishop filled their lives, dominated them from childhood, laid out for them exactly the kind of women he expected them to be, and made it virtually impossible for them to be anything else. I gather he drove away all suitors and kept Celeste to be his intellectual companion, and Angeline to be his housekeeper and hostess when necessary. By the time he died they were far too old to marry, and totally dependent on his views, his social status and his money. If Clemency, in her outrage, threatened to destroy everything on which their lives were built, and faced them not only with old age in total public disgrace but a negation of everything they believed in and which justified the past, it is not hard to understand why they might have conspired to kill her. To them she was not only a mortal threat but a traitor to her family. They might consider her ultimate disloyalty to be a sin that warranted death."

"They might well," Drummond agreed. "Other than that you are left with some as yet unnamed slum profiteer who was threatened by Clemency's uncovering work. I suppose you have looked into who else's tenements she was interested in? What about Lutterworth? You said he's socially ambitious — especially for Flora — and wants to leave his trade roots behind and marry her into society? Slum profiteering wouldn't help that." He pulled a sour face. "Although I'm not sure it would entirely hurt it either. A good few of the aristocracy made their money in highly questionable ways."

"Undoubtedly," Pitt agreed. "But they do it discreetly. Vice they will overlook, vulgarity they may accept — with reluctance, if there is enough money attached — but indiscretion never."

"You're getting very cynical, Pitt." Drummond was smiling as he said it.

Pitt shrugged. "All I can find out about Lutterworth is that his money was in the north, and he sold nearly all his interests. There never was any in London that I can trace."

"What about the political aspect?" Drummond would not give up yet. "Could Clemency have been murdered because of some other connection with Dalgetty and his Fabian tracts — and Lindsay the same?"

"I haven't traced any connection." Pitt screwed up his face. "But certainly Clemency knew Lindsay, and they liked each other. But since they are both dead, it is impossible to know what they spoke about, unless Shaw knows and can be persuaded to tell us. And since both houses are burnt to the ground, there are no papers to find."

"You might have to go and speak to some of the other members of the society — "

"I will, if it comes to that; but today I'm going to Lindsay's funeral. And perhaps I can discover what Clemency did on her last day or two alive, who she spoke to and what happened that made someone so angry or so frightened that they killed her."

"Report to me afterwards, will you? I want to know."

"Yes sir. Now I must leave, or I shall be late. I hate funerals. I hate them most of all when I look around the faces of the mourners and think that one of them murdered him — or her."

Charlotte also was preparing to attend the funeral, but she was startled to have received

513

a hand-addressed note from Emily to say that not only would she and Jack attend, and for convenience would pick Charlotte up in their carriage at ten o'clock, but that Great-Aunt Vespasia also would come. No explanation was given, nor when they arrived, since it was now five minutes past nine, would there be any opportunity to decline the arrangements or ask for any alternative.

"Thank heaven at least Mama and Grandmama are remaining at home." Charlotte folded the note and put it in her sewing basket, where Pitt would not find it, simply as a matter of habit. Of course he would ultimately know they had all attended, but there was no way she would be able to pretend to Pitt it was a matter of personal grief, although she had liked Lindsay. They were going because they were curious, and still felt they could discover something of meaning about Lindsay's death, and Clemency's. And that Pitt might not approve of.

Perhaps Emily knew something already? She and Jack had said they would probe the political questions, and Jack had made some contact with the Liberal party with a view to standing for Parliament when a vacant seat arose that would accept him as a candidate. And if he were truly serious about continuing Clemency's work, he might also have met with the Fabians and others with strong socialist beliefs — not, of course, that they had the slightest chance of returning a member to the House. But ideas were necessary, whether to argue for or against.

She was busy dressing her hair and unconsciously trying to make the very best of her appearance. She did not realize till she had been there half an hour and was still not entirely satisfied, just what an effort she was making. She blushed at her own vanity, and foolishness, and dismissed the wrenching thoughts of Stephen Shaw from her mind.

"Gracie!"

Gracie materialized from the landing, a duster in her hand, her face bright.

"Yes, ma'am?"

"Would you like to come to Mr. Lindsay's funeral with me?"

"Oh yes, ma'am! When is it, ma'am?"

"In about quarter of an hour — at least that is when we shall be leaving. Mrs. Radley is taking us in her carriage."

Gracie's face fell and she had to swallow hard on the sudden lump in her throat.

"I 'aven't finished me work, ma'am. There's still the stairs to do, and Miss Jemima's room. The dust settles jus' the same though she in't there right now. An' I in't changed proper. Me black dress in't pressed right — "

"That dress is dark enough." Charlotte looked at Gracie's ordinary gray stuff working dress. It was quite drab enough for mourning. Really, one day when she could afford it she should get her a nice bright blue one. "And you can forget the housework. It'll not go away — you can do it tomorrow; it'll all be the same in the end."

"Are you sure, ma'am?" Gracie had never been told to forget dusting before, and her eyes were like stars at the thought of just letting it wait — and instead going off on another expedition of detecting.

"Yes I'm sure," Charlotte replied. "Now go and do your hair and find your coat. We mustn't be late."

"Oh yes, ma'am. I will this minute, ma'am." And before Charlotte could add anything she was gone, her feet clattering up the attic stairs to her room.

Emily arrived precisely when she said she would, bursting in in a wildly elegant black gown cut in the latest lines, decorated with jet beading and not entirely suitable for a funeral, in that although the lace neckline was so high as to be almost to the ears, the main fabric of the dress was definitely a trifle fine, showing the pearliness of skin in an unmistakable gleam more fit for a soiree than a church. Her hat was very rakish, in spite of the veil, and her color was beautifully high in her cheeks. It was not difficult to believe that Emily was a new bride.

Charlotte was so happy for her she found it hard to disapprove, sensible though that would have been, and appropriate.

Jack was a couple of steps behind, immaculately dressed as always, and perhaps a little easier now about his tailor's bills. But there was also a new confidence about him too, not built solely on charm and the need to please, but upon some inner happiness that required no second person's approbation. Charlotte thought at first it was a reflection of his relationship with Emily. Then as soon as he spoke, she realized it was deeper than that; it was a purpose within himself, a thing radiating outward.

He kissed Charlotte lightly on the cheek.

"I have met with the Parliamentary party and I think they will accept me as a candidate!" he said with a broad smile. "As soon as a suitable by-election occurs I shall stand."

"Congratulations," Charlotte said with a great bubble of happiness welling up inside her. "We shall do everything we can to help you to succeed." She looked at Emily and saw the intense satisfaction in her face also, and the gleam of pride. "Absolutely everything. Even holding my tongue, should it be the last resort. Now we must go to Amos Lindsay's funeral. I think it is part of our cause. I don't know why, but I am convinced he died in connection with Clemency's death."

"Of course," Emily agreed. "It doesn't make any sense otherwise. The same person must have killed both of them. I still think it is politics. Clemency ruffled a great many feathers. The more I investigate what she was doing, and planning to do, the more I discover how fierce was her determination and how many people could be smeared with the taint of very dirty money indeed. Are you sure the Worlingham sisters did not know what she was doing?"

"No — not absolutely," Charlotte confessed. "I don't think so. But Celeste is a better actress than Angeline, whom I find very hard to think guilty, she seems so transparent, and so unworldly — even ineffectual. I can't think of her being efficient enough, or coolheaded enough, to have planned and laid those fires."

"But Celeste would," Emily pressed. "After all, they have more to lose than anyone."

"Except Shaw," Jack pointed out. "Clemency was giving away the Worlingham money hand over fist. As it happens she had given all her share away before she died — but you have only Shaw's word for it that he knew that. He may have thought little of what she was doing and killed her to stop her while there was still some left, and only learned afterwards that he was too late."

Charlotte turned to look at him. It was an extremely ugly thought which she had not until this moment seen, but it was undeniable. No one else knew what Clemency had been doing; there had been only Shaw's own word for it that he had known all along. Perhaps he hadn't? Perhaps he had found out only a day or two before Clemency's death, and it was that discovery which suddenly presented him with the prospect of losing his extremely comfortable position both financially, for certain, and socially, if she should make it public. It was a very good motive for murder indeed.

She said nothing, a chilling, rather sick feeling inside her.

"I'm sorry," Jack said gently. "But it had to be considered."

Charlotte swallowed hard and found it difficult. Shaw's fair, intense and blazingly honest face was before her inner eye. She was surprised how much it hurt.

"Gracie is coming with us." She looked away from them towards the door, as if the business of going were urgent and must be attended to. "I think she deserves to."

"Of course," Emily agreed. "I wish I thought we should really learn something —

but all I can reasonably hope for is a strong instinct. Although we might manage to ask some pertinent questions at the funerary dinner afterwards. Are you invited?"

"I think so." Charlotte remembered very clearly Shaw's invitation, and his wish that she should be there, one person with whom he could feel an identity of candor. She thrust it from her mind. "Come on, or we shall be late!"

The funeral was a bright, windy affair with more than two hundred people packing the small church for the formal, very stilted service conducted by Clitheridge. Only the organ music was faultless, flowing in rich, throbbing waves over the solemn heads and engulfing them in the comfort of a momentary unity while they sang. The sun streamed through the stained-glass windows in a glory of color falling like jewels on the floor and across the rigid backs and heads and all the variegated textures of black.

Upon leaving Charlotte noticed a man of unusual appearance sitting close to the back, with his chin in the air and seemingly more interested in the ceiling than the other mourners. It was not that his features were particularly startling so much as the intelligence and humor in his expression, irreverent as it was.

His hair was fiercely bright auburn and although he was sitting, he appeared to be quite a slight man. She certainly had not seen him before, and she hesitated out of curiosity.

"Is there something about me which troubles you, ma'am?" he asked, swiveling suddenly around to face her, and speaking with a distinctly Irish voice.

She collected her wits with an effort and replied with aplomb.

"Not in the least, sir. Any man as intent upon heaven as you deserves to be left to his contemplation — "

"It was not heaven, ma'am," he said indignantly. "It was the ceiling that had my attention." Then he realized she knew that as well as he, and had been irking him on purpose, and his face relaxed into a charming smile.

"George Bernard Shaw, ma'am. I was a friend of Amos Lindsay's. And were you also?"

"Yes I was." She stretched the truth a fraction. "And I am very sorry he is gone."

"Indeed." He was instantly sober again. "It's a sad and stupid waste."

Further conversation was made impossible by the press of people desiring to leave the church, and Charlotte nodded politely and excused herself, leaving him to resume his contemplation.

At least half the mourners followed the coffin out into the sharp, sunny graveyard where the wet earth was dug and the ground was already sprinkled over with fallen leaves, gold and bronze on the green of the grass.

Aunt Vespasia, dressed in deep lavender (she refused to wear black), stood next to Charlotte, her chin high, her shoulders square, her hand gripping fiercely her silver-handled cane. She loathed it, but she was obliged to lean on it for support as Clitheridge droned on about the inevitability of death and the frailty of man.

"Fool," she said under her breath. "Why on earth do vicars imagine God cannot be spoken to in simple language and needs everything explained to Him in at least three different ways? I always imagine God as the last person to be impressed by long words or to be deceived by specious excuses. For heaven's sake, He made us. He knows perfectly well that we are fragile, stupid, glorious, grubby and brave." She poked her stick into the ground viciously. "And He certainly does not want these fanfaronades. Get on with it, man! Inter the poor creature and let us go and speak well of him in some comfort!"

Charlotte closed her eyes, wincing in case someone had heard. Vespasia's voice was not loud, but it was piercingly clear with immaculate enunciation. She heard a very soft "Here, here" behind her and involuntarily turned. She met Stephen Shaw's level blue eyes, bright with pain, and belying the smile on his lips.

She turned back to the grave again immediately, and saw Lally Clitheridge's look of steel-hard jealousy, but it aroused more pity in her than anger. Had she been married to Hector Clitheridge there would certainly have been moments when she too might have dreamed wild, impermissible dreams, and hated anyone who broke their fantastic surface, however ridiculous or slight.

Clitheridge was still wittering on, as if he could not bear to let the moment go, as though delaying the final replacing of the earth somehow extended a part of Amos Lindsay.

Oliphant was restive, moving his weight from one foot to the other, conscious of the grief and the indignity of it.

At the far end of the grave Alfred Lutterworth stood bareheaded, the wind ruffling his ring of white hair, and close beside him, her hand on his arm, Flora looked young and very pretty. The wind had put a touch of color into her cheeks, and the anxiety seemed to have gone from her expression. Even while Charlotte watched she saw Lutterworth place his hand over hers and tighten it a fraction.

Over her shoulder to the left, at the edge of the graveyard, Constable Murdo stood as upright as a sentry on duty, his buttons shining in the sun. Presumably he was here to observe everyone, but Charlotte never saw his gaze waver from Flora. For all that he seemed to observe, she might have been the only person present.

She saw Pitt only for a moment, a lean shadow somewhere near the vestry, trailing the ends of a muffler in the breeze. He turned towards her and smiled. Perhaps he had known she would come. For the space of an instant the crowd disappeared and there was no one else there. It was as if he had touched her. Then he turned and went on towards the yew hedge and the shadows. She knew he would be watching everything, expressions, gestures, whose eyes met whose, who spoke, who avoided speaking. She wondered if anything she had learned and told him was any use at all.

Maude Dalgetty was standing near the head of the grave. She was a little plumper than in her heyday, and the lines were quite clear in her face, but were all upward, generous and marked by humor. She was still a beauty, and perhaps always would be. In repose, as she was now, there was nothing sour in her features, nothing that spoke of regret.

Beside her, John Dalgetty stood very straight, avoiding even the slightest glance to where Quinton Pascoe stood equally rigid, doing his duty by a man he had liked but quarreled with fiercely. It was the attitude of a soldier at the grave of a fallen enemy. Dalgetty's was the pose of a soldier also, but he was mourning a warrior in a mutual cause. Never once in the service did they acknowledge each other.

Josiah Hatch was bareheaded, as were all the men, and looked pinched as if the wind bit into his bones. Prudence was not with him; neither were the Worlingham sisters. They still held to the belief that ladies did not attend the church funeral or the graveside.

At last Clitheridge wound to a close, and the gravediggers began to replace the earth.

"Thank God," Shaw said behind Charlotte. "You are coming to the funeral luncheon, aren't you?"

"Of course," Charlotte accepted.

Vespasia turned around very slowly and regarded Shaw with cool interest.

He bowed. "Good morning, Lady Cumming-Gould. It is most gracious of you to come, especially on a day so late in the season when the wind is sharp. I am sure Amos would have appreciated it."

Vespasia's eyes flickered very slightly with

an amusement almost invisible.

"Are you?"

He understood, and as always the candor was on his tongue instantly.

"You came because of Clemency." He had known he was right, but he saw it in her face. "It is not pity which brings you here, and you are right, the dead are beyond our emotions. It is anger. You are still determined to learn who killed her, and why."

"How perceptive of you," Vespasia agreed. "I am."

All the light vanished from his face, the frail humor like sunlight through snow. "So am I."

"Then we had better proceed to the funerary meal." She lifted her hand very slightly and immediately he offered her his arm. "Thank you," she accepted, and, her hat almost sweeping his shoulder in its magnificent arc, she sailed down the path towards her waiting carriage.

As had been done for Clemency, this gathering was held in the Worlingham house also, from very mixed motives. It was impossible to do it, as would have been customary, in Lindsay's own home, since it was a mere jumble of scarred beams resting at violent angles amid the heaps of burned and broken brick.

His dearest friend, Shaw, was in no better a position. He could hardly offer to hold it in Mrs. Turner's lodging house. It was not large enough and was occupied by several other people who could not be expected to have their house disrupted for such an event.

The choice rested between the Worlinghams' and the vicarage. As soon as they realized that, Celeste and Angeline offered the use of their home, and of their servants to make all the necessary provisions. It was a matter of duty. They had not cared for Amos Lindsay, and cared still less for his opinions, but they were the bishop's daughters, and the leaders of Christian society in Highgate. Position must come before personal feelings, especially towards the dead.

All this they made plain, in case anyone should mistakenly imagine they supported anything that Amos Lindsay had said or done.

They received everyone at the double doorway into the dining room, where the huge mahogany table was spread with every kind of baked meat and cold delicacy. The centerpiece was formed of lilies with a heavy, languorous perfume which instantly reminded Charlotte of somnolence, and eventually decay. The blinds were partially drawn, because today at least the house was in mourning, and black crepe was trailed suitably over pictures and texts on the walls, and around the newel posts of the stairs and over the door lintels.

The formal proceedings were very carefully laid out. It would have been impossible to seat everyone, and anyway since Shaw had invited extra people as the whim took him (including Pitt, to the deep indignation of the Worlingham sisters and the vicar), the servants did not know in advance how many there would be.

Therefore the food was set out so that people might be served by the butler and maids who were standing waiting discreetly just beyond the door, and then stand and speak with each other, commiserate, gossip and generally praise the dead until it should be time for a few prepared words, first by the vicar, then by Shaw as the departed's closest friend. And of course they could partake of a few of the very best bottles of Port wine, or something a little lighter for the women. Claret was served with the meal.

"I don't know how we are going to learn anything now," Emily said with a frown of disappointment. "Everyone is doing precisely what one would expect. Clitheridge looks incompetent and harassed, his wife is trying to compensate for him all the time, while being aware of you and Dr. Shaw, and if looks had any effect your hair would have frizzled on your head and dropped out, and your dress would hang on your back in scorched rags."

"Can you blame her?" Charlotte whispered back. "The vicar doesn't exactly make one's pulse race, does he."

"Don't be vulgar. No he doesn't. I would rather have the good doctor any day — unless, of course, he murdered his wife."

Charlotte had no effective answer for that, knowing it could be true, however much it hurt, so she turned around sharply and poked Emily in the ribs, as if by accident.

"Humph," Emily said in total comprehension.

Flora Lutterworth was on her father's arm, her veil drawn back so she might eat, and there was color in her cheeks and a faintly smug smile on her pretty mouth. Charlotte was curious to know what had caused it.

Across the room at the far side, Pitt saw it too, and had a very good idea it had something to do with Murdo. He considered it highly likely that Murdo would not find it so difficult to pursue Miss Lutterworth. In fact he might very well discover that it happened in spite of any ideas of his own, and it would all be much easier than he had feared.

Pitt was dressed unusually smartly for him. His collar was neat, his tie perfectly straight — at least so far — and he had nothing in his jacket pockets except a clean handkerchief (Emily's silk one was only for show), a short pencil and a piece of folded paper so he might make notes if he wished. That was quite redundant, because he never did; it was something he thought an efficient policeman ought to have.

He realized Shaw had invited him precisely to annoy Angeline and Celeste. It was a way of establishing that although the function was held in the Worlingham house, this was Amos Lindsay's funerary dinner, and he, Shaw, was the host and would invite whom he chose. To that end he stood at the head of the table, very square on his feet, and behaved as if the servants offering the baked meats and claret were his own. He welcomed the guests, especially Pitt. He did not glance once at the grim faces of Angeline and Celeste, who were in black bombazine and jet beads, standing behind him and a trifle to one side. They smiled guardedly at those they approved of, such as Josiah and Prudence Hatch, Quinton Pascoe, and Aunt Vespasia; nodded civilly to those they tolerated, like the Lutterworths, or Emily and Jack; and totally ignored those whose presence they knew to be a calculated affront, such as Pitt and Charlotte — although since they came separately and did not speak to each other, the sisters did not immediately connect them.

Pitt took his delicious cold game pie, jugged hare, and brown bread and butter and homemade pickle, liberally apportioned, and his glass of claret, finding them extraordinarily difficult to manage, and wandered around half overhearing conversations, and closely observing faces — those who were speaking, and more particularly those who were alone and unaware they were being observed.

What had been the precise course of events on the day or two before Clemency Shaw's death? Some time earlier she had discovered the source of the Worlingham money, and spread and given away her own inheritance, almost entirely to relieve the distress of those who were the victims of appalling misery, either directly to assist them, or indirectly to fight the laws which presently enabled owners to take their excess profits so discreetly that their names were never known nor their public reputations smeared with their true behavior.

When had she shared this with Shaw? Or had he discovered it some way of his own, perhaps only when her money was gone, and they had had a furious quarrel? Or had he been wiser than that, and pretended to agree — No. If he had hidden his response, it must have been because he thought there was still a substantial majority of the money left — enough to be worth killing her to save.

He looked across the heads of two women talking, to where Shaw still stood at the head of the table, smiling and nodding, talking to Maude Dalgetty. He looked very tense; his shoulders were tight under the fabric of his black jacket, as if he longed to break into action, punch the air, stride backward and forward, do anything to use that wild anger inside him. Pitt found it hard to believe he would have contained his temper so well that Clemency, who must have known his every expression, inflection of voice, gesture, would not have understood the power of his rage, and thus at least some shadow of her own danger.

What must she have thought when Josiah Hatch announced that there was going to be a stained-glass window put in the church dedicated to the old bishop, and depicting him as one of the early Christian saints? What an intolerable irony. What self-control had enabled her to keep silent? And she had done so. It had been a public announcement, and if she had given even the slightest hint that she knew some hideous secret, as a member of the family she would have been listened to, even if not entirely believed.

Was it conceivable that everyone had kept

silent about it — a conspiracy?

He looked around the room at the somber faces. All were suitably grim for the occasion: Clitheridge harassed and nervous; Lally smoothing things over, fussing around Shaw; Pascoe and Dalgetty studiously avoiding each other, but still padded out by bandages under their mourning clothes — Dalgetty's cheek stitched and plastered. Matthew Oliphant was speaking quietly, a word of comfort, a gesture of warmth or reassurance; Josiah Hatch's face was white except where the wind had whipped his cheeks; Prudence was more relaxed than earlier, her fear gone. Angeline and Celeste were quietly angry; the Lutterworths were still being socially patronized. No, he could not believe in a conspiracy among such disparate people. Too many of them had no interest in protecting the reputation of the Worlinghams. Dalgetty would have delighted in spreading such a richly ironic tale, the ultimate freedom to speak against the established order of things — even if only to infuriate Pascoe.

And Amos Lindsay, with his Fabian socialist sympathies, would surely have laughed loud and long, and made no secret of it at all.

No — assuredly nothing had been said when the window was announced. And all plans had gone ahead for it, money had been raised, the glass purchased and the artists and glaziers engaged. The Archbishop of York had been invited to dedicate it and all Highgate and half ecclesiastical north London would be there at the ceremony.

Pitt sipped his claret. It was extremely good. The old bishop must have laid down a remarkable cellar, as well as everything else. Ten years after his death, Theophilus's share gone, and there was still this quality to draw on for an affair which was not really more than a duty for Celeste and Angeline.

The Worlingham window must be costing a very considerable amount of money, and according to the family, part of the purpose of it was to show the great regard in which the whole of Highgate had held the bishop. Therefore it was to be funded with public money, collected from the parish, and any other people whose remembrance of him was so clear that they wished to contribute.

Who had organized that? Celeste? Angeline? No — it had been Josiah Hatch. Of course, it would be a man. They would hardly leave such a public and financial matter to elderly ladies. And it would be more seemly if it did not come from one of the immediate family. That left the two grandsons-in-law — Hatch and Shaw. Hatch was a church sidesman, and had a reverence for the bishop that exceeded even that of his daughters. He was the old bishop's true spiritual heir.

Anyway, the idea of Stephen Shaw working on such a scheme was ludicrous. He had disliked the bishop strongly in his lifetime, and now on learning of the true source of his wealth, he whose daily work took him to the victims of such greed, despised him with a passion.

Pitt wondered what Shaw had said to Hatch, when Hatch asked him for a contribution. That must have been a rich moment: Hatch holding out his hand for money for a memorial window depicting the bishop as a saint; and Shaw newly aware that the bishop's fortune came from the wretchedness of thousands, even the exploitation and death of many — and his wife had just given away every penny she inherited to right at least a fraction of the wrongs.

Had Shaw kept his temper — and a still tongue?

Pitt looked again across the crowd at that passionate, dynamic face with its ruthless honesty.

Surely not?

Shaw was banging the table, his glass high in his other hand.

Gradually the buzz of conversation died and everyone turned towards him.

"Ladies and gentlemen," he said in a clear, ringing voice. "We are met here today, at the kind invitation of Miss Celeste and Miss Angeline Worlingham, to honor our departed friend, Amos Lindsay. It is appropriate that we say a few words about him, to remember him as he was."

There was a faintly uncomfortable shifting of weight in the room, a creaking of whalebone stays, the faint rattle of taffeta, someone's shoes squeaking, an exhalation of breath.

"The vicar spoke of him in church," Shaw went on, his voice a little louder. "He praised his virtues, or perhaps it would be more accurate to say he praised a list of virtues which it is customary to attribute to the dead, and no one ever argues and says, 'Well, no, actually, he wasn't like that at all.' " He raised his glass a little higher. "But I am! I want us to drink in remembrance of the man as he really was, not some hygienic, dehumanized plaster replica of him, robbed of all his weaknesses, and so of all his triumphs."

"Really — " Clitheridge looked pale and dithered between stepping forward and interrupting physically — and the more restrained action of simply remonstrating, and hoping Shaw's better taste would prevail. "I mean — don't you think — ?"

"No I don't," Shaw said briskly. "I hate

the pious whimperings about his being a pillar of the community, a God-fearing man and beloved of us all. Have you no honesty left in your souls? Can you stand here and say you all loved Amos Lindsay? Balderdash!"

There was an audible gasp of indrawn breath this time, and Clitheridge turned around desperately as if he were hoping some miraculous rescue might be at hand.

"Quinton Pascoe was afraid of him, and was horrified by his writings. He would have had him censored, had he been able."

There was a slight rustle and murmur as everyone swiveled to look at Pascoe, who turned bright pink. But before he could protest, Shaw went on.

"And Aunt Celeste and Aunt Angeline abhorred everything he stood for. They were — and still are — convinced that his Fabian views are unchristian and, if allowed to proliferate though society, will bring about the end of everything that is civilized and beneficial to mankind — or at any rate to that class of it to which we belong, which is all that matters to them, because it is all they know. It is all their sainted father ever allowed them to know."

"You are drunk!" Celeste said in a furious whisper which carried right around the room.

"On the contrary, I am extremely sober,"

he replied, looking up at the glass in his hand. "Even Theophilus's best burgundy has not affected me — because I have not drunk enough of it. And as for his superb Port — I have not even touched it yet. The very least I owe poor Amos is to have my thoughts collected when I speak of him — although God knows I have enough provocation to get drunk. My wife, my best friend and my house have all been taken from me in the last few weeks. And even the police, with all their diligence, don't seem to have the faintest idea by whom."

"This is most undignified," Prudence said very quietly, but still her voice carried so at least a dozen people heard her.

"You wanted to speak of Mr. Lindsay," Oliphant prompted Shaw.

Shaw's face changed. He lowered the glass and put it on the table.

"Yes, thank you for reminding me. This is not the time or the occasion for my losses. We are here to remember Amos — truly and vividly as the living man really was. We do him a hideous disservice to paint him in pastel colors and gloss over the failures, and the victories."

"We should not speak ill of the dead, Stephen," Angeline said after clearing her throat. "It is most unchristian, and quite unnecessary.

I am sure we were all very fond of Mr. Lindsay and thought only the best of him."

"No you didn't," he contradicted her. "Did you know he married an African woman? Black as the ace of spades — and beautiful as the summer night. And he had children — but they are all still in Africa."

"Really, Stephen — this is quite irresponsible!" Celeste stepped forward and took him firmly by the elbow. "The man is not here to defend himself — "

Shaw shook her loose, bumping her abruptly.

"God dammit, he doesn't need a defense!" he shouted. "Marrying an African is not a sin! He did have sins — plenty of them — " He flung his arms expressively. "When he was young he was violent, he drank too much, he took advantage of fools, especially rich ones, and he took women that most certainly weren't his." His face screwed up with intensity and his voice dropped. "But he also had compassion, after he'd learned pain himself: he was never a liar, nor a bigot." He looked around at them all. "He never spread gossip and he could keep a secret to the grave. He had no pretensions and he knew a hypocrite when he saw one — and loathed all forms of cant."

"I really think — " Clitheridge began, flapping his hands as if he would attract every-

one's attention away from Shaw. "Really —
I — "

"You can pontificate all you like over everyone else." Shaw's voice was very loud now.
"But Amos was my friend, and I shall speak
of him as he really was. I'm sick of hearing
platitudes and lies, sick and weary to my heart
of it! You couldn't even speak of poor Clem
honestly. You mouthed a lot of pious phrases
that meant nothing at all, said nothing of what
she was really like. You made her sound as
if she were a quiet, submissive, ignorant little
woman who wore her life away being obedient, looking after me and doing useless good
works among the parish poor. You made her
seem colorless, cowardly of spirit and dull of
mind. She wasn't!" He was so furious now,
and so torn by grief, that his face was suffused
with color, his eyes were bright and his whole
body trembled. Even Celeste dared not interfere.

"That was nothing like Clem. She had more
courage than all the rest of you put together
— and more honesty!"

With difficulty Pitt tore his attention from
Shaw and looked around at the other faces.
Was there any one of them reflecting fear of
what Shaw was going to say next? There was
anxiety in Angeline's face, and distaste in
Celeste's, but he could not see the dread that

540

would have been there had they known of Clemency's discovery.

There was nothing in Prudence's profile either, and nothing in the half outline of Josiah except rigid contempt.

"God knows how she was born a Worlingham," Shaw went on, his fist clenched tight, his body hunched as if waiting to explode into motion. "Old Theophilus was a pretentious, greedy old hypocrite — and a coward to the last — "

"How dare you!" Celeste was too angry to consider any vestige of propriety left. "Theophilus was a fine, upright man who lived honestly and charitably all his life. It is you who are greedy and a coward! If you had treated him properly, as you should have, both as his son-in-law and as his doctor, then he would probably be alive today!"

"Indeed he would," Angeline added, her face quivering. "He was a noble man, and always did his duty."

"He died groveling on the floor with fistfuls of money spread all around him, tens of thousands of pounds!" Shaw exploded at last. "If anybody killed him, it was probably whoever was blackmailing him!"

There was a stunned and appalled silence. For deafening seconds no one even drew breath. Then there was a shriek from Angeline, a stifled sob from Prudence.

"Dear heaven!" Lally spoke at last.

"What on earth are you saying?" Lutterworth demanded. "This is outrageous! Theophilus Worlingham was an outstanding man in the community, and you can have no possible grounds for saying such a thing! You didn't find him, did you? Who says there was all this money? Perhaps he had a major purchase in mind."

Shaw's face was blazing with derision. "With seven thousand, four hundred and eighty-three pounds — in cash?"

"Perhaps he kept his money in the house?" Oliphant suggested quietly. "Some people do. He may have been counting it when he was taken by a seizure. It was a seizure he died of, wasn't it?"

"Yes it was," Shaw agreed. "But it was flung all over the room, and there were five notes clutched in his hand, thrust out before him as if he were trying to give it to someone. Everything indicated he hadn't been alone."

"That is a monstrous lie!" Celeste found her voice at last. "Quite wicked, and you know it! He was utterly alone, poor man. It was Clemency who found him, and called you."

"Clem found him, and called me, certainly," Shaw agreed. "But he was lying in his study, with the French doors open onto

542

the garden — and who is to say she was the first person there? He was already almost cold when she arrived."

"For God's sake, man!" Josiah Hatch burst out. "You are speaking about your father-in-law — and the Misses Worlingham's brother! Have you no decency left at all?"

"Decency!" Shaw turned on him. "There's nothing indecent in speaking about death. He was lying on the floor, purple-faced, his eyes bulging out of his head, his body chill, and five hundred pounds in Treasury notes held so fast in his hand we couldn't remove them to lay him out. What is indecent is where the bloody money came from!"

Everyone began to shift uncomfortably, half afraid to look at each other, and yet unable to help it. Eyes met eyes and then slid away again. Someone coughed.

"Blackmail?" someone said aloud. "Not Theophilus!"

A woman giggled nervously and her gloved hand flew to her mouth to suppress the sound.

There was a sharp sibilance of whispering, cut off instantly.

"Hector?" Lally's voice was clear.

Clitheridge looked red-faced and utterly wretched. Some force beyond himself seemed to propel him forward to where Shaw stood at the head of the table, Celeste a little behind him and to his right, white to the lips and shaking with rage.

"Ahem!" Clitheridge cleared his throat. "Ahem — I — er . . ." He looked around wildly for rescue, and found none. He looked at Lally once more, his face now scarlet, and gave up. "I — er — I am afraid I was the one with — with, er — Theophilus when he died — er, at least shortly before. He — er — " He cleared his throat violently again as if he had some obstruction in it. "He — er — he sent a message for me to come to him — with one of the — er — choirboys who had — er — " He looked imploringly at Lally, and met implacable resolve. He gasped for air, and continued in abysmal misery. "I read the message and went over to his house straight-away — it sounded most urgent. I — er — I found him in a state of great excitement, quite unlike anything I had ever seen." He shut his eyes and his voice rose to a squeak as he relived the utter horror of it. "He was beside himself. He kept spluttering and chok-ing and waving his hands in the air. There were piles of Treasury notes on his desk. I could not even hazard a guess how much money. He was frantic. He looked very unwell and I implored him to allow me to send for the doctor, but he would not hear of it. I am not sure he even grasped what I was saying.

544

He kept on insisting he had a sin to confess."
Clitheridge's eyes were rolling like a frightened horse and he looked everywhere but at the Worlinghams. The sweat broke out on his brow and lip and his hands were wringing each other so hard his knuckles were white.

"He kept on thrusting the money at me and begging me to take it — for the church — for the poor — for anything. And he wanted me to hear his confession . . ." His voice trailed away, too agonized at the memory to find words anymore, as if his throat had closed.

"Lies!" Celeste said loudly. "Absolute lies! Theophilus never had anything to be ashamed of. He must have been having a seizure, and you misunderstood everything. Why in heaven's name didn't you call the doctor yourself, you fool!"

Clitheridge found his tongue again. "He was not having a seizure," he said indignantly. "He was lunging after me, trying to grasp hold of me and force me to take the money, all of it! There were thousands of pounds! And he wanted me to hear his confession. I was — I was mortified with embarrassment. I have never seen anything so — so — so horrifying in my life."

"What in God's name did you do?" Lutterworth demanded.

"I — er — " Clitheridge swallowed convulsively. "I — I ran! I simply fled out of that ghastly room, through the French windows — and across the garden — all the way back to the vicarage."

"And told Lally, who promptly covered up for you — as usual," Shaw finished. "Leaving Theophilus to fall into a seizure and die all by himself — clutching the money. Very Christian!" Still, honesty moderated contempt. "Not that you could have saved him — "

Clitheridge had collapsed within himself, guilty, hideously embarrassed and overcome with failure. Only Lally took any notice of him, and she patted him absently as she would a child.

"But all the money — ?" Prudence demanded. She was confused and appalled. "What was all the money for? It doesn't make sense. He didn't keep money at home. And what happened to it?"

"I put it back in the bank, where it came from," Shaw answered her.

Angeline was on the edge of tears.

"But what was it for? Why would poor Theophilus take all his money out of the bank? Did he really mean to give it all to the church? How noble of him! How like him!" She swallowed hard. "How like Papa too! Stephen — you should have done as he wished. It was very wrong of you to put it back in the bank. Of course I understand why — so Prudence and Clemency could inherit it all, not just the house and the investments — but it was still very wrong of you."

"God Almighty!" Shaw shouted. "You idiot woman! Theophilus wanted to give it to the church to buy his salvation! It was blood money! It came from slum tenements — every penny of it wrung out of the poor, the keepers of brothels, the distilling in gin mills, the masters of sweatshops and the sellers of opium in narrow little dormitories where addicts lie in rows and smoke themselves into oblivion. That's where the Worlingham money comes from. The old bishop bled every drop of it out of Lisbon Street, and God knows how many others like it — and built this damn great palace of complacency for himself and his family."

Angeline held both her hands to her mouth, knuckles white, tears running down her face. Celeste did not even look at her. They were quite separate in their overwhelming shock and the ruin of their world. She stood strong-faced, staring into some distance beyond everyone present, hatred and an immense, intolerable anger hardening inside her.

"Theophilus knew it," Shaw went on relentlessly. "And in the end when he thought he was dying it terrified the hell out of him. He tried to give it back — and it was too late. I didn't know it then — I didn't even know that ass Clitheridge had been there, or what the money was for. I simply put it in the bank because it was Theophilus's, and shouldn't be left lying around. I only discovered where it came from when Clemency did — and told me. She gave it all away in shame — and to make whatever reparation she could — "

"That's a lie! Satan speaks in your mouth!" Josiah Hatch lunged forward, his face scarlet, his hands outstretched like talons to grip Shaw by the throat and choke the life out of him, and stop his terrible words forever. "You blasphemer! You deserve to die — I don't know why God has not struck you down. Except that He uses us poor men to do His work." Already he had carried Shaw to the ground with the fierceness of his attack and his own despair.

Pitt charged through the crowd, which was standing motionless and aghast. He thrust them aside, men and women alike, and grasped at Hatch's shoulders, trying to pull him back, but Hatch had the strength of devotion, even martyrdom if need be.

Pitt was shouting at him, but he knew even as he did so that Hatch could not hear him.

"You devil!" Hatch spoke from between his teeth. "You blasphemer! If I let you live you'll soil every clean and pure thing. You'll spew up your filthy ideas over all the good work that has been done — plant seeds of doubt where there used to be faith. You'll tell your obscene lies about the bishop and make people laugh at him, deride him where they used to revere him." He was weeping as he spoke, his hands still scrabbling at Shaw's throat, his hair fallen forward over his brow, his face purple. "It is better that one man should die than a whole people wither in unbelief. You must be cast out — you pollute and destroy. You should be thrown into the sea — with a millstone 'round your neck. Better you'd never been born than drag other people down to hell with you."

Pitt hit him as hard as he could across the side of the head, and after a brief moment of convulsing, wild arms flailing and his mouth working without sound, Josiah Hatch fell to the ground and lay still, his eyes closed, his hands clasped like claws.

Jack Radley pushed his way from the side of the room and came to Pitt's aid, bending over Hatch and holding him.

Celeste fainted and Oliphant eased her to the ground.

Angeline was weeping like a child, lost,

alone and utterly bereft.

Prudence was frozen as if all life had left her.

"Get Constable Murdo!" Pitt ordered.

No one moved.

Pitt jerked up to repeat his command, and saw out of the corner of his eye Emily going towards the hallway and the front door, where Murdo was patrolling.

At last life returned to the assembly. Taffeta rustled, whalebone creaked, there was a sighing of breath and the women moved a little closer to the men.

Shaw climbed to his feet, white-faced, his eyes like holes in his head. Everyone turned away, except Charlotte. She moved towards him. He was shaking. He did not even attempt to straighten his clothes. His hair was standing out in tufts, his necktie was under one ear and his collar was torn. His jacket was dusty and one sleeve was ripped from the armhole, and there were deep scratches on his face.

"It was Josiah!" His voice was husky in his bruised throat. "Josiah killed Clem — and Amos. He wanted to kill me." He looked strained and there was confusion in his eyes.

"Yes," she agreed, her voice soft and very level. "He wanted to kill you all the time. Lindsay and Clem were only mistakes — because you were out of the house. Although perhaps he didn't mind if he got Amos as well — he had no reason to suppose he was out, as he did with Clemency."

"But why?" He looked hurt, like a child who has been struck for no reason. "We quarreled, but it wasn't serious — "

"Not for you." She found it suddenly very painful to speak. She knew how deeply it would hurt him, and yet she could not evade it. "But you mocked him — "

"Good God, Charlotte — he asked for it! He was a hypocrite — all his values were absurd. He half worshiped old Worlingham, who was a greedy, vicious and thoroughly corrupt man, posing as a saint — and not only robbing people blind but robbing the destitute. Josiah spent his life praising and preaching lies."

"But they were precious to him," she repeated.

"Lies! Charlotte — they were lies!"

"I know that." She held his gaze in an uncompromising stare, and saw the distress in his, the incomprehension, and the terrible depth of caring.

It was a bitter blow she was going to deal him, and yet it was the only way to healing, if he accepted it.

"But we all need our heroes, and our dreams — real or false. And before you destroy someone else's dreams, if they have built their lives on them, you have to put something in their place. Before, Dr. Shaw." She saw him wince at her formality. "Not afterwards. Then it is too late. Being an iconoclast, destroying false idols — or those you think are false — is great fun, and gives you a wonderful feeling of moral superiority. But there is a high price to speaking the truth. You are free to say what you choose — and probably this has to be so, if there is to be any growth of ideas at all — but you are responsible for what happens because you speak it."

"Charlotte — "

"But you spoke it without thinking, or caring — and walked away." She did not moderate her words at all. "You thought truth was enough. It isn't. Josiah at least could not live with it — and perhaps you should have thought of that. You knew him well enough — you've been his brother-in-law for twenty years."

"But — " Now there was no disguising any of his sudden, newfound pain. He cared intensely what she thought of him, and he could see the criticism in her face. He searched for approval, even a shred; understanding, a white, pure love of truth for its own sake. And he saw at last only what was there — the knowledge that with power comes responsibility.

"You had the power to see," she said, moving a step away from him. "You had the words, the vision — and you knew you were stronger than he was. You destroyed his idols, without thinking what would happen to him without them."

He opened his mouth to protest again, but it was a cry of loneliness and the beginning of a new and bitter understanding. Slowly he turned away and looked at Josiah, who was now regaining his senses and being hauled to his feet by Pitt and Jack Radley. Somewhere in the hallway Emily was bringing Constable Murdo in, carrying handcuffs.

Shaw still could not face Angeline and Celeste, but he held out his hands to Prudence.

"I'm sorry," he said very quietly. "I am truly sorry."

She stood motionless for a moment, unable to decide. Then slowly she extended her hands to him, and he clasped them and held them.

Charlotte turned away and pushed between the crowd to find Great-Aunt Vespasia.

Vespasia sighed and took Charlotte's arm.

"A very dangerous game — the ruin of dreams, however foolish," she murmured. "Too often we think because we cannot see them that they do not have the power to destroy — and yet our lives are built upon them. Poor Hatch — such a deluded man, such false idols. And yet we cannot tear them down with impunity. Shaw has much to account for."

"He knows," Charlotte said quietly, raw with regret herself. "I told him so."

Vespasia tightened her hand on Charlotte's. There was no need for words.

THORNDIKE PRESS hopes you have enjoyed this Large Print book. All our Large Print titles are designed for easy reading, and all our books are made to last. Other Thorndike Large Print books are available at your library, through selected bookstores, or directly from the publisher. For more information about current and upcoming titles, please call or mail your name and address, for ...

THORNDIKE PRESS
PO Box 159
Thorndike, Maine 04986
(800)223-2336
207-948-2962

DATE			